The
iAmerican

MIKAEL CARLSON

Warrington Publishing
New York

Warrington Publishing
P.O. Box 2349
New York, NY 10163

Printed in the United States of America
First Edition
ISBN: 978-0-9897673-7-8 (paperback)
         978-0-9897673-6-1(ebook)

Cover design by Veselin Milacic

Also by Mikael Carlson:

- The Michael Bennit Series -
The iCandidate
The iCongressman
The iSpeaker

For my father, Ronald, the most honorable man I have ever known.

Dedicated on his behalf to "We the People."

While the exploits of Michael Bennit in *The iAmerican* can stand on their own, a reader will get far more out of his story by starting with the beginning of his journey. To that end, I encourage anybody who purchased this book to read the first three installments of the series beforehand.

"Social media is itself as temporary as any social gathering, nightclub or party. It's the people that matter, not the venue. So when the trend leaders of one social niche or another decide the place everyone is socializing has lost its luster or, more important, its exclusivity, they move on to the next one, taking their followers with them."
— Douglas Rushkoff

"As more people use social media to tell the story of the future, the wants and needs of more people will be reflected."
— Simon Mainwaring

"99.5 percent of the people that walk around and say they are a social media expert or guru are clowns. We are going to live through a devastating social media bubble."
— Douglas Rushkoff

-PROLOGUE-
MICHAEL

Circumstance can be a twisted, spiteful thing. Seriously, what are the odds that the man who Kylie just informed us moments ago is the architect of my assassination now stands outside the door in my outer office? It's the kind of creepy thing usually reserved for one of Brian De Palma's psychological thrillers.

While the Speaker of the House and I were mugging for the cameras at a press conference less than an hour ago, Kylie was hearing from my archnemesis, James Reed, that the man I was sharing the podium with was the one responsible for ordering our deaths. She tried to stop the press conference before it started, but it was too late. Now the damage is done, and we are faced with what exactly to do with this new information.

Sarah is one of my junior staffers and has no idea why we are all wearing a look of horror on our faces. When she knocked and opened the door to let us know that Speaker Albright was here to pay a visit, there is no way she could know what Kylie just told us. She has to be confused as why I haven't instructed her to let our newest political ally in.

Not wanting the discussion among Vince, Vanessa, Chelsea, Kylie, Cisco, Terry, and me to be heard by anyone outside our office, I motion Sarah to come in. She complies, closing the door behind her as the confusion morphs into a look of genuine concern. That will only get worse, I'm sure. This conversation is going to be … spirited.

"You can't meet with him," Vince commands, in no mood to hide his disdain.

"It's the Speaker of the House. He can't *not* meet with him," Chelsea defends, looking at our current dilemma more from a political and protocol perspective. She is growing into this role. That's what a chief of staff is supposed to do.

"He was responsible for trying to have us gunned down on the steps of the Capitol a little over a month ago. Do you seriously want to let him in here?"

On the final day of the session before Christmas and the convening of a new Congress, I was giving a press conference on the steps of the Capitol following the defeat of a rules bill Albright had championed. If it had passed, it would have been a damaging blow for me, Cisco, and all the other icandidates who had won their races the previous November and were getting ready to join our ranks. The press conference was meant to be a simple question and answer session with the media, until Jerold Todd Bernard pulled out a 9mm handgun and started blasting away at us.

I was hit in the shoulder, and although I'm healing, I still have countless hours of physical therapy and wearing my left arm in a sling because of him. My closest political ally, Congressman Francisco Reyes from Texas, was shot in the leg and needed immediate surgery to repair his femoral artery. Blake Peoni, the stooge from Winston Beaumont's staff turned Chelsea's love interest, was shot twice in the back and only recently came out of his medically induced coma. Marilyn Viano, the former senator who helped launch the campaigns of my hundred icandidates before turning on me, was shot in the head and killed.

"Fine, Chels, go ahead and let him in. I got something for him," Vince says, pounding his fist against his hand.

Vince, one of the three remaining students from my B period American history class that started me on this journey, is always ready for a fight. With his Italian heritage and violent temperament, he would have fit right in one of the Godfather movies. Except the third one which sucked.

"We don't know for a fact if what he said is even true. All we have is James Reed's word for it. Are you telling me you trust that man?" Chelsea fires back at Vince.

"If Kylie and Spooky Terry over there believe him, it's enough for me," Vince responds, eliciting a glare from my girlfriend's investigative counterpart.

Terry Nyguen works in some unnamed job for some unnamed think tank here in Washington. He has never been clear about his motives for helping us, but he's been an ardent supporter since my first reelection campaign when he warned us that we could become targets. I'm not sure I trust him, but he is a veteran and former member of the United States Navy's elite Dev Group, better known as Seal Team Six. Those credentials are good enough for me, even though as a former Green Beret I've been taught to hold squids with a certain level of derision.

"I hate to interrupt, sir, but the Speaker is waiting," Sarah interjects sheepishly from her spot just inside the door. "What should I tell him?"

"Cisco, you've been quiet so far. What do you think?" I ask, turning in his direction. Whether it's his Latino blood, Texan heritage, or just being a common man among elites, my friend and colleague has never been shy about giving me his opinion. His silence during this argument is a little unnerving.

"I'm still trying to process this. It's your call, Michael."

"If you face him, he'll know," Kylie whispers to me after my pause runs too long. She's right, I can't act my way through this.

From the moment I met Kylie in the parking lot of the Perkfect Buzz coffee shop in Millfield, back during my first campaign, she's had an uncanny ability to get inside my head. In the time we have spent since then, I've learned that she knows me better than I know myself. Because of that, I trust her judgment about these things implicitly.

"Sir, I really need to give him an answer," Sarah pleads.

This is an impossible situation. I can't risk blowing off the man who may be the strongest political ally I have ever had and be wrong. On the flip side, as Kylie pointed out, I don't know how I will react when I face him. As much as I would love to grab him by the throat and beat the truth out of him, this is not Fort Bragg and I'm not in Special Forces anymore. We play by a different set of rules in Washington, D.C. Out of any better alternatives, I decide on an approach I almost never use. I lie.

"Tell him we are in the middle of a personnel crisis that needs my immediate attention and that I'll catch up with him later."

"Yes, sir," Sarah says with a nod that fails to mask the perplexed look on her face. An instant later, she retreats back into my outer office to relay the excuse, closing the door behind her.

"Personnel crisis?" Vanessa asks me.

"It is one, of a sort."

"So now what do we do?" Chelsea posits, looking to form some sort of plan of action.

"You mean other than chasing the fat bastard down the hallway and beating him to a pulp?"

"Settle down, Vince. You're assuming he's guilty, and we don't know that yet."

"Aw, come on, Congressman!" Vince shouts. "All the crap we've had to deal with from him for the past two years and you're doubting he's capable of this?"

"There's a big difference between being a political adversary and the mastermind of the worst assassination attempt since Ronald Reagan," Chelsea retorts, coming to my defense.

"Oh, please. You don't know him at all then."

"I've sat with him, talked to him, and looked into his eyes. I know him better than you, Vince, and that's why I'm willing to give him the benefit of the doubt."

"I never pegged you for naïve, Chelsea."

"You'd better watch your tongue, Vince, before I rip it out."

"Enough! Both of you!" I bark, conjuring up my old military command voice. I can tolerate strong opinions, but I hate when things get personal.

Vince may technically work for Chelsea, since she's my chief of staff, but they have more of a brother-sister relationship. She is nurturing to him and he is protective of her, especially as it relates to her newfound interest in Blake Peoni. They have a great working relationship, but like all siblings, both real and imagined, they are prone to argue like cats and dogs now and then. I have never seen any of their arguments this extreme, though.

"Kylie, Terry, you guys are the ones who met with Reed. Do you think he was telling the truth?"

They had both worked hard investigating whether there was any sinister involvement surrounding the shooting. The police had settled on the lone gunman theory and, although it had not been made public, had all but closed the case. Kylie adamantly believed someone was pulling Jerold Todd Bernard's strings. With the help of Terry, she managed to uncover enough evidence to prove it. That trail led right to the doorstep of James Reed.

"Reed is one of the shadiest characters in this city, but, in this case, I don't think he has a reason to lie," Terry opines, refusing to look me in the eye. He isn't taking any pleasure in that conclusion.

"We didn't initially believe it either," Kylie continues for him. "But the more I look at it, the less upside I see. He had a certain smugness during our whole conversation with him. He couldn't wait to pull out the evidence and show us, but managed to draw the whole thing out just long enough to where it wouldn't make a difference. I think he's telling the truth."

Kylie is a brilliant investigative journalist and has made a living being right about these things. I just don't want to believe it either. James Reed, the Kentucky native turned managing partner of the lobby firm Ibram & Reed, is sly enough to pull a ruse like this off and make it believable. The question that needs to be answered is does he have the goods on Albright, or is this some elaborate hoax meant to divide us?

"There's no reason for him to lie, Michael," Cisco concludes, finally coming to grips with our new reality.

"Cisco, I can think of a half-dozen of them. At the top of the list is to create dissent among us. And if that's what he's trying to do, it's working."

"So, what are we supposed to do? Ignore the fact that we're working with the same man who shot both of us and landed her boyfriend in a coma for weeks? Because you may have been shot before back in your army days, but it's a new experience for the rest of us. I'm not okay with cozying up to the guy responsible for it."

"Neither am I," Vince chimes in.

"Me either," Vanessa agrees.

"You guys are incredible," Chelsea says, her head moving side to side in disgust. "You've already made up your minds and we don't even have all the facts."

The room descends into chaos. We were all traumatized by the shooting on the steps and, despite the therapy sessions, have repressed our emotional responses to it in one way or another. Finally learning the truth, or at least something that sounds like the truth, about what really happened that day has ripped open the sutures on our emotional wounds. It's given some of us a target for our anger, even if it turns out to be the wrong one. The arguments whirring around this room are not logical ones. They are emotionally charged and filled with overtures of hatred and revenge.

"Okay, enough!" I bark once again, bringing the room to a begrudging silence. "We can argue about this for the next week and we'd still be in the same spot. We need confirmation that Reed was telling the truth."

"He has the evidence. Let's get it from him," Vince offers.

"No, we need independent verification. We can't trust anything Reed has."

"A second source," Kylie adds, putting it in a journalistic context.

"Exactly."

"How do we get that?" Vanessa questions, not sold on the idea.

"I can get it," Terry volunteers quietly. Somehow, I don't doubt it.

"How? From who?" Vince demands.

"Easy. I'll find Albright's staffer. How I get the information out of him is … well, you probably don't want to know that."

The evidence Reed claims to have in his possession implicating Speaker Albright is a disposable cell phone that purportedly was used to give the go order for Bernard to gun us down. Albright got rid of the phone when the deed was done, but an intrepid member of the Speaker's staff, that Reed keeps on his private payroll, rescued the device from the trash right before the shooting. It's exactly the kind of battlefield intelligence we need. If the staffer talks, we'll get our answers … and our target.

"I hate to bring this back up, but what if Terry is able to confirm he wasn't lying?"

"Chels—"

"No, she's right, Michael," Kylie cautions. "You went on television and asked the country to trust Albright—to trust the both of you. What happens if he was behind it?"

Everyone in the room stares at me, but I have no answer for them. If Terry is able to confirm what Reed told Kylie, it would be an act of betrayal I can't yet fathom. I'm quick on my feet, but under these circumstances, I am at a complete loss for what to do.

"You can't storm the castle wall until you cross the moat," I say, stalling. "Right now, we need to give Terry time to do … whatever it is he does to get information. Once we know if Reed is being straight with us, or not, we can talk about courses of action. Until then, not a word of this gets uttered to anyone."

It was not what everyone wanted to hear, but they accept it and start to file out of my office. I feel a chill run up my spine, causing the hairs on the back of my neck to stand rigidly at attention. With so many independents joining us for the new session of Congress after upset victories in the last election, we were optimistic it would lead to a promising start. Even recovering from gunshot wounds, the thought of having a positive impact was a welcome respite from the turmoil of my first term. Now, I get the sense that this new nightmare will make the frustration of my first years here seem like the good old days by comparison.

PART I

THE GOVERNMENT OF THE PEOPLE

-ONE-
CHELSEA

I remember a saying the congressman used in the classroom when a school day was dragging. He would quote Einstein, who said, "When you are courting a nice girl an hour it seems like a second. When you sit on a red-hot cinder a second it seems like an hour. That's relativity."

The days in Washington can fly by when you're busy, which we usually are. Unfortunately, in the two days since the press conference, and the mother of all bombs Kylie dropped about Albright, time has stood still. Even the time I spend at Blake's bedside does not whir past like it normally does.

As much as I like watching the big game with my father, I have wanted to spend every free moment I can with Blake. His awakening from the coma he'd been in since the shooting was a gift I don't plan on squandering. Besides, he's every bit the football fan most guys are, only he has to watch from the confines of the George Washington University Medical Center.

Vince and the congressman headed up to Connecticut yesterday to work out of the district office in Danbury for the two days before Super Bowl weekend officially starts. It's as much to avoid running into Speaker Albright as anything else. Kylie joined them, not wanting to be in the city by herself for the big game. She wasn't much of a sports fan when we first met, but

Michael's affinity for football has worn off on her since they have been dating.

When Terry contacted me that he had news, we decided not to travel north and set up a late night videoconference over Skype instead. He joined me in the office along with Vanessa, who I'm surprised didn't tag along with Vince to Danbury. Although they are still being secretive about it, I know they have to be dating. Gossip about their relationship status is all the rage among the congressman's staff here in D.C.

The conference chimes and Kylie, Michael, and Vince connect from Danbury. A few moments later, Congressman Reyes joins from his home in Texas. Once everyone gets through the initial greetings, Terry wastes no time getting down to business.

"It's Albright's phone," he relays to us without any preamble. He's not big into small talk.

"How do you know?" Congressman Reyes asks, wanting the details.

"As I mentioned before, Congressman, none of you are going to want to know that information. Trust me when I say there is no doubt about the truth. Albright was involved in the attempt on your lives."

"There's always doubt when James Reed is involved, Terry," Congressman Reyes interjects. "We're talking about a guy who tried to have one of his staff members frame Michael to get him expelled from the House. If he was capable of that once, what makes you think he wouldn't try it again? He's not wired to tell the truth."

The congressman's run-in with Ibram & Reed employee Tyler Logan at a Danbury restaurant seems like an eon ago. The young lobbyist had tried to get him to accept a bribe while ensuring someone, posing as a member of the public, was ready to take pictures of it. Fortunately for us, Mister Bennit had smelled a rat and had one of my former classmates capture the whole thing on video. In spite of clear evidence exonerating him, he only survived the expulsion vote on the House Floor by a couple of votes.

Reed had denied being involved during his testimony in the subsequent investigation, if you can call the hearing the House conducted that. He had so many former members of the committee in his hip pocket that the inquiry was brief, shallow, and futile. There had been far more interest in the coming election than there was protecting one of their members from a despicable campaign to destroy him.

"Fine. If you really want to know, Congressman Reyes, I had a … conversation … with the mole Reed had placed on Albright's staff. He explained in detail how he found the burner phone and turned it over to another of Reed's minions."

"A conversation? He willingly talked to you?" Congressman Reyes continues to question.

I study Terry as he pauses and gives the question some thought. I get the impression his methods were less than honorable, and he probably doesn't want to implicate anyone on this videoconference if others ever uncover what he did.

"I can be very persuasive," he replies after a long moment.

"I'm not sure I want any more detail than that, Cisco," the congressman explains. "I don't think you should either."

"We have to operate under the assumption everything he said is true," Terry continues. "The staffer said he heard the call to Jerold Todd Bernard and retrieved the phone when Albright tossed it in the receptacle to get rid of it."

"That's kind of a dumb thing to do, isn't it?" Kylie asks, looking for a hole in the story.

"It's sloppy, but there was more risk getting caught with the phone later. Albright couldn't have known about the NSA's capabilities and would have no reason to think the call he made could be traced back to within the walls of the Capitol."

"And there was no reason to think that someone would retrieve it in time if it had. It would go out with the trash that evening and would be long gone before anybody even realized what they were looking for."

"Precisely."

The knowledge of a call made to the assassin was uncovered by Terry early on and that information still hasn't been released publically by the Capitol Police. Withholding that information only stoked Kylie's belief that they were going to stick with the lone gunman story and ignore any evidence that pointed in a direction to the contrary.

Her devotion to the investigation and the congressman's focus on his job had almost torn their relationship apart. I've seen plenty of my friends go through bad breakups, but this one would have been especially horrible. Mister Bennit is like a second father to me and Kylie is like the mother I lost so many years ago. Their split would have killed me emotionally.

"Wouldn't he have wiped his prints?" Vince asks, getting into the whole true crime spirit of this thing.

"He should have but apparently, in the heat of the moment, he didn't. Not that it matters. He probably left DNA on it either way," the congressman responds, beating Terry to the punch.

"Regardless of whether it is true or not, Reed's going to go public with this. Today's media is not interested in the truth as much as they are ratings," Vanessa correctly surmises from next to me. "What do we do?"

"Nothing," Cisco demands. "We don't do a damn thing. If we come clean with this, it will destroy us."

"Faster than if we do nothing and it comes out?" Kylie retorts, astonished he would suggest keeping this a secret.

"Assuming it will come out at all. I don't think—"

"It's going to come out, Cisco," Kylie argues.

"We don't know that."

"James Reed didn't give us this information out of the kindness of his heart. He did it to try to bury us with it," the congressman snaps.

"Yeah, bury us by destroying the most powerful political alliance in the country the moment we step in front of the Washington press corps. When you admit that the man you helped remain as Speaker of the House is the same man who tried to *murder* you, it's not going to be a real trust-builder with the American people."

"What's the alternative?" Vince inquires. "Deny everything?"

"And ignore the fact the man tried to have us killed? Respectfully, you're crazy, Congressman."

"You think I'm happy about that idea, Vanessa? I will have a limp for the rest of my life because of what that bastard did. But this is more important. The icongressmen are finally poised to make a real difference in the political process in this country. I'm not willing to see that fail."

"At the expense of justice?" I ask. I got a concussion on the day of the shooting, but now I'm wondering if maybe Cisco hit his head harder on the steps than I did. This is not like him. He sounds like the politicians we were elected to replace.

"At the expense of *anything*."

"I can't believe you're saying that, Congressman." It's true. I can't.

"I have barely slept the last three days thinking about this. It is the only solution."

"Lack of sleep may be clouding your judgment," Congressman Bennit suggests.

"And your wanting to be completely transparent is clouding yours. You're forgetting, Michael, that we are politicians and this is the game."

"A game we have devoted every ounce of energy trying to change."

"And we will. That's my point. To do that, we have to be both relevant and present. We go public with this on our own, we lose the former and, in a couple of years, probably the latter."

"Who's making the assumptions now, Cisco?"

Since the moment Congressman Reyes joined us in Washington, following his own special election, I have never seen a moment where the two of them weren't on the same page. I know they have their disagreements on issues, but never anything this dramatic. Even through a videoconference I can tell they are getting angry with each other, and that is sending a shiver down my spine.

"Ask yourselves something. Why hasn't he gone public yet? It's been three days. Why hasn't he run to the police or the media?"

Everyone on the videoconference goes quiet. I look to Terry and Vanessa sitting in the congressman's inner office with me. They have the same blank stares Vince, Kylie, and the congressman have. There is no answer to that question.

"Okay, I'll answer it," Cisco says, breaking the silence. "He's waiting to see what we do. He has our king trapped and wants to see what piece we move next, before he goes for checkmate."

"Cisco, we swore an oath. We promised the American people—"

"Michael, I know what you're going to say, but I need you to hear me out on this because I have never seen anything clearer than I see this. If we tell the truth, it's the end of the independents. Are you willing to make that exchange?"

-TWO-

MICHAEL

"It's the end of us if we don't," I tell my friend. "We will turn into everything we swore not to be if we bury this."

I would love to know what Chelsea is thinking right now. Now I am wishing I had told them to meet us up here for the meeting. My chief of staff gives off a distinct vibe through her body language that tells me everything I need to know about what's going on in her head. I noticed it the first day she ever sat in my classroom. Although I can see her face in this videoconference, I just can't pick up her non-verbal communication over Skype.

"You need to think about doing this for the greater good," Cisco fashions as a very stiff response. Now I can't control my frustration.

"Are you kidding me with that garbage? Every politician who has been in Washington for far too long utters those same words to explain their shady, and often illegal, actions. Hell, Johnston Albright probably justified his decision to try to kill us that way. The president taking executive action without Congress is along the same line."

"We are different than them and you know it!"

"Nobel prize-winning economist Milton Friedman once warned of mixing benevolent purpose with government. He stated that, 'Concentrated power is not rendered harmless by the

good intentions of those who create it.' To put it more succinctly for you, 'The road to hell is paved with good intentions.'"

"You and your quotes," Cisco dismisses. "I've been shot. I've already been to hell and back. I don't want it to be for nothing."

"Nobody does," I reply.

"Then you need to start thinking about the big picture, Michael."

It's strange being at odds with him. I don't think it's ever happened before. Another eerie silence ensues on the conference. My staff has been working with me for so long that they know the argument between Cisco and me is the main event on the fight card and that they shouldn't get involved. Even Kylie is content to let me have it out with my colleague. He may not want to hear my quotes, but he's going to get a story.

"I don't want this to be our Desert One."

"Our what?"

I'm sure he'll regret asking that a couple of minutes from now. I half expected one of my former students to chime in with their usual, "Here comes today's history lesson," comment, but I think they understand there's a time and place for levity, and this isn't it.

"President Jimmy Carter ordered the launch of Operation Eagle Claw on the twenty-fourth of April, 1980, in an attempt to rescue the fifty-two diplomats held captive at our embassy in Tehran. The White House had avoided military action ever since the embassy takeover on November fourth and Carter had exercised tremendous restraint in his dealings with Iran. Unfortunately for him, the global praise he received for not overreacting began to subside as his lack of response looked more like indecision and weakness.

"To make a long story short—"

"This is short?" Cisco sneers.

"To make a long story shorter," I continue, "the mission was a disaster. Eight helicopters were sent to the rendezvous, but only five arrived operational. The operational parameters were blown, so command made the decision to abort the rescue attempt. As the forces prepared to leave the rally point, one of the helicopters collided with a fuel-laden transport filled with servicemen. Both aircraft were destroyed and eight servicemen perished in the conflagration. The place the incident happened was called 'Desert One.'"

"My God, Michael, will you please get to the point?"

"The White House announced the failed rescue operation the following day," I continue, ignoring his whining. "At that point, hostages were scattered across Iran, making any other attempts futile. Carter had his chance and blew it. As a result, Americans lost faith in him and his presidency. He lost to Ronald Reagan in the 1980 presidential election."

"So what? It has no relevance—"

"Cisco, what looked like a prudent move in the beginning ended in complete disaster because Carter wasn't willing to take decisive action early on. What makes you think it will end differently for us?"

Silence blankets the group on the conference again, as Cisco continues to glare at me over our video connection. I've seen the look he's giving me before. It started with Winston Beaumont at my first debate when I had him tripped up over the qualifications for a member of the U.S. House of Representatives. I have seen it a few times since and never expected it from him.

"You can come up with all the historical mumbo jumbo you want, but this is a mistake," my friend and colleague decrees with an acidity in his voice that the normally jovial representative from Texas is feeling anything but right now.

"Cisco, listen—"

"No, you listen! You want to make this decision on your own, fine. I'm not going to be a part of it. This is where we part ways."

His face disappears from the screen with a click of a mouse button. That's the other problem with videoconferences—it's too easy for people to leave them. He got angry and ended his participation in our discussion. I have the feeling that's not all between us that's ended.

-THREE-

JAMES

I'm not really a monuments kind of guy. Washington is a city with a monument devoted to anyone who made a contribution in American history. Tributes to those who fought our wars are fine, but the ones to the generals and political leaders have to go. If the people ever knew the truth about most of them, they would rip those statues down faster than Saddam Hussein's came down following the fall of Baghdad during the Iraq War.

While I loathe the arrogant homage to times long gone and figures long dead these stone and bronze eyesores depict, I do like the various museums the city has to offer. The Smithsonian Institute is one of the largest and most prestigious curators of artifacts on the planet. I need a long walk to clear my mind and, given the fact that it is below freezing outside, one of the museums on the National Mall fits the bill.

The National Museum of American History displays the social, political, cultural, scientific, and military heritage and experiences of the American people, meticulously collected since its founding in 1964. Among the items on display are Dorothy's ruby slippers from *The Wizard of Oz*, a piece of Plymouth Rock, Muhammad Ali's boxing gloves, and Archie Bunker's chair from one of my favorite television shows, *All in the Family*.

The crown jewel of the museum is the original Star Spangled Banner that flew above Fort McHenry in Baltimore's harbor at the height of the War of 1812, when Francis Scott Key was inspired to write his famous poem. It's really a nice piece of history to behold.

I wander around the second floor, mindlessly admiring relics of Americana while my mind is preoccupied with other notions. Well, one other notion, at least. Michael Bennit.

The renegade congressman from Connecticut has been a man of action since the day his plane landed in Washington following his special election. He was made of Teflon last summer, but finally he is showing the chinks in his armor. Michael Bennit has demonstrated his ability to think quickly in the heat of the moment and his current indecision is very uncharacteristic. The question is, why? Is he waiting for me to make my move?

I have been waiting for the last two days for him to go public. It would be the Michael Bennit thing to do. There was no doubt in my mind that Mister Honor himself would fall on his sword and the police would come, seize the evidence, and lead me away in cuffs. That was how it was supposed to happen; only it hasn't.

Is he hoping my revelation to Kylie will just blow over? He can't be stupid enough to bury his head in the sand like some ostrich and hope this storm passes him by. So why has he been silent? Is he trying to find out if my evidence is the Real McCoy?

Not that he can. Kylie is a capable journalist, but she doesn't have the investigative skills to track that down. Maybe her henchman, Terry Ny-something could. I don't know what his background is, but I don't see how he could have any better success.

So, again, what is he waiting for? He has to be waiting for me. Maybe there is an opportunity here. I resigned myself to the very real possibility I'd be locked in a prison cell by now. Withholding evidence of a crime, especially one as high profile as an assassination attempt on a sitting congressman, is an activity that can result in a lengthy stay in a federal penitentiary. I never doubted that Bennit would run to the police immediately after Kylie gave him the information I told her and her stooge. What does it say that he didn't?

Could Bennit be corruptible after all? Power is a strong elixir, and the original icongressman has taken more than a few sips since he's been here. Once ignored, now he's the most powerful politician in this town. Maybe he's not the most powerful ever, but is, at a minimum, the most politically potent legislator the country has seen in decades. Maybe he's not as willing to give that up as I thought he would be. It's not like I haven't been wrong about him before.

The people have turned to him in overwhelming numbers to fix a system they believe is broken. They have faith in him. He has to know going public will destroy that forever. It won't matter that that he was almost killed a little over a month ago. Sympathy is a short-term emotion in America these days. The media loves a scandal, and given Michael's popularity, this one will be huge. If he flaunts the law by remaining silent, he'll be portrayed as just another shady politician who lied to the people. He will have betrayed the fragile trust so many Americans have come to invest in him and they will hate him for that.

His chief of staff is sharp, even for a twenty-something. She has to be telling him the same thing I'm thinking, and if she isn't, surely Michael's girlfriend is. Kylie Roberts is a seasoned professional who has uncovered more than a few nefarious plots in her short journalism career.

So assuming he's been told that, he's decided to remain silent. That's very interesting. He listens to his staff. He trusts them. What advice are they giving him?

It doesn't matter. There's an opening here to exploit and I need to press my advantage because I have nothing to lose. This museum is filled with underdog stories; men and women who were all but defeated and still found a way to beat the odds and prevail. I can be one of them. I can be the man who corrupts the incorruptible iCongressman.

When Bennit got to town, I launched an audacious plan to ensure I could call the shots in this town for years to come. I wanted to copy the example he had set through his social media campaign experiment, to get a group of people I could manipulate elected to Congress. I wanted nothing less than to find a way to control the U.S. House of Representatives. I failed, but maybe now I still can.

-FOUR-
KYLIE

"You've been quiet since we left the office. I figured coming here would cheer you up."

"It has."

"Yeah, I can tell," I say with a smile in a futile effort to brighten his dour mood.

After the videoconference ended, we left the office and came for a late dinner at one of our favorite little haunts. Vera's Trattoria is one of several great restaurants on Mill Plain Road, and the place we go when we want good Italian or are craving a pizza.

"It's been a tough day, but I'm sure you've seen worse."

"You know, I went to Ranger School before I went to Special Forces Selection. One of our first days there, we ran an obstacle course where they made us low crawl through freezing, muddy water for three hundred meters under barbed wire. The whole time, instructors bawled at us to crawl faster and to keep our faces in the mud. When we finished, some unfortunate sap made the mistake of asking one of the instructors when we would be stopping for the day. He grinned like a devil and said, 'What do you mean, stop? The sun isn't even up yet.' It was the longest day of my life. This feels just as bad."

"You're afraid you won't be able to patch things up with Cisco? Because, whether you want to admit it or not, you have an epic bromance with him that puts Adam Levine and Blake Shelton to shame."

"I know. This is different somehow, though. I don't know how to explain it. This whole situation sucks."

I hate seeing Michael this way. National politics can beat down the most enthusiastic and optimistic of people. I'm afraid he is in danger of joining their ranks.

"You're caught between the proverbial rock and hard place. What are you going to do?"

"I have no idea." His indecisiveness is starting to get on my nerves. He needs to make a decision and go with it.

"Wrong answer, airborne. You're a Green Beret. You've been forced to make decisions under fire before, so make one. What is your gut telling you to do?"

"Eat dinner," he responds, before ripping off another bite of his pizza slice.

"I'm being serious, Michael."

"So am I. You can't compare combat with what I'm going through now." I suppose I can't dispute that.

"Okay, but you've been in bad situations more than a few times since your election. Each time, you went with your instinct, which was usually the last thing people expected. It's worked out every time."

"This is different."

"How so?"

"Because I knew what had to be done. In this situation, I don't know. I'm at a loss."

"I think you know what you have to do. You know you need to jump on a flight this weekend."

"I thought about going down to Carolina to see him. I'm not sure it's a good idea."

"And flipping a table at an ethics hearing and telling the chairman to shut up before you jamb his microphone down his throat, was a good idea in your mind?"

"Touché."

"Good. So it's settled."

"Not entirely. True leaders, I mean the great ones, have all faced incredible adversity: George Washington, Lincoln, FDR, Kennedy, Reagan …"

"Lumping yourself with greats now, are you?" I smirk.

"No, never, but I understand the weight of their decisions. I know they were forced to do things they didn't want to. For example, each of them had to ask someone for something they didn't want to. George was forced to tell Martha he would be off fighting the revolution, Lincoln had to—"

"Uh oh."

"What?"

"I'm suddenly getting the feeling I'm being set up for something I'm not going to like."

"I promised you once that I would never ask you to do this again, but I have to. I need you to write an article."

"You're right, you promised," I warn him.

Michael ran his first campaign entirely on social media and, to prove a point, never took a stand on a single issue. It was an experiment to see how closely the American people were paying attention to what their prospective leaders were saying. The results were definitive—he lost by less than a hundred votes.

To ensure people got the point of what he was trying to do, and warn future generations of the dangers of such apathy, he had me write an article that was picked up and run in every major newspaper in the country. It was devastating, but honest, and people reacted to it by, overwhelmingly, electing him following Beaumont's resignation.

"I need you to write the story—the *whole* story—of everything that's happened since the shooting. If the truth is going to come out, I want the people to hear it from us."

"I thought you hadn't made a decision."

"I haven't, but I want the option should I need it. I don't want to ask you at the last minute and cause you to rush it."

I hate the idea of this. He had promised to never put me in a position where something I write could destroy his career. And, just like back then, I'm compelled to try to get out of it using any excuse I can find.

"Let's assume I agree to write this. What do you want me to do with it? I don't have a job, remember?"

"We'll cross that bridge when we get to it."

"Or burn the bridge," I caution him, because that's exactly what we're going to be doing.

-FIVE-

CHELSEA

"Good morning, sunshine!" I announce as I walk into his room.

"You're up early for a Saturday morning," Blake responds, beaming as he sees me shed my coat and toss it on the window ledge.

He's looking much better than he did even a few days ago. Only a couple of weeks removed from the medically induced coma that allowed the multiple surgeries on his back to heal, the ashen face I stared at following the shooting has more color in it. He's inclined on his bed with the television on, instead of lying flat on it comatose, and has the cafeteria menu next to him, so I know breakfast will be arriving shortly. Things are looking up nicely indeed.

"I couldn't sleep. I'm still upset over what happened between the congressmen yesterday. How are you feeling? You're looking a lot better."

"I'm beginning to go nuts," Blake says, waving his hand. "I can see why your boss snuck out of here when nobody was looking. I'm jealous."

Mister B slipped out the door of the hospital early on Christmas Eve morning and fled to Arlington Cemetery to visit the grave of an old army buddy who had been killed on a mission they were on. The hospital went nuts when they found out and called Kylie, who tracked him down there and escorted him back. Unfortunately, Blake was shot in the back twice and can barely get out of bed. I don't have to worry about him going anywhere.

"Keep working with the physical therapist and you'll be out of here before long," I tell him, bending down and giving him a kiss.

That simple action is still very new to me, and very weird. Blake and I hadn't been dating long before he got shot shielding me from the bullets Jerold Todd Bernard aimed in my direction. It was the noblest thing anyone has ever done for me, and especially surprising considering our history.

Blake Peoni rose up the ranks of Congressman Winston Beaumont's staff to become his right-hand man. He was also the hatchet man, charged with doing the unsavory mudslinging and leaking personal information about opponents to the press that the voting public hears about every October. One of his most damaging tasks was spreading the lie about me having an affair with Mister Bennit, my teacher at the time.

I hated him for that. I even threatened him, with a knife my father gave me, on the bridge at Briar Point State Park. To his credit, he has worked every day since then to regain our trust. Blake came clean about the lie, but not in time for us to win the election.

A year later, he brought in his aunt, former senator Marilyn Viano, to help run the icandidates and warned of her duplicity when she crossed us. Somewhere in the middle of all that I stopped resenting him and started falling in love. Life is strange.

"Not soon enough. What about you? How are you holding up? You were pretty upset when you called me last night."

"I feel like I'm caught in the middle of a tug of war between two titans."

"They're still not talking?" he asks with a tone of concern.

"I don't know. I haven't spoken to the congressman yet today. They're acting like a stubborn old married couple, so I doubt it."

"Do you think Congressman Reyes has a point? I mean, do you think he's right about going public ruining everything you guys built?"

I exhale deeply. "Yeah, that's what makes this so hard. I understand Mister B's position, but I see Congressman Reyes's side of it, too. I understand why everyone is so torn. It kills me to think that Reed could actually win this round."

"Do you think this is a game?" Blake asks, gingerly shifting in his bed to face me better, as I pull up a chair to his bedside.

"No, I think what the congressman is trying to do effects real lives. Reed treats it as a game though, and he keeps score."

"Everyone keeps score in Washington, Chels. Fortunately, or unfortunately, so do voters."

"I'm not so sure about that."

"Okay, maybe you're right about that, but America sees what Michael is trying to do here."

"None of that will matter if word of this gets out. We can fight it with social media, but the mainstream newscasts will control the narrative. At best, all we'll manage to do is confuse the American people and they'll lose the faith in us we've fought so hard to earn."

"Isn't that Reyes's position?"

"Yeah," I whisper under my breath, avoiding Blake's stare.

"But?" he asks, trying to look me in the eyes.

"But if we bury it, we're no better than anyone else who's come here and failed to deliver on their promises."

"It's a problem, there's no doubt about that. Nobody ever said governing was easy. Want some advice?"

"I'm not here for your looks or charm," I respond with a wink.

"Ouch. You know what your greatest asset is?"

"I have nice legs?"

"I mean Congressman Bennit and his staff's greatest asset," he answers, rolling his eyes. Does he not think I have nice legs?

"No, what?"

"Your collective ability to think outside the box and do the unexpected. Social media campaigns, table flipping, organizing House members to elect a Speaker … everything you guys have done is unpredictable."

"Not everybody would say that's a good thing."

"The people saying that are the ones who lost to you. I should know because I was one of them once. I watched Beaumont implode because of it."

"I could have used this pep talk right after the shooting." It's true. I couldn't wait to be able to talk to him again.

"Sorry, I was … uh … unconscious."

"I needed your help and you're going to use the lame 'I was in a medically induced coma' excuse? Weak, Blake, very weak," I tell him, accompanied with a playful light punch to his shoulder.

"You did just fine on your own."

"I suppose, but you have no idea how nice it is to have you back. If it weren't for my friends, I don't know how I would have made it through all that."

"You must miss them with all this going on," Blake observes, giving my hand a couple of affectionate caresses.

"I do. We weathered a lot of storms together. It's weird not having them around anymore."

The core group of us, Vince, Vanessa, Brian, Amanda, Emilee, Xavier, and I, were the ones who met at Briar Point to plan the campaign the summer between our junior and senior years of high school. A lot has happened since that day. While most of them went off to college, they still managed to stay involved. When we said our good-byes a couple of weeks ago, we knew it was probably the last time we would all be in the same room together.

"Do you think they miss all this?" he asks.

"Part of them I'm sure does. They have to get on with their lives, and they realize that. I think they'll all be content to play the role of the Russians in World War One."

"Huh?"

"The Russians. They fought valiantly for years during the Great War until the Bolshevik Revolution when they decided to sit the rest of war out to handle their own business. I think the gang's going to do much of the same."

Blake just stares at me and shakes his head, while wearing a stupid grin. I have no idea why he's looking at me that way.

"What?"

"Nothing. You're starting to sound just like your boss. I'll say this much—Michael Bennit must have been one hell of a history teacher."

-SIX-

MICHAEL

Unlike the first visit to this backwoods retreat, I have no problem finding his driveway this time. I steer my rental car up to the front of the house and park in roughly the same spot as Kylie did when the two of us and Chelsea paid Speaker Albright a visit only a few short weeks ago.

The early morning flight out of New York was a quick one, aided by only having a carry-on and no checked luggage. I was lucky to find a seat on this flight when I went to book it following my dinner with Kylie at Vera's. Once I knew I was leaving to come here, I couldn't sleep. I don't know if it was out of anticipation or trepidation, but the uneasiness hasn't subsided now that I'm here.

I make my way onto his front porch and go to knock on the front door when I notice it cracked open. I open it a little farther and step across the threshold into the foyer where we were greeted by Mrs. Albright, only now she's nowhere to be found.

"Hello?" I call out, just in case.

I cock my ear to listen for a response, but all I hear is the faint melody of some classical piece coming from down the hall. I follow it, stopping at the sturdy door that marks the entrance to Albright's study. I'm about to open the door and burst in before another idea pops into my head.

I've only engaged in breaking and entering twice in my life. The first was during my misspent youth, when I exercised some poor judgment in joining a couple of friends in breaking into a neighbor's garage. The second was during my deployments in Iraq and Afghanistan, when my Special Forces unit searched countless villages looking for insurgents. Now there'll be a third.

There are more efficient ways of breaking down a door than kicking it, but using breaching tools are not nearly as gratifying. Taking a step back, I draw my leg back and up and thrust it forward with all the might I can muster. The result is the same as it was with the dilapidated hovels in Iraq. The door explodes open as splinters of wood from the doorjamb tumble through air.

The room is what a bookworm would dream of for a man cave. Ceiling-to-floor bookcases filled with cloth-bound books cover every wall in the room. A thick layer of cigar smoke hangs in the air of the otherwise ornate and beautiful space, now marred with one very broken door.

Albright stares at me with a mix of shock and fear. He looks like he's been on a week-long bender. Never the picture of health, his gut is even more bloated from excessive drinking. The normally well-dressed politician is clothed like he just finished a long day of panhandling on a New York street. He's disheveled and, by the way he is trying to steady himself, inebriated. It's not what I expected to find.

"That really wasn't necessary, Michael," he says after composing himself. "The door wasn't locked."

"It was far more satisfying than knocking politely."

"My door would disagree, but you certainly know how to get someone's attention. Drink?" he asks, as he lifts and shakes the decanter sitting on his desk. Apparently the journey back and forth to the wet bar ten feet away was too taxing for him.

"It's ten in the morning, Johnston."

"I can add it to your coffee if it would make you feel better. I know your addiction to lattes."

"You did it, didn't you? You had Jerold Todd Bernard try to kill me." There's nothing like the direct approach.

"Oh, I should probably make this a double," he says, filling his tumbler. "You found out the day of our press conference, didn't you?"

I don't bother responding. The words of his answer rattle around my head. It wasn't a denial. It wasn't outrage that I could insinuate such a thing. It wasn't anything more than an outright admission of guilt. And now I have a bigger problem—controlling my own anger.

"I knew something was wrong when you had your staffer send me away. How did you find out?"

"Reed," I respond through clenched teeth.

"And you believed him?" As if he's one to talk about trusting people.

"No, we had to confirm it," I snap.

"How?" he inquires, sounding more like someone wondering how I pulled off an upset in my fantasy football league. I use the opportunity to get the last bit of confirmation I need before I throttle him.

"Reed has a mole on your staff. He gave him the burner phone you tossed in the trash receptacle."

Albright's ruddy complexion goes stark white. He gazes at me with a look of disbelief, before shaking his head and slugging the entirety of his drink back. He sets the empty tumbler down in front of him and wipes his mouth with his sleeve. This guy is a mess.

"I should have known."

"Why did you do it?" I don't really care about how he didn't know Reed planted paid informants on his congressional staff.

Understanding why he chose to betray is what I came here to find out.

"Does it matter?"

"It's the only thing standing between you and the worst beating of your life."

"Spoken like a true soldier," he mutters, leaning back in his executive chair.

"Are you going to tell me or am I going to have to get the duct tape and hammer and find out Jack Bauer style?"

"No wonder you are so popular. You know how to get things done, and that's what people in this country want right now. Come here for a moment," he says, rising out of his chair and gesturing me to follow him to a bookcase on the wall on the opposite side of his spacious study.

"The biggest problem with reaching the top of any profession is it is a long fall back to the bottom. It's what I was facing after the November elections and the failure of the rules bill," he explains, finding the book he was looking for and pulling it off the shelf.

Many of the volumes in this study are ancient-looking cloth- and leather-bound masterpieces, no longer circulated by modern book publishers. This particular shelf, however, contains more modern works still in their contemporary paper dust jackets.

"I was going to be out as Speaker," he continues, "and my own party, which I dedicated my entire adult life to supporting, was going to either cast me out of politics or feed me to the wolves. It was an unwinnable situation, and I blamed you."

"So you thought you'd even the score by having me killed! By trying to kill my staff, who have mostly just begun to live their lives! That was your solution?"

"Desperate men do desperate things, Michael. You, of all people, know that." He hands me the book.

I take it and stare at the cover. For most people, his message would be completely lost. When you hand a biography of Aaron Burr to a former history teacher, it's another form of communication.

Aaron Burr was elected to the U.S. Senate in 1791 and, nine years later, he ended up as vice-president after an unsuccessful bid for the presidency. The election was a constitutional test not dissimilar to the one I caused in the House. A tie in the Electoral College with Thomas Jefferson left the House of Representatives to determine the winner. Burr's rival, Alexander Hamilton, supported Jefferson and ultimately secured the presidency for him. Back then, there were no party tickets as there are today, and the loser Burr became vice president.

As the end of his term approached in 1804, Burr lost the election for governor of New York and again blamed Hamilton for the loss. Eager to defend his honor, he challenged his nemesis to a duel and killed him. He was absolved of any charges, but the public screamed murder and his downward spiral began. Three years later, he was charged with conspiracy and his political career was ruined.

"Do you think this begins to justify your actions?" I demand, waving the book inches from his puffy face.

"No, it doesn't. I wasn't thinking straight, but I told Jerold to only target you and Viano. He was never supposed to endanger anyone else."

"Are you serious?" I shout, flinging Burr's biography across the room like a Frisbee and sending it crashing into a very expensive-looking vase on the coffee table. "When bullets are flying, even the professionals don't know exactly where they'll hit. That's why there is always collateral damage in war and always will be!"

"I know. I told you, I wasn't thinking clearly. And thank you for that. I always hated that vase."

"You think this is some kind of joke to me, Johnston?"

"No, I know it isn't, but I resigned myself to my fate once I realized you knew the truth. It's why I left the front door open and sent my wife up to Columbia on a shopping trip. I had a feeling you'd be coming."

"Coming for revenge?"

"Or for answers."

-SEVEN-
SPEAKER ALBRIGHT

Michael Bennit can be a volatile man, but I don't think he would be dumb enough to act on his physical threats. Part of me wishes he would though. He needs answers to get closure. He just is so angry he doesn't see that yet.

"Michael, you have questions. I have the answers. This will be the last opportunity you ever get to ask them, so use it wisely."

"How did you know Jerold Todd Bernard?" He isn't wasting any time at all.

"Bernard was one of Reed's henchmen that he used to funnel illegal money to candidates. To avoid generating a trail that could lead back to Ibram & Reed, these payments were transferred through proxies. If any of them ever got caught, he would have plausible deniability and could wash his hands of the whole thing."

"I know that part. What happened to him to make him the man he became?"

"Bernard was one of Reed's best and most reliable assets, but politics is a tough business. Doing what he was doing, you're bound to run afoul of pretty powerful people. One of them made it his personal mission to destroy him."

"Who?"

"It doesn't matter who, just that he succeeded. The rich and powerful are accustomed to getting their way, Michael. They also act like insufferable infants when they don't. In this instance, the person in question lost his race and, once he got wind of the money that was illegally channeled to his opponent, blamed poor Jerold. To get even, he took everything from him with a snap of his fingers and the ordeal made Jerold a broken man."

The rich and powerful can make destroying someone's life really that easy, and it happens far more often than people know. Average Americans have their problems—raising their kids, paying their mortgage, dealing with the occasional family dispute. The wealthy live in a whole different universe, and it can be an ugly one.

"So how do you fit in?" Michael asks, apparently still trying to put all the pieces together in his head.

"I'd known Jerold Todd Bernard since my very first campaign, so I tried to help him out in any way I could. Money, work, housing, you name it. I did everything in my power to help him pick up the pieces and get on with his life. Only—"

"By putting a gun in his hand?" Michael interrupts.

"It wasn't that simple. All the king's horses and men wouldn't have put that man back together either. He came to me at the beginning of last fall, depressed and suicidal. I offered to get him help and support, but he had made up his mind. He wanted to end it all."

"So instead of a simple suicide, you turned him loose on me, promising a suicide by cop in return."

I look down, more as a reflex than because of a conscious decision. I was angry and desperate and able to rationalize away any trepidation I had at the time. Now I've never felt more shame than I do right now.

"Look me in the eyes, Johnston." I can't bring myself to do it. "Look at me! Tell me that's what you did!" he demands in a voice filled with rage hot enough to boil water. I force my eyes up to meet his.

"Yeah, that's what I did," I whisper. "At the time I thought it would solve both our problems and he agreed. So I gave him instructions as to the best way to target you."

"Then you gave the 'go' order."

"There was no such thing. I just needed to tell him where and when you were going to make your statement to the press. You were a marked man long before that and nothing was going to stop him."

"You didn't try."

"No, I didn't."

Michael scoffs and walks back across the room to the window behind my desk. I don't bother following him. At this point, the more distance between us the better. I don't want to find out I'm wrong about him getting physical.

"Knowing what you did, why did you decide to work with us?" he finally asks, after an awkward silence that felt like it lasted a lifetime.

"It was never my plan, obviously. Remember what Chelsea said about me being nervous when you guys last visited after Christmas? About the reason for it being because I didn't know how much you knew?"

"Vaguely."

"She could not have known how right she was. I thought you were there because, somehow, you'd figured out I was behind the whole affair. It wasn't until she asked if I knew who was responsible that I realized you weren't on my trail."

"And you denied having any knowledge of it."

"Denial is not only a reflex in politicians, it's programmed into our DNA. So yeah, I denied it. I thought maybe this storm would pass like so many others have."

"You still haven't answered my question," Michael deadpans.

"I joined you because you offered. At first, it was just to get back in the game and maybe keep you from learning the truth about who was behind the assassination. Then something happened. You awoke a part of me that had gone dormant long ago. Because of you, I realized why I had run for Congress in the first place. You reminded me what it was like to make a difference in people's lives again. After that, I had meaning in my own."

"You should have found out before Marilyn Viano was murdered and my friend almost bled out right in front of me. You should have found out before Chelsea ended up with a concussion and her boyfriend ended up shot twice in the back and in a coma. You should have found that out before you tried to kill *me*, Johnston."

"Yes, I should have, and I will live with those regrets for the rest of my days. I know what I did will never be forgivable, no matter how many times I tell you how truly sorry I am. I cannot bring Marilyn back, and I can't undo the damage I've done. The question now is, where do we go from here?"

Michael goes back to looking out the window. I'm sure part of him still wants to use me as the slab of beef from *Rocky*, but there's less of a chance of that now. Unfortunately, there are fates worse than a beating. I get the feeling he has one of them in mind.

"I don't know," he says, after another painful silence. "You're going to pay for this crime. With God as my witness, you're going to rot in a prison for what you had done that day.

For killing Viano, for shooting me and Cisco, and for landing Blake in a coma because of his wounds."

"I'm sorry for all of that. I truly am."

Michael moves around from the back of the desk and I meet him in the center of my beloved study. His eyes are piercing, and unlike most politicians who act tough or threatening, he actually is. Michael Bennit may be the most trustworthy politician in Washington, but he's also by far the most intimidating.

"My students were like my own children when I was a teacher. That's the kind of bond many educators form with their pupils. You endangered some of them and are going to pay for that. God might find it in his heart to forgive you, but know in your heart that I never will."

He moves past me and out the shattered door to my study. I hear the echoes of his footsteps as he moves down my hallway to the front door like a man with a purpose. Through actions I only have myself to blame for, I gave him that purpose.

"Maybe in the next life you will, Michael," I mutter to myself.

-EIGHT-

JAMES

Rarely has America ever been united outside of war or unthinkable tragedies like 9/11. We are an opinionated people, and politicians feed off those opinions to advance their own agendas. The media are unwitting accomplices in that game, and they can always be counted on to widen that divisiveness.

For the past couple of decades, the battle between Democrats and Republicans has ruled the headlines. With the introduction of Bennit's freshly elected icongressmen in the House, the independents have become a unifying force despite our best efforts to portray them as otherwise. The political conflict is now being framed by the media as the House of Representatives verses the White House. The Senate has not yet joined the fray, but politicians are sensitive to the whims of the people and the media whose reports they watch and read. Senators jockeying for position in the food chain will be dragged into the power struggle sooner or later.

Fear over the impending battle is the only reason I can think of as to why I would be summoned to the West Wing by Diane Herr. As the president's chief of staff, she is his top advisor and will want options on the table on how to deal with the marauding congressmen, capable of blocking his agenda and blurring his vision for America. At least that's why I think I'm here on a Saturday morning.

I pass through security and am escorted through the lobby of the working part of the White House. When the building is portrayed on television, there are always staffers running around as if government operates at a breakneck pace. Nothing could be farther from the truth. In fact, television portrayals of life at this street address are almost comically wrong.

For anyone who has ever seen *The West Wing* on NBC, even the layout between that set and the real thing are vastly different. The most noticeable is the lack of a policy "bullpen" like there was on the show. In fact, about the only similarity between the television depiction and real life is the geographical relationship between the Oval Office and the Roosevelt Room, which I was just shown into. I am right across the corridor from the center of national executive leadership.

The windowless space is really nothing more than a glorified conference room approximately twenty-five feet wide and thirty-five feet long featuring a table that seats sixteen. President Richard Nixon dedicated the room in honor of Theodore Roosevelt under whose administration the West Wing was built. It is typically used by White House staff, but given its close proximity to the Oval Office, it regularly serves as a waiting area for people preparing to meet the president. I doubt I am one of those people today.

"Good morning, James. I apologize for being late. Please, have a seat," Diane says, breezing in with an annoying nonchalance considering how long she has kept me waiting.

"I'm not sure it still is morning, Diane," I tell her, without any effort in hiding my contempt at her tardiness. Having already spent too much time studying the portraits of both Theodore Roosevelt and Franklin Roosevelt displayed in the room, I choose my seat at the table and crash down into it.

"Again, I'm sorry. It couldn't be avoided. Can I get you anything?" Yeah, lunch.

"No, I'm fine, thanks," I tell her as she slides into a seat directly across the table from me and sits pleasantly to the side with her legs crossed. "So, what is this about?"

"During some of our recent strategy sessions, there have been some concerns raised about the independents in the House. It has stoked some pretty heated disagreements and I wanted to get some perspective from people outside of the administration."

"So you came to me."

"Yes, among others. I'm looking for some insights into the independent icongressmen."

"Diane, it's not only the independents you have to worry about. It's everyone willing to join the caucus Bennit started, and that includes the Republicans *and* the Democrats. Representatives from both parties are eagerly participating in it."

"Fight Club. What a stupid name. Do you happen to know what are they discussing?" Normally I would think she's trying to confirm her own information, but I'm betting she's asking because she has no more of an idea than I do.

"Diane, you saw the movie. You know the first rule of Fight Club. The members of that caucus are taking that secrecy very seriously. Nothing is leaking out."

"Fight Club" is the moniker of the caucus Bennit set up for the icongressmen that has been joined by alarming numbers of Republicans and Democrats. With the promise of no cameras, press conferences, or leaks, he has provided a forum for representatives to express their opinions without having to filter their words or edit content out of fear of the media. Nothing has leaked out of the meetings to date, thus keeping to the first rule of Fight Club which states that nobody talks about Fight Club.

"You know, I'm scheduled to face off against Bennit's chief of staff on one of the Sunday morning political shows tomorrow."

"You're mixing it up with Chelsea Stanton? That ought to be interesting." I will have to remind myself to tune in for that. Tomorrow is the Super Bowl, but those two squaring off will be the game to watch for me.

"Yes, it should be entertaining for the folks back home to watch me wipe the floor with her."

"Be careful not to underestimate her, Diane," I warn. Not that she'll listen.

"I'm not. She's young and inexperienced. And, to my knowledge, she's never participated in a show like this, whereas I have."

"We all thought that about Bennit too. Yet he won his debate against a seasoned incumbent his first time out, and has politically outmaneuvered almost every prominent politician in Washington since."

"I'm not going up against him."

"No, but she's quite literally one of his students. Now, I know y'all didn't invite me here for debate pointers against a twenty-year-old. What can I do for you and the president?"

"No, you're right, we didn't. The president and I need to know what it will take for Bennit and his icongressmen to support his agenda."

"Y'all are asking me?"

"It wasn't my idea, it was Glenn's."

Again with the first name. Diane has been close friends with the president for a long time. Whenever she wants someone to know she's speaking for him, his first name gets used in conversation. This is one of those times.

"I thought the independents would be boxed in during the election for Speaker. They wanted Bennit and everyone believed they wouldn't settle for less. That's typically what happens after a wave election—new members believe they have a mandate and won't compromise. Bennit changed that when he got them to support Albright for Speaker. These guys mean business. They are out to tackle problems and are willing to seek compromises to pass bills that will help solve them."

"The president doesn't see much room for compromise in his agenda."

"You're starting to sound like his predecessor."

"It may be the only thing he has in common with a Republican. The only bipartisan consensus we've managed to reach over the past three decades is the unchecked expansion of presidential power. The previous occupant of this office brought that to a whole new level, and we plan on taking advantage of that."

"Diane, he was widely called an 'elected king' by the time he left office, and the American people didn't react well to it. What was his approval rating when he left office? Forty percent?"

"The only people who will care if the president expands his powers are the ones from the other party who aren't going to vote for us again anyway. That's how it works and you know it."

"Are you willing to bet his presidency on that? Because I think y'all are being overly optimistic that the American people aren't going to pay attention. Bennit's social media crusade is changing the rules of the game."

"That's for us to worry about." Worrying about that should be keeping them up at night and, if it isn't, they aren't taking it seriously enough.

"Fine. So why am I here?"

"We have support for what we want to do. We'll do it ourselves if we have to, but Glenn knows getting congressional support is an easier path. The Senate is already on board. We just need traction in the House."

"And you're asking my advice on how to get it?"

She nods, and I am beginning to think that there is a path back to power for me after all. If I can deliver the White House a couple of victories, I can use that newfound value to reinsert myself into a position of influence. That's a refreshing thought, since three days ago I was convinced Bennit would run to the police and I'd be heading to prison for withholding evidence of a crime.

"You need to hand them legislative defeats. Don't let a single bill they pass become law. The resulting deadlock will beat the spirit out of them, and if you manage to pepper in a few wins of your own, y'all will force the social media experiment to fail. People will realize the promise of the icongressmen was an empty one and y'all will score gains in the midterms that render the survivors of their cause ineffective."

"That's a well-articulated plan, James, only you've said it yourself that Michael Bennit is a coalition builder. I don't want to ask the president to have to veto everything they pass." She's right. I have said that in the past, and he is one.

"What about the Senate? You said they are on board with executing the president's agenda. Have them block passage or pass their own version and make sure the House version gets hacked up in the conference."

A Congressional Conference Committee, composed of senior members of the House of Representatives and the Senate, is created when the chambers pass different versions of a piece of legislation. The members are charged with negotiating a compromise bill that will be returned directly to the floor of both houses of Congress for a vote. The president can kill legislation championed by the House by ensuring the Senate is uncooperative in agreeing to a bill.

"We can do that, but it won't work forever. You said it yourself. This is a new political climate and those self-preservationists in the Senate are not going to block reasonable legislation."

Self-preservationists are a good descriptor of the men and women who make up today's upper house. Aren't all politicians that way, including Michael Bennit? What would he be willing to trade? An idea springs into my head. I have more leverage than I thought with the iCongressman. He has to be convinced of my information I gave to Kylie by now. He's waiting on me to make a move, because he doesn't want to make it himself. I can use that.

"Diane, I think I may be able to help your situation," I tell her, unable to suppress the growing smile on my face.

"How?"

"By getting the independents to go along with much of your agenda."

"And how are you going to get the unimpeachable Michael Bennit to do that?"

I lean back in my chair, enjoying the moment. For the first time in days, I feel like a man with a new lease on life. I'm in the driver's seat again, and I have no intention of giving it up.

"Simple. I'm going to make him an offer he can't refuse."

-NINE-
KYLIE

With Michael catching a flight this morning to confront Albright down in Charleston, I have had plenty of time to organize my notes to start writing the article he wants. What I really was doing was stalling. I've struggled to bring myself to start working on this because I know it could mean the end of his political career if it ever gets printed.

It is past noon now and I need to get away from my laptop for a while after spending the morning questioning my sanity for agreeing to this. I grab my coat and keys and jump into the car for a short trip into town. I figure I can use my break productively and work on knocking off another item on my to-do list.

Being shunned by most major national newspapers comes with a serious downside—they won't entertain printing an article from me. I had great success when I freelanced during Michael's first campaign, but my final article made them feel used, burning a lot of my remaining bridges in the process.

The Washington Post took a chance on hiring me, but my determination to get to the bottom of the assassination attempt resulted in them firing me as well. If Michael asks me to submit this article, none of the big papers are getting it. They'll sit on the sidelines while a smaller publication gets the credit for printing an article that could fundamentally change how Americans perceive their leaders for the next ten years.

Since I can't immediately get wide distribution, I will have to hope online blogs pick it up and cause it to get reported by the network and cable news programs. To do that, I need to find someone willing to take a chance on me and sell them on the prospect of a once in a lifetime scoop. I have the perfect paper in mind, and I don't even have to drive far to reach it.

The *Millfield Gazette* has an office in the center of town, on a steeply sloped road that heads down toward the river. I select a spot right in front of the building, ensuring I fully engage the parking brake before turning the engine off. Leaving the warmth of my vehicle and braving the ice cold New England air, I trudge to the door and walk in.

The office is about as small as the paper's circulation. The *Millfield Gazette* is a local, hometown paper in every sense. It primarily reports on town events, school sports, and local politics. Since it has such a small staff, I figured I would find at least one of the editors in the office on a Saturday and I'm not disappointed.

"Kylie Roberts?" a voice asks from the doorway of an office off the main work area. I'm a little taken aback. The large, disheveled, middle-aged man seems to know exactly who I am and I don't remember ever meeting him.

"Uh, yeah," is all I manage to stutter out. Way to leave an impression, Kylie.

"Sorry, I didn't mean to throw you off guard. Your name and reputation precedes you. You're something of a legend in the minds of people in this office. Michael Bennit's first campaign is still remembered with awe and reverence around the water cooler here. I'm Randy Sprague, editor-in-chief."

"Pleased to meet you, Randy. It was a very interesting time."

Michael's first campaign was the textbook example of a media circus, in no small part because of me. At the height of what became known nationally as "Bennitmania," his students were being chased by paparazzi and everyone was clamoring for the first live interview with the political recluse known as the iCandidate. Covering it all, to the best of their ability, was the small hometown paper that was used to board of education meetings and varsity football games. Through it all, they did a really nice job measuring the effect the campaign was having on their small town.

"Yes it was. What brings you here today? And don't think my staff won't be insanely jealous that I got to meet you."

"I have a proposition for you, Randy."

"A proposition? Okay, you have my attention. Please, have a seat. I'd offer you some bad coffee, but … well, it's really bad and I don't want to scare you off."

After passing on his offer of undrinkable sludge, I explain the article Michael wants me to write to Randy and offer a few highlights about the content without getting into any specifics. I then give him my opinion as to what it's going to mean to the people and the political landscape of the country. He listens intently, not interrupting for even a single question. When I'm done, he leans back in his chair, staring at the wall behind me.

"Basically, I'm here because I need to know if you want the first crack at it printing it," I say in conclusion, after his lack of an immediate response becomes unnerving.

"Wow. That's some offer. Not that I'm not appreciative, but if you say this is going to be an earth-shattering exposé, why not go to one of the major papers?"

"If you know my reputation then you know my history with them, Randy. This is a once in a lifetime chance. Don't pass it up on my accord."

I'm willing to admit that I'm not much of a salesperson, but I think I'm doing a pretty adequate job. Not that the opportunity to print this doesn't sell itself. He just needs to have the guts to say yes.

"Kylie, we have a small circulation in Millfield and an even smaller budget. I can't afford to pay your freelance fee—"

"Then don't. I don't want financial compensation for this. It won't cost you a thing." That triggered the obligatory look of apprehension.

"I don't know."

"Can you imagine the circulation increase and prestige potential this will bring? It will be picked up by every newscast in the country, local and national. Every newspaper will want to rerun it."

"Yeah, maybe, but this is starting to smell like a propaganda job, especially since you don't want to get paid for it." Okay, maybe I'm not doing such a good job at selling it.

"I promise you, it's anything but."

"I'll need to see the article first," Randy argues. Despite the small-town charm, he's your typical newspaper editor.

"I wouldn't expect you to print it blind. Of course you'll see it and have input on changes."

"You know if this is half of what you say it is, it would be a real coup for us. It could even be bigger than Congressman Bennit's first campaign."

"It sounds like you're all out of excuses."

"When will it be ready?"

"It's hard to tell. This is a sensitive and politically charged piece. It could be a week or it could be a month from now. We can discuss when it should go to print because the timing may require some … finesse."

It will actually require a lot of finesse since there's no guarantee I will write it or that Michael will decide it needs to be printed. Unfortunately, I can't let this editor know that. Newsmen don't like large amounts of uncertainty when planning the layout of their publications. As much as I want to be straight with Randy, the truth is not an option. If Michael decides to move forward, I need to have a plan in place to get it printed and this is my best shot. If he chooses not to, the only damage done will be some very unhappy editors at the *Millfield Gazette*. Under the circumstances, I can live with that.

"That's not much lead time, Kylie, especially since I don't know how many column inches it will be or whether I can even—"

"Are you really going to let layout concerns ruin this for you? Do we have a deal, yes or no? I need to know right now so I can move on to the next paper in line." I think they call that the hard sell.

"We have a deal, contingent on me reading and approving the article. Is that acceptable?"

"Yes. I'll send you my draft as soon as it's finished. We'll talk again then. Enjoy the Super Bowl tomorrow."

We shake hands and I leave the office as quickly as I can before he changes his mind. Now I have to stay determined not to change mine. Until then, I'm content scratching that item off the to-do list.

-TEN-
CHELSEA

I've never been on a Sunday morning political show before. In fact, most of the kids my age are still hungover from their Saturday night college binge drinking sessions to bother watching one, should they even have the interest to do so. I guess I'll never win an award for being normal.

The Sunday morning talk shows were once the mainstay of American politics. Shows like NBC's *Meet the Press*, CBS's *Face the Nation*, and ABC's *This Week* provided opportunities for interviews that our leaders would use to set the national political agenda. The shows started becoming too gossipy, relied on repeatedly hosting the same guests, and started becoming stale while fading in importance. Add the omnipresent specter of cable news and the go-anywhere reach of mobile devices, and the shows have lost much of their relevance.

Not all of it though. In an attempt to revitalize its ratings, the show I was invited to is now taped live at its Washington, D.C., studios and has provided some of the most hard-hitting interviews seen over the past year. Kylie loves the new direction, claiming it is bringing back the spirit of true journalism. Congressman Bennit has appeared on it a couple of times, and was more nervous for them than he was before his first debate.

Hearing that did little to calm my own nerves. Knowing that politicians rarely pick a fight with each other on national broadcasts, the program quickly learned that staff members have no such reservations. So the top of the show may be reserved for the most powerful and influential political figures, but the fireworks begin during the second segment when staff members get their turn.

"Are you ready, Miss Stanton?" the production assistant I know only as Cindy announces from the door leading into the makeup room.

"As ready as I'll ever be," I tell her, getting out of my chair and following her out into the studio.

As the technicians outfit me with my wireless microphone, I cannot get over how small these places really are. They look much bigger on television than they are in real life. I'm about to sit when Satan's handmaiden walks in.

Slender and in her mid-forties, she's pretty in a Cruella de Vil kind of way. There is very little I would consider feminine about her. Her short black hair and form-fitting pantsuit leads me to believe she wishes she had been born with a y-chromosome.

"Hi, I'm Diane Herr, it's a pleasure to meet you, Chelsea," she says with her hand extended while forcing a polite smile. I know what she really wanted to say, and it wasn't nice.

"It's nice to meet you as well," I reciprocate. I know what I want to say to her too, and it isn't nice either.

We settle in as everyone takes their positions. Since this particular show went to the live format instead of the prerecorded one favored for so many years, the timelines are tighter and everyone seems to run around in a state of panic.

"Welcome back, everyone," the moderator says when the red light below the camera lights up.

"In this segment, we are joined by White House Chief of Staff Diane Kerr, and Chelsea Stanton, chief of staff for the assumed leader of the independents in the House of

Representatives, Michael Bennit. Thanks to both of you for joining."

"Thanks for having us," we both say at the same time. Ugh.

"Diane, let's start with you. The president has made overtures in his inaugural address, and several speeches since, about his willingness to circumvent Congress to advance his agenda. Is it his desire to bypass the legislative process?"

"The president believes deeply in wanting to meet the needs of the American people. For decades, Congress's failure to act on substantial legislative initiatives has crippled our progress as a nation and we have lost our standing in the world because of it. Since Congress cannot do what's necessary, the president is willing to exercise the full authority of his office to do what's right for our citizens."

"I don't think anyone would disagree with the dysfunction in Congress over the past several decades," I interject, "but I think we should be wary of any president who uses it as an excuse to fundamentally expand his powers—"

"That's not what he's doing." Did she just really interrupt me? Can she not see the color of my hair? It's on now.

"That is exactly what he's doing," I snap back acidly. "He's also basing this power grab on the inaction of previous congresses and not taking into account that there is a strong and growing coalition being built to address those issues."

"You're talking about Michael Bennit and the caucus he created that united the independents and a number of moderate Democrats and Republicans?" the host asks.

"Yes, I am. The independents who were elected ran on a platform not based on rigid ideology, but of working together to solve issues. Despite what the president thinks, the people aren't looking for him to enact legislation with the stroke of a pen. They want their elected representatives to set aside their partisanship and be capable of working with each other."

"Diane, do you think Congressman Michael Bennit is capable of restoring a sense of order and function to a very broken Congress, and is the president willing to work with him and Speaker Albright?"

"I'm not sure what Chelsea was paying attention to last November, but the *people* elected the president. Fifty-three percent of them chose him to lead this country. You can't possibly believe that a representative from a *small* district in Connecticut is in a better position to know what's best for the country than the president of the United States is."

Vince warned me that I would need to come out swinging or she would eat me alive. Vanessa told me to find a balance between confident and arrogant. Forget it. I'm a redhead and there is no off switch for that. It's time to take Vince's advice and slam the condescending bitch.

"Actually, last November I was watching ordinary citizens, running their campaigns on social media, defeat seventy-six of the most entrenched incumbents in the House. They did so because of our citizens' desire to end partisan politics and seek out compromises and solutions to the issues our country faces."

"The country doesn't want compromise, they want strong leadership."

"I don't expect you, as the president's chief of staff, to understand what the people want when you forget that it was the Electoral College that elected him to office, not the people."

The blood drains from Diane's face when she realizes her error. Take that. I can almost hear the laughter coming from Blake's hospital room and I can guarantee the congressman and Kylie shared a high five in their living room up in Millfield.

"That's semantics," she argues, trying to save face. "Everyone knows the Electoral College is more nostalgic than factual."

"Nostalgic? Tell that to Al Gore," I say with an irrepressible grin.

Vice-President Al Gore lost the election to George W. Bush in 2000 after winning the popular vote but losing the crucial Electoral College votes in Florida. The margin there was razor thin, and yes the United States Supreme Court gets much of the blame for ending the contentious recount, but had the presidency hinged on simply the popular vote, the man who "invented the Internet" would have been president.

"Diane, I understand your desire to ignore the fact that the Electoral College is part of our election process," I continue, taking advantage of her loss of words. "The Constitution is a pesky document for a president who has already made it clear that he wants to rule by executive order. The fact is, congressmen in the House have the most intimate relationship with the people and, as a body, are in the best position to forge the solutions to problems."

"Chelsea, are you saying Michael Bennit is going to make good on his pledge for Congress to take a more proactive approach in setting the legislative agenda for this country?" the moderator questions, acting more like a referee than a facilitator.

"As he stated in his press conference at the end of the last session, it was the Founding Fathers' expectation that the Legislative Branch would be the engine that propelled government."

"And the president's job is to steer it." Diane is desperate to seize the initiative back. Not so fast.

"If by steer it you mean ensure that laws passed by Congress and signed into law are fully implemented and enforced by the Executive Branch, then I completely agree with you." If looks could kill, I would be taking another ride to George Washington University Medical Center, only as a corpse this time.

"Diane, does the president view his role as something more akin to an elected king, as some have suggested?"

"Of course not. He has simply stated that he will do everything in his power to fill the vacuum the complete absence of congressional leadership has created to make government work for the people."

"What I believe Diane is trying to say is that the president's approach will be the same one his predecessors have used. He will come up with bills that appease his base and steamroll them through Congress along party lines. For those he can't, he'll bypass the legislative process altogether and sign executive orders to advance his radical agenda. Does that sum it up, Diane?"

I ask that final question with all the sweetness and sincerity I can muster. I want to try to sound like I'm being helpful. I don't know if I pulled it off to the cameras, but I've never seen someone angrier.

"I think that Michael Bennit's *young* chief of staff is vastly oversimplifying things." Oh, she went there. After playing the age card, I don't let her continue.

"How am I oversimplifying the president's own words? I'm sure you were right there during his inaugural address when he said, 'We cannot wait any longer for those sworn to conduct the business of the people to end their procrastination and make hard choices to address the issues of our time.'"

"You're taking that line out of context from a much larger speech," Diane complains.

"The context was the president setting the stage for taking unilateral action, if necessary, to advance his sole vision for America. How is that not the behavior of an elected king or despot?" That word even got her more flustered.

"Using that term is a cheap political ploy and that was not what he was trying to convey. The president is not trying to be a king or a despot. He was commenting on Congress's failure to act on issues over the past couple of decades. He is prepared to act to solve problems facing this country. It's why people elected him."

"They also elected him to uphold and defend the Constitution of the United States, not ignore it by issuing executive orders when it suits his political purpose."

"He's not doing that!" She's edging closer to the cliff. Time to give her a push.

"Okay, so when we begin passing bipartisan bills in Congress that work to solve the 'problems facing this country,' we can count on his support and watch him sign them into law?" Gotcha.

Diane, one of the most respected and outspoken political operatives in the county, comes down with an acute case of laryngitis. She starts to say something, but words just can't manage to make it out of her mouth. I hope my father set his DVR for this.

"How about it, Diane?" the moderator prompts, not wanting the awkward pause to cause viewers to lose their interest.

"We will look at each law on a case by case basis and the president will make his own determination whether a particular bill is in the best interests of the people."

"So that's a no, then? You won't support bipartisan legislation that passes both houses of Congress?" I'm not letting her off that easy.

"I think it's premature to draw any conclusions as Congress hasn't managed to pass anything, Chelsea."

"Yet."

"We will have to end it there. Diane Herr, Chelsea Stanton, thanks for joining us today," the moderator decrees, putting the White House chief of staff out of her misery.

"My pleasure," I state. Diane just nods.

The moderator sets up the next segment and sends the viewers into a commercial break. I sit in my seat, a smile on my face not reciprocated by my colleague. The wait for the red light on the camera to click off seems eternal.

"And, we're out," a producer relays from offstage.

No sooner than the words escaped his lips than Herr rips off her microphone set and stomps off. I wait for a technician to help with mine, glancing over at the next guest to occupy my seat.

"Well, that was fun. Are you sure you've never done this before?" the moderator asks.

"No, why?"

"Because I just watched a girl barely out of high school take apart the most powerful chief of staff since Karl Rove, and he was called the 'Architect.'"

"It was beginner's luck."

"Oh, I doubt that."

He's right. It's a byproduct of working with Congressman Bennit. No student would have survived his American History class without knowing how to debate. It's why we passed the Tylenol around fifteen minutes into class.

"Okay, let's just say I had a great teacher," I tell him with a wink before leaving the set.

-ELEVEN-

MICHAEL

Maybe my brief trip yesterday to the relative warmth of the Carolinas messed up my tolerance, or maybe it's the wind chill, but it's downright frigid out here. Kylie said it was cold yesterday, but it's bothering me more today than cold temperatures usually do. At least I'm dressed for the weather.

I was not about to wear a suit, tie, and overcoat for this meeting, although history would indicate there is little doubt he will. I've never seen the man in casual dress before and prefer to believe he sleeps in one of his five-thousand-dollar suits. The man with the Kentucky roots has a severe sense of style, but hopefully no tolerance to the cold.

"I got a call on the way here," James Reed tells me after parking his expensive rental and walking up to me while buttoning up his coat to protect against the biting wind. "I was told your chief of staff dismantled Diane Herr on one of the morning political shows an hour ago."

"I know, I watched it," I say with almost fatherly pride. When he reaches me, neither of us offer a handshake, and not because it's cold out.

"The irony is, I warned Diane not to underestimate her in a meeting we had yesterday. I guess she didn't listen."

"There's a lot of that going on in Washington."

"This is a beautiful spot, Congressman," Reed says, admiring Briar Point State Park.

"This is the parking lot, Mister Reed," I tell him. "Come on, I'll show you beautiful."

"Diane Herr is a brilliant political strategist, but a little too smug for her own good. She needed to be knocked down a peg or two," Reed offers as we walk down the path towards the river.

"There's a lot of that needed in Washington, too. I may have agreed to meet you, Mister Reed, but I didn't really want to. Let's get to the point of why we're both here, shall we?"

"What's the matter, Congressman? You don't want to be seen canoodling with the enemy? This is how business is done. It's like the Allies and the Germans coming out of trenches during Christmas at the start of World War One. I'm assuming you know the story."

Of course I know it. On Christmas Eve in 1914, German and British troops sang carols to each other across the battlefield. At dawn on Christmas Day, German soldiers emerged from their trenches crying out "Merry Christmas" in English as they walked toward allied lines. The soldiers assumed it was a trick, but since the Germans were unarmed, decided to greet them in the no man's land between. The men exchanged token presents including cigarettes, plum puddings, and other comforts of war, before singing carols and even playing a friendly soccer game. The Christmas Truce of 1914, as it came to be called, was probably the last example of such behavior between enemies in wartime. The next day, they went back to killing each other.

"It's a romantic story, but you know what many of them also did? They buried their dead. The short ceasefire created an opportunity for the somber task of retrieving the bodies of fallen comrades who had perished between the lines."

"I didn't know that. Let's hope it doesn't come to that between us."

"It almost did, remember? I spent last Christmas in a hospital and Marilyn Viano was buried shortly after it."

"Wow. This is a nice view," James tells me, as we reach the bridge and admire the scene. Chelsea would kill me if she ever knew I took this despicable man to her favorite spot.

The view of the center of Millfield from the iron bridge is stunning, with smoke curling from the chimneys on white roofs dusted in snow from last night's flurry. The two majestic church steeples reach for the sky, in a setting that is pure New England.

"It is. This is also a great place to hide a body," I warn. There would be no shortage of offers to help me bury him, although the hole would need to be massive. We'd have to rent a backhoe.

"I know you want me to get to the point, so here it is. I want a truce, Congressman."

"That's a tough request to consider with you hoisting a guillotine over my outstretched neck."

"You're talking about this nasty business with Albright? Yes, he's not a good man, is he? Y'all should choose your friends more carefully."

"Sage advice coming from the man who has none," I fire back. I'm not in the mood for his opinions.

"Now I know where your chief of staff gets her fiery wit from," he proclaims with a chuckle.

"Or maybe I got it from her and the rest of my former students. You don't last five minutes in a classroom without one." And that's the truth.

"Politics is a nasty business," Reed concludes, shifting gears on the conversation and once again turning his head to admire the view. "With all the agendas and partisanship and ideological divides in this day and age, you never know who you can trust. But the people seem to trust you. It would be a shame to destroy the last vestige of hope people seem to have in our federal government, simply because you made the mistake of trusting Johnston Albright."

"Well, there's not much I can do about that once you go to the police with the phone." I play along with him only because this conversation will never end if I don't, and my car heater is beckoning. Not to mention that it's Super Bowl Sunday and Kylie is back at the townhouse with enough junk food to make a die-hard tailgater proud.

"That can be avoided," he offers, turning to face me. This ought to be interesting.

James Reed is a snake oil salesman, and he has a new concoction he's going to try to convince me to buy. It will cure all my ailments, but only if I can meet his price. In the end, it will be too expensive and not work at all, but I might as well hear him out.

"Oh yeah, how?"

"By deciding to work with me instead of against me."

-TWELVE-
JAMES

Bennit has a lot to lose. If I had made him this offer even a year ago, he would have told me where I could stick it. Now that he's gotten a taste of power and influence, he's realizing they create a strong elixir that gives you an incredible high and has nasty withdrawals when it's gone.

"Work with you how?"

"I would be open to making an arrangement similar to the one I had with many of your predecessors and most of your current colleagues," I explain.

"You want to dictate votes."

"Congressman, you have always overstated my impact on the legislative process. All I want from you is your agreeing to meet and discuss matters of importance to my clients with me. How you vote on the final product is your business."

"Yeah, right," is all he mutters in return. He's not buying it, but at least he's thinking about the proposal. That's something.

"Whether you believe me or not is your choice. The truth is I don't buy votes like you're so inclined to think. The donations I make into political campaign coffers only buys me access, which is why my firm supports both parties. With the right level of access, I can let the merits of my argument sway our elected representatives. That's what I do. It's what all lobbyists do." Well, it almost sounded true.

"And if I refuse?"

"You don't want to refuse. This is a one-time offer."

"I don't want to be in the same city as you, Mister Reed, let alone work with you."

"Congressman, you have a bright staff. Listen to them. Y'all know as well as I do that once the information about Albright's involvement goes public, it will destroy you and the other independents. Do you really want to be a footnote in American political history? The great iCandidate who destroyed a bright political future for trusting the wrong man?"

"As opposed to the one who sells his soul like so many others before him?" he argues.

"I'm sorry you think of it that way. My deal is a fair one and I'm not asking much in return."

Bennit is struggling to say yes to my offer, even though his morality is putting up a strong fight. He knows this is the only way out, evidenced by his failure to tell me no. I have managed to box him in for the first time since he came to Washington. God, I love my job.

"Why are you offering me a deal at all? You've wanted to destroy me since the day I set foot in Washington."

"That's true, I have. Since then, you and your staff have earned my respect. Y'all have proven yourselves to be worthy adversaries. People are beginning to figure out that you're not some yahoo that rode into town because of a fad, including the folks at 1600 Pennsylvania Avenue who advise the president."

"You're referring to your meeting at the White House yesterday?"

"Yes. I was summoned there because the president is scared of y'all. You and the icongressmen have formed powerful ties with the moderates and nobody can predict what you're capable of. The White House can't tolerate that uncertainty, so Diane

Herr is looking for any way she can to neutralize the House. Together, we can use that to our advantage."

"How?"

There's no point in disclosing too much. Maybe I will tell him what I have in mind once he accepts the deal. Whether he likes it or not at the point is irrelevant. Once he agrees to my terms, I'll own him.

"We can discuss that once we've reached an agreement."

"And the burner phone? What happens to the evidence against Albright?"

"I'll keep it. In a safe place, of course."

"Oh, I don't think so," Michael emphatically objects. I didn't think he would go for that, but it's his problem.

"Congressman, Johnston Albright's involvement in the assassination never has to be disclosed to anyone. I am keeping the evidence to ensure you don't double-cross me. That's non-negotiable, but trust me when I say, if we reach an accord here, I hope there is never a reason for it to ever see the light of day."

"And what about the Speaker of the House? What happens to him?"

"I can leverage what I know to get him to leave politics if you're uncomfortable working with him. I can't imagine you would be, considering he ordered someone to murder you in cold blood. The GOP has already hinted to the press that he has medical issues. That was the groundwork of their own attempt to force him from the party before you reinstalled him in the top leadership post in the House. I can easily use that to … remove him… from the situation."

I'm elated that Bennit is thinking about this as hard as he is. I figured it was a long shot, but glad I went with my instinct to make the pitch anyway. The man who is always so sure of himself is now anything but. Some lyrics by Kenny Rogers pop into my head. Right now, in this moment, my tormentor doesn't know whether to hold 'em, fold 'em, walk away, or run.

"I need time to think it over."

"I'll give you a few minutes."

"That's not going to work. I'll consider your offer, but if you force me into a decision now, the answer's no and we can both go down together. Is that what you want?"

"Fine," I tell him, thrown off a touch by the ferocity of his response. "I wanted a decision now, but I'm a reasonable man. If you need time to realize the benefits of this, I'll accommodate you. Time is a small price to pay for your consideration of my offer. However, there's a limitation on this arrangement. I'll give you a week to decide and not a day longer. My secretary will call you to make arrangements for us to meet with your decision."

"What's the matter, Mister Reed? Are you afraid to do it by cell phone?" I smile at the dig.

"I hope we can set aside our past differences and learn to work together," I tell him, ignoring the jab at my methods. "Enjoy watching the big game tonight, Congressman."

As I meander up the path that leads from the bridge to the parking lot, I'm thrilled with how that went. He's going to agree, and I'm back to where I should be. I guess I was right—politicians are all the same. Manipulating them will always be as easy as breathing.

-THIRTEEN-
KYLIE

The front door opens and I hear the keys crash into the dish at the entrance as I make the final preparations for our Super Bowl spread at the kitchen counter. He passes me, grabbing a handful of potato chips before fishing a cold Sam Adams out of the fridge.

"Don't judge me. It's my cheat day," he says, giving me a kiss before plopping down on the couch. This can't be good. He never drinks at midday, even on a Sunday before watching football.

"Cheating on your normal diet has never entailed chugging a beer," I observe, as he drinks almost half of the bottle. "I guess your meeting with Reed didn't go well. Do you want to talk about it?"

"Not really."

He then goes on to explain the whole meeting with Reed anyway. The man has a set on him to even consider making Michael that offer. Arrogance is as much a part of Washington as the Lincoln Memorial is, but this brings new meaning to the term audacity.

"You're not seriously considering taking him up on his deal?"

"He's offering me an out," Michael replies with a shrug.

"Sure he is, making you nothing more than a marionette in the process. He'll own you and you know it."

"He claims all he wants is access."

"Yeah, I'm sure that's the case. At least until you do something he doesn't like and he pulls the envelope holding the phone out of his drawer and dangles it in front of your face, saying, 'Remember this?'"

"Maybe he'll give me the evidence in return for my cooperation," the love of my life defends.

"Sure, of course he will. Because when someone tries to sell you the Brooklyn Bridge, they give you the title to it. Have you lost your mind?"

"Yeah, I probably have, but there's no harm in weighing all the options. Cisco's going to argue that taking the deal preserves the intent of the icongressmen."

"Their intent was to serve the American people, not live a lie. Is that really what you want to do?"

The long pause that ensues does not inspire confidence. It's not the awkward silences we shared for a month following the shooting, when we couldn't agree on each other's actions. As scary as that was, this may be several degrees worse. It indicates something I've never seen in him—indecision.

I know he doesn't want Albright to get away with ordering Viano's murder, but he also realizes the decision is not so cut and dry. Cisco made a good argument and is willing to risk their friendship to back it up. He wants to do the right thing, but with so much at stake, I don't think he's sure what the right thing is anymore. Welcome to Washington, D.C.

"The nice thing about being a part of a special operations team in a war zone is you can always count on the guy next to you," he says, zoning out and regressing into a dark place in his mind he'd probably rather not visit.

"And now?" I ask, using a gentle voice meant to bring him back to the present.

"Johnston Albright betrayed me, Kylie. Not just by ordering the shooting. He at least tried to justify that. No, he embraced me when we returned to Washington. He agreed to join us and worked side-by-side with me knowing what he had done. How can someone do that? How can you …? Can you begin to imagine how rotten and black a soul must be to be capable of that?"

I don't respond. I can't. I've never been one to trust people to begin with, so I can't relate. This type of treachery can't sit well with a man who was willing to trust his life to his brothers in arms on a daily basis when he was deployed overseas to combat zones. I do know a thing or two about betrayal though. Out of all the crimes one person can inflict on another, this one cuts the deepest and leaves the most visible scars.

"How's the article?" Michael asks, suddenly shifting topics. Soldiers are not typically known for their ability to share their emotions and feelings. The fact that he admitted as much as he did to me is progress in my mind.

"It's coming along. It will probably be my best ever, not that I want to see it printed. Although, it's looking better than any of the other options right now," I lament.

"I don't want it to be printed either, but like I said, if we end up having to tell the story, I want you to tell it."

"You know, you're the only man who manages to make me regret my career choice."

"But you're so good at it," he chides playfully.

"You know, you're going to have to make that decision sooner or later," I state after another awkward pause. "The arrangement I made with the editor yesterday is not going to last forever. If he doesn't see a draft in the next week or two, he's going to think we're playing him and back out."

"And if he does see it too soon, he could let the whole world know when we don't want them to. All of our options are bad ones, Kylie. Albright deserves prison for what he did and Reed should join him for withholding evidence. But Cisco is right, too. The cost is a steep one. The people will never trust me or any of the independents again. The political damage will ensure more gridlock in the government because our enemies will ensure that's exactly what happens. We will have failed in everything we set out to do."

"That's all probably true, but you missed one important thing. The longer you wait to decide, the worse they will get. What do you want me to tell the paper if you decide to make this deal with Reed?" Of course I'm hoping he says he won't make one with him, but it's his choice and I know he's considering it.

"Tell him that I chose Door Number Two."

-FOURTEEN-
SPEAKER ALBRIGHT

Damn, it's cold out here. The breeze blowing in from the harbor is doing a wonderful job further chilling already unseasonably cold air. I knew on the ferry ride out here that I would regret having not brought a warmer jacket. Turns out I was right.

After the boat docked, I hurried the short distance to the sally port and the shelter from the wind the massive brick walls of Fort Sumter were guaranteed to provide. Named after the heroic Revolutionary War general Thomas Sumter, this is one of a series of fortifications built following the War of 1812 to protect the harbors along the southern U.S. coast from naval attack.

It's past noon now and my stomach is grumbling. I should have packed a snack along with bringing a warmer jacket. The fort is nearly deserted, given the fact it is below freezing on a Super Bowl Sunday. The desolate atmosphere is fine by me. It's the reason I came here—to be alone with my thoughts.

This place is one of my favorites in the world. When the growing divide between the North and South erupted into armed conflict, the first shots in anger from Confederate artillery came here on April 12, 1861. The garrison at Fort Sumter surrendered thirty-four hours later. The yanks would try and fail for nearly four years to take it back.

The resilience of the defenders showed in holding the fort is a source of pride here in Charleston. Although I am a member of the United States government, I will always be a southerner at heart. My chest fills with pride when I think how noble the men from my state battled, first across the river at Fort Moultrie against the British in the American Revolution, then here during the Civil War. Their willingness to sacrifice and endure given the long odds makes my own political troubles feel so small.

It would be easy for me to blame Bennit for all my misfortune. I was a superstar in the Republican Party before he burst on the scene. Sure, guys like Harvey Stepanik wanted my job, but it wasn't anything I couldn't handle. Michael Bennit, and my party's reaction to him, changed everything and I was dumb enough to go along with it. Because of him, my political career was ruined. He destroyed the one thing I cared about—being a player on the national political stage.

Only that thinking is flawed, because he didn't destroy anything. I did. It's stupid of me to think any of this is Michael Bennit's fault. At his core, he's an honorable guy. A former soldier and teacher who believes in the Constitution and the people it was written to govern. He was only trying to do what he thought was best for them. He didn't set out to destroy me, I did that to myself.

He even tried to bring me back into the fold. By extending a hand of friendship and involving me with the icongressmen, Bennit made me feel the passion for helping the people that I had lost long ago. Something that James Reed, and men like him, have beaten out of every fresh-faced politician who ever stepped off a plane at Reagan National.

Now I've managed to jeopardize everything. My actions are inexcusable, no matter how I try to justify them to myself. It's a hard reality to accept. I'm the third most powerful man in the country, but what I really am is a thug. I tried to have a colleague murdered and a former senator died in the process. I am responsible for innocent people being wounded and putting a gun in the hands of a man down on his luck so he could end his life and my problems all in one moment. If all that wasn't bad enough, now I have to live with the notion that I jeopardized the most promising political movement the country has ever seen.

I can't let that happen. I need to stop James Reed any way I can. But how? Would I only be making a bad situation worse? How could I? How could I sink lower than I already have? *Newsweek* once called me the most promising young politician in the country when I first got elected. Whatever happened to that man? I may never have an answer to that question, but it's not really important. What is important is stopping James Reed once and for all. But again, how?

I climb up to the top level of the bastion, where cannons once protected the shoreline, and admire the view of the harbor. The wind whips at my face as I look to the sky above the fort and imagine what it must have been like to be manning this post on that fateful April day. Did the men here all want to surrender, or did they want to fight? Did they plead for their commander to raise the white flag, or was that his decision? What would I have done?

It doesn't matter. I wasn't there in April of 1861, but I am here now. The decision I make now will define who I am, and there is only one solution I can think of. Reed has power over Michael and I need to take it away from him. I have to make amends for what I did. It may never restore my relationship with Michael, but at least it doesn't handcuff him from doing the great things he will go on to do. Things I should have done.

I now have the clarity that I was looking for by coming here. I take a deep breath and close my eyes, enjoying the first moment of peace I've had since Michael Bennit kicked down the door to my study twenty-four hours ago. I have reflected on it, and I have prayed for guidance. Now I have received it. Now I know what I have to do.

-FIFTEEN-

CHELSEA

"Hey, boss."

"Hey, Chels! It sounds like you're calling me from a submarine. Where are you?"

"Walking down a corridor in the Rayburn Building."

The Rayburn House Office Building is the biggest and most prestigious of the offices housing members of the United States House of Representatives. It's also devoid of carpet or anything to absorb sound. Footsteps sound like a teenager beating a bass drum in a marching band and trying to have a conversation in this echo chamber requires more than the usual concentration.

"Please tell me you're not at the office on a Sunday—especially *this* Sunday."

"Not all work stops because of the Super Bowl."

"Yes it does," the congressman retorts. "My first act as president would be to declare the Monday following the game a national holiday. Who are you there to see?"

"The Three Amigos."

"Are you kidding? They're huge football fans. They won't be there."

The Three Amigos is the moniker I gave the chiefs of staff of some moderate New York Democrats. It started because they were always together and I could only remember one of their names. Once I came to learn they all had the name Chris, I decided it was easier to keep referring to them that way around the office. Now everyone on the congressman's staff calls them that.

"Yes they will. They're in mourning because their team sucks. Trust me, they'll be here."

Our office, and those of most of the icongressmen, are next door in the Cannon Building. The Rayburn Building may be the office most congressmen want to end up in, but our building is the fortress for the social media independent movement. Despite the appeal of the newer, more spacious Rayburn offices, I like where we are as much as the congressman does.

"If you say so. I figured you would be out celebrating the shellacking you put on Diane Herr earlier this morning."

"I'm using my emotional high to get a few things done, Besides, I think you were more excited about it than I was when you called me," I tell my mentor. I was barely off the set when my phone rang and he started gushing like a proud parent. Even my father was more retrained with the praise than he was.

"I'd like to think you owe that performance to being a student in my class. In fact, I plan on taking full credit for it," the congressman jokes.

"Thanks, and yeah, I even told the moderator that I learned from the best. Vince called me earlier and said the only way it would have been more entertaining was if I had mooned her."

"That sounds like something he would say. What are he and Vanessa up to?"

"Vince is out and about, making sure all the press knows how bad I owned the president's chief of staff. Vanessa is working the social media angle."

"In case I've never told you, it's a lot of fun watching you guys work. Why are you paying our friends from New York a visit?" the congressman asks, referring to the state where the districts that the principals of the Three Amigos are located.

"I got a call from several of the icongressmen congratulating me on embarrassing Herr. One of them told me that we have a consensus on five bills in the House. They should make it through committee and get to the floor within the next couple of days and I wanted to start getting some help in lining up support in the Senate."

"Which bills?

"Corporate   tax   reform,   inner-city   rehabilitation, infrastructure spending, small business incentives, and … uh … the restoration of net neutrality."

"Net neutrality won't pass the Senate yet. Focus on the first four and see where you get."

"Will do, Congressman. Representative Parker will help with the Republicans, so I am going to enlist the help of the Three Amigos to convince their principals to help line up some Democratic Senate cosponsors."

"All right, good luck. There's part of each of those bills tempting enough to bring the Senate together to approve them, but it won't be easy with the president's brand of partisan politics."

"I guess you should be lucky that I've never signed up because I thought this job would ever be easy, sir. I'll be in touch."

Pocketing my phone, I march into Amigo One's office and drop my purse on the credenza along the wall. The three chiefs of staff of moderate New York Democrats are always in each other's offices, so it is a process of elimination to find them. I nailed it on the first attempt this time.

"Hello, boys," I say, removing my coat and scarf.

"Don't you love how she just waltzes in here like she just won the mirror ball trophy from *Dancing with the Stars*?" The fact he used that analogy is making me wonder if Amigo Three really isn't that into watching the pregame show.

"The door was open."

"Most people schedule meetings."

"Most people are home eating Cheetos and drinking beer by now. I don't watch much football and you guys root for a team that can't manage to—"

"Okay, okay, okay, don't say it. We don't allow Jets bashing here, especially from a Giants fan. Are you here for our help or our advice?"

"Both, actually. Your bosses joined the caucus and like working with us, right?"

"Yeah …" Amigo Two says.

"Oh, here it comes," Amigo Three chimes in.

"What is your boss' relationship with the Senate?"

"You both owe me twenty bucks," Amigo One tells his counterparts. "We had a wager on if you would come to us to help drum up bipartisan support in the Senate."

"I hate losing to him," Amigo Two tells me, as he slaps a twenty on the desk. "Getting any support in the Senate is a tall order."

"The president is pushing his own agenda there," Amigo Three adds, pulling out a bill of his own and handing it to his friend. "I don't think the Democratic Senators will want to take him on."

"Okay, well, thanks for your time. I guess when you joined the Fight Club, it was only to impress the voters back home. Now that real work is involved, I understand you're not interested in helping."

"Buckle up, gents; she's taking us on a guilt trip."

"And it will be a very long ride if you don't just let me get my way."

"It's not that simple, Chels," Amigo Two argues. Talking to them would be so much easier if they weren't all named Chris.

They share a brain, metaphorically speaking, so it only makes sense that they share first names as well.

"Yes, Chris, it is," I fire back. "You joined the caucus to make a difference, but we could get the best law since the Magna Carta passed through the House and it will never make it to the Oval Office without the Senate. If we don't get them on board, we might as well not bother showing up for work."

"It's going to cost us a lot of political capital. Capital we don't have," Amigo Two offers up as an excuse.

"He's right. Guys over there owe us favors, but not that many—"

"You've allied yourselves with the most popular politician the country has seen in decades. How much more juice do you need to pull this off?"

"She's getting good at this job," Amigo Three says to the others.

"I have good mentors."

"Thanks," Amigo One beams.

"Oh, yeah, I suppose you guys are included," I say with a wink.

"I'm beginning to miss the old Chelsea. You know, the one that walked around Capitol Hill like Little Bo Peep looking for her sheep."

"It turns out I left them alone and they came home wagging their tails behind them. Exactly the lesson you three will learn if you don't just agree with me now."

"We're not saying we won't help, but it's a fool's errand. The Democrats in the House working with Bennit is one thing because he has more pull than gravity. The president has the Dems in the Senate chained to the wall like Sloth from *The Goonies*."

"So I need you to be my Chunk, hand them some rocky road ice cream, and get them to help us find One-Eyed Willie."

"You've seen *The Goonies*? Were you even born when that movie came out?" Amigo Two asks, his mouth gaping open.

"I work long hours and there isn't much on at night by the time I get home. Now, stop stalling. Are you guys going to help, or end up wishing you had when I'm done?"

The three of them exchange looks in the way they know I hate. They have been friends and coworkers for so long that they could have whole non-verbal conversations with each other. It's infuriating.

"Fine. We'll talk to our bosses. You know the president is going to veto these bills even if they pass. They're going to be too moderate for him and we won't have the votes to override, no matter how convincing we are."

"Then he is going to have an even bigger problem with the American people."

"He's going to make good on his threats to issue executive orders and dare us to stop him," Amigo One predicts.

"Then that's what we'll have to do," I conclude.

"Is Bennit up for that fight?"

"And before you answer with something snarky, Chris is asking a serious question. We are talking about taking on the president and his legislative agenda. If we get hung out to dry on this ..."

"He might think he's an imperial president, but he shouldn't start polishing his crown just yet. So long as Michael Bennit is in Congress, the chief executive had better remember why his branch comes second in the articles of the Constitution."

-SIXTEEN-

MICHAEL

Like most guys, I love football. Unlike baseball where I share a love of the Yankees with Kylie and only watch them devoutly, I will watch any football game on television from pros to high school. If they televised the championship of the Millfield Parks and Recreation Flag Football League, I'd watch it.

Kylie's dispatched me to the grocery store to do some last minute shopping, because I'm still cranky following my meeting with James Reed and have been driving her nuts. At least that's how I'm justifying it. The real reason is I was supposed to stop on my way home from the meeting.

Kylie is not much of a cook, but has managed to learn to make a mean chili in the Crock-Pot. She has a family recipe, claiming it's the only useful thing her estranged mother ever gave her. Unfortunately, she forgot the secret ingredient which is why I'm here. Not one to let an opportunity get wasted, I decide to pick up a container of real French onion dip instead of the nasty low-fat kind she wants me to eat.

"I'm a little concerned that my congressman is struggling shopping for groceries. If you can't do something that simple, how can I expect you to revive the economy?" Chalice asks, coming up beside me as I scan the labels for the dip with the most fat in it.

"Easy. When I fail, I have four hundred and thirty-four other people to blame. How are you, Chalice?" I ask my former boss.

Chalice Ramsey is the chair of the Social Studies department at Millfield High School and was my guardian angel when I taught there. I was public enemy number one for the tyrannical principal, Robinson Howell, and Chalice did her best to run interference between us. She is a great educator, was an excellent boss, and since I have been in Congress, a trusted confidant.

"I'm good. I hate football, but you know what the key to a happy marriage is?"

"Uh, supporting your spouse's addiction to physical sports?"

Chalice has been married forever, and everything I know about her husband boils down to his infatuation with contact sports. Hockey, football, rugby, lacrosse … if it involves hitting someone with something, it's in his wheelhouse. He thinks basketball players are pansies and baseball is full of prima donnas lacking the testosterone needed to call themselves men. I think his views are shortsighted, but to each their own.

"No. Separate televisions."

"I thought it was separate bathrooms that kept a marriage happy?"

"That ranks a close second. You're not your usual self. What's got you tied into knots?"

"Just your typical political crisis of conscience."

"And here I was thinking politicians had no conscience. If it has you questioning things, it must be bad. Do you want to share?"

"Yes, because I always prefer my therapy sessions to be held in the dairy section of my local supermarket."

"Don't sass me, Michael. You know I hate that," Chalice says, causing me to conjure my first smile of an otherwise dreadful day.

"You've seen all the polls and read all the articles. Politicians are nothing more than greedy thugs looking out for their own best interests, yada, yada, yada. It would be so much easier if that was true," I explain.

"Are you telling me it's not?"

"No, at least it never starts that way. Most of the people who get elected to political office start off with honorable intentions. Somewhere along the line, they get corrupted. Sometimes their own egos give in first. For others, their political party changes them. In some cases, it's the system itself that does it and, in rare instances, circumstances dictate their fate. In the end, it's impossible to serve the people and not get sucked into doing something you'll regret for the rest of your life, even if it's for the right reasons."

"I'm not sure why you're so surprised. You're a student of history, Michael. You know what power can do to people."

"Yes, I do. And I also thought it was easy to resist so long as a person stayed true to his or her moral compass. Those who didn't were weak-minded. Now I am beginning to understand it's not so cut and dry."

"Everyone wants the One Ring of Power."

"Chalice, you've been hanging around Jessica, haven't you?"

The Rings of Power in J. R. R. Tolkien's Middle-earth are magical rings intended to subvert the races of men, elves, and dwarves to his power. The One Ring, bearing only the hidden inscription of the incantation Sauron spoke when he made it, was the ruling ring that controlled the others. Though dragon-fire could destroy the others, the One could be unmade only by casting it into the fires of Mount Doom where it was forged. Jessica, my ex-fiancée, current English teacher in the building, and always one of Chalice's favorite people, was a huge fan of the Lord of the Rings books. I had watched the movies.

"Your situation is not new. You know that. History is not made up of reruns, but all the new shows have the same themes."

"That's a new take on my line."

I have always been a proponent of the line, "History does not repeat itself but the themes in history do." For me, it was the foundation of how I taught history. Every time I talk to Chalice I miss it that much more.

"Your replacement used it in his class last week." Ouch. I don't like thinking about someone in my classroom.

"I have no doubt that this theme is repeating itself, but I don't know who could have had it worse."

"I don't know what you're going through for sure, but how about Benedict Arnold?"

Benedict Arnold was a hero during the American Revolution following British General John Burgoyne's surrender at the Battle of Saratoga. He would become one of the most infamous traitors in U.S. history after he tried to turn over plans for the defense of West Point to the British. Arnold never felt he received the recognition he deserved and, tired of his perceived mistreatment by the Patriots, sold his allegiance for money and a command in the British Army. In a twist of fate, the plot was discovered before any damage was done to the cause. To this day, his name is synonymous with "traitor."

"Okay, I'd like to think it's not that bad, but there's more irony to that analogy than you know."

"Good, and, if all else fails, I provided you with a plan of action. If things go really bad, you can do what Arnold did and move to London."

After the war, Arnold moved to England, where he died fifteen years later. The British never accepted him and often regarded him with the same ambivalence the Colonists did, which had prompted him to switch sides in the first place. That may have been a cruel fate for Arnold, but I like to think of it as poetic justice.

"I can't stomach eating fish and chips every day," I tell her, prompting the roll of her eyes I used to receive on a daily basis at Millfield High.

"Do you really want my advice, Michael? Stay true to yourself. You have a good compass and will know what direction to go. You'll make the right choice."

Wise words from a wise woman. I don't have the heart to tell her the truth. In this case, there is no right choice, only the least bad one.

-SEVENTEEN-
SPEAKER ALBRIGHT

"Are you sure you don't want to come with me?" my wife says, sitting on the living room couch next to me. "I'm sure everyone would want you to watch the game with them. It will be fun."

Our church decided to hold a Super Bowl party for parishioners not interested in watching the game at home or subjecting themselves to a rowdy party of drunken fans. My wife and the ladies' group volunteered to help set up for the party, so she feels obligated to go. I'm sure she thought I would agree to join them, but I'm just not up to it.

"No, I think I'll pass. You go on ahead."

"I'm worried about you, Johnston. You're not yourself lately."

"I'll be fine. Have you ever known me not to bounce back better than ever?"

"No, you're the most resilient man I know," she reassures, although still with a hint of concern in her voice.

"And you're the most wonderful, loving, and beautiful woman I have ever met. I love you with all my heart."

I give her a kiss and a long hug that I wish could last for hours. She has always been a rock for me to lean on. I could never have made it to where I am today without her.

"Well," she says after our embrace ends, "I probably will leave at halftime so we can watch the rest of the game together if you want."

"That sounds nice." I give the love of my life another kiss. "I'll see you for the second half."

I watch my wife leave out the front door, closing it behind her. That woman is a saint to have put up with me all these years. She has stood by me through every up and down life has ever thrown at me.

I get up off the couch, walk down through the hall and into my beloved study through the battered door. The items I packed when I returned from Fort Sumter are still tucked away neatly in the old knapsack that is resting inconspicuously on my red leather chair. I grab the bag, sling it over my shoulder, and head out the back door of the house. The temperature is brisk, but not cold enough to deter me from being outdoors. I meander my way down the long boardwalk leading from the back door of my house to the crick that runs through my backyard.

I love this spot. When we bought this property thirteen years ago, the brick structure, with its pitched ceilings and arched doorways, was a symbol of beautiful Southern-style architecture. As nice as the house was, this spot along the Bull Creek was the real reason I bought it.

Settling in on a wooden bench, I take a sip of brandy from my flask, savoring the warmth and flavor of it as it travels down my throat. I open the backpack and reach in, clamping my hand around what I'm looking for. Once it's in my grasp, I pull out the thick photo album.

Flipping open the cover, the first page of the book is dominated by our official engagement photo. She was a real Southern belle and looked so beautiful that day. I continue leafing through the dozens of pictures and remembering what wonderful moments each of those were. She was an amazing bride, and has been an even better wife. I couldn't have asked for a better partner in the entire world.

Finished, I set the book down and once again reach into the bag and pull out a second album. Opening the cover, this one is comprised of shots taken through my political career. There were pictures from my first campaign, first day in Congress, and the day I became Speaker of the House. My wife took many of them. Life in the national spotlight can be tough, but she never wavered in her support of my political aspirations.

When I get to the end, I pull out the envelope containing the single white sheet of paper tucked between the last page and the back cover. I didn't bother to lick the glue on the envelope to seal it. Pulling the white cotton stationary out and unfolding it carefully, I reread the words I wrote by hand a couple of hours ago, right after I returned from the fort.

There is something romantic about handwritten letters. In the days of computers, e-mails, texts, and laser printers, communication has gotten far too impersonal. Satisfied that everything is captured in writing and just the way I want it to be, I return the paper to the envelope and stick it back in its place in the album. I set the book on the wooden bench, right on top of the previous one.

I take a look back at my house and then at the lazy river before me, and just lose myself in my thoughts for a while. It's getting colder now as the late day sun nestles behind the trees. Fighting a shiver, I swallow the remaining brandy from my flask and reach for the only item left in the bag. It's time.

-EIGHTEEN-
KYLIE

The game is over, another big game blowout which made the halftime show entertaining by comparison. Michael helped clear the debris of the evening—the remainder of the veggies and dips returned to the fridge, the chips returned to the pantry, and the chili bowls and platters stuffed into the dishwasher now on its rinse cycle.

Despite him needing to catch an early flight to Washington tomorrow, neither of us is tired enough for bed. Content just to sit on the couch with each other, I watch the post game analysis on television while he opens up his laptop and surfs the news sites.

I glance at the article he's reading about Friday's White House press briefing. The drumbeat is the typical one coming from the executive branch these days. It drones on about how all of the ills this country faces are Congress's fault and how the president plans to fix things himself.

"The media is quick to try to drive the wedge between us, aren't they? There is absolutely nothing new in this article, yet they treat it like breaking news."

"Conflict means ratings and circulation. They have spent so much time dividing us as a people; the division between the legislative and executive branches of government is a fresh approach for them."

Michael scoffs and surfs to a new story on the Politico website. "Of course you don't see this on mainstream media sites. A Quinnipiac poll, about the public's faith in Congress, shows 'Americans that have a great deal or good deal of faith in our abilities to make laws that will positively affect the nation' have gone up by thirteen percent."

"And look, Americans are attributing the increase to your leadership," I observe, ignoring the boring postgame autopsy of what went wrong for the losers and reading along with him.

"Nothing like having to live up to high expectations," he says, closing the laptop and setting it aside.

"Americans are feeling a little buyer's remorse over electing our current president," I explain. "They are going to continue turning to you. It's a lot to burden one congressman with, but if you believe the people on the streets, they think they finally have their man."

"I'm not so sure I am their man or that they should turn to me. This thing with Albright … I mean, if it gets out … can the American people deal with another failure in this government? At what point do they lose faith in the whole system?"

"Nothing is ever easy, is it?" I curl up next to him on the couch. Even our relationship hasn't been easy lately. Regardless of what he is going through, I'm not about to let this tear us apart. I will support him in whatever decision he makes, regardless of whether I agree with it.

"It could all so easily fall apart. I mean, whichever way I go, it could all end up in disaster."

"I suppose that gives you a little more understanding of what all your favorites in history went through now that you are making it yourself."

"You couldn't have paid me enough to fill Washington's or Lincoln's shoes. I have no idea how they did it."

Lincoln and Washington never set out to be great men. They had the misfortune of being leaders at a time in history where circumstances dictated they rise to the challenge. I suppose you could make the same argument for Roosevelt during World War Two. In those cases, the fate of the entire nation rested on their shoulders. I cannot even begin to fathom the stress they must have endured, and I'm sure Michael feels the same way. The current predicament Michael is in is taking enough of a toll on him. I couldn't imagine what it would be like to be Martha Washington or Mary Todd Lincoln and watch their husbands endure so much.

"Have you heard from Cisco?" I finally ask him.

"No. But I can imagine his opinion hasn't changed any."

"Maybe there will be some sort of omen that will help you find your way."

I hear Michael's cell phone ring from the other room. Damn, I was just getting comfortable snuggled up to him. I move out of his way as he fights his way off the couch and walks over to the counter in the kitchen to retrieve it.

"It's Chelsea," he says after checking the caller ID before pressing send on the phone to connect the call.

"Please don't tell me you owe some bookie thousands for betting wrong on that debacle," he tells her with a smile on his face. It disappears quickly and I know something is wrong.

"How did you hear?"

He listens intently without interruption as Chelsea relays the details of whatever is going on. He looks pained, so this really cannot be good. When his jaw tenses and he rubs his temples with his thumb and middle finger, I know it's really bad. I can't fight the urge to sit up a little straighter on the couch as I brace for the bad news I know is coming.

"Okay, I'm out of here on the first flight in the morning and will head straight to the office. Try to get some sleep. I get the feeling tomorrow is going to be a long day."

"Honey, what's wrong?" I ask with a fair amount of concern and urgency as he hangs up the phone. He takes a moment before looking at me.

"Johnston Albright."

"What about him?"

"He committed suicide."

PART II

BY THE PEOPLE

-NINETEEN-
JAMES

"Damn him! Damn that man!" I scream at the television as the anchor relays the breaking news. The scene is a nondescript one. The images they are showing are nothing more than a disco's worth of red and blue police strobes a half mile away from the camera and in front of what I presume to be the house of the Speaker of the United States House of Representatives. Given the sensitivity of the situation, that's probably as close as they were allowed to get.

"There is no word on whether a note was left yet, but sources close to the Albright camp have stated off the record that the Speaker of the House may have had a serious medical issue and that may be the reason for his suicide."

A medical issue. If the anchor only knew just how wrong he is. There's no doubt in my mind that Albright left a note, and even less uncertainty about what it will say. He's going to point toward the same mysterious medical issue for his death that I would have used to force him from office.

"Again, breaking news has just arrived in our studios that the Speaker of the House, Johnston Albright, is dead at the age of fifty-three of an apparent suicide at his home in South Carolina," the anchor summarizes for the viewing audience.

In the span of a week, I have gone from the inevitability of prison to the feeling of being on top of the political world again, to utter hopelessness. The president is seeking my counsel through his chief of staff, and I am a whisper away from owning Michael Bennit, who is the most powerful and respected man in D.C. right now.

Albright just gave Bennit an out and created an added complication for me. How the hell am I going to use his actions as leverage now? I can't go after a man who's dead. This suicide has put everything I've worked for in jeopardy. Even with the burner phone, Michael could claim he didn't know anything about it.

He will take a massive political hit, but I would look worse for smearing a dead man should I decide to go public with it. Suddenly, prison looks like a real possibility again because I'm the one withholding evidence. Bennit could deny he knew anything about it and even pass it off as framing him since I've tried it before. I wonder if he knows that.

I flip through the channels and it's the same story on every network. Regular programming has been interrupted to bring the latest news about tragedy within the ranks of their government. I punch in the channel for CNN on the remote and a moment later nearly the same image pops up, only with a reporter on the scene.

"Do we know who found him?" the attractive anchorwoman asks the onsite field reporter, who looks like he was just torn away from a tailgate party.

"My understanding is that Speaker Albright's wife found him when she returned from a church gathering he did not attend," the reporter answers. "There are no further details of where in the house he was, or how he took his own life."

"Has anybody you talked to indicated that there were any signals … or any signs that he was depressed or contemplating suicide?" She is clearly off the script and just looking to burn time until they learn something more.

"No, in fact, the people we have managed to talk to say they've seen a different side of the Speaker since he began working with Michael Bennit and the independents in Washington. I would go so far as to say they were stunned at the news and never would have expected something like this."

"Has his wife made a statement yet?"

"No, there is no news on his wife, nor has she said anything in public. I can imagine she is traumatized by this—"

I click mute, knowing they don't have any more useful information. If they think she's traumatized … I have never felt so deflated in my life. I was so close, I could almost taste it.

If I stay the course and manage to succeed in making an arrangement with him, I could pull the strings of a man more powerful than Albright ever was. Bennit could easily end up as Speaker of the House when they hold a new election for the position. In fact, I would put money on it. His willingness to give up running for the top spot in the House endeared him to many of his colleagues. He might still not have the experience, but he has the momentum.

The downside is, if I don't pull this off, I have to go through with my threat of making all this public. Even if he denies the knowledge about the burner phone, which he probably will, Bennit will be publically eviscerated for aligning himself with a murderer and not knowing it. I will still take him down politically and it will be a much harder fall than ever. The only problem is I fall with him. In the end, I look like a bad guy, and still go to prison for not coming forward with the evidence in my possession.

It would be mutually assured destruction, and as a soldier and a history aficionado, Bennit must understand the concept. Known colloquially as "MAD," it's a military and national security strategy the United States employed against the Soviet Union in which full-scale use of nuclear weapons would effectively result in the destruction of both the attacker and the defender. The result of any nuclear exchange would be no victor; only total destruction.

The rationale of the policy was to promote deterrence. I still have the leverage to do the same, despite Albright's suicide. I can bring the lies about Albright's health and his complicity in the assassination to light if I need to. It would finish me, but the scandal I could create, even if Bennit denies everything, would be enough to permanently tarnish his otherwise glowing reputation. He has more to lose than I do, and won't want to start a war he cannot win. He'll agree to my terms. He'll have to.

-TWENTY-

MICHAEL

"I figured you'd be here early," the big man from Alabama says as he enters my office.

"Yeah, I caught an early morning flight out of Connecticut and came straight here from Reagan National."

"I suppose we all raced back after hearing the news last night," Congressman Parker laments. "It's not every day you lose the Speaker of the House. Have you heard any of the details?"

"Only what the news is reporting. He shot himself with a 9mm handgun in his backyard and his wife came home to find him dead. Apparently he left a note, but authorities haven't released the details."

"No, they haven't, and they won't until later today after the FBI briefs key members of Congress. We've had to endure way too much tragedy lately. I pray our fortunes change soon."

If God listens to anybody, it's Congressman Thomas Parker. He's an ordained minister from a family of Southern Baptist preachers who served as chaplains in almost every war the United States has fought since the British burned Washington. He was a nightmare for me during my first year here, but through a miraculous twist of fate, saved my hide from expulsion and we've been on good terms ever since.

"I think some Americans would disagree with you, but that's a conversation for another time. Is this a social visit? I mean, I'm hoping one of these days you are going to drop in just to say hello and not give me bad news. Is today that day?"

"Not exactly. I was wondering if you were ready for your big day."

"What are you talking about?"

"You really don't know. I thought as much."

"I'm really not going to like this, am I?"

"After the election of the Speaker, a document is delivered to the Clerk of the House as soon as practical. It contains a list of members in the exact order in which each shall act as Speaker Pro Tempore should the elected Speaker not be able to execute his or her duties."

Parker has been around the U.S. House of Representatives for a long time and is one of the utmost authorities in its rules of operations. If he is reciting this to me now, there's a good reason. One that I cringe to hear.

"Okay … I have a bad feeling I know what's coming next."

"Your name is at the top of that list. Under the rules, in the case of a vacancy in the Office of Speaker, the next member on the list will serve as Speaker on a temporary basis until a new election is held to fill the position. You'll be sworn in, about a half hour from now," he says, checking his watch.

"You've got to be kidding me."

"I'm not. As Speaker Pro Tempore, you will exercise the authorities of the Office of Speaker as necessary."

"Congressman, it isn't your job to come up here and tell me this."

"No, it isn't. People were afraid you would make a run for it. I volunteered to come up and share the news with you … and physically restrain you if necessary," he says with a smile.

"With due respect, sir, you'd never catch me if I decided to run." I play along, hoping this is a joke, but knowing some of my colleagues, it isn't.

"I know. That's why I'm between you and the door." Crap. He is. "Michael, you're a good man and a great American. I know you'll do a fine job. Now, let's go down to the House Floor. The clerk is going to gavel it into session, and after the blessing, you are going to be sworn in. For all intents and purposes, you will be the Speaker of the United States House of Representatives."

* * *

I don't have the first idea about what I am doing. I have only been in Congress just long enough to figure out how to do my own job, let alone run the whole House of Representatives. Unfortunately, I can't tell anybody that. I can't let on that I am completely clueless.

Combat was easier, and far simpler. You learn the tactics and familiarize yourself with weapons and procedures for one purpose—to kill the guy trying to kill you first. Soldiers in battle don't spend time worrying about the politics that put them there. Political discussions by troops in war are the figments of the overactive imaginations of Hollywood screenwriters. The instinct in battle is to survive, and to protect the guy next to you so he can too. That's it.

Politics is not that cut and dry. Having a leadership position is even more demanding. You have egos to massage, agendas to both advance and deflect, media to appease, special interests to battle and, above all, a sitting president who would do away with Congress in a heartbeat if he thought he could get away with it. It's a battle fought on many fronts.

Now, instead of sitting on the periphery of it, I am smack in the middle of the firestorm. I don't see myself being effective in this role, which is why I was almost pleased when the first three votes for Speaker deadlocked in January. It gave me the excuse to compromise and turn the reins of political leadership over to someone more seasoned who I thought I could trust. Murphy's Law saw to ruining that otherwise brilliant plan.

I stop into the Speaker's office to pay respects to Albright's staff, who are noticeably shaken at the news of his death. As much as I want to be consoling and sympathetic, I struggle with being either for three reasons his staff don't know. The first is the undeniable fact that he ordered me killed. The second is multiple people in this room are on James Reed's payroll. The third reason, and most important, is that one of those people knows the truth about what happened.

"We need to talk," Cisco says, coming up from behind me and escorting me into Albright's inner sanctum, which I now suppose is mine for the time being.

"Close the door behind you," I warn as we enter. "And speak softly. These walls have ears."

I go over to the wet bar and sniff from the decanter sitting there, as he complies with my request. Satisfied the amber liquid isn't motor oil or something, I pour a drink in a weird-shaped tumbler.

"Want one?" I ask my friend.

"It's eleven in the morning."

"Yeah, I know."

"Kylie would not be pleased," Cisco warns.

"Yeah, I know that too," I deadpan, taking a sip.

"You know you're drinking a dead man's scotch, right?"

"Considering what he's put me through, I think I deserve it," I defend, as I move around to behind his desk.

"Do you mean you deserve it because of the shooting or because he made you his replacement should something happen to him and didn't tell you?"

"Both, actually. What's on your mind, Cisco?"

"Albright left a note. Do you know what it says?" I can tell by the tone in his voice that he's war gaming something.

"No, but we have a briefing later today. I suppose we'll find out then."

"This place creeps me out a little," Cisco says as his head and eyes wander around the spacious room. "Do you think he planned the attack with Bernard from this office?"

"I have no idea and I'd rather not think about it."

"Does that mean you're not going public with it either?" There it is. That's why he asked about the note.

"Cisco—"

"Everybody knows you're going to be the next Speaker now, Michael, and I don't mean pro tempore, whatever that really means. You are going to have the power to affect real change whether you want to or not. The stakes are even higher than they were when we first found out about Albright's involvement in the assassination."

"It's not about power or this position—"

"It's all about that to these people. It certainly is to the president. We may be devoted to the voters back home, but our political enemies aren't. We need you in this position. We need you to be the iSpeaker we wanted in the first place."

"What difference do you really think that is going to make?"

"The president is on the warpath. He has the bully pulpit and is using it to paint us as bumbling fools. America needs a strong leader to face off against his power grab. Someone they know and trust. They need you. You are going to be the one America sees behind the president at the speech tomorrow night."

"Don't remind me of that, please."

I take a sip of my scotch. I swear I will never develop a taste for this stuff. The president is addressing Congress tomorrow night and, as tradition dictates, the Speaker of the House, or acting Speaker, sits behind him on the rostrum along with the vice-president, who is the leader of the Senate. I hate the idea of that but I'll worry about it tomorrow. What Cisco is advocating is a bigger concern right now.

"If I say nothing to America about Albright's involvement, and bury the truth instead, do I really deserve their trust?"

"It's for the greater good."

"That's the same argument despots and tyrants use. It doesn't matter to me whether I am the Speaker, serving in his capacity temporarily, or just a schmuck on the Floor of the House. Nothing has changed, Cisco."

"We worked *so* hard to get to this spot. I can't believe you are willing to throw it all away over something the American public doesn't need to know. All that talk about making a difference will be nothing more than hollow words. You say nothing has changed? Something has changed, Michael."

"Oh, yeah? What's that?" I ask him, as he sulks toward the door.

"Our friendship if you go public."

-TWENTY-ONE-

CHELSEA

"Well, that was interesting," I say, following the president's speech to the joint session of Congress.

For whatever reason, the president's remarks were not a formal State of the Union Address, although most of the American public would never notice a difference between the two. Perhaps he didn't feel it was appropriate to comment on the state of our union since he was only sworn in a couple of weeks ago. Not that any of us believes it would stop a man who is getting measured for a crown and ordered a scepter from Amazon.

"Didn't he say the exact opposite of what his chief of staff argued with you about on Sunday?"

"Welcome to modern politics, Vanessa," Vince laments. "You say one thing to one group, another thing to a different one, and hope the confusion it causes makes everyone throw up their hands in disgust and quit paying attention."

"Unfortunately, that's a winning recipe," I declare.

"At least the congressman didn't make any crazy faces behind the president during the speech," Vanessa offers with a smile. We all know it's something he was capable of doing.

"Or worse, fall asleep," Vince adds.

"He would never do that," I argue. "Remember what he did to that poor kid in class who fell asleep once during his lecture on Civil War Reconstruction?"

Vince and Vanessa both laugh at the memory. The subject matter was so dry that, despite his best efforts, even our beloved teacher couldn't make it interesting. Sleeping was the biggest taboo in that class and one of our classmates made the mistake of nodding off.

"I didn't know a Super Soaker could shoot that far," Vince beams, recalling how a stream of water from the powered up squirt gun hit the dozing student right in the forehead. It sounds cruel, but we all knew the rules and the consequences for breaking them. Even the kid who got a bath was okay with it.

"He never slept in class again after that."

"Yeah, but I remember Mister Bennit had to trade in the water cannon for a Nerf gun once Principal Howell found out." Fortunately, he never had to use the Nerf gun on us, even though foam arrows weren't as intimidating as the prospect of getting drenched with water.

"I wonder what all the teachers and administrators back in Millfield think of seeing their former coworker sitting behind the president. I think he looked good there," Vanessa opines.

"He won't think so. He likes cameras about as much as giving speeches, which is to say not much at all."

"Americans don't know that," Vince argues. "I'm sure a poll is coming, but I'm willing to bet they liked seeing him up there a lot."

"That's more than we can say for the reaction to the president when he entered."

The relationship between the executive and legislative branches has historically been contentious, but this president's attitude toward Congress in the opening days of his administration is downright hostile. The chief executive got a frosty reception from the assembled legislators in the room when he was announced and made his way down the center aisle. All newly elected occupants of the White House get a honeymoon period where the media goes easy on them and legislators play nice. Considering the tenor of his Inaugural Address, that honeymoon period ended as soon as it began. Even the Democrats in the chamber weren't as enthusiastic in their applause as they have been in the past for a member of their own party.

"It's only going to get worse if somebody doesn't step up to challenge him," Vince decries, always itching for a fight. "If not, he will take it upon himself to determine the course of the nation for the good of the people."

"You want us to mix it up with him, Vince?" I ask.

"Everybody is going to be looking to us, Chels. Who else is going to do it? We can agree to fight or we can line this president up with Muammar Kaddafi, Saddam Hussein, Josef Stalin, Pol Pot, and Adolf Hitler. They all said their actions were for the people's benefit."

"Whether the president likes it or not, Mister Bennit's running the show now. The Senate is supporting the White House's agenda for now, but if he expects the House to act on his proposals, he needs us," Vanessa explains.

"So, what's your point, guys?"

"Chels, the congressman is starting to lose his identity," she bemoans. "He doesn't have the fire he once had …"

"He's not acting like the guy who flipped a table last summer and dared everyone to bring it on, plain and simple. He's starting to act like every other politician in this town," Vince rants.

"And sound like it, too," Vanessa finishes, pointing at the television where the congressman is stammering through a post speech interview with reporters.

"And what would you like me to do about that?" I ask, feeling my redhead temper flare up.

"You're his chief of staff. If he's wandering off the path and needs a flashlight to find his, get to Home Depot and find him one. You're the only one who can, and if you're not willing to, we may watch him change into something we don't like right before our eyes."

-TWENTY TWO-
MICHAEL

"Mister Speaker, what did you *really* think of the president's address?" Apparently my whitewashed first answer was too politically correct for them.

I will never get used to being called "Mister Speaker." It's unfortunate that acting in that role, along with being the leading voice of the independents, makes talking to the media after a presidential address unavoidable. It doesn't mean I have to like it though.

"I think he was very articulate," I answer, being coy on purpose.

"Anything else?" The press corps is relentless.

"He brought up some issues that we've been derelict in discussing for a long time," I add.

"What about his alluding to going around Congress if they don't act on his proposals?"

"We are working on legislation to address many of the issues he mentioned. I think he will have the opportunity to sign them into law."

"Not his specific proposals though?" another reporter questions.

"There is no one man with all the right answers in this country, but I appreciate his desire to do what's right by the

American public." I think that was non-partisan enough to placate the reporters and get them off this subject.

"So, you support the president's insistence on taking executive action if Congress fails to act on his proposals?" Okay, maybe not.

"I didn't say that."

"So what are you saying, *Mister Speaker*?"

I think it's a dangerous affront to the republic we live in, but I can't say that. I can't risk alienating support in the House by making a stupid comment I'll regret later. I think back to when Albright said if I thought this job was easy, I could have it. I realize now that I absolutely don't want it.

"Republicans are screaming at what they perceive to be a power grab by the Democratic president. Some of them have even hinted at impeachment because of it. Would you support that?"

It figures the media would bring this up. I guess I took too long to answer the last question. All they are looking to do here is further divide a government which has been fractured to the point of ineptitude for decades. I need to stomp down this impeachment talk before it becomes the narrative.

"Impeachment of a president is reserved for high crimes and misdemeanors. It's not prudent to talk about how Congress would or wouldn't react to an abuse of executive power."

"The Republicans disagree. Do you think you can achieve unity in the House, knowing that they will not support the president?"

Now I am beginning to lose my temper. "We will never achieve unity. What we are looking for is consensus."

"Okay, will you be able to reach a consensus in the House knowing that Republicans will not cooperate with a Democratic president," another reporter argues.

"It may be erroneous to frame the problem as a partisan one, although I understand the reasons for doing it."

"I don't hear the Democrats arguing for impeachment, Mister Speaker. How is it not a partisan argument?"

"In this case, the Republicans are reacting to an overreach of executive power. If it was a Republican in the White House, the Democrats would be saying the same thing. When we get to a point where this Congress sets aside ideological and partisan differences, and reaches the conclusion that the president has overstepped his authority, we will have those types of conversations. Until then, we have a lot to prove to the American people and I think our focus needs to stay on that."

The press corps exchange glances and smirks, and I realize this interview is a disaster. The very notion of Republicans and Democrats working together on anything is laughable to most people. We have had some success with it in the caucus, but nobody talks about Fight Club.

I fumbled this, and the reason is clear to me. There is too much on my plate. Albright is dead and the contents of his note will be made public tomorrow right before the promised meeting with my least favorite lobbyist. It's time to start making some decisions and living with the consequences, and first up to bat is what to do about James Reed.

-TWENTY-THREE-

KYLIE

I only half listened to the president's address. Some journalists need absolute silence with no interruption when they write their articles. Others can do it amidst whatever chaos is going around them. I prefer something in between.

I kept the television on for the background noise, but mostly just in case my maverick boyfriend decided to do something crazy during the speech. He is the acting Speaker of the House now, and should be above such skullduggery, but this is also a man who flipped a table in a congressional hearing. You really can't put anything past him.

I take a sip of my Merlot and think about how I want to finish this article. The main body of the piece is complete but I'm struggling with the last part of the exposé. I set my wine glass down on the coffee table after making room among the pages of notes spread haphazardly over it.

One of the most important parts of writing anything well is wanting to. I don't, at least not this article. I know why Michael wants me to write it, but that doesn't make the task any easier.

I glance up to see that his interview has ended and the vultures have found another carcass to chew on. This one is Harvey Stepanik who has diarrhea of the mouth about what the president had to say. That's the animosity the press have come to expect between the Republicans and Democrats in Washington.

Normally I would dismiss the words that come out of any politician's mouth. It's much more useful to pay attention to what they do. I'm a journalist and have a reason to be jaded and cynical, but Americans have become the same way. Nobody believes there is an honest politician out there, no matter what they say in public. Michael has given people a reason to hope they're wrong, and it may have been the last chance to convince them they're wrong.

This article will destroy that trust as soon as it's printed. It will be Exhibit A for every one of his political enemies to point to claiming he is a fraud, or untrustworthy, or makes poor decisions. It won't matter to anyone that he took the hard road and was honest with them. The truth is no longer valued in this country, not like it once was.

I hate the idea that one mistake could turn the reins of power back to the political elites who have been abusing it for so long. The divide between the political parties in this country is more than ideological—it has become personal. Every issue is framed as a win or a defeat, and never is a law discussed in the context of what is right for the people. As a result, the people have become just as divided as if we were standing on opposite sides of a great chasm with no one willing to build a bridge between us. Well, one person was willing, but this story could put a hasty end to that dream.

Of course, I could be wrong. The first time I wrote an article I thought would be damaging, it ended up propelling him into the office he now holds. At his request, I chastised him for the impersonal approach of his social media campaign and lambasted him for not taking a stand on issues. It drove home the point he wanted to make—that social media to organize and communicate is a wonderful tool, but America has to demand that communication be substantive and base their votes on things that matter.

I thought the article would destroy him if he ever decided to run again, but, in a surprise, America got the point. When he ran in the special election, they challenged him on his views and liked what they heard. That formula was replicated and catapulted the seventy-six icandidates into office in the last election. I hope we have the same good fortune with this article, should it ever get printed.

I have to believe he knows what he's doing. The strain of the last month nearly destroyed us, and I'm not willing to sacrifice our relationship again. For the first time in my life, I have a man I love with all my heart. In the wake of the shooting, my own crusade nearly cost me everything I value. So if he wants me to do this, I will stand by him, but I fear for what that might mean for his career in the long run.

-TWENTY-FOUR-
CHELSEA

Now I know why the congressman drinks so much coffee. I feel like I haven't slept in days. Between working with our own staff and coordinating with Albright's former one, there just aren't enough hours in the day for me to get all of my work done. Thank God for caffeine.

I stop by to see Blake at the hospital most mornings, despite having so little time, and this morning was no different. I needed to talk about last night's speech and what I think we are going to be up against. He is improving everyday and I'm hopeful he'll be released from the hospital in the not too distant future. He shared some of his insights, and we're on the same page with what's happening and what we think the congressman should do moving forward.

The conversation ran long and I'm very late getting to the office. When I do get there, I say a quick hello to the junior staffers and head into my cramped office. As I settle into my chair, I notice Sarah followed me in.

"Chelsea, I'm sorry to bother you, but Vince and Vanessa asked me to tell you that they ran out to get the scoop on how Congress is feeling about last night's speech."

"I think we know what that is, Sarah."

"Yeah, but I think they are seeing how much support we can get because of it in the Senate."

"Okay, that makes more sense," I say with a nod.

"I got the impression last night that even the Senate wasn't happy with the president, even the Democrats."

"They aren't, but whether that means anything for us is the mystery. Where's the congressman? Is he in yet?" I ask, knowing I need to talk to him as soon as possible. He got eviscerated by the media in the wake of his post-speech interview, and we need to discuss how to handle the fallout. If Vince and Vanessa haven't started fielding more questions about it yet, they will before long.

"He was here and then rushed out with his security detail trying to keep up. He didn't say where he was going."

"That sounds like something he would do."

The U.S. Secret Service was originally formed to investigate counterfeiting of currency, but their role was expanded following the assassination of President McKinley to protect the life of subsequent presidents. That role was extended to include other government officials, well-known politicians, visiting dignitaries, and former presidents. The Speaker of the House does not usually have such protection, unless a threat exists to the president or vice-president and it's felt that the line of succession must be preserved. In the case of Congressman Bennit, he was already the subject of one assassination attempt and, with the apparent suicide of the previous Speaker, someone thought having a detail assigned to him was a good idea. I hope those agents didn't think it would be a cushy assignment.

"It must have been amazing having him as a teacher," Sarah says after a moment. I realize I've never really talked to her. I try not to cozy up to the staff, even though we all maintain good working relationships.

"Amazing is one word for it. Terrifying is another. His exams would literally make students cry. I've seen it."

"He ran for Congress because you all aced a final or something, right?"

"Yup."

"Was it hard? The test, I mean?"

"Yeah, I think it was the hardest we had that year. It was a cumulative exam covering over two hundred years of American history, but the entire class studied every waking moment for it. Everyone wanted to win the bet, even though most of my classmates didn't join the campaign."

"And now here you are. You're the chief of staff for the Speaker of the House."

"Speaker Pro Tempore," I correct, knowing that myself and the congressman are the only two drawing the distinction.

"Can I ask you another question, Chelsea?"

"Sure."

"Congress expects us to fight the president. The media wants him to do it and an increasing amount of letters, e-mails, and social media comments are asking him to. Why isn't he?"

I realize the strangeness of this. Sarah just earned a master's degree in political science and she's asking me about political strategy. The world is so upside down.

"The congressman is a doer. It doesn't matter what the mission is, he wants to get it accomplished and has very little use for turf battles. He knows a fight with the president isn't going to leave him much time for anything else. If we get dragged into a protracted battle with the White House, we'll never get any legislation passed and the American people will suffer for it."

"Does he have a plan?" The question causes me to let out a little laugh.

"Sorry, I didn't mean to—"

"No, no, no. It's not you I'm laughing at. It just reminded me of something. When we were all in school, every Friday one of us would ask if Mister Bennit had plans for the weekend. One time, he shared a quote with us by Eisenhower that always stuck with me. He said, 'In preparing for battle I have always found that plans are useless, but planning is indispensable.' I never realized there was a difference until I started working here."

"What is the difference?"

"Planning helps set the direction of where you want to go, and that remains static. A plan is how you actually get there, and that can change a lot. The congressman hasn't shared a plan with me, but I can promise you that he's done the planning and knows exactly where he wants to go."

-TWENTY-FIVE-
JAMES

In 1861, theater manager John T. Ford leased the abandoned First Baptist Church on Tenth Street and created a popular venue for theatrical and musical productions. In the days following the end of the Civil War, Abraham Lincoln visited the aptly named Ford's Theatre for a performance of *Our American Cousin* and was shot by Confederate collaborator John Wilkes Booth. Lincoln died the next morning across the street at Petersen House.

The theater remained closed for more than one hundred years before officially reopening in 1968 as a national historic site and working theatre. The reason I chose this place is symbolic. What better place in Washington to meet a man who survived an assassination attempt than the building where one didn't?

I'm here fifteen minutes early, but Michael Bennit is equally punctual. He arrives five minutes after I sit down, complete with an armed security detail who take their posts a respectable distance away. Neither of us says anything immediately, instead choosing to soak up the atmosphere of this amazing and historic building.

"Part of me wants to bill you for the cost of the ticket to get in here."

"Aw, come on, I figured you would like this place, Michael. As a history teacher, you have to be a Civil War buff. Are you sore that they charged you admission? Did you have to pay for the goons, too?" I ask after he doesn't respond, pointing over my shoulder at the severe-looking bodyguards in suits who I assume belong to the Secret Service.

"Actually, I did. At least they let me use my military discount for being a veteran."

"Did you tell them why you were coming here?"

"They don't ask questions like that, apparently. I told them I needed to come here and here we are."

"I half expected you to say you tried to ditch them."

"Who says I didn't? Unfortunately, they were briefed about my escape from the hospital and were ready for it. So are we here to talk about my protective detail or can we get this over with?"

"Power down your phone first," I instruct him, getting rewarded with the look I imagine most teachers master giving their misbehaving pupils.

"Fighting a little paranoia about recordings, are you, James?"

He used my first name. That's a first. I'm not sure if that's good or bad as he powers off his iPhone, letting me watch before placing the device back into his coat pocket.

"Have you pondered my offer?"

"Yeah, I'm still on the fence." Sure he is.

"This is a bad time to fight indecision. You need to make a choice."

"Or else what? You'll bore me with another story about your Uncle Buster and his coon dog?"

Reed had treated Kylie and me to that gem at Viano's memorial service. The story was a colorful way of telling me I needed to control her. Anybody who knows Kylie realizes how laughably implausible that is. I almost dare him to bring up a similar story for me, but it doesn't look like he's going to take the bait.

"No, but even he could understand the benefits of this arrangement."

"Did you hear the media report on the contents of Albright's note?" Michael asks, staring straight ahead towards the stage John Wilkes Booth jumped onto from the balcony after shooting Lincoln.

"Yes, I heard. It said pretty much what I thought it would. Y'all aren't naïve enough to believe it, I hope."

"It doesn't matter what I believe."

"No, it doesn't. Albright tried to give you some deniability, but it doesn't change anything between us," I lie convincingly. "We both know what happens to your political career if I turn that phone over to the police and Albright gets fingered as the mastermind behind the assassination attempt on you and the death of Marilyn Viano."

"It changes everything, James. You'll go to prison, too. You're willing to risk that again?" he asks me.

"I was prepared for it the moment I showed the phone to your girlfriend and her henchman," I respond. "I thought you would both go running to the police and you surprised me when you didn't. Now that I think to ask, why didn't you?"

Michael continues to stare ahead at the stage and doesn't respond. Now I know I have him. It's time to close the deal.

"You don't have to answer that. I already know the answer. Everyone thinks these kinds of decisions are easy until they are forced with making one. You want to do what's best for your constituents and the American people. I get it, and I want the same. All I'm asking for in return is to be a part of that process. So, what's your decision? I need an answer."

"I have no choice but to go along, do I?"

"We are not ten years old. We've been around long enough to know there is always a choice, but this is the best alternative and you know it. You will still be the man who can save the federal government from itself. So it's a yes?"

"Yes."

"Excellent. I'm glad we could find common ground in this ... situation."

"You need to understand something, James. We may have an agreement, but my dedication to this country will always win. If you want access, you'll get it. But if you think I will ever betray the principles I stand for, you'll find out just how wrong you are."

"I can live with that," I respond, fighting to suppress a huge smile. I've heard that before.

I can live with puritanical inclinations for now, anyway. The farther he goes down this path, the more painful it will be to retreat. I'll play his game and, before he knows it, he will have no choice but to play mine.

"And one more thing, James. If you cross me, I will become your biggest nightmare."

"You have been a thorn in my side since you got here. I was resigned to the fact I was going to prison because of you. Trust me, Michael, you already are," I say, rising out of my seat. "You made the right decision. I'll be in touch."

-TWENTY-SIX-

MICHAEL

"Congressman Parker is waiting for you, Mister Speaker," Albright's secretary states as I walk into his former office in the Capitol.

As my promotion to this position is only temporary as of now, I asked the departed Speaker's staff to remain on board to run this office until the election is held for a permanent replacement. They have been running the office for years and are better suited for it than my staff is. Their immediate responsibilities have also included making the political arrangements for Albright's funeral. There are no aspersions among them that once that task is complete, and a new Speaker of the House is elected, they will have to make arrangements for employment elsewhere.

"Okay, thank you."

"Good afternoon, Congressman," I tell Parker as I enter the office. "I apologize for being late."

"You're the Speaker of the House now," he tells me. "If you apologize every time you're late for a meeting, you will be saying 'I'm sorry' an awful lot."

I shake the giant paw he calls a hand and offer him a seat in front of the massive oak desk. His face is serious, and the uneasiness of another problem being added to my already full plate begins settling in. With all the drama in this town, how hard would it be for C-SPAN to have the number one reality television show in the country?

"What's on your mind?"

"Partisan ugliness."

"Is there ever a time partisanship is pretty?" I ask, trying to lighten the mood. It doesn't work. Parker is all business for this meeting.

"I've spent some time talking to the more radical elements of the Republican Committee," he explains. "They are seriously talking about impeachment."

"When isn't one of the parties talking about impeachment when the president is from the other party?"

There is truth to that. Only two American presidents have ever faced that unpleasantness. Both Andrew Johnson and Bill Clinton were impeached by the House of Representatives for charges levied against them, although neither was removed by the Senate and both were allowed to keep their jobs. Richard Nixon certainly would have been impeached and removed had he not resigned from his office in disgrace over the Watergate scandal.

In our modern political atmosphere, the president is threatened with impeachment on a yearly basis by members of the opposite party. George W. Bush was threatened by the Democrats for leading us into the Iraq War on faulty intelligence, and Barack Obama faced the same peril over his handling of foreign affairs, including the Benghazi attack, ISIS, and the Russian invasion of Ukraine. While there may or may not have been legitimate concerns about the handling of those events by both men, the drumbeat for removal from office was a largely partisan one.

"Normally I would agree with you, but this isn't just another Republican against Democrat battle. It's more than that, as you know. This is about the survival of the fundamental structure of our political system."

"Yes, but that's not how it will be treated by the Democrats and the media, especially if it's the most extreme factions of your party making the push."

"Unfortunately, it is. Harvey Stepanik is leading the charge. He's going to insist articles of impeachment are brought to the Floor. What will you do if he drafts them?"

This is not what I need right now. Harvey Stepanik is pushing this agenda to set himself up for a run for president. Radical elements of his party, who hate the current occupant of the Oval Office, will descend on the polls in huge numbers during primary season to vote for a candidate seen as taking him on. This is why nothing gets done in Washington. Everyone is too busy focusing on long-term career goals to care about Americans and their near-term problems.

"I'll allow a vote, because that's what I promised to do in this chamber. But we shouldn't be under any illusion about how this is going to play out. The Republicans will introduce the resolution and the Democrats will have a field day using it against you. The media will kick it around like a soccer ball, and in the end, it won't come close to passing.

"As a result, the Republicans look like bitter obstructionists and the president becomes more powerful than he already thinks he is. He will point to the failure as more congressional dysfunction, throw his hands in the air and claim he can't work with us. By the time the next presidential election comes around, he will have taken even more executive action than he would have before the attempt to remove him."

"That's an ominous analysis," Parker agonizes.

"I'm not done yet."

"I was afraid you were going to say that."

"Stepanik will thump his chest about the noble defeat and use the exposure to win the Republican nomination for president. He'll be a darling among the party faithful, but have no crossover appeal whatsoever. He'll lose independents by … call it a three to one margin, women by two to one, and have no chance at courting the African-American or Latino voting blocs. In the end, the electoral map won't change much, except you'll lose a few more traditionally red states like North Carolina that have been wavering in recent elections anyway. It will be an electoral romp and another four years for the president all because the egomaniac Stepanik got a visit from the Good Idea Fairy and people followed him blindly."

"You're getting good at this, Michael. I agree with all of that," Congressman Parker lauds after listening to my synopsis. "It's a bad road to go down for my party and for the country."

"Can you talk your colleagues out of supporting impeachment?"

"The Republicans in the Black Caucus, yes. As for the others, I don't know. They want to take action so their supporters back home don't think they are handing the president a blank check."

"There are probably some interim steps, short of an impeachment battle, you can discuss with them. But ultimately, the long-term solution is not the easiest one. We have to change how we look at politics. If this becomes a red versus blue, Republican verses Democrat argument against the expansion of executive authority, it's going to fail."

"You're thinking about unifying the entire House against the president? Including Democrats?"

"No. We need to unify the entire Congress against him, including the Senate."

"Michael, you have to know that will never happen."

"It has to, or we might as well get used to calling the president 'Your Majesty.'"

-TWENTY-SEVEN-

KYLIE

"You've had a rough day," I tell Michael as he plays with the food on his plate more than eats it.

"Yeah," he says, stabbing the chicken filet with a fork as if it was still alive and clucking.

He's in a foul mood and I thought a night out at this little bistro would do him some good. I was wrong. If anything, it has given him more time to think and that is making things worse.

"So you've agreed to a pact with the devil and fought against a course of action you would love to take against a guy you think is a tyrant. What are you going to do for an encore?"

"I was thinking about practicing some necromancy with Johnston Albright, so he can find another guy to take a shot at me."

"That's not funny," I scold.

"None of this is funny," he states, placing the fork at the top of his plate. "Did you finish the article?"

"I have a few final touches yet to make, but yeah, it's done. Are you going to go through with having it printed?"

"I have no idea."

"Do you understand the consequences of that action if you do?"

"I can only hope they react like they did last time."

"Honey, I love you, but don't hold your breath. Whether you realize it or not, the media has been friendlier to you than almost any politician in the past fifty years. They have never really challenged you as a candidate or a representative, even though you made them look like clowns after the first election. For whatever reason, they still give you the benefit of the doubt."

"I feel there is a 'but' coming."

"But there are a few that are itching to take you down a few pegs. You've seen their OpEds. As your power grows, the natural inclination of the mainstream media will be to knock you off your pedestal and take great joy watching you fall. You're going to be handing them the perfect excuse to do that."

"I know. This whole thing is an enormous gamble if I decide to do it, but isn't it a better solution than working with Reed?"

"Don't you mean working *for* Reed? It's a risk either way, and the outcomes are unpleasant with both of them."

"The bigger the risk, the bigger the reward."

"Or the bigger the crash. This is a dangerous game you're playing. You know that, right?"

He takes a long pull on his beer, sets the glass down, and dabs the corners of his mouth with a napkin before placing it back in his lap. One of the few things that can tear him away from enjoying a good beer is the opportunity to regale me in an even better history lecture.

"I'm just lining the troops up on the battlefield for my own personal Battle of Cowpens."

"I'm assuming I'm about to get today's history lesson, so get on with it."

"It shouldn't be a shock by now," he says with a wink before starting. "In the latter part of the Southern Campaign of the American Revolution, an ailing General Daniel Morgan was on the run from Banastre Tarleton and his force of about eleven hundred fifty men. He managed to get himself pinned against the flood-swollen Broad River in South Carolina and decided to make a stand against the British at a well-known crossroads called the Cowpens."

"Question," I say, actually raising my hand for effect. "Why was it called the Cowpens?"

"The term 'cowpens' was used to refer to pastureland kept clear of undergrowth by grazing cattle."

"Oh. Simple enough."

"Anyway, the Battle of Cowpens was fought in January 1781, and became a turning point of the war in the South. Morgan managed to earn one of the few Colonial victories of the entire war.

"The whole battle was over in less than an hour. At the end, the brash, young Tarleton, hated among the Patriots there, fled the field with a handful of his men. The British endured staggering losses while Morgan only suffered a tiny fraction of the British casualties."

"Okay, this is about the time where I have to ask what the point is."

"Morgan risked everything, used some very unconventional tactics on the battlefield, and managed to force a result nobody in the world expected. British General Cornwallis was forced to give up on the Carolinas and retreated to Virginia with his weary army. Nine months after the fight at Cowpens, the British Army surrendered at Yorktown."

"Nope, I'm still not getting it. What's your point?"

"Morgan and his troops won a surprising victory that changed the complexion of the entire war. I'm hoping and praying this ends the same way."

"So where are you going to fight your Battle of Cowpens?" I ask, prodding him to tell me the decision I think he's finally made.

"The last place karma would ever expect me to."

-TWENTY-EIGHT-
CHELSEA

This press briefing room was used twice before, leading to events that altered our lives. It is the same room Speaker Albright announced his investigation into the congressman, leading to the table flip, a viral social media campaign, and the success of the icandidates in the election.

The second time was when Congressman Bennit stood with him in front of the media and proclaimed the desire to challenge the increase in presidential power only a week ago. Now I am about to watch the congressman use it to possibly end his career. I swear this room is cursed.

I leave and join Vanessa in the small, sparsely used corridor that runs adjacent to the room. It is typically only occupied by the members and their staffs who are heading to the room for a briefing or making the final reading of their notes just beforehand. The congressman should be using it to join us any moment.

"We're all set," Vince says after he enters through the same door I did, making sure he closes it behind him to avoid the curiosity and prying eyes of the Capitol press corps. "Except for needing a keyboardist to play a funeral dirge as the congressman takes the podium."

"You don't know what he is going to say any more than I do. Try to be optimistic, Vince."

"Yeah, that's going to happen," he replies with no shortage of sarcasm. "It's standing room only in there. I felt like a ticket taker at a Yankees–Red Sox game when they started pouring in."

"If coverage is what you wanted, Chels, it's what you got," Vanessa adds. "It's going out live on the cable networks. Networks might break in, depending on what he says."

"Why this room?" Vince asks, shaking his head and clearly as disgusted to be here as I am.

"The congressman specifically requested us to have it here. I don't know why, but he has his reasons. He told me if the room was unavailable, we would wait to hold the announcement until it was."

"That's an unusual request. Since when does Mister B care where he addresses the press, unless …?"

"Unless he's about to do something stupid," Vince finishes for Vanessa.

Unlike when I felt out of the loop as his chief of staff, I don't want to know what he's planning this time. He didn't offer to tell me, and I didn't ask. I didn't want to be in a position to have to talk him out of whatever course of action he had decided to take. I have a feeling I know what he's about to do, but Mister Bennit has never been what I call predictable.

"Well, we're minutes away from finding out."

"He's running late," Vince says to the both of us, nervously tapping his watch. "He's never late."

"He should be here in a mom—"

"Is he doing what I think he's doing?" Congressman Reyes shouts as he stomps up to me like a bull charging a matador. He's angrier than I have ever seen him.

"I'm not sure what he's saying, Congressman."

"Don't lie, Chelsea!" he screams, sticking his index finger in my face. "You know exactly what he's saying."

That's more than enough aggressiveness to get my redhead temper flaring. Vince even takes a step closer, glaring at our ally, or former ally, as the case may be. Vince is protective of me in a brotherly way, and he sees trouble.

Since the day Congressman Reyes found out with the rest of us that Speaker Albright was behind the plot to kill us, he's been a different man than the one I met when he first came to Washington. He was combative about what action to take, aloof when we didn't agree with him, and now combative again. I'm not sure I want to see what follows that.

"Get out of my face," I tell the congressman in no uncertain terms. He removes his finger, but he's still too close for comfort.

"You are his chief of staff, Chelsea. His senior advisor. You bear the responsibility for his political well-being and, I'm telling you, you can't let him do this."

"You're right. I'm his chief of staff and my job is to do what he asks. In this case it was to set up a press conference. What he says during it is his business."

"You won't convince me he didn't tell you." I don't give a damn whether he believes me or not.

"Congressman, I'm not going to try to convince you of anything. I'm sorry if you feel like you're out of the loop, but that's between the two of you. He didn't share the specifics of what this is about with me, and that's the end of this conversation."

I'm not interested in making a scene yards away from the entrance to the room holding the assembled Washington press corps. Reporters can sniff out conflict like bloodhounds. The last thing we need is a tiff like this leading the six o'clock news. I start to walk away before I'm grabbed and spun around.

"What the …? Let go of me!" I demand, as I try to jerk my arm away. Cisco's right hand is clamped on my arm like a vice. I'm not going anywhere. Vince takes another step closer with a fist balled when I hear a voice give a firm and grave warning from behind me.

"Cisco, let ... her ... go."

-TWENTY-NINE-
MICHAEL

I can't believe what I am seeing as Cisco looks at me in surprise. Chelsea struggles to get him to release his grip, and out of reflex, he clenches onto her forearm even tighter. I close the remaining five steps between us and now he gets to find out how protective of his students this former teacher and Green Beret is.

"Michael, I—"

There's no coming up with excuses now. It's too late for that. The hallway is empty except for the five of us, but I wouldn't care if the world was watching. I grab the wrist of his hand clenched to Chelsea's arm and my fingers automatically move to the pressure points on his wrist I was looking for. Squeezing my fingers against them, his hand involuntarily opens, releasing Chelsea, who immediately backs away.

Seizing the initiative, I transition into a reverse wristlock by sliding my palm up to the back of his hand and wrap my fingers across the fleshy part of his palm below the little finger. I twist Cisco's hand to the right, while stepping toward him and placing his now immobilized hand against his chest.

I apply downward pressure and use the combination of leverage, strength, and adrenaline to slam him against the wall. Leaving his arm pinned against his chest, I lean forward, using my body weight to add additional pressure to the joint. The whole move only took about two seconds.

"Now, what's this about?" I demand, moving my head within inches of his grimaced face. I ease the pressure slightly to allow him to compose himself.

"You ... you know what this is about. You met with Reed and didn't consult me. You're going to destroy—"

"And any of that gives you a right to assault my chief of staff?" I ask through clenched teeth, applying some more pressure to let him know I'm not happy with his response.

"I ... I overreacted."

"Oh, you think? You are my friend, and I've always welcomed and appreciated your counsel. But you've lost your way, Cisco. And by hurting Chelsea, now you've lost your mind."

I release my grip on his hand and give him a quick short shove against the wall before disengaging. I was waiting for him to take a swing, but instead he backs a step or two away. Smart choice. Maybe now it's dawning on him that he's lost control of his emotions.

"I ... uh ... I'm—"

"You need to get out of this town and clear your head. At a minimum, you need to get the hell out of my sight. Don't ever let me find out you threatened a member of my staff ever again."

Cisco shakes his hand to get the blood circulating back into it. He looks at Chelsea like he wants to offer an apology, but nothing comes out of his mouth. He turns and heads out, away from us and the entrance to the briefing room.

"Are you okay?"

"Yeah, I'm fine. He's stronger than he looks," Chelsea says, still visibly shaken from the ordeal. "I've never seen him act like that before."

"Me neither," I tell her, worried that there's something seriously wrong with my friend.

"Thank God you got here when you did, Congressman. I was about to send him on a trip back to the hospital. You were much more subtle than what I had in mind," Vince confides.

"We'll talk about what happened later and why. Are you sure you're okay, Chels?"

"Yes, sir, I'm fine. Let's just get this over with."

* * *

"Thank you all for coming," I tell the room full of reporters and journalists.

Vince has outdone himself. The briefing room is lined with cameras, packed full of journalists and is standing room only. It's a severe departure from the announcement of our first campaign when we held an online web chat and only three members of the media showed up.

Even with the low turnout, that day was a complete disaster. Vince took too much personal responsibility for the debacle and quit the campaign. I wonder what he'd be doing now if he didn't come back. Hell, I wonder what I would be doing, because I doubt it would be this.

"It's been a difficult time in the House with the death of our colleague and leader four days ago. The loss of Speaker of the House Johnston Albright is a tragic one, and something the American people never could have seen coming. All of our heartfelt condolences go to his wife and I would like to thank the media for respecting her privacy during this very difficult time.

"As you all know, I'm known to pay a little bit of attention to what's going on in social media," I say, getting rewarded with laughter from the press corps. "I have seen some conspiracy theories about Albright's death that have begun to get circulated on those sites and wanted to clear some of them up before they really begin to gain any credence in the minds of the public."

I see some eyes roll and I know many of the journalists in the room are expecting another ride in the Capitol spin cycle. That's the way dispelling rumors goes in this town. Boy, are they in for a surprise.

"The first is what ailments the Speaker of the House may have had. I have heard everything from terminal brain cancer to Parkinson's disease. As has been reported, he wrote in his suicide note that he was suffering from ALS. I can tell you, beyond a shadow of a doubt, that what he wrote is not true."

The gasp from the media is quickly replaced by looks of confusion. That got their attention. I'm disputing the words written by his own hand, and now they're wondering why. I guess they know now that this isn't your typical, boring Washington press conference.

"He wrote that to protect me," I continue. "He knew what the truth would mean and created a lie that wouldn't be questioned. He needed to distance himself from his office and from me, and felt that taking his own life was the only way to do that. So I can tell you that his suicide was not the result of ALS, cancer, or any other mystery illness."

I take a deep breath. My entire political career may end with the next words that come out of my mouth. I am basing this on the faith that Americans will understand and that they deserve the truth.

"He committed suicide because he learned that I found out he was the man who ordered my assassination."

-THIRTY-

KYLIE

"That's quite a story, Kylie. I'm assuming you're here telling it to me now because of that," the chief says as she points over at the television mounted on her office wall.

Chief Deana Hayes runs the Capitol Police from its headquarters located in a boxy, seven-story structure on D Street. She broke into law enforcement on the gritty streets of Chicago and is as tough as they come because of those experiences. Having navigated the waters here in the nation's capital, I'm willing to bet those days were easier, if not safer.

I glance over at the muted flat screen where the media is going out of their minds shouting questions. Michael must have dropped the bomb about Albright. I'm not sure which one of us has the tougher job right now, me or him.

"Yes."

"Kylie, are you sure you don't want a lawyer here? You just admitted to me that you conspired with Congressman Bennit to sit on information critical to a police investigation. That's obstruction."

"Yes, ma'am. We're aware of that."

Deana shifts uncomfortably in her chair. She didn't expect that response. In a city where everybody puts their unique spin on everything, honesty throws everybody off their game. This woman has seen it all as the head of the Capitol Police, except this. The truth is that rare around here.

"Okay, why didn't you come to me sooner with this?"

"We didn't know the truth. You know about Reed's history with Michael. We were afraid that he could have fabricated the whole thing, so we—"

"What makes you think he didn't?"

"We had … independent verification."

"From whom?" Deana pries, leaning back in her chair. She doesn't like the fact that someone else was investigating this outside of her department one bit. If my goal was to keep us out of jail, I'm not doing a good job of it.

"I'm not at liberty to say."

"Oh, you're not?" Yeah, I'm really not doing a good job at all.

"No, ma'am. How we determined whether it was truthful is irrelevant. You can determine the validity of our claim for yourself once the evidence is in your possession."

"We will, Kylie, trust me. And I will also be looking to get to the bottom of exactly how you determined for yourselves whether this was worth bringing to us. That leads me to the problem I have here. You should have brought this to me immediately. We are in a better position to determine the authenticity of this cell phone Reed has in his possession. I should arrest you and Michael Bennit for that reason alone."

"Then arrest us." This woman loves to threaten me and I have never responded well to them.

"By your cavalier approach, you're making me think you don't believe I will."

"Deana, I left our apartment fully believing you would. Michael is under the same opinion. We know we've made mistakes, and we decided together to face the consequences for them."

"How noble of you," she condescends.

I don't bother responding. There's nothing more to say. Part of the conversation Michael and I had at dinner was what the consequences for our actions would be if he decided to go public. Being charged for withholding critical information from a police investigation was a very real possibility.

"You know, you could have asked for immunity for this information. If what you told me is true, you're basically handing me information that closes one of the highest profile cases we've ever had. It's information we may never have gotten on our own. In fact, now that I think of it, you could have gone public with this story before informing us and made quite the name for yourself."

I think back to Michael's hospital room at G.W. when I started this odyssey. It was always about getting to the truth. I knew there was more to the story of the assassination, even if everybody, including my boyfriend, thought I was crazy.

"The article on your desk is going to be printed tomorrow because we want the whole truth told. My goal isn't to embarrass you or the Capitol Police, nor am I interested in making a name for myself. When I saw the love of my life lying in that hospital bed, I was only interested in getting to the bottom of who was behind the assassination attempt. I did that.

"Now I'm handing that information to the people who can do something about it, and he is in front of the media telling the American people that the man he took into his confidence, and worked side by side with, tried to have him killed. Believe me, ma'am, you tossing us in prison is the least of our concerns."

Deana turns her head to watch what's going on at Michael's press conference. It looks like he's running the gauntlet. The media are not unlike a school of sharks—when they smell blood in the water, they aggressively attack. Right now, Michael is chum.

"Lieutenant Utley?" she shouts at the tall, handsome, and well-built African American officer waiting outside the door.

"Remember the day you accosted me on my way to Capitol Hill?" she asks as she turns her attention back at me. Suddenly, I start to feel like chum too.

"I vaguely remember it." I remember her threatening me more. I have been diligent in sorting my recyclables ever since that day, just in case.

"Yeah, Chief?" Lieutenant Utley says from the doorway. I think I'm about to find out what the inside of one of her cells looks like.

"I knew there was a reason I should have just arrested you. It would have made my life much easier," she says with a smile that she never flashes. "Lieutenant, I need you to get a search warrant for the offices of Ibram & Reed."

"Roger that, ma'am."

"While you're at it, get an obstruction of justice and interfering with a police investigation arrest warrant for James Reed. I'm convinced we'll need it."

"Yes, ma'am," he answers, leaving in a rush. When the boss wants a warrant, I imagine it's a race to see how fast you can get it to her.

"You're free to go, Miss Roberts."

I get out of my chair and head to the door, thrilled that I am not being sized for a prison jumpsuit. For me, day-glow orange will never be the new black. I almost made it out of her office before she stops me.

"Kylie? One more thing," she adds, causing me to turn around at the door. "Don't leave town in case this doesn't check out and I need to make you the resident of an eight-by-six room."

-THIRTY-ONE-
MICHAEL

"Mister Speaker, you knowingly sat on this information about Albright's involvement for a week?"

"Yes." It's a straightforward response, without qualification or excuse. I'd say more, but it's also the third time I've answered that question.

"Are the Capitol Police involved now?" the well-groomed reporter in the front of my lynch mob follows up.

"They were made aware of this information just prior to this press conference."

"Do you think they could charge you with obstruction of justice?"

"I can't speculate on what they will or won't do. At a minimum, I am sure I'll be having an uncomfortable conversation with them about it."

Poor Kylie. She was left to face the wrath of the Capitol Police alone. Even though she volunteered to do it, I still feel horrible that I'm not there facing this together with her. Although, given the hostility here, I doubt she'd feel the same way. This is brutal.

"Congressman Bennit, how do you expect people to trust you after this? You stood up here with the Speaker a week ago and asked us to trust him."

"Yes, I told the American people he could be trusted. I believed that I could work with him to change the political landscape of this country. Despite our political differences, I thought he was a man of honor and character. I was wrong and I expect to be judged for that."

"If you were wrong about that, why shouldn't we believe you are wrong about things in the future?" another journalist asks, taking his turn in the inquisition.

"If you believe leaders don't make mistakes, then you have unrealistic expectations about what leadership is and who leaders are. Above all else, we are human and, as such, prone to err. True leadership is not about never making a mistake. It's about admitting them, learning from them, and making sure to never make the same one again."

"Doesn't that depend on the mistake, Mister Speaker?" a female reporter asks from the middle of the school of sharks.

"Some mistakes have more dire consequences than others, yes."

"And your mistake?"

"I don't have the right to make that judgment. That's up to the people to decide."

"Do you *expect* people to support you knowing what you told everyone today?"

"Do you mean after I publically embraced the man who tried to kill me, wounded my friends and members of my staff, killed a former senator, and then buried that information for a week? Or do you mean because I allowed a powerful lobbyist to try to court me into making a deal to sweep the whole thing under the carpet in return for influence?"

The question throws him off his game. I can deal with criticism of my actions, but I don't respond well to sarcasm, especially from the holier-than-thou members of the Washington press corps. I realize it comes with the territory when you're forced to deal with the modern media, which is why I was happy to be the .

"Yes," he croaks. "All of that."

"I don't know what people will think. What I do know is that it's easy to back someone when they are succeeding. It's much harder to stand next to them when they fail. When I was teaching, I used to tell my students that failures were more important than successes in life. Not because anyone wants to fall short, but because when we do, we learn who we are. Failure is the ultimate test of character.

"Mine was tested over the past seven days. Johnston Albright ended his life because he thought it would give me the opportunity to stand before you and deny everything I have just told you. Knowledge of the evidence about Albright could have been refuted and my hands would have been washed of the whole thing.

"My political enemies would have used the allegations against me to create confusion and dissent. In the end, the American people would have to endure yet another political scandal without knowing who to believe. The only other alternative was to enter into a deal with James Reed and exchange the loyalty to my constituents for his silence to save my own hide. But the American people deserve more than another bought and paid for politician making laws that affect their lives. I'm not here because I expect anything from the people.

"Any way I present it to you today, I failed in some way. I admit those failures, and I alone will accept the consequences of them. You have all kept asking what I expect of the people. How I think they should respond to my admissions today. It's the wrong question, and you're asking it to the wrong person. I'm not here to tell you what I expect of my constituents or the American people. I'm here because I want them to know what they should expect of me."

-THIRTY-TWO-

JAMES

"I have rejected James Reed's offer," I watch Bennit announce on the television from my seat behind the desk. "I'm here now, telling the truth about who was the mastermind behind the shooting last December and the real reason for Johnston Albright's suicide. I may have failed in my obligation to investigators, but I will not fail in my obligation to the American people. Whether they are willing to accept my failures or reject me for them is a decision they alone will make."

That lying bastard! He sat next to me and accepted my deal, knowing he was going to go public anyway. Bennit is throwing himself on his sword and begging for mercy from the American public while leaving me to twist in the wind.

"Mister Reed?"

"What is it, Marcy?" I snap, after punching the button on my intercom.

"I'm sorry to bother you, sir, but the phone lines are jammed with requests for a comment on Michael Bennit's allegations. Is there anything you want me to tell them?" Yeah, that I am going to kill the man myself when I see him.

"Tell them I'm not available for comment at this time. Please hold all my calls and cancel any appointments. I don't want to be disturbed."

"Yes sir," Marcy says sheepishly, as the intercom clicks off.

I turn my attention back to the television. Look at him. He's taking the full brunt of the Washington press corps and not flinching. Every question the reporters are asking is getting a straightforward answer. Nothing is getting dodged. Someday, when they write the book on Michael Bennit, this press conference will be a defining moment with its own chapter.

I've never seen a politician, at the apex of his power, be ready to give it all away so willingly. It would be inspiring if it wasn't a shame. The president will use this to destroy Michael Bennit and bring him closer to gaining the power he covets. Political enemies in Congress Bennit didn't even know he had will surface to cleave their piece of flesh from his carcass. The media will eviscerate him just because he's the freshest fodder. The unflappable Michael Bennit isn't so invincible after all.

The quick, violent rap on my door precedes its more violent opening. What the hell? Did she not hear my instructions?

"Marcy, I told you I didn't want to be distur—"

"We don't really care. I am Detective Larson and this is Detective Taylor. We're with the Capitol Police."

"We have a warrant to search these premises, Mister Reed," Detective Taylor says, waving the folded paper in the air. About ten uniformed officers strut into the room, including the chief of police.

He doesn't waste any time. He knows what he's looking for, and knows right where to find it as he heads straight to the drawer in my desk. Giving it a good jerk, it doesn't budge.

"It's locked," he observes after a couple more quick tugs to be sure.

"Do you have the key for this?" Detective Larson asks in a commanding voice.

There is no point fighting it. They will only destroy a perfectly good desk getting into that drawer. I reach into my pants pocket and produce the key. He seizes it from me, and moments later uses it to open the secured space in my desk that no other set of eyes has ever seen. The other goonish officer in the cheap suit slips on a set of protective gloves and retrieves the manila envelope and the precious contents inside. Opening it, a single nondescript back cell phone slides out of the envelope and into his hand. He gives his counterpart a nod.

"James Reed, you are under arrest for obstruction of justice and conspiracy. You have the right to remain silent. Anything you say or do can be used against you in a court of law. You have the right to an attorney. If you cannot afford an attorney, one will be appointed to you. Do you understand these rights as they've been read to you?"

Yeah, I understand them, I don't say as my hands are cuffed behind me. I understand them very well.

-THIRTY-THREE-
CHELSEA

That was one of the more epic press conferences you'll see in this town. After about an hour of grilling the congressman, the questioning died down as word spread among the media about breaking news of the police arriving at Ibram & Reed. It must have been fun watching cable news network anchors balance those two stories.

I got a 9-1-1 text from Sarah asking us to get back to the office as soon as we could. I signaled the congressman and he ended the conference, promising to grant as many interviews and answer as many questions he can for whoever wants them. We hustled back to the office, part of me expecting to get jumped by Congressman Reyes on the way. He must be fuming over this.

When the congressman, Vince, Vanessa, and I walk into the office, the staff is buzzing like angry hornets after someone knocked over the hive. Everyone is frantic, talking, shouting, and moving about like commuters at Grand Central Terminal in New York at rush hour.

"Holy crap," Vince states after taking in the scene, capturing what I'm sure we're all thinking.

"Can you say boiler room?" Vanessa tacks on, referencing the term used to describe the daily work scene in some shady 1980s' brokerage houses.

"Thank God you guys are back," Sarah says in simultaneous relief and exasperation. "The phones went crazy here right in the middle of the press conference."

"I bet they did," Mister Bennit confirms, not showing the least bit of surprise at the anarchy we walked into.

"Media requests are pouring in for interviews and reporters are calling nonstop with questions. We don't know what to tell them."

"Vince, start a calendar and set up interviews. Tell them we have to limit them to fifteen minutes due to volume. Outside of standing obligations you know we can't break, fill every other slot up."

"Got it," Vince confirms, as he removes his suit jacket and scampers off to organize the troops.

"What else do you have, Sarah?"

"Social media is blowing up. Twitter is going bonkers and Facebook feeds are filled with posts about us. Some of them are good; some … well, not so good."

"Vanessa?"

"I'm all over it. What are people saying on Twitter?"

"I don't know. I've been trying to manage this mess. I was told it ranges from the congressman being a fraud to the only man they ever plan on electing president."

"That's a wide range," the congressman says, almost sounding amused.

"Hashtag BennitFraud and hashtag Bennit4Prez are both trending. Our accounts are blowing up with comments and questions. We can't keep up with it."

"We could have used Brian, Peyton, and the others right about now," he observes.

I don't know how he can be so calm. I wasn't gutted on national television by the press and I'm a wreck. The police could be coming to arrest him at any moment for obstruction, and he's acting like he doesn't have a care in the world. I guess that's the feeling when the weight of the world has been lifted off your shoulders.

"Speaking of which, Congressman, you might want to consider calling them and having a talk. They have to be getting blindsided by this."

"Yeah, that's a good idea. I'm in my office if you need me."

I watch the congressman head into his office and close the door behind him. I know he wants nothing more than to engage the people on social media like he has so many times before, but now is not the time. He might be the symbol of placidity after the hour-long tussle with the press corps, but it's left him mentally and emotionally drained.

"Anything on what the other politicians are saying?" I ask my junior staffer after I'm sure he isn't going to reemerge from his office.

"No, not yet."

"Okay, that's not all bad," I say to myself. "They're probably huddling with their staffs to figure out how to respond."

"What will they say?"

Yes, what will they say? The congressman is so concerned about the people's reactions. I'm willing to bet he never considered how his colleagues would respond. I can only guess how this will turn out, but it's an educated one.

"Our enemies will be the first to make statements. The rest won't say anything until they figure out which way the political winds are blowing. How the American people react will go a long way to determine how they do."

"What do you think Americans will do? I mean, what will they think?"

"I honestly don't know this time. The media is going to drive this story. There's no telling which way the people will go on this. America likes an underdog, but they also like watching the mighty fall. The same people who grew up reading *The Little Engine That Could* took pleasure in Tiger Woods's club-wielding wife and Brittney Spears shaving her head."

"Could it be that bad?"

"It could be worse."

"What do you need me to do?"

The chaos that gripped the office has become a little more organized, but the frenetic pace hasn't subsided. So much to do. We have a window of opportunity before our enemies jump all over us, but it's closing rapidly.

"Just make sure everyone is doing their jobs. I need to call some friends on the Hill and find out what they're thinking."

"Chelsea, are we going to be okay?" Sarah asks as I begin to retreat to my office.

"I don't know. Let's get to work and find out."

-THIRTY-FOUR-

KYLIE

I get an uneasy sense of déjà vu. The last time I saw the lights of this many police cars in one place, EMTs were loading the love of my life into the back of an ambulance. The scene in front of me is giving me anxiety as I fight my own version of post traumatic stress disorder.

Jumping into my car the moment Deana let me go from her office, I raced over here to get a prime spot to view the spectacle. I wanted to be here when they led the bastard out in handcuffs. I want him to see me and know that he didn't win. It doesn't take long. I didn't even remember to text Michael an update until I got here.

The frenzy sweeps through the mass of media on the scene like the wave in a football stadium when Reed is led out. To his credit, he doesn't try to hide his face under a jacket like so many under arrest are prone to do. He struts out with his police escort like he's proud of what he's done. A few seconds later, he is guided into the back of a waiting squad car.

I didn't get my wish. He couldn't have seen me this far away from the entrance. I didn't get the chance to look him in the eye and let him know he lost. There was no opportunity to silently convey the message that we would not be manipulated and would not be cowed. Then again, he probably already figured that out.

"Well, this will be in the news cycle for weeks."

"Bill! What are you doing down here?" I ask my one-time colleague and long-time friend.

"I heard Bennit was throwing a presser and got the feeling it was going to be something epic. Of course, it would have been easier if someone had given me a heads-up instead of leaving me to gaze into my crystal ball."

"Sorry, we were a little busy."

"Yeah, I'll remember that. Anyway, I left Capitol Hill when I got word that the police were descending on the offices of Ibram & Reed. Since I didn't see you there as your boyfriend was baring his soul to America, I figured you'd be here."

"You were right."

"I usually am. Let's take a walk."

Nobody will ever characterize Bill Gibbons as being insecure. Self-confidence comes with the territory when you are one of the best political journalists in the country. I found him to be obnoxious when we worked together, and I still do. Unfortunately, I owe him. He was the one who pointed me in the direction of Michael's campaign when my post *New York Times* days consisted of eating Fritos and engaging in self-loathing.

It's freezing out, but the thought of Reed being carted away for mug shots is keeping me warm. We walk away from the chaos and into nearby Franklin Square. With all the activity in front of the twelve-story building that houses Ibram & Reed catching the attention of any casual passerby, the park is deserted.

"How did the press conference go?"

"Michael was amazing, as usual, but the media are going to crucify you guys."

"Probably."

"Does he have a plan to deal with the fallout?"

That's a good question. In all the conversations we had about this, planning for how to deal with the aftermath wasn't a part of any of them. Maybe he figured he would let his staff work on those details.

"I have no idea, but, if I know his staff, they are working on that right now."

"Another social media outreach?"

"He wouldn't be the iSpeaker if there wasn't one," I offer playfully.

"Will he resign?" Bill isn't sharing my good mood.

"Only if his constituents demand it, but you didn't seek me out here for answers to questions I'm sure Michael has already answered. What's really on your mind?"

"Did you write a story?"

We get passed by a couple of beautiful women, but Bill doesn't even turn his head. That's out of character for a man who would earn gold if chasing skirts ever becomes an Olympic sport. He's locked into this conversation, which means he has more than questions—he has an agenda.

"I wrote *the* story."

"Who's printing it?"

"Bill, Alex Trebek asks less questions than you are. Why do you care?"

"Actually, he technically gives the answers, but it's not important. I'm asking because I want it for *The Times*."

"News flash, you're a journalist, not an editor. You don't get to make the determination about what they print."

"No, I don't, but they're going to want it, even with your name on the byline. You need to get the article into a paper with a massive distribution, and I'm offering to make that happen."

"Who says I didn't?"

"Because I know you, Kylie. You and Bennit are perfect for each other because you're both mavericks. It's either going into a small-town publication or on an online blog. Either way, it will never have the reach of what I'm offering."

I laugh, first a chuckle, and then rising almost into hysterics. It takes a full minute for me to regain my composure. Bill just stands and watches me, not amused.

"What's so damn funny?"

"I worked for the *New York Times* and got fired for trying to expose a scandal that would end up leading to the rise of the most influential politician in the country. I then got fired from the *Washington Post* for trying to expose the conspiracy behind the assassination of that politician, which has led to the suicide of the Speaker of the House and the arrest of the most powerful lobbyist in America."

"So what?"

"Now the one article they actually *want* to print is the one that could end the career of the man I love."

"That's not what this is about. You've proved your point to them, Kylie. Now let them work for you. I don't think your article will end anything."

He's right. Despite all out speculation, neither of us knows what this article will mean. It could destroy him, could save him, or it could be completely ignored. I have my feelings on the subject, but the only way to find out is to get it printed and read by as many people as possible. I am just not going to use them to do it.

"No. Neither the *Times* nor the *Post* deserves this exclusive. They can take a backseat on the story of the decade for a while."

"Okay," he responds impassively.

Wait, what? I expected more of a fight from him. One of the primary reasons for Bill Gibbons's success is that he doesn't take no for an answer.

"That's it? Okay?"

"Yup. I made the pitch my editor instructed me to make and now I'm going to make the pitch I want to make."

"What's that going to entail?"

"Helping you."

-THIRTY-FIVE-
MICHAEL

My years in the military made me a morning person, by training if not by choice. It's a great time to work out and get the blood pumping, but I already feel energized this morning. Forgoing exercise for the time being, I headed over to the Cannon Building from our apartment with my security detail two hours before usual. The lights were on when I arrived. No matter how early I get to the office, one of my staff members always beats me here.

"Good morning, Congressman. You have a visitor," my legislative correspondent says in greeting. With the bills we have getting ready for the House Floor, I know why he's here early. "He's in your office."

"Okay, thanks." That can only mean one person.

I stroll into my inner office and see Cisco making himself comfortable on one of my sofas reading the newspaper. I recognize the page immediately. The paper was Friday's *Washington Times* with the reprint of Kylie's article.

"Are the minstrels still singing, Cisco?"

"More than ever."

"What are you doing here so early?" More like what are you doing here at all?

"I wanted to beat Chelsea here so I could avoid her redheaded rage," he relays, folding the paper and placing it on the small coffee table.

"She's not the only person you need to fear here," I answer in an ominous voice that didn't require acting lessons. It's been a week since he grabbed her outside the press briefing room and I'm still livid at him.

"I know. I screwed up."

"That's an understatement."

"I owe all of you a major apology and I wanted to start with you. What happened with Chelsea was inexcusable. You're angry about it and should be. I've been a jerk since the day we found out about Albright."

"You just figured that out?"

"I stopped seeing the therapist not long after the shooting."

That's a new revelation. Posttraumatic stress is not restricted to men coming home from combat, although the wars in Iraq and Afghanistan helped the medical field understand it more and raise awareness. Anybody experiencing high levels of trauma can be affected by it and, because of that, we all spent some time on a shrink's couch as a preventive treatment called psychological debriefing.

"Why would you do that?"

"I thought I was fine. I didn't think I needed help."

"Most of the guys I served with said the same thing. Then came the endless motorcycle accidents at a hundred miles an hour, countless cases of spousal abuse, and numerous suicides."

"The psychologist told me that. In my case, it was behavioral changes manifesting in rage against anyone and everything, especially who and what I cared for most," he states, starting up while recalling the words from memory.

Cisco seemed perfectly normal after the shooting when I visited him in his hospital room. The mind is mysterious place that we are only beginning to understand. Unlike an arm or leg, it's tough to know when someone's is broken. It's even harder to try to fix.

"I don't want you to think I'm using that as an excuse for what I did … for what happened with Chelsea. I … I need you to forgive me for acting like an ass."

"I accept, but it's not my forgiveness you really need, brother. There's a certain redhead in this office that still wants to challenge you to three rounds in a ring."

"I'd lose."

"Yes, you would."

The tense silence between us is a new experience. Everything about Cisco is lighthearted, and I hate that our friendship has turned this ugly. I understand what he's going through, and I do forgive him, but it doesn't mean I'm less angry, nor will I be able to forget it.

"Kylie's article was brilliant."

"I'm glad you think so. I thought she made me come across as a naïve idiot."

"No, you look like the honest guy Americans want representing them. This last week is a testament to that, despite what the media is saying."

America's shock at the news subsided quickly. The television media were quick to paint a picture, but it was only part of the story. All of them were kicking me, but were divided as to how hard. The more partisan champions in the press from both sides beat the drum to destroy me while others were more forgiving.

When Kylie's article ran in the *Millfield Gazette*, the voters in my district got the bigger picture. When the online blogs started commenting on the report, it gained the attention of the network and cable news shows. Before long, all the major news outlets wanted to print a copy. Kylie finally acquiesced to allowing the major metropolitan papers to reprint it, and on the Sunday following the press conference, the article ran in every major newspaper and online news site in America.

As America dove in, the story went viral. All of the information was out there, and that was our intent. People had the information they needed to figure out if I was a naïve schmuck, a typical politician who flaunted the law, or just a guy who made some honest mistakes. Then it became a waiting game to see how they decided.

Social media has become the barometer of the American attitude about almost everything. If you want to know what's hot, what's not, and what has America's attention, look at someone's Facebook news feed or what's trending on Twitter. Sites like Reddit and Digg propagate stories at lightning speed, and there's nothing like YouTube, Vine, or Instagram for sharing the visuals.

Over the past week, the media has been trying to shape public opinion against me, only it's not working. If the social media measure is to be believed, most people understand and support how I handled the incident and accept my reason for not running straight to the police. Many of them are equally forgiving of my alliance with Albright. Polls conducted by respected organizations like Gallup and colleges like Marist and Quinnipiac showed a drop in my approvals, but not a dramatic one. I am not a big reader of opinion polls, but for once they published one I cared about. Over eighty-three percent of respondents said "yes" to the question, "Is Michael Bennit trustworthy?"

None of that is slowing my political enemies from taking me to the woodshed. The president is taking full advantage of the scandal. White House briefings sound more like Waldorf and Statler hurling one-liners insulting the cast of the *Muppet Show* than something you would expect coming from the office of the leader of the free world. The president thinks trying to tear me down will save his own flailing approval rating and is throwing everything he can at the effort.

"Look, I was wrong, Michael. About everything," Cisco concludes with sincerity.

"Hold on, let me record that."

"I'm serious. I should have trusted you."

"Cisco, I have always appreciated your counsel. I don't always make the right choices, but I didn't become a congressman just so I could get reservations at good restaurants. Lying would have made our jobs here more convenient in the short term, but the price was too steep in long term."

"I realize that now. I just wanted ..." Cisco starts to say before averting his eyes. He knows he was willing to trade principles I believe should be nonnegotiable, and if James Reed understood me at all, he'd have known I was lying to him at Ford's Theatre when I fooled him into thinking I would compromise mine.

"You didn't want to lose the ability to make a difference here. You were afraid the truth would undo everything the icongressmen are accomplishing."

"Yeah."

"It still might. It's only been a week and the jury is still out as to how Americans will ultimately react to this. All we can do is continue to be the representatives they elected. The rest will work itself out, one way or another."

"I suppose. Do you think Chelsea will accept my apology?" he asks, shifting gears in the conversation again. I know it must be weighing on his mind.

"Probably, but you're going to owe her. She collects favors like baseball cards around here now."

"I can cut her grass. Or clean her pool."

Cisco has used that type of self-deprecating humor since the day I met him. He's proud of his Latino roots and loves poking fun at the stereotypes of it. Since the shooting, he's been much more serious than he ever used to be. Maybe this is a sign that the old Cisco is finally starting to find his way back.

"You can offer, but outside of the fact that she rents and her place doesn't have a pool, she'd never accept. She would never want you to be anything less than you are."

"Oh, yeah? What am I?"

"A distinguished United States Congressman. Now let's get back to it. These bills aren't going to get themselves through the House and we have a lot of work to do to convince the Senate."

-THIRTY-SIX-
CHELSEA

"Hi, honey, Happy Valentine's Day," I tell Blake as I enter his hospital room carting an oversized jug of gourmet jelly beans. Blake doesn't have much of a sweet tooth, but he does have a weakness for the small, kidney-shaped confections.

"Thanks! I tried to go shopping for you, but the nurses caught me in the stairwell." I'm not sure if he's kidding or not, but that brings up another subject.

"The same nurses who told me when I stepped out of the elevator that you're giving them a hard time?"

"No more than usual," he replies. "I'm just tired of being cooped up in here."

"You're not missing much outside. The weather is lousy."

"That's not what I meant. This … this isn't how I planned on spending our first Valentine's Day."

"Blake, you're alive. That's enough for me."

I give him a kiss. For a man who was shot twice in the back, he's doing remarkably well. The physical therapy is helping his mobility, and he's healing remarkably fast under the circumstances. Bullets cause a remarkable amount of trauma in the body, and it took several surgeries by some of the best doctors in the country to repair the damage to his internal organs.

"And they'll let you out of here when you're ready."

"It's been a month and a half. Believe me, I'm ready. I don't know how guys who were wounded in combat could have stayed at Walter Reed as long as they did. My father never would have survived the hospital had he been injured in the Gulf War."

"Speaking of which," I say, digging through my purse for the small box I put in there. "I have one more gift for you."

"Is it a cloaking device so I can sneak out of here?"

"No, but you'll appreciate it just as much."

I find the box and hand it to him. He opens it, and a tear comes to his eye. I had a feeling it would have that effect on him.

"I … rescued it … from the police evidence room," I inform him, omitting the details.

"Please tell me you didn't break in and steal it."

"I didn't," I say with a smile, as I help him affix the small triangular pin to his hospital gown.

I'm a little fuzzy about why this insignia of the Second Armored Division means so much to him, but he has worn it every day I can remember since our first election. He was wearing it the day he was shot, and it ended up in the custody of the Capitol Police until today.

"Thank you for this. It's a wonderful gift. You're amazing. I didn't think I would see you here so early today."

"The congressman ended the session and then gave everyone on the staff the rest of the day off."

"Since when does that stop you from working?" Blake asks, knowing full well the number of hours I put into this job. It's no wonder why so many staffers on Capitol Hill are young. The pay is lousy, hours long, and it demands a lot of energy.

"It didn't. I had a productive meeting with some of the House Democrats first."

"Getting them on board or talking to them about the Senate?"

"Both. It was easier than I thought it would be."

"That's because the president's popularity has plunged farther than a supermodel's neckline. Even Democrats are distancing themselves from him."

"The president is prodding them to attack Mister Bennit. He's doing everything he can to organize the Democrats to use the scandal against him."

"Of course he is. He sees his influence in his own party waning."

"Who would have thought that a week ago?"

"Between Congressman Bennit doing a gazillion interviews, Kylie's article, and the staff's social media outreach, you collectively did an amazing job getting information out to a usually apathetic public. You set a new standard for political crisis management," Blake compliments, clearly impressed with the effort we put in.

This past week was a hectic one. When the congressman wasn't doing interviews with everyone who wanted one, he was on social media talking to the people. He even flew home and hosted open forum town hall meetings in three towns in the district, to let his own constituents vent. No questions were off limits, and it was a good thing, because they didn't hold back.

Our political opposition arranged for a couple of people to try to embarrass him at these forums, but their whole plan backfired when one of their hired accomplices admitted on camera, in the middle of the meeting, that she had been paid to go there and try to humiliate him. Undaunted, the congressman had told her to ask the question anyway, which she reluctantly did. The whole episode ended up with almost a million views on YouTube and the clip was shown all over the mainstream media. The fact that Congressman Bennit ended up answering the question made his stock go up that much higher.

"Taking the crisis head-on was his idea, not mine."

"Yeah, but you made it happen and were smart enough not to talk him out of it. Most chiefs of staff would have tried. Many of them would have insisted."

"To be honest with you, I thought about it. I never would have guessed Americans would have reacted this way. I've seen scandals in the past destroy public figures, especially when it's all the media ever talks about."

"The media doesn't have the power to shape opinions like it used to. They still have influence, but social media has given people an outlet to discuss what's going on and form opinions on their own. It's like buying a product online. All the advertising on the planet won't stop shoppers from going straight for the reviews to see what their peers are saying. That's what the public is learning to trust, and nobody can change that."

"I still thought this would destroy him. Everyone did."

"If this had happened to any other politician three years ago, it would have," Blake concludes. "That's how much you've changed things. You thought voters would be upset because he let them down. That was true, but what you didn't realize is that by coming forward with the truth, you validated everything they believed about him in the first place."

"I guess."

"Sweetie, in the end, Americans don't really care that he sat on the information for longer than he should have or worked with Johnston Albright in the first place. They care that he had the integrity to do the right thing."

"I suppose that's the stuff people think a Speaker of the House should be made of."

Blake pulls himself up a little straighter in his bed. He wears a more serious look on his face and I begin to think I said something wrong. He looks into my eyes.

"Honey, the American people don't give a damn about the Speaker of the House. Most of them couldn't tell you who Johnston Albright was before his suicide. You need to get used to the idea of something."

"What's that?"

"People aren't rallying behind Michael Bennit because they want him to be a leader in Congress. They are supporting him because they want him to run for president."

-THIRTY-SEVEN-

JAMES

"You look well for a man who was recently incarcerated. No unpleasant experiences in the shower, I hope." I get the urge to smack the condescending grin off the smug jerk's face. Instead, I just ignore his comments.

"Is there some symbolism behind meeting me here? You're comparing me to a sinking ship?"

The RMS Titanic was the largest ocean liner built in her day and sank on her maiden voyage in 1912, killing around fifteen hundred people. The disaster still ranks as one of the worst peacetime maritime disasters in history, and by far the most notorious. The most recent box office film featuring the sinking grossed hundreds of millions of dollars, despite being little more than a ridiculous love story.

The Titanic Memorial is a simple granite statue of a half-dressed man erected next to the Washington Channel in southwest Washington. It's dedicated to the heroic efforts of the men on the ship who would eventually drown or freeze in the North Atlantic, as the women rowed away in all the available lifeboats. Coincidentally or not, this statue of a man with arms outstretched looks a little like Kate Winslet's pose on the bow with Leonardo DiCaprio in the movie.

"Not at all. I like this place. It's quiet," Harvey Stepanik observes, looking around at the complete absence of humanity.

And it's cold today. If the frigid temperatures were not enough to keep tourists away, it's the fact that people come to the nation's capitol to see the more prominent landmarks like the White House and Lincoln Memorial. Nobody comes to Washington to visit a monument to a ship that wasn't even American. The story of the unsinkable ship sliding under the sea makes for good storytelling, but tourists won't spend valuable time seeing a commemoration to it.

"I also appreciate that it honors the men who gave their lives so that women and children might be saved."

He needs something from me. That's the theme of this meeting. Normally I would drag it out of him for expediency. However, since I may not be a free man for much longer, I might as well enjoy this.

"So here we are again," he says after it becomes apparent that I won't say anything. "I have another opportunity to be Speaker of the House." There are no limits to this man's ambitions.

"What makes you think you have a chance this time?" I scoff. Lindsay Lohan has a better chance of becoming Queen of England than he does leading the lower chamber of Congress.

"The race is wide open. Democrats can't find a consensus candidate and Michael Bennit is crippled."

"Bennit is going to win."

"Not after that scandal he won't. He's lost too much support and—"

"You need to stop listening to the media and start listening to the voters. The media has settled on their narrative, but the word on the street is much different."

"The voters don't pick the Speaker, the members do. They are not going to choose a guy with no experience to—"

"He's already doing the job, Congressman. He's going to win."

"He won't if you can get the Democrats to support me."

"Why would I do that?"

"Because the president is weak, that's why. You know it, I know it, and they know it. With your powers of persuasion, we believe Democrats may be convinced to jump ship and hedge against him by voting in a strong Republican."

"Y'all are dreaming," I say with a laugh. "Bennit may have ushered in a new era of bipartisanship, but they won't go that far."

"You haven't asked them."

"You're right, and I won't."

"Oh, that's right. I keep forgetting you're under indictment and probably going to prison. You couldn't convince a fireman to climb a tree to save a cat."

"Then why are we here talking?" If Harvey isn't planning on me barnstorming for him like I did a month ago when the new Congress formed and elected a Speaker, then what does he have in mind?

"Because you still have leverage. You know where the bodies are buried and who was wielding the shovels. And most of all, James, you have nothing to lose. If you help us, by using that information as ransom for the votes of the Democrats, we'll do our best to return the favor."

He's right. I have enough dirt on almost every politician in Congress to pull it off. Well, almost every politician who is not an icongressman. It's not the type of information that would earn a prison stay, but more than enough to throw a monkey wrench in any reelection chances.

"So you want me to use what I know to threaten the Democrats in the House into supporting you for Speaker."

"You've done far worse, James, and we both know it."

"If I do this, how do I get a guarantee you will uphold your end of the bargain?"

"You don't. When I am elected Speaker, you'll get my word that I will do everything I can to get the charges against you reduced or dropped entirely. That's the only guarantee you're going to get."

"That's not good enough."

"It'll have to be, because that's all you're getting. It's your choice, James. I don't even need an answer. Bennit scheduled the vote for a new Speaker on Wednesday of next week. If I win, I'll know you came through. Then come see me when I move into my new office on Thursday and we'll talk some more."

"You're not scared of meeting with a disgraced lobbyist? Imagine what people will say."

"The only thing people are paying attention to right now is Michael Bennit, and that's the problem. I don't really want to work with you, James, but right now I see an opportunity for us to help each other. If you help me, I'll be the third most powerful man in the United States government. At that point, I won't care what people say. Good luck to you, James."

He walks away and I head back to my town car. There is a seedy side of politics that most Americans choose to ignore. Most people like sausage, but not too many want to know how it's made. The same is true for politics. If they found out how their government really operated, most of them would never trust their elected officials again.

I climb into the backseat next to the figure who has been my shadow since the moment I got released. He has to be one of the scarier individuals I have ever crossed paths with. Not because he has threatened me with violence, but because he doesn't have to. He could freeze water with a single stare.

I don't like our arrangement, but I'm not in a position to argue either. Only a few months ago, I was the one making the deals with people who had no choice but to accept them. How the times have changed.

"Did you get what you wanted?" I ask him, tapping my chest where the wire I'm wearing is located.

"Yes."

"Are you done with me then, Mister Nyguen?"

"No, Mister Reed, I'm afraid we're only getting started."

-THIRTY-EIGHT-
KYLIE

It's amazing what an exclusive exposé with massive national appeal can do for a small newspaper. My exclusive article was a circulation and advertising bonanza for the *Millfield Gazette*. So much so that they've hit their advertising goal for the year and it's only February.

The media exposure the newspaper got after the article ran was off the charts, and every reprint on the web and in the national dailies made mention of them. The resulting windfall will allow them to add some staff and reduce the workload on the overburdened team. To celebrate, they insisted I come to the office for a small fête with the staff.

After an hour of ego-swelling congratulatory offerings, I head down the street to the place where it all began. The center of Millfield is as quaint as a New England town can get. It's also cold. February is not a fun month to live here unless you're a polar bear … or a moose.

"Hi, Kylie! What can I get for the world's most famous reporter?" Laura gushes from behind the counter as I enter the shop.

"I'm hardly famous, Laura," I correct, sure I'm blushing a little.

Laura is the longtime owner of Millfield's favorite hangout. The Perkfect Buzz is huge by coffeehouse standards, elegantly decorated with comfortable furniture that creates a warm, inviting atmosphere. With Laura's permission, the staff made it ground zero for Michael's first election effort. When the campaign went viral, it became the most renowned independent coffeehouse in the country.

"Oh, don't be so modest, dear. You and your boyfriend are the closest thing we have to celebrities in this little town."

"Well, then this celebrity would like a cup of your boldest blend," I tell her with a smile.

"Coming right up."

After a couple of minutes, I have my steaming cup of Java and retreat into the corner of the seating area. There aren't a lot of customers here, and I would rather avoid the prospect of seeing anyone I know. I park myself into an overstuffed chair next to a man buried in a copy of last week's *Gazette* and oblivious to my presence. I finish nestling in to enjoy my coffee when he lowers his newspaper.

"Nice article," the familiar voice barks, almost causing me to spill my hot drink on myself.

"Geez, Terry, you scared the crap out of me!"

"Sorry."

"No you're not."

"You're right, I'm not. The last part of this is genius where you subtly weave in how we all make mistakes and how we should expect the same of our politicians. That admitting to our failings is the character everyone claims they want out of the people who lead us. It was priceless."

"I'm glad you liked it, but what the hell are you doing up here? Shouldn't you be using your spook skills to uncover the next conspiracy? I'm sure there's a Miss Scarlet planning to off Michael in the Conservatory with the candlestick somewhere."

"I was always more fond of Colonel Mustard."

"Of course you were." Everyone has a favorite character in the board game Clue.

"Actually I was looking for you."

"It couldn't wait until I get back to Washington?"

"Unfortunately, no."

"Okay, well I'm not about to start guessing, so out with it."

"Is Michael going to run for Speaker of the House?"

"They have a Fight Club meeting on Friday, but yeah, I'm sure the icongressmen will want to nominate him. Why?" I'm a suspicious person by nature, but Terry brings it out of me at a whole different level.

"Your political enemies are moving against you."

"How do you know that?"

He just looks at me. Some people have a gift for communicating without ever saying a word. Terry Nyguen's stares speak volumes.

"Okay, so what you're saying is I don't want to know. Fine. How are they moving against us?"

"They're searching for dirt that can be used to blackmail representatives into electing Harvey Stepanik as Speaker of the House."

Harvey Stepanik. I wouldn't trust that man to fold my laundry. He is everything people despise about politicians. His mindset is the exact same as Winston Beaumont's, and that makes him dangerous, if not formidable.

"Other than what we've already admitted to, what else is there to find on Michael? It's not as if people haven't been looking for something to use against him since his first campaign."

"They aren't looking for dirt on you guys. They're targeting anyone who might support you."

"Okay, so what do you expect us to do about it?"

"Nothing. I have it handled."

"So you flew up to Connecticut to tell me something not about us that we don't need to do anything about. You're a strange bird, Terry."

"Nothing is as it seems, Kylie, and I don't know what lengths the extremists on either side of the aisle will do to get their power in the House back. I also don't know what the president might be planning. I know of this particular plot, but that doesn't mean I know them all."

For a brief moment, I think about telling Terry about Reed's attempted extortion of Michael but change my mind. He probably already knows anyway. So I try a different question.

"Why are you doing this?"

"It's my job."

"Your job at a think tank?"

"I told you when we first met that the people I work for want to protect independent candidates. That hasn't changed, other than the protection extends to independent congressmen as well."

"Okay, are we in any danger?" The question sounds scarier to me after I ask it. I don't know if I want the answer this time.

"There are no physical threats to you at this time, but the political stakes are as high as ever. Michael dodged a bullet when he came clean with his alliance with Albright. It was the smartest thing he could have done, but that doesn't mean the party faithful on both sides won't be looking for other ways to take him down, especially if he ends up as Speaker of the House."

"Okay, so what do you need us to do?"

"Just be smart. I'll handle the rest."

-THIRTY-NINE-
MICHAEL

It's easy to get carried away in our Fight Club meetings. This being the day before the vote I scheduled to elect a new Speaker of the House, everyone thought it was appropriate that we hold a special meeting to talk about tomorrow. What I was hoping would be a quick meeting turned into anything but, as discussions about various legislative initiatives seeped into the conversation.

"You're back," Chelsea says from her desk as I stroll into the outer office.

"I am. What are you still doing here?"

"Just catching up on some things," she replies, as I take a seat across from her desk.

"Where are Vince and Vanessa?"

"They left an hour or so ago to catch a late dinner."

"Ah. So they went on a date."

"Not that they'll admi—Wait, what? Did they tell you?"

"Of course not. They've kept that secret better than the CIA could."

"Then how do you know? I mean, I've been friends with them for years and they still haven't officially told me."

"Chels, I was a high school teacher. You think we didn't know who was dating who in our classes? It only takes about two months of teaching before those blips start showing up the radar. Teenagers don't need to change a Facebook status to let the world know, because you were all horrible at hiding it."

"And Vince and Vanessa? How long do you think they've been a couple?" Chelsea asks, amazed I know more about what's going on with them than she does.

"Since the summer after you graduated."

"It's just embarrassing I didn't know that."

"You can't win them all."

"Are the icongressmen going to nominate you tomorrow?"

"They seem intent on it." I sigh. Here we go again.

I've been through this before, and I didn't enjoy the process the first time. Although I have a better chance than last time, there is a very good chance we could end up in a protracted stalemate this go around. Fortunately, Congress is not bound to elect a new Speaker before conducting our business like when the term first started. It doesn't seem possible that it was only almost two months ago. So much has happened.

"Don't sound so enthusiastic."

"I hate the idea of moving the office if it comes to that. Are you excited about the prospect?"

"Being the chief of staff for the Speaker of the House can't be any more terrifying than what I walked into when I first showed up down here."

I grab a stress ball off her desk, give it a good squeeze or two, and then toss it in the air. I catch the foam sphere and turn it over in my hand, inspecting it. I'm not sure what stress this little tchotchke is supposed to relieve. If it was a stress voodoo doll, I could see it.

"Can I ask you a question, Chels?"

"Sure."

"Why did you, Vince, and Vanessa join my staff? Each of you could have gone off to any college or university you wanted. Why come here?"

"I don't really know. I suppose after running two campaigns, the thought of just being a lowly freshman going to classes didn't have much appeal for me. Vanessa felt the same way, especially since she wasn't going to get a sports scholarship to the schools she wanted to go to."

If Xavier was the male athletic phenom in their class, Vanessa was his female counterpart. Both of them were three sport stars, although Xavier excelled in basketball while Vanessa ruled the softball diamond. Like all my staff, a hundred schools were lined up for her to attend but none of them wanted her to play softball there.

"And Vince?"

"Come on, Congressman, can you imagine Vince in 'Introduction to Art History'?"

"You're right. He would spend his lectures defacing his textbook by drawing nipples on the Venus de Milo."

Chelsea lets out a laugh and it's good to hear. Since the shooting, she hasn't laughed as much as she used to. Blake is on the mend and she has really settled into her job, and her old sense of humor is starting to reassert itself. It's good to see.

"So joining my staff was college avoidance for you? Is that why you came back for this term instead of starting at Harvard?"

"Yes … I mean, no."

"You're starting to sound like my colleagues, Chels."

"How do I explain this? I wasn't afraid of going off to school; I just didn't *only* want to be a college student. After our senior year, I would have felt the same way I did after you lost your first campaign."

"Depressed?"

"Normal. I wanted to do more; to be more than just another face in a huge lecture hall."

"You wanted to keep making a difference."

"Yeah. The others felt the same way, too. Peyton, Brian, Emilee, Amanda, Xavier ... It's why they spent so much time in college helping us. When you have the chance to be involved in running campaigns and shaping laws and helping people on a national level, it becomes ..."

"Addicting," I finish for her. Chelsea nods her head.

"Now, can I ask you a question?"

"Shoot."

"Why did you decide to run again after the first campaign? You made your point to America and fulfilled the obligation of our bet. Why did you do it again?"

"I needed the money," I deadpan, drawing out a smile.

"No, really."

"You've worked for me going on two years this June. Why are you asking me now?"

"Now seemed like an appropriate time to ask, considering your question."

Chelsea and I have always maintained something of a teacher-student relationship despite her being my closest political advisor and the young women who runs my entire staff. It dawns on me that she has probably wanted to ask that question for a long time and could never bring herself to do it. It's amazing how far we've all come.

"Fair point," I tell her. "Honestly, at first it was because I don't like losing. In the Special Forces, failure is never an option. You're trained to do what it takes to succeed, because if you don't, your trip home will be in a flag-covered box."

"And I thought my job had pressure."

"Most civilians say that," I say with a wink. "Anyway, I wanted to prove a point in our first campaign, but as soon as we started again, I realized just how desperate the country is for politicians they feel they can trust. I've never cared about power or money. I joined the army to make a difference. I became a teacher for the same reason. I figured I could do the same here. It wasn't until I got here to the Emerald City and pulled the curtain back on the wizard that I realized how hard that would be."

"And now you're the frontrunner to be the Speaker of the House. What a ride this has been."

"I wouldn't take your lap belt off just yet, Chels. I think there are plenty more twists and turns left before this train pulls back into the station."

-FORTY-
CHELSEA

"Did I miss the start?" Vanessa asks, as she rushes in with boxes of donuts and coffee.

"No, the congressman just gaveled in the session. You're just in time."

We are gathered around the television in the outer office. The whole Washington staff is here, and a couple of staffers from our district office who drove down to be a part of the action. Looking around at the group, we are all roughly the same age, give or take a few years. The Michael Bennit youth movement is in da house.

"Well, here we go again," Vanessa decrees, as she sets the goodies down on a desk. "Is Vince back yet?"

"No, he called. He's en route," one of my colleagues tells her.

I purposely decided to watch the proceedings from the office instead of the gallery like last time. Without Brian, Peyton, Amanda, Emilee, and Xavier being around, it just wouldn't feel right. Not that this is much better. I miss having them around, and I really wish Blake was here.

"Any bets as to how this goes?" one of the staff says as everyone digs into the donuts and the coffee pours like a beer tap at happy hour.

"I have ten that says the congressman wins by over twenty votes," my legislative assistant says.

"We all have ten on that," another staffer challenges.

"Guys, if you're going to bet, make it interesting," I interject. "Vanessa, what did your straw poll come up with?"

Vanessa ran around polling the members' staffs on how their principals would vote. She didn't talk to all of them, but using the same methods pollsters do to come up with approval ratings based on a sample, I'm guessing her forecast will be hyper accurate. I don't know what her margin of error is, but she'll be within it.

"I have him winning by thirty-seven."

"There you go, guys. The over-under is now thirty-seven."

The staff begins to make their wagers when Vince breezes in through the door. He gets my attention and beckons me over to my office. The concerned look on his face is disconcerting. He's rarely ever this serious.

"What's up, Vince?"

"I talked to a reporter from ABC who owes me a favor. He told me that there's a story floating around that the congressman has been approaching members of the Democratic Party and blackmailing them in return for their vote for Speaker."

"What?" I demand, exasperated.

"You heard me."

"Blackmail with what?"

"Apparently, the story goes that the congressman made a deal with our favorite lobbyist after all. Reed gave him the goods on almost every member of Congress and, in return, he would give him the access he wanted. Only Mister B turned on Reed and now is using that information to scrounge the votes to remove the 'pro tempore' from his title."

"You've got to be kidding me."

"I said the same thing. The media aren't running with this yet. They're skeptical, but less so than they would have been a month ago. I'm confident they'll figure out the whole thing is a lie, but some might report it if he wins convincingly."

"It's a lie built out of a lot of small truths. The congressman did have a deal with Reed."

"What?" Now it's Vince's turn to be shocked.

"He accepted Reed's offer the day before he went public to throw him off the scent of what he was about to do. From what Kylie told me, Reed also entered into a deal with Stepanik to make him Speaker."

"Okay, you've been holding out on me. "

"I'll fill you in about the whole thing later. It's a brilliant tactic, actually. This will be the first news about the new Speaker of the House, and it will come fresh off another scandal."

"Do you think the president is behind it?"

"Or Stepanik is. Either way, we're going to have a major problem."

"Are you going to text the congressman and let him know?"

I think back to our conversation about why he decided to run and how I needed to keep my lap belt on for a ride. Now I know what he was referring to. Maybe he knows what's going on and maybe he doesn't, but the next hour is going to be an interesting one.

"No. We're going to sit back and watch the fireworks."

-FORTY-ONE-

KYLIE

"The next order of business is the election of the Speaker of the House of Representatives for this session of Congress. Nominations are now in order. The clerk now recognizes the gentleman from Kansas."

This isn't as fun without having James Reed here to annoy. The last time I was in this gallery, my sole purpose was to let him know I was going to take him down. This time, my heart and mind are both in the right place.

"It is my honor to present for election to the Office of Speaker of the House of Representatives the name of Thomas Parker from the great state of Alabama."

"The clerk now recognizes the gentlewoman from California," he announces from the rostrum, as the moderate Republican who offered Parker's name departs the podium in the Well of the Floor.

"As chair of the Republican Conference, and upon a majority vote of that conference, I present for election to the Office of the Speaker the name of the Honorable Harvey Stepanik from Ohio."

Short, sweet, and to the point. Everybody seems eager to get down to business. Even more noteworthy, she used the word "majority" instead of "unanimous." It's an important distinction, and a possible reason why the nominations are not nearly as flowery and flamboyant as they were in January.

"The clerk now recognizes the gentlewoman from California."

"It is my privilege to nominate, through the vote of Democratic Caucus, the name of the Honorable Brian Lockwood of the Commonwealth of Virginia for the Office of Speaker of the House of Representatives."

The dull nominations continue without any fanfare whatsoever. The names offered as nominees include another Republican, two more Democrats, and of course, Michael as the sole independent. Congressman Reyes even toned it down this time when he announced the nomination.

"The names of the Honorable Thomas Parker, Harvey Stepanik, Brian Lockwood, Jennifer Preston, Carleton Huntington, Phillip Chandler, and Michael Bennit have been placed in nomination. Are there further nominations?"

Isn't that enough? For a legislative body that almost seems to be starting to gel, it's not evidenced by the number of nominations. The division is not in the center of the ideological spectrum. Of the six nominees other than Michael, all of them would be considered on the extremes. The only one I know he has any real interaction with is Parker who, despite his staunch conservatism, is willing to debate and work with the icongressman and other moderate members of the Fight Club.

"There being no further nominations, the roll will now be called, and those responding to their names will indicate by surname the nominee of their choosing. The Reading Clerk will now call the roll."

As during the last three votes in January, the names of each voting member in the House start getting called alphabetically. It only takes a few moments for the Reading Clerk to reach the name the whole chamber, whole government, and whole country want to hear. Everyone with any interest in politics is waiting to see how Michael votes, especially considering nominees used to abstain. He broke that tradition in January, and the question everyone wants answered is whether he'll do it again. It wasn't a popular move among the members the first time.

From the gallery, I study the body language of the members below. There's a lot of uncertainty in the room, and if there's one thing politicians loathe, it's uncertainty. I survey the House chamber with my eyes, moving back to the rostrum just in time to hear the next name on the roll call.

"Michael Bennit."

-FORTY-TWO-

MICHAEL

I can hear my heart beat inside my chest. It's pounding as hard as the first time I jumped out of an airplane over Fryar Drop Zone at Fort Benning, and as loud as it did when I waited in silence as a Taliban patrol passed my hide site in Afghanistan. This is another moment of truth, just like those times were.

It's a cliché, but you really can hear a pin drop in the room. There is not a sound. No coughs. No sneezes. No whispers. It is completely silent and I know every man and woman have their eyes riveted on me.

Somewhere in the back, cameras are beaming this image everywhere. Cable news is carrying it live. Millions more will get notifications on their smartphones. Tens of millions will tweet about it and share Facebook posts they see on their news feeds. In the span of a day, three hundred million Americans and hundreds of millions more people across the globe will know what I did right now.

I focus on the American flag hanging behind the rostrum. The stars and stripes is more than just a piece of material—it is the powerful symbol of a dream that unites a nation. A dream of liberty and a dream of freedom. I inhale deeply.

"Parker."

The room erupts into a cacophony of noise. They didn't see that coming. There was no warning. I didn't have my staff brief any of the others, including the other independents. Nobody knew what I was about to do, not even Kylie. The decibel level of the resulting din forces the Reading Clerk to pause and the Clerk of the House to bang the gavel to try to restore order.

The icongressmen closest to my seat all recover from their shock and give me nods. I don't know if they realize why I just did that, but most of them are willing to play follow the leader. The stares I am getting from the Republicans, and even more so the Democrats, aren't quite so warm and supportive.

"I'm letting you throw my next surprise party," Cisco whispers to me as the noise in the room returns to a more conversational level. "You could've at least told me."

"What fun would that be? Besides, I only decided for sure I was going to do it twenty seconds ago."

"You are the ultimate maverick. Look over there. The Democrats are pissed," Cisco observes as he gives a nod in the direction where the Democrats are assembled on the Floor.

"Yeah, so are a lot of the Republicans."

"Do you care?" That causes me to grin.

"I wouldn't be much of an independent if my purpose in life was to make them happy."

The roll call continues and the effect of my vote is almost instantaneous. The icongressmen begin to vote for Parker, joined by countless Republicans. Outside of a dozen or two of the moderate Democrats who are taking the "why not?" approach, the remaining members of their party are dividing their votes among their nominees.

"You realize that you may be the only nominee for Speaker in history not to get a single vote."

"It wouldn't be the first time I made history here."

-FORTY-THREE-

JAMES

I can only watch in horror as the vote concludes. They can spend all the time they want tallying the vote. Anyone watching and listening to the parade of representatives make their selection knows the result.

"The tellers agree in their tallies that the total number of votes cast is four hundred thirty-two," I watch as CSPAN's camera zooms in on the clerk as he makes his announcement. By comparison, listening to Ben Stein read the dictionary would be more entertaining than listening to congressional proceedings.

Three members of the House did not show up for the vote. I knew two would be absent because they are both undergoing medical treatments; one for a heart attack and the other cancer. The third guy must have decided this wasn't important enough to attend. I will have to find out who that was as the clerk continues reading the results.

"The Honorable Thomas Parker of Alabama has received two hundred seventy-five; the Honorable Brian Lockwood of Virginia, one hundred seventeen; the Honorable Harvey Stepanik of Ohio, twenty-one; the Honorable Phillip Chandler of Maine, twelve; the Honorable Carleton Huntington of Alaska, four; the Honorable Jennifer Preston of California, three; the Honorable Michael Bennit of Connecticut has received no votes."

"Figures," I grumble at the television. Bennit getting shut out was the result I was looking for the first time we went through this. Serendipity ...

"Therefore, the Honorable Thomas Parker of the State of Alabama, having received the majority of the votes cast, is duly elected as Speaker of the United States House of Representatives," the clerk announces, concluding the vote.

The room begins a rousing applause as I change the channel to CNN, then FOX. The breaking news graphic filled the screen on both, as I'm sure it does on MSNBC. The result will be the lead story on every major news broadcast tonight. None of the political pundits' predictions included this.

I heard through the rumor mill that a story was circulating through the press corps that Bennit was trying to blackmail Democrats using information I provided him. It's a laughable assertion, and not only because of his unimpeachable character. Who would ever think I would give up information without the promise of anything in return?

There's only one place I can think of this rumor originating and that's from the White House. Just like Harvey tried to take advantage of my arrest and fall from grace to extract information from me, Diane must have figured she would use my tarnished name to discredit Bennit as soon as he got elected as Speaker.

Of course, Bennit had other plans. The man is like Jumanji—you roll the dice and never know what effect you're going to get. He's as unpredictable as a squirrel crossing an interstate, and everyone who has tried to predict how he'd react to a given political situation only winds up embarrassing themselves.

I watch as Thomas Parker is escorted to the dais by the House Majority and Minority Leaders to be sworn in. He's always been a strong conservative, but never much of a party cheerleader. For that reason, he was never seriously considered by his fellow Republicans for any of the top leadership positions in the house. Then he allied with the icongressman. Now he's the man.

Poor Harvey Stepanik looks like he wants to throw up. Despite sharing a similar ideology and both hailing from the same party, there isn't any love lost between him and the new Speaker. He didn't want to lose to Michael Bennit or any of the Democrats. I can guarantee he really didn't want to lose to Thomas Parker. It's like being the point guard on your high school varsity basketball team and losing a pickup game of one on one to your little sister.

I'm sure the staff at the White House is fighting their own waves of nausea. The president needed a Democrat to win, although the party members dividing their votes made them losers from the moment the roll call started. Michael Bennit may have been a nightmare for them along the lines of Freddy Krueger, but Thomas Parker is Jason. Or Michael Myers. Whoever the Halloween guy was.

The African-American community is going to go crazy over this. We've had a black president, but not since the 1800s have we had one as Speaker of the House. As I watch him get sworn in, I can't help but think he's not the man his party thinks he is.

Thomas Parker may be a Republican, but he's also a proud member of Bennit's Fight Club. So does this mean the GOP really controls the House, or do the independents? It's a consideration I hadn't thought about. Did he and Bennit strike a deal? It's unlikely, but not implausible.

Bennit voted for Parker because now the Republicans get the blame if things go south in Congress. He can continue pushing the independent agenda while Parker fights the White House and the rest of the far-left Democrats. As much as I hate to admit it, that's ... brilliant.

Normally I would be looking for an angle in this situation. I'd be searching for some opportunity to exploit to gain more influence or control. Unfortunately, there's no point in that any longer. My game is over, regardless of what I keep telling myself.

I'm out of cards to play. With Terry Nyguen watching my every move, there's nothing more I can do to salvage my importance or keep my influence. I've lost, and the best thing I can hope for now is to stay out of jail. I'm on the sidelines now, and I'll get to watch, from a distance, what transpires over what promises to be a very interesting year.

PART III

AND FOR THE PEOPLE

-FORTY-FOUR-
CHELSEA

"Look at this motley crew," the Speaker exclaims as we walk into the office.

The second half of the congressional session is barely a week old, making a strategy discussion a top priority. With Albright's suicide, the congressman's dealing with the news of his complicity in the assassination attempt, and the election of Parker as Speaker of the House, we didn't get much time to plan at this point last year. This is a midterm election year and every member of the House will weigh their decisions based on the reception they'll get from voters next November. The sad reality of American politics is that the window to get anything accomplished is incredibly short for this reason. The same mechanism meant to keep representatives accountable to the people also grinds the process to a halt.

"Good morning, Mister Speaker," the congressman says, shaking the big Alabaman's hand.

"Mister Speaker," I say, following suit.

"It's good to see you again, sir," my other half adds, completing the greetings.

"Blake, it is great to see you up and about. I've said countless prayers for your speedy recovery over the past year."

"Thank you, sir. I'm thankful God seems to have answered them favorably." His words cause the ordained minister to grin with approval.

Blake is not overly religious but, like Mister Bennit, has the utmost respect for those who are. I've heard the Speaker and Congressman Bennit discussing religion in the office countless times as their professional relationship has turned into a friendship. They were insightful arguments, and the perfect exemplar of how two men who do not agree on everything can still have intelligent debate without hating each other.

"It must have been a long year for you," the Speaker says to Blake.

"Lots of physical therapy, but it could have been a lot worse. Plus I had a great woman at my side ..."

"Aw, thanks!"

"Nagging the whole time," he finishes.

"How long before they're married?" Speaker Parker asks the congressman as I smack Blake on the arm.

"They practically are," Mister Bennit says with a smirk.

"Please, everyone, have a seat," Speaker Parker offers.

We take our places at the long table in his personal conference room. Blake gingerly lowers himself into his seat, trying to avoid any abrupt motion that could cause injury. It's been a little over a year since the shooting and his recovery has been a rollercoaster ride. Blake couldn't get out of the hospital fast enough, and his eagerness resulted in two setbacks late last spring, which made the stay even longer.

"So, Michael, is this year going to be the same as last year? Watching all of our hard work get vetoed away by the president or left to die in the Senate?"

"There's a good chance, unless we manage to shake things up. There isn't much interest in passing anything these days."

"Seventeen bills got vetoed by the president," Blake confirms. "Twice that number made it through both houses of Congress but died when we couldn't reach a consensus in the conference. Nearly a hundred bills passed the House and were never even considered by the Senate. It was obstructionism at its best."

"Seventeen vetoes," the Speaker muses. "That has to be some kind of record."

"Not even close. FDR had over six hundred, so he has a ways to go."

"Yeah, but he was in office forever, Blake," I argue.

"Okay, Truman had two fifty," Blake fires back.

"Grover Cleveland beat him with four fourteen in his first term." We all look at Congressman Bennit, wondering where he got the exact total from a president who served well over a hundred years ago.

"What? I did a little reading over the holidays."

"So any idea what you want to do about it?" the Speaker posits, trying to get everyone back on task.

"The president has an approval rating in the low forties and falling," Blake informs us. "He needs to arrest the fall if he has any chance of keeping the Senate during the midterms."

"My colleagues aren't going to be eager to help with that," Parker concludes. He's right. The Republicans are giddy over watching the president decline in the polls.

"No, they won't, but are they happier to watch him sign more executive orders than he already has?"

"No, which is why I wanted you guys to know that the GOP is seriously considering impeachment again."

"They've been talking about that in Judiciary forever," I say.

The House Judiciary Committee received the remit at the end of last summer to begin the formal inquiry into the issue of impeachment based on the president's use of executive orders and alterations of laws that were passed. If Speaker Parker is correct, the Judiciary Committee will send another Resolution consisting of the Articles of Impeachment to the full House for debate. The media will go nuts, America will groan, and we'll be caught in the middle.

"They're playing politics with it. Nothing energizes a base more than political hardball," the Speaker scoffs.

"It won't pass the House."

"I know, but Stepanik doesn't care. Americans aren't happy with the president and he thinks giving him a good kick will score him some political victories that will lead to net gain for Republicans in the fall."

"At the expense of the icongressmen," the congressman clarifies.

"If they vote against it, yes. He thinks you guys may lose a chunk of the middle no matter how you and the other independents justify it to the people on social media."

"Stepanik is smart," I tell everyone. "This is a no-lose situation for him. If the resolution passes, he forces the Senate to decide the president's fate. If it fails, he can point the finger at a group that promised to unite and accomplished nothing for failing to remove the biggest hurdle."

We knew coming here that this was going to be a rough climb. After the promise of the icongressman, the Fight Club, and the election of Parker as Speaker of the House, we were optimistic last year that we could score some wins for the American people. It wasn't to be.

The scandal that marred the beginning of the year quickly subsided, and America watched as Congress finally got down to business. The House got together to pass a record amount of bills, mostly through a level of collaboration and compromise not seen in generations. What few bills made it through a hostile Senate died on the president's desk.

The result in America was what anyone would expect. A population that feels it was let down by Obama's hope and change called it quits on our promise of a new era as well. We know this year is the last chance to turn it around, but it's off to a lousy start.

"Please, Michael, tell me you have some historical anecdote that works well for this situation."

"I don't, but I do have a quote."

"This ought to be good," I whisper to Blake.

"Sun Tzu once said, 'The opportunity to secure ourselves against defeat lies in our own hands, but the opportunity of defeating the enemy is provided by the enemy himself.'"

"Chelsea, would you mind translating that for me?"

"Mister Speaker, I think what the congressman is trying to say is maybe we can make politics work for us, for a change, by using it to get enough votes to override some vetoes."

"How? We can't even get enough support in the House to overturn a veto. And forget getting the Senate on board."

"Leave that to me, Blake."

Blake and I exchange glances. Neither of us has any idea where he is going with this. Like most of the congressman's plans, it is sure to turn some heads.

"Okay, what do you need me to do, Michael?"

"I need you to encourage the Republicans to introduce the articles of impeachment."

"That's supposed to help?" the Speaker asks incredulously.

"Trust me," Mister Bennit responds with the smile we used to get in class before he pulled out a pop quiz.

"Blake, can you call the Architect of the Capitol? We may have to ask him to start bolting down the furniture before tables start flying again."

-FORTY-FIVE-
KYLIE

I double-check the address on my smartphone again. It reads 800 F Street, NW, just as it did the last six times I checked. The building isn't the one I thought it was. When I got the e-mail from Terry to meet him at this address, I immediately thought it was a little weird he wanted to link up at the National Portrait Gallery. I dismissed it because Terry Nyguen is a couple beers shy of a six-pack anyway. Only when I got here did I realize I was in the wrong place.

The building I should have been looking for is only steps away from the MCI Center and happens to be the only public museum in the United States solely dedicated to the art of espionage. I read the sign and let out a sigh. Yeah, this is much more fitting for the man we call Mister Dark and Mysterious.

"Really, Terry? The International Spy Museum?" I ask as I sense he's snuck up on me once again.

"I find your lack of interest a little disappointing, Kylie. This is one of the greatest museums you will ever visit. Imagine twenty thousand square feet filled with the tools of the trade owned by some of the most infamous spymasters of all time. It's enough to make a man weep."

"It's enough to make me want to scream. I am not letting you drag me through there, so what do you want to do?"

"Are you sure? It's warmer in there than it is out here."

Early January is not the time to be wandering around the city like a lost tourist. Washington may be warmer than New York, but not by much. I am more of a spring and summer girl. Save the frigid air for the polar bears … and the Scandinavians.

"The choice between freezing to death and dying of boredom isn't much of a choice at all, but at least this coat is warm."

"Fine. Maybe after hitting up a Starbucks you'll be in a better mood," he declares as we start walking. At least now he's speaking my language.

"So can you tell me why we're here, or do we have to wait until we find an empty parking garage?" I ask, leveling a not so subtle reference to the meetings Woodward and Bernstein had with Deep Throat during the Watergate scandal.

"Here on the street is fine. I'm not sure I will be telling you anything you probably don't already know."

"Okay, out with it. Is Michael in any danger?" It's becoming my default question to this man.

"He will always be a target, Kylie, but there are no credible threats against him."

"Well, that's good at least," I mumble with a sense of relief.

"For now, anyway."

"You are such a killjoy. Are you finally coming clean about what you really do for the think tank you claim to work for?"

"No, but I am here on the behalf of some colleagues who specialize in doing analytical work and research for us on domestic political figures."

"Do you always have to speak so cryptically? Which political figures are you talking about?"

"It doesn't matter. What matters is what they have to say about the current occupant of 1600 Pennsylvania Avenue. Here's a question for you, Kylie. If I asked you what the biggest threat to the American way of life is, what would your answer be?"

"I don't know. Apathy, Al Qaida, debt, failures in education ... take your pick."

"Any of those is a viable answer. Now, if I ask that same question to the president of the United States, the response I'd get is Michael Bennit."

"What? That's ridiculous!"

"I agree, but we have a very strong belief that the he considers Michael the number one threat to his administration. He believes that his agenda is the best course for America, and he will destroy anyone in his way of advancing it."

"By destroy, you mean ...?"

"No, I don't think he would go as far to have someone take a shot at you and Michael again."

"Why not? It didn't seem to stop the Speaker of the House when he felt his grip on power was slipping away."

"Good point. But as I stated, there's no credible physical threat against you guys. There is a political one, though. He's looking for dirt."

"You told me last year people were looking for dirt when you scared the crap out of me at the coffee shop. This is politics and everybody is always looking for something to use against someone else. Opposition researchers make a very good living for that reason. Michael has nothing to hide."

There is one benefit to dating a man with a public profile—if he was doing something behind my back it would be flashed all over the front page. Researchers have investigated every aspect of Michael's life, looking for anything his political enemies can use against him. Every inquiry they've ever made has come up empty. If they haven't found something by now, they're not going to.

"I didn't say you need to worry about Michael."

"Good, because I'm not. Winston Beaumont dug to China looking for anything during his first race and only ended up with a very deep hole. There's nothing to find."

"On him, at least. But Michael is a coalition builder, and if you can't take him out ..."

"You take everyone working with him out."

"There are more skeletons in the closet in Washington than there are in the catacombs of Paris. The president is going to find and use them against anyone with the audacity to work with the independents."

Terry knows the specifics. He knows the who, what, where, when, and why, but isn't going to tell me. I don't bother asking as much as the journalist in me is screaming to.

"That could just as easily blow up in the president's face."

"He's not looking at it that way. Congress is getting increasingly popular and he has a lower approval rating at this point in his presidency than any of his last ten predecessors. Desperate times call for desperate measures, and he is going to go on the offensive to stop the freefall."

"Why are you telling me this?"

Terry stops in the middle of the sidewalk and searches his surroundings through his dark Oakley sunglasses. Something is bothering him more than usual. That thought alone is unnerving.

"This president is a particularly ruthless one. He's not going to play ball and compromise with Congress. It's his way or no way at all, and that is a very dangerous thing in this country. Michael has done an amazing job bringing people together, and it's making the White House look bad. I don't want to see him get blindsided by a knockout punch that could end the fight once and for all, because I don't know if I can stop it this time."

-FORTY-SIX-

JAMES

Thirty-seven percent. That's the current approval rating of the president of the United States. For the first time in memory, Congress has a higher approval, even if it is only by one point. Anything in the thirties is abysmal but, for Congress at least, it is a lot better than the teens they've been polling at over the past decade. The president must be getting desperate.

When Stepanik approached me last year to use my knowledge of his colleagues' illegal and nefarious activities against them to install him as Speaker, it was a laughable request. Why would I use it to help him with the promise of nothing in return? I should send him a fruit basket or something as a thank you, because it did give me an idea though.

I knew Terry Nyguen couldn't watch me forever. Now, a year into this congressional term with no substantive legislative accomplishments, Bennit is going to be forced to get aggressive. If the president gets scared enough, he'll know where to come for help. And when he does, I'll be ready.

"James, are you listening?"

"No, not really."

"You should probably take—"

"What? Take this more seriously? I'm sorry, are you the one who's been indicted and is facing a long prison term?"

The suit doesn't answer. Of course he doesn't. He's only an associate on my legal defense team and I'm the client who pays an exorbitant fee for him, his fellow associates, and his boss to do their jobs. I don't pay for some paralegal to read pages of text to me that would cure the worst case of insomnia.

"I didn't think so. I am taking this very seriously, but y'all are boring me to tears. Keep me out of that courtroom. That's the only thing you need to worry about."

"We have drawn the discovery process for your case out as long as we can, James," my well- dressed, high-priced lawyer tells me from across the conference room table. Milton Adelstein is the best in the business when it comes to defending important people and his impressive track record of keeping his clients from facing the consequences of their bad decisions. Or at least the ones they got caught doing.

"Draw it out longer," I demand.

"We can't," another member of my extensive legal team chimes in. "They already set the trial date."

"It's been a year. We can't push it off longer," the associate argues, trying to look important for his boss.

"File to dismiss."

"We've done that three times, Mister Reed. The judge isn't going to dismiss this case. At least, not without proper … reason."

"I wasn't implying we bribe him, young man," I tell the snot-nosed kid who's out of his depth trying to play with the adults at this table. Although, the idea of buying off the judge crossed my mind a while back and I seriously considered it for a while.

"I hope not. It's why you're here in the first place."

"Milton, I hired you to defend me in this case because I expect you to get me off the hook. Now, can you or can't you?"

"You were caught with the evidence in your possession. It's a losing battle and I think you need to consider a deal from the prosecutor."

"No."

"James, I've been doing this for a long time. I've seen it all and I know how this is going to end. This is an unwinnable case. If you want to avoid serious jail time, you need to plea down."

"I said no."

"The DA made an offer, but it comes with a time limitation. If you change your mind too late, the deal goes away," Adelstein's associate says. "It's a fair deal. If you don't take it and gamble with a trial, the outcome will be far worse."

I have at least one more ace up my sleeve. There is more than one way to get out of a prison term in this country. All I need is for Congress to do what they always do—something stupid.

"No deals. You're my legal team and I pay you to abide by my wishes. Continue to stall as long as you can."

"And then what?" Milton asks.

"Then we go to trial."

-FORTY-SEVEN-
CHELSEA

Blake comes in and sits in the chair across from my desk without as much as a kiss on the cheek. As much as I enjoy getting them, we save the displays of affection for non-work hours. I'm technically his boss now since he accepted the congressman's offer of a position on the staff once he got released from the hospital. I don't want the others to see me canoodling with him in the office.

"It's official. The Republicans have introduced articles of impeachment to the House Floor."

Great. Under the Constitution, the House of Representatives is endowed with the sole power of impeachment involving the president, vice president, or other federal officers. After debate, if the articles are approved, they are sent to the Senate, which has the exclusive power to try all impeachments and remove the offender if found guilty.

"How many counts?"

"Seven."

"The seven deadly sins. How righteous of them. The GOP must be going for broke on this. That's a lot of counts."

"The members in the Judiciary Committee threw the book at him, metaphorically speaking," Blake answers.

"That didn't take long. We met with the Speaker, what, like a week ago?"

"Something like that, yeah."

"Did the icongressmen on the committee vote for it?" I'm afraid to hear the answer, although I already know it.

He nods. We knew some of them might go along with this. Our success was predicated on making a difference in people's lives. In the past year, we have nothing to show for our efforts. The independents are frustrated, and now they see an opportunity to take it out on the source of that frustration.

"Well, we did ask Parker to help this along. I was just hoping none of the independents would vote for it."

"They had a hard time saying 'no' and didn't want to explain their abstentions back home. They like to vote on things."

"Yeah, I know."

"You know, I don't know how much advice I can give you on this, Chelsea. I've never been through one of these."

"Me neither," I smile. I wasn't even in kindergarten when Bill Clinton was impeached.

Congress had held serious discussions of impeachment of the president only four times in our history. Andrew Johnson was impeached when Congress became disgruntled with his handling of post-Civil War matters, but he had remained in office after he was acquitted in the Senate by one vote. Congress had also introduced a resolution to impeach John Tyler over state's rights issues, but the resolution had failed.

In more recent times, Congress was debating the impeachment of President Richard Nixon over the Watergate break-in when he resigned from office. His removal from office would have been a no-brainer. Bill Clinton was impeached by the House on charges of perjury and obstruction of justice over lying about his affair with White House intern Monica Lewinsky. Like Johnson, he had dodged a bullet in the Senate.

"Did you guys hear?" Vince asks as he and Vanessa storm into my small office.

"About the impeachment? Yeah."

"I guess you can kiss this year being productive good-bye. The media are already off and running with it," Vanessa laments.

"We can't think like that."

"Think like what? That we're totally screwed? That the reason Americans are so angry is because of crap just like this?"

Vince is getting emotional, and I would be too if I were in his position. He wasn't in the meeting we had with the Speaker. Other than Blake, nobody on the staff has any idea what game the congressman is playing. I don't even know all the particulars.

"We have to be ready in case something changes." Okay, that was weak.

"Seriously? What's going to change, Chels?"

"I don't know, but I've learned that chance favors the prepared. Let's be prepared."

"Fine, but I've learned something, too," Vince decrees. "I've learned that the American government cannot manage to get out of its own way."

-FORTY-EIGHT-
KYLIE

When you live with someone, you instantly know what kind of mood they are in by the way they open and close the door when they get home from work. If they're angry, it's quick and violent. If they are tired, it's lazy and slow. If they had a good day, it's energetic. If it was frustrating, it was like how Michael just entered.

"Hard day at the office, honey?" I ask him as he crashes into the couch without bothering to remove his suit jacket.

"Aren't they all these days?"

"Good point. Do you want to talk about it?" I say, without looking up from my computer.

"Not really. I assume you heard that the Republicans pushed articles of impeachment to the House Floor today."

"I did. You were smart to hand Parker the Speaker position and let the big guns run the House." I get a grunt in return.

Michael is a great leader, but he's not an administrator and not a politician in the normal sense of the word. He only wants to make a difference and has no tolerance for the infighting that seizes Congress up in an unmanageable gridlock. He is a man struggling to unite people in a place where deep division is the eleventh commandment. Trying to run the House of Representatives would have made him miserable.

"You're writing?" he asks, finally noticing the open laptop perched in my lap on the couch.

"Yeah, I can't let you be my sugar daddy forever. I need to earn my keep. I figured I could write about this crazy rumor I heard that you plan to support a group of icandidates running against established senior senators. Do you care to comment?"

"Am I on the record?"

"Yes. Then I'm going to ask you why you didn't empty the dishwasher before you left this morning."

"Then no comment."

"To which one?"

"Both. Either of those questions can only get me in trouble."

With a wink, he gets up, takes his jacket off, and goes to the fridge. He pulls out a bottle of water, and I'm pleased he didn't go for the Sam Adams. It's easy to adopt bad habits in a job like his.

"Okay, is it true?" I ask him, as he uncaps the water and swallows half of it before bothering to take a breath.

"That depends. Are you Kylie Roberts the soon-to-be Pulitzer Prize winning journalist, or Kylie Roberts, the love of my life?"

"Can't I be both?"

"No comment." At least he smiled.

"Fine," I say, closing my laptop. "We're off the record."

"Yes, I'm planning to run them against the senators up for reelection this fall."

"All of them?"

"The ones not willing to cooperate with us. So yes, as of right now, pretty much all of them."

"Will you give me a quote for this?" I ask, reopening my computer. There's a story here after all.

"Sure. Can it wait?"

"Yup. I only just started. But while I'm waiting, can you answer another question?"

"I'm sure this question is going to be equally disturbing."

"That depends on how you answer it. Are you planning on running for president?"

"If I was, don't you think I would have sat down and talked to you about it first?" he asks, sitting back down on the couch next to me.

"You mean before making a life-altering decision that would subject us to unending scrutiny, a complete lack of privacy, and unrelenting criticism? I would hope so, but you didn't answer the question."

"Well said, and you're right, I didn't answer it. No, I'm not planning on a run for the White House. Why?"

"There's a rumor out there."

"Oh boy, one I haven't heard! I didn't think there was any room in conversations for rumors not concerned with what's going on in Congress. Where did you get it from?"

"A couple of beat reporters and a White House senior correspondent mentioned it to me in passing."

My revelation causes him to smile, and I know something is up. I am not as involved with Michael's political dealings as I was a year ago. We decided it was the best thing for my career if I kept my distance from him and his staff on Capitol Hill. As a result, I'm not in the loop on whatever he has planned. Maybe he is more of a politician than I'm giving him credit for.

"Well, would you run?" I prompt.

"I don't think Americans are ready for that yet. I'd hate to have to try to flip the Resolute desk in the Oval Office to make a point. But honestly, I really haven't thought about it." I'm not sure how much I believe that.

"Well, sweetie, you might want to," I tell him as I go back to writing the article. "The questions are coming."

-FORTY-NINE-

MICHAEL

"Thank you for joining us tonight, Congressman. I have one more question before you go. There are rumors circulating that you are contemplating a run for the White House. Is that true?"

Crap. I almost made it through this interview without him asking. For a country that purports to hate politics, there is no shortage of programming jamming the airwaves with politically themed shows. Most of them, this one included, air on the twenty-four-hour cable news networks. It would be easy to dismiss that as them needing content for prime-time broadcasts, but their ratings are not unimpressive.

I wanted the rumor of my impending presidential run out there, but not in such a public way. Kylie surprised me last night when she told me she had heard the rumor. Now I'm being asked about it live in this Washington studio.

"Have you ever seen a politician in this town that doesn't on some level dream about being president?" I deflect artfully.

"Does that mean you're running?" the anchor persists.

"We haven't even gotten to the midterms yet. It's too early to be talking about subjecting the American people to speculation about another presidential election year. They equate conversations like this to seeing Christmas decorations in stores in September," I joke, even though I'm actually serious.

"Come on, Congressman, yes or no? You offered a colorful analogy, but people want to know. Polls on the subject have you as a frontrunner in any hypothetical race."

There are polls on this already? How could anyone know who they are voting for in an election three years from now? I'm beginning to think people are already forgetting the lesson I tried to teach during my first election.

"I appreciate the question, but there isn't any yes or no answer to it right now. It's just too early, but you hear that all the time from every politician who thinks they're a contender, so I'll make a deal with you. When I decide, I'll call you up and you can have me back on your program to give you an answer."

"Deal! I'm going to hold you to that," the anchor beams.

"I have no doubt you will."

"Thanks for coming on the program, Congressman Bennit."

"Thanks for having me."

* * *

"No dinner plans with Kylie tonight?" Cisco says as we take our seats and the hostess hands us menus and takes our drink orders.

"She's working tonight and I didn't want to bother her. Apparently, getting mentioned for a Pulitzer means everyone wants you to write for them."

"That sounds a little like what happened when I got elected to Congress."

"What do you mean?"

"I mean that nobody cared who I was or what I'd done before I got elected to come here. Everyone just assumed I was a day laborer or something. That's the problem with Latinos being the most stereotyped culture on earth."

"Most cultures would find that debatable," I interrupt.

"Whatever. After I dropped off the paperwork to get on the ballot for the special election, I went back home and thought about the journey my life had taken that led me to run for Congress. Only then did I realize my nanny was black, my pool boy was Asian, and my landscaper a white guy. That's when I knew I could campaign on my terms and not worry about the outcome. I knew I'd already made it in the world."

I laugh, but he's probably serious. Cisco overcame a lot of challenges to make it here. Other than the trauma from the shooting he's still dealing with, it's why he was so resistant to doing anything that would derail the independent movement. When I go, he'll be the one left carrying the torch.

"Kylie is a great writer and an amazing woman. A Pulitzer will only let the world know what you already figured out a long time ago," Cisco concludes after taking a sip of his beer.

"You're a man of incredible wisdom," I tell him with a smile.

"Do you think anyone will recognize us here?" he asks, surveying the inside of the restaurant.

I changed into street clothes and met him here following my live interview. Washington is not unlike Hollywood—people trying to make the big time like to be noticed, and once you get there, you do everything you can not to be. Between the casual dress and dining off the beaten path at a Georgetown burger joint, I think we're safe from our version of the Washington paparazzi.

"I sincerely hope not," I tell him, clinking his pint glass before tipping back my Guinness.

"Are the rumors working?"

"Yeah, a little too good, I think. Who did you tell, anyway?"

"Nobody special. Just the usual congressional chatterboxes. You need to blame Vince and Vanessa for the overexposure of this particular rumor. They have this town totally wired for sound."

"I never cease to be amazed by that. You know, Vince quit my campaign once because he didn't think he could do the job."

"Yeah, well, I think he's found his calling now. I wish I had him and Vanessa on my staff. Would you ever be willing to trade for them?"

"They're not baseball cards, Cisco," I tell him with a laugh. Chelsea, Vince, and Vanessa are more than my staff. They are my former students and valued friends. In short, they're priceless and there's nothing he could offer in a trade for them.

"Do you think starting these rumors will have the desired effect?"

"Of scaring the president? Yeah. I think he only needed a nudge to become completely unglued." I have no idea if this plan will work, but I won't deny having fun antagonizing that man.

"And this is the nudge?" I tip my beer in his direction and give him a nod. "What if it was to ever become more than a nudge?"

"You mean like really running for president?"

"Yeah, why not?" Cisco is being a little coy about this. We have been on unsteady ground since the day in the hallway with Chelsea. We have both forgiven him and gotten past it, but he's been far more careful in his interactions with us since. The Cisco of old would have been beating me over the head with this.

"Kylie asked me the same thing last night."

"What did you tell her?"

"I was ... ambiguous."

"To a reporter?" Cisco says with a laugh. "I doubt that, unless you were just warming her up to the idea."

"I wasn't."

"When are you going marry that girl? It will be so much easier to call her the First Lady than the First Fiancée or First Girlfriend, or the—"

"Stop there," I warn with a laugh. "Don't I have enough on my plate already, my friend?"

"Aw, if you like, you need to put a ring on it."

"Cisco …"

"I know, I know. Sorry. Do you know why this rumor is taking off?" he asks, sipping his own beer.

"No, enlighten me."

"It's because everyone wants it to be true."

"Not everyone, Cisco, not everyone."

-FIFTY-

JAMES

"Why did you want to meet here?"

"It's a nice night for a walk."

"If by nice night you mean freezing to the point where I can't feel my face, then yes, it is."

"It's not that cold out," Diane offers, dismissing my discomfort. Sure, it isn't if you're already cold-blooded.

I'm not sure why I'm cursed with clandestine meetings at monuments around the city. Eleven months ago it was Harvey Stepanik trying to enlist my help at the Titanic Memorial. Now Diane Herr is going to make some proposition to me here. At least Terry Nyguen doesn't have a wire on me like last time. He's been watching my every move over the past year, so I wasn't surprised that he contacted me within a few hours of Diane asking for this meeting.

"I love this place," she continues. "It's my favorite monument. Did you know my grandfather fought in World War II?" I don't ask her for what side, even though I want to.

The World War II Memorial honors the millions of Americans who served during the war, the more than four hundred thousand who died, and everybody on the home front who supported the war effort. The Second World War is the only twentieth-century event commemorated on the central axis of the National Mall, located between the Lincoln Memorial, Washington Monument, and within sight of the White House.

"No, I didn't know that." Nor do I care.

"He was a marine in the South Pacific. He took part in the whole island-hopping campaign before being injured on Okinawa and earning a trip back to the States."

"The South Pacific, eh? At least it was warm there. Maybe as warm as your office would have been, so why didn't we just meet there?"

"You already know the answer to that, James. If you need me to spell it out for you, it's because you're a disgraced lobbyist under federal indictment and we can't have you traipsing through the West Wing. The media have us under siege and our poll numbers are already low enough."

"You forgot the president being in danger of getting impeached."

Diane waves a dismissive hand. I would expect nothing less from the president's chief yes man. Or in this case, yes woman.

"Y'all aren't worried about the impeachment?" I prod.

"Nope. It's just another smear tactic aimed at getting the president off message."

"Don't play games, Diane. I know that's why I'm here."

"I'm sorry to disappoint you, James, but we're not afraid of getting impeached. We're afraid of the man we think is really behind it."

"Harvey Stepanik?" I'm stunned. He couldn't scare a baby rabbit with chainsaw.

"Hardly. That man couldn't find his way out of an open closet. No, I was talking about Michael Bennit."

"That's a bit of a reach," I say with a snicker. Is she serious?

"Is it? You were the one who once told me never to underestimate him. You should be happy I'm taking your advice for a change."

We fall silent as we pass a couple of tourists braving the cold temperatures to take in the beauty of this monument and its dim yet peaceful lighting. It gives me a moment to pause and reflect on her statement. I don't think Bennit is behind this. He's not politically savvy enough to play the game at that level.

"I did say that, but it doesn't mean he's running around jumping tall buildings in a single bound, either."

"So you don't think we should be worried?"

"No, y'all should be terrified. The last person the president would want to tangle with is Michael Bennit. So, you think he is somehow linked to the impending impeachment?"

"Yes, we believe he is the controlling vote and using the momentum to catapult him into an independent bid for the presidency." That's news.

"And y'all know this for sure?"

"We have heard enough rumors being circulated in the press briefing room, leaked out from people who know. He's going to use the impeachment against us, and we need to prevent that from happening at all costs. We can't wait for a Senate trial if it goes that far. We know we'll win, but the president doesn't want to have to debate the iCongressman with an impeachment hanging around his neck, should he make a run at the White House."

"I find that very implausible but, if he runs, you need to know what y'all are up against. Bennit used to be a social media candidate who had mainstream appeal. Now he's a mainstream candidate with incredible social media appeal. He doesn't need a huge organization with campaign offices and lots of staff because he owns the Internet. He'll spend a tiny fraction of what you do on the race and still beat you by double digits, regardless of whether the president faces impeachment or not."

"Thanks for painting such a rosy picture, James," Diane sneers.

"I'm not going to stroke your egos. Since you and the president are convinced y'all have Bennit's motives all figured out, what do you need from me?" I suppress a smile. I know exactly what's coming next and have planned for it. Everything is coming together.

"How much dirt do you have on the Republicans?"

"Which ones?"

"All of them, but especially the members in the House."

"I have enough."

"James, we are way beyond vague ambiguities now. Define enough," Diane commands.

"I could cause a half dozen to resign, humiliate another twenty-five or so to the point where they don't have a prayer at getting reelects, and embarrass the rest. Why?"

"I may need you to use that information."

Same crap, different monument. This all sounds so familiar because it is. I knew the president's minion would come crawling to me for help, just like Harvey Stepanik did at the Titanic Memorial. I may no longer have any influence, but I do have knowledge, and knowledge is power.

"Why would I do that?" I play along.

"Because what we offer in return is the one thing you need most right now—a full pardon for your crimes."

"You're assuming I'll be found guilty."

"There's no doubt in anyone's mind about that. Glenn will catch a lot of heat over it, but he's willing to bail you out of your situation if you'll return this ... favor."

There's the first name again. God, I hate it when she does that. It gives me the out I need, though, just not the one she's looking for.

"Okay, it's a deal. How do you want me to handle it?"

"Any way you see fit. Oh, and James?" she turns back to me as she heads back to the White House looming in the distance. "This offer is contingent upon success."

"Who makes that determination?"

She smiles. "We do. Have a good evening, James."

She heads east off the grounds of the memorial and I follow fifty feet behind her until she makes a right after crossing the street. I continue on straight, putting some distance between us before pulling out my cell phone.

"Yeah?" the voice on the other end of the line answers as I glance over my shoulder to ensure Diane Herr is heading back towards the White House following the path that runs along Seventeenth Street. Good, she is.

"Mister Nyguen, I just left the meeting with Diane Herr and you asked me to call you when it was over."

"Yes, I did. What did she want?" This guy is all business.

"Nothing that concerns Michael Bennit, if that's what you're worried about," I explain to him as I stroll up the curved path towards the Washington Monument.

"Everything concerns me, Mister Reed. And whatever I'm concerned about should be of utmost importance to you."

"Fine. It's late and I'm assuming you don't want to discuss this via cell phone." I've only met him a couple of times, but it's enough to know he likes the super-secret spy stuff.

"Very perceptive, Mister Reed."

"Where do you want to meet?"

"How about right here?"

"What?" I shout as I reach the flags at the base of the Washington Monument. I search for him on the surrounding sidewalks in all directions, but all I see are couples out for a stroll and a small group of tourists walking towards the Lincoln Memorial. "What do you mean, right here?"

"Turn to your right. See me now?"

Crossing the grass a couple of hundred feet away from the direction of the Sylvan Theater Stage is a shadowy figure dressed in dark clothing. Even in the light of the National Mall, he is practically invisible against the backdrop the copse of trees near the stage provides. Calling him was the best thing I could have done because I never would have known he followed me here. Like an idiot, I am still holding the phone to my ear when he finally reaches me, long having disconnected the call and pocketed the phone.

"I told you, Mister Reed, I am always watching you," he comments, noticing my stunned expression as he shows me a palm-sized set of some high-tech version of binoculars before tucking them in his pocket.

"So I have come to learn," I tell him as I regain my composure and put my own phone away.

"Now, tell me all about it," he commands as he turns and walks up the National Mall towards the Capitol.

-FIFTY-ONE-
KYLIE

Anybody who frequently works from home understands the need to get out once in a while. While it's nice to avoid the daily grind of a commute to and from work, being cooped up in the house all day can wear on you. I'm tired of staring at my laptop and need to get out of here for a while.

We have plenty of coffee in the house. Michael's caffeine addiction ensures the pantry is properly stocked at all times, but a trip to Starbucks is an excuse for me to get out and stretch my legs. The closest one is in Union Station, and is about a mile walk from our apartment in the NOMA section of Washington. While it's a little chilly to be out for a stroll, I decide to brave it anyway.

The central rail hub of the capital is quieter this time of day, so the wait in line is not a long one. The line during rush hour can easily extend out the door and cost twenty minutes of your time. I place my drink order and am waiting as the barista applies her trade to fulfill the orders of the four people in front of me, when my world gets turned upside down.

"Fancy meeting you here," the voice that sounds just like my sister says from behind me. When I turn, I'm shocked to see a slimmer, but otherwise stunning Madison Roberts standing there. Damn, it is her. I'm not sure if her stumbling in here at the precise moment I show up is a coincidence or whether she somehow followed me here, but it doesn't matter. Out of instinct, my claws come out.

"Who let you out of prison?" I ask, loud enough so anyone standing within thirty feet can hear.

"I guess we're dispensing with the pleasantries early, eh, sis? It's good to see you, too."

"I thought you still had some time on your sentence."

"Reduced for good behavior and all that," Madison replies. "You know how it is."

"Actually, I don't. I've never been imprisoned."

"I'm sure you've never been to one, either. Imagine, I'm locked up for almost two years and I never once got a single visit from my dear older sibling." Yeah, I'm sure thinking about me not visiting kept her up at nights.

"I sent cookies." I actually did. I even splurged and put M&Ms in them.

"Kylie, everything you have ever baked in your entire life has been inedible. Even if by some miracle they were, I couldn't trust you not to add rat poison to the recipe." Now I'm mad at myself for not thinking of that.

"Mom says hi, by the way," Madison continues, changing to another sore subject with me.

"I doubt that."

I haven't talked to my mother since the allegations against Winston Beaumont went public. Madison was always her favorite, and there was no room in her life for the child who sent her princess to prison. It doesn't matter that she was abetting a criminal or engaged in something illegal. It also doesn't matter that, during a moment of weakness, I tried to warn her and got fired from my job in return. Nope, nobody crosses my mother's precious little angel without feeling her wrath, or in my case, getting disowned.

"You're right, she didn't. She wants nothing to do with you."

"The feeling's mutual. So, what brings you back to Washington?"

"Job opportunities."

"Here? I would have thought you could find a job stripping pretty much anywhere."

"Much faster than you could," my younger sister fires back, feigning a laugh or two. "No, I have talents that are in demand in this town."

"There's no arguing that, but when employers hire people to assist in a conspiracy, they'd prefer them not to get caught. But hey, I could be wrong. I might be underestimating the number of openings around for convicted felons."

Madison is one of those people who can dish it out and not take it in return. Nothing puts her on edge faster than acting the same way around her as she treats others. And by acting the same way, I mean smug, demeaning, and arrogant.

"You're so proud of yourself, aren't you, Kylie?" she snaps.

"For taking down a sleaze bag like your former boss? You're damn right I am. I consider that one of my greatest achievements. You going down with him was icing on the cake."

"You know, I did a lot of reading in prison, Kylie. I know all about your escapades with your boyfriend. I have never seen a politician who thinks he's more self-important than Michael Bennit."

"If you say so."

I find that hard to believe, since her former employer thought he was the center of the universe. Michael, on the other hand, is one of the least egocentric people I have ever met. Madison doesn't have a high opinion of soldiers or teachers, so it's no wonder she thinks that.

"Compromise, compromise … ugh! He's like a broken record. He wants everyone to give up what they believe in just so he can pass laws to make himself look good. And do you know what the worst part of it is? He destroys anyone who stands in his way. Poor Johnston Albright."

Madison has always known how to push my buttons. Maybe I'm having a bad day, or maybe it's because I haven't seen her in a long time. Either way, she's doing an exceptionally good job of it today.

"Madison, as usual, you have no idea what you're talking about."

"Oh, I think I do. Just remember something, Kylie. Bennit doesn't have a monopoly on doing what's right for the American people. You may think you have a lot of support, but there are a lot of people out there who think this country is far better off without him in politics."

"I know that, Madison. We spent a Christmas in the hospital because of it, or didn't you hear?" I swear, if she makes a single comment about him not finishing the job that day, I will strangle her myself in the middle of this coffee shop.

"I'm not talking about crazy people. I'm talking about senior politicians and government officials who believe your husband is taking us down the wrong road. Oh, I'm sorry. I forgot … you're not married yet."

"I see prison did very little to humble you, Madison," I say through clenched teeth, as I fight to control my anger. "You can come up with all the snarky comments you want. You've always been better at them than I am. But do you want to know what the biggest difference between us is?"

"No, but I can't wait to hear it," she says, rolling her eyes.

"I'm happy. You see, it's not about Pulitzers, or money, or power and prestige. It's about putting yourself out there to make a difference. You'll never understand what happiness is because, for you, it's always about reaching the next level or climbing the next rung on the ladder. You'll never find happiness because once you figure out that life's not about that, it will destroy you."

"Thank you for those astounding insights, Doctor Phil. I'll be sure to keep that in mind," she says, as she brushes some imaginary lint off her shoulder.

The barista finally hands me my drink. I wanted to enjoy it here and do some people watching, but the sooner I get out of this place, the better. This city is not big enough for the both of us, let alone Union Station. I enjoyed living here much more when I knew she was locked up.

"You do that," I say to her, as I turn to leave.

"Kylie, one more thing before you go," she calls out, stopping me.

"What?"

"I'm back, whether you like it or not. There is no shortage of your political enemies who will be looking for the expertise I can offer. I know your weaknesses, Kylie, and I know Michael Bennit's. So, you're right. I am 'reaching for the next level' and 'climbing the next rung on the ladder.' Right now, they mean taking you and your saintly boyfriend down.

"Whatever makes you happy, Madison," I say with a smug tone I reserve only for people I despise.

"I know you want me to wallow in misery, but let me be very clear on something," she says, getting uncomfortably close to me. "I don't care if it takes a decade or it happens tomorrow, but watching you fall will make me *immensely* happy."

-FIFTY-TWO-

MICHAEL

"I expected to see clove hooves and a tail," Blake whispers to Chelsea as our early morning guests arrive to my office. I was thinking yesterday was a weird day, with Kylie running into her sister and me getting a call out of the blue from Mister Dark and Mysterious himself. The last thing I would have expected is to start a work day meeting with Goldfinger here.

The group exchanges greetings and we sit in the small seating area in my office. The Majority Leader and Speaker of the House sit on the couch Cisco likes to install himself on, while Vanessa, Blake, Chelsea and I take seats in the surrounding chairs. Vince stands along the wall like he's my own personal Secret Service detail.

"So, what is this about?" Stepanik asks, impatient and clearly unhappy to be sitting in this office.

"Gentlemen, the House and Senate Republicans are about to be the target of a massive and very damaging smear campaign," I tell them point-blank.

"That's nothing new, Michael," Harvey sneers.

"That's true, it isn't. The source of this alleged damaging information might be worth noting."

Harvey looks at Speaker Parker like I'm wasting his time. He's about to find out how wrong he is. If I know anything about Congressman Stepanik, it's his hands are among the dirtiest of anyone in Congress.

"Where is the information coming from?" Speaker Parker asks, knowing I wouldn't ask him and the House Majority Leader up here without a very good reason.

"James Reed."

Stepanik goes white as a ghost. Take that, you smug piece of crap. There's nothing like watching an arrogant man with a hyper-inflated ego deflate before your eyes.

"Wha … why would he want to do that?"

"To deliver a political advantage for his current benefactor. You know the drill, Harvey. You tried to do the same thing for the same reason."

He looks like he is going to be physically ill. Two birds with one stone, the old adage goes. With a couple of quick statements, I substantiated my information and let him know what a complete and total scumbag he is. Speaker Parker just glares at him. There is no love lost between the two men, and this will further the Speaker's belief that Harvey Stepanik represents everything that is wrong with the Republican Party.

"How did you—"

"It doesn't matter how we know you met with him at the Titanic Memorial and asked him to blackmail Democrats in exchange for their voting you in as Speaker," I interrupt. "You know exactly what kind of information Reed has accumulated on the members of Congress. Some of it is only embarrassing. A lot of it is borderline illegal and will be enough to keep the media fixated on it while the Justice Department investigates for a long time. You know how much both of those groups love us. Then there's the House Ethics Committee who will—"

"What is the information and on whom?" Harvey asks, unable to hide the nervous tone to his voice as he cuts me off mid-sentence.

"I don't have the particulars, Mister Leader, nor do I care to know them. I was only given the broad strokes."

"Do you think this is about the impeachment?"

"Probably," Blake says after I turn to him. "The targets are the ranking GOP members of the House, not the Fight Club, as it would be if this had something to do with legislation."

"How do we know the president is involved?" Speaker Parker asks in an even tone.

"The request made to Reed came from the White House," Chelsea answers.

"Who?"

"It doesn't matter," I chirp. "Someone who is senior enough over there to be acting on behalf of the president."

"This is bad, Michael. It's an election year," Speaker Parker warns in a foreboding tone.

"Bad? It's a disaster!" Stepanik says in a panicked voice that contrasts with the Speaker's calmness. "If this information came out today we couldn't recover in time for election day."

"You'll lose control of the House and the ripple effect would cost you seats in the Senate," Blake surmises while Chelsea nods her head in silent agreement.

Outside of my two guests, Blake is the most politically experienced person in the room. When Chelsea approached me last summer with a request to offer Blake a job, I didn't hesitate to say yes. Although I have concerns about tensions that could arise between them affecting their work, the thought of matching his experience and drive with her insight and spirit was too irresistible.

"You can take Blake's analysis to the bank, Harvey," I tell the majority leader, not bothering with the formalities anymore. "A Democrat-controlled Congress and the White House is a triple threat to the GOP and your party's personal nightmare."

"Thank you for pointing that out as if I didn't already know that," Harvey blurts out in frustration. "I didn't just walk in off the street yesterday. I am fully capable of doing my political analysis so stop treating me like I'm a political invalid."

"That wasn't my intent," Blake argues in his defense.

"Sure it wasn't," Stepanik sneers, turning to me. "Did you ask us up here just to rub this in, or do you have some sort of plan?"

-FIFTY-THREE-
CHELSEA

That man was the kid in kindergarten who ran around chasing girls and pulling their hair. He is a control freak, egomaniac, and unlike his distinguished colleague who I have grown to like and respect, a despicable person. Part of me wishes the congressman wasn't giving them the heads-up on what could be coming.

He called us last night and asked us to meet him an hour before this already early meeting started. In Washington, there is no such thing as normal work hours. I strolled in at six and was still the last one here. He outlined what he had been told and what he was planning to do with the information. So yes, Congressman Sleezebag, of course he has a plan.

"I have an idea that will cut the president off at the knees, but it's going to require some sacrifices from your party."

"We're not giving up on the impeachment. In fact, I'm more determined to move forward knowing this."

"No one is asking you to alter your current course of action, Mister Leader," the congressman states.

"Although you're an idiot if you don't," I'm compelled to tell him. I should be more respectful to a sitting member of Congress, but I just can't be in this case. I'll blame it on my generation and, if that doesn't work, my hair color.

I glance at Blake in time to see the corner of his mouth rise in a half grin. There is something to be said about being professional and a statesman. Mister Bennit has to play that role here, no matter how bad he wants to throw Stepanik out the window. I, however, have no such restrictions.

"Idiot? Who the hell do you think you are, talking to me like that," he barks at me, moving out of his chair aggressively.

Instinct kicks in with the others in the room: brotherly from Vince, sisterly from Vanessa, fatherly protectiveness from the congressman, and Blake wanting to shield me from harm once again. Maybe it is still the trauma from the shooting that keeps us on edge, but Stepanik freezes in place as everyone moves around me like a phalanx.

"Settle down, Harvey, for your own safety," Speaker Parker says, reaching up and placing his hand on Congressman Stepanik's shoulder and easing him back into his seat. The congressman and Blake sit back down, but Vince hovers next to me just in case.

"She can't talk to me that way!"

"Harvey, considering you were conspiring with Reed against her boss and mentor, she can talk to you any way she pleases. You should be grateful that we are here at all."

"What does she know?" Stepanik questions. This man's arrogance is astounding.

"Chelsea is only twenty-one and has a more seasoned political mind than you'll ever have, so you might want to hear her out."

"Thank you, Mister Speaker," I say once I have their attention again. "If you really want to go through with the impeachment, Congressman Stepanik, then have at it. I'm sure it will make for great drama in the press. It will also fail."

"No it won't. We will make sure—"

"Yes, it will," Blake chimes in, "whether you want to hear that or not. The charges are weak, at best. Even if you could get enough support from the independents in the House to reach a simple majority, he'll never get removed by the Senate. You know this and, if you don't, Chelsea labeling you an idiot is being generous."

"You people are unbelievable," Stepanik mumbles, sitting back and folding his arms across his chest in a textbook defensive posture. "Almost eighty percent of this country thinks the president is taking us down the wrong path. Fifty-five percent say he is overstepping his authority. How can you argue with those numbers? They come from the American people who you claim you are here to serve."

"You conveniently left out the rest of that poll, congressman," Vanessa observes, joining in the fray. "Seventy-one percent of the country believes impeachment isn't justified. We can read poll numbers too."

"Those numbers will change once we outline our evidence," he responds, glaring at her. Vanessa is not easily intimidated, and, when she is, it's not by men the likes of Harvey Stepanik.

"Maybe, but not by Election Day."

"Okay, so do you have a better idea?" Congressman Stepanik asks, turning to Mister B. I'm not sure if he is ceding the argument or just eager to say whatever will get him out of this room fastest.

"Yeah, we do. It's time to fight the battle we came here to wage. If you want to beat the president, you need to help me override the vetoes in the House."

"You're kidding me? You really want me to support the bills the moderates are passing? You've lost your minds."

"Mister Leader, a sizable chunk of your party voted for them in the first place. It would only take a handful of representatives from either side to get the override we need in the House. We can work on the Senate later."

"It's not possible."

The awkward silence of the inevitable impasse settles over the room. In war gaming before this meeting, we figured this is as far as the conversation would get. Everything from here on out is the congressman's job, and he'll be ad-libbing it. Of course, that's what he's always been best at.

"Mister Leader, why do you hate us so much?" the congressman asks, drawing a stunned look from his colleague.

"Excuse me?"

"You heard me. Why do you hate us so much? Is it because we're not as conservative as you are, or is there more to it?"

"I ... we don't believe in the same things," Congressman Stepanik stutters.

"Like what, a good education for our kids, clean water, low taxes, a healthy business environment, or a sound immigration policy? Are you against all those? I only ask because you voted against each of them before they went to the Senate."

"No. In each of those cases, the bills went too far or not far enough," the leader of the Republicans in the House defends. "That's the problem with you moderates—you only do things half way. You can never make the tough decisions to get the country on the right course."

"And that's the problem with the extremes, Mister Leader. They think their way is always the right way, with no room for discussion or compromise. The bills we passed weren't perfect, but they were progress. And by doing so, we are halfway closer to our goal."

"All evidence to the contrary."

"Yet still closer than the all or nothing approach the parties have adopted that have been a disaster in this country," I state, causing Vince to move a step closer in case the majority leader decides to go berserk again.

"We are past the time for half measures in this country, young lady. We have real problems that require real, attainable solutions that fix them."

"I agree, Harvey, which leads us back to where we are now," Congressman Bennit retorts. "Your articles of impeachment are a half measure because you know they have no chance of accomplishing anything. It's political theater, and deep down, you know it. If you're so determined to take action against the president, why aren't you willing to listen to an alternative?"

"Why should I?"

For a grown man and elected representative, Harvey Stepanik is nothing more than a sniveling child. How the people of Ohio bring themselves to vote for him time and again is a mystery to me. Of course, I say that about a lot of people I meet here. I'm sure America does too.

"Why should you? Because behind Door Number Two is a scenario where the president wins and you'll be back home this time next year, polishing your résumé. When you do," Congressman Bennit says, leaning forward, "I want you to think about this day and wonder what would have happened had you just heard us out."

"Harvey," Speaker Parker consoles, "the decision you make right here, right now, may determine the future of our party for the next decade." The man knows how to stroke an ego when he thinks it's needed.

"Okay, fine. I'll listen, but I'm not making any promises."

"You don't need to. I'm glad you stayed, Mister Leader, because I think you're going to like this next part."

-FIFTY-FOUR-
JAMES

"David, it's been a long time. It's good to see you again!"

"I wish I could say the same," he says, entering my office. "You've been a busy man lately. That's especially confusing to me since I was assured that you'd be running a low profile while you wait for your court case."

"And I have been. Don't believe everything you hear."

"Oh, I don't, but I can't help but wonder why you would be meeting with the White House chief of staff at all considering the charges you are facing." Crap. Who has he been talking to?

"David, I met with her at the request of the president. And as for the charges against me, I fully expect the case to be dismissed. It's nothing more than a thinly veiled smear campaign against me," I tell him with the expectation that he has no real clue what is going on.

David Karmitz is one of the partners in the firm, although he has never been involved in any of its day-to-day operations or dealings. He pops his head in the office once in a while when he's in town, but otherwise just sticks with his pro bono work and collects a paycheck. It's good to be the only son of the other founding partner.

"James, I fully understand what this firm does can be a dirty business, and there is no shortage of vindictive people out there willing to use their positions and their money to exact revenge."

"That's the truth." At least he gets it.

"It's why I had no issue with you remaining at work while your case made its way through the courts so long as you stayed behind the scenes. I'm not here to discuss any of that, though," he relays to me.

"So if you're not here to talk about the charges against me, what brings you to town today?"

"To fire you," he deadpans.

"What?"

"You heard me, James. Don't stand there with your mouth gaping like a moron. I'm terminating your employment, effective immediately."

"You don't have the authority!" I bark, more as a defensive reflex than because of any actual fact.

"I do, and you know it. The other partners are in agreement. You're out."

"Y'all can't do that! I built this firm. It would be nothing without me."

"We can do it and we did."

"Why, because I've been indicted? It's not the—"

"I told you, James. It isn't about the indictments against you. It's about your activities since. Clandestine meetings held with the House Majority Leader and the White House chief of staff. Leveraging privileged information in return for favors. Attempting to blac—"

"You son of a ... You have no idea what you're talking about. I did no such thing. Those were business meetings, and they were aboveboard. You'd know that if you actually spent any time in this building. You're nothing more than an absentee landlord. Now you think you can just waltz in here and fire me? It's not your name on the door. It's your father's ... and mine."

"It was my father's ... and now it was yours. He's long since passed, and I trusted his faithful partner to manage things in his stead. But you failed, James. You were corrupted and you corrupted everyone around you."

David walks to the window near my desk, with its picturesque view of the park below. Facing indictments, and possibly prison, I have feared my days of enjoying it were in danger of coming to an end. Now it may have.

"Do you know why my father put his first name on the door and not his last?" he asks.

"Because he didn't like the way your last name sounded. He told me he was afraid people would stereotype us because of it."

"That was what he told you, but it couldn't be further from the truth," David snickers. "It was in case this firm ever did something morally questionable. He didn't want impropriety to tarnish the family name. He died without that ever happening, but must be thankful the name Karmitz isn't on the stationery. Unfortunately, that doesn't mean we are completely shielded from what you've done."

"I've done nothing! It's you who your father would be ashamed of! The prodigal son who feels the need to repent for his own past misdeeds by working for free on the backs of the men and women who slave away to make this firm what it is."

How dare he? A man with his colorful background has no business lecturing me about tarnishing anything. David is a hollow shell of what the elder Karmitz was, and the single source of his father's greatest disappointment.

"My father built this firm because he thought lobbying for special interests was a noble thing. Advocacy is an inherent right of the people, and we were paid to be their voice in Washington. What you did was turn it into a farce. He wouldn't be ashamed of me. He'd be ashamed of what his pupil became, so now I am taking the action he would have."

"You have no right acting in your father's name."

"You can make that argument, James, but regardless, I am acting in the name of the board. Leave now, or I will have security escort you out."

"If you do this, I'm going to teach this town a lesson they'll never forget and burn this firm to the ground in the process! There will be so much information leaked to the press, newspaper printers will run out of ink. I know where all the bodies are buried, and I'm willing to draw maps."

"You are going to do no such thing. You may have the goods on almost every elected official in this town, James, but you know what I have?"

A shiver runs down my spine. In the years since his father's death, I have only known David as the weak, timid man who couldn't walk in his father's shadow. His tone now is confident, and even aggressive. He knows something. Maybe he knows everything.

"That's right, James. I know all your dirty laundry. Every shady dealing you have ever had while an employee under this roof. What the police have on you is nothing compared to the scope of the treachery I can unveil."

"You don't have the balls. It would take you, your family name, and even your father's precious firm down too," I threaten.

"You're forgetting, James. I was an absentee landlord who decided to come back to town and found his rental was trashed. I have plausible deniability."

I fill with rage. It's anger over the situation, but also at the thought that I got outmaneuvered by this legal hippie. David Karmitz doesn't have the intelligence to fold my socks, let alone manage to uncover what he claims to have.

"I won't stop you from fighting your current charges, James. You're going to jail, whether you want to admit that to yourself or not."

"How noble of you."

"But if I hear you used a single piece of information against a politician from either party, or an independent, I am going to have a story to tell when I march down to see the Capitol Police. By the time I'm done, you'll be in prison for so long that the authorities will have to start making funeral arrangements for you."

In the span of five minutes, my world has been turned upside down again. I pride myself in not being blindsided by things. The only person who has ever been able to pull it off is …

"Did Michael Bennit put you up to this?"

"No," he says with a guttural laugh. "That man is the closest thing to a white knight this country will ever see get elected. Let's just say I got a tip from a mutual acquaintance of ours. I guess something positive comes out of these Washington think tanks every now and then."

I know in an instant who he means. The same shadowy figure who has stalked me to ensure I keep my mouth shut and find out who wanted the information and why. The same man who promised to make my life hell in prison if I didn't cooperate is now making sure I take what I know to the grave.

"Terry Nyguen."

-FIFTY-FIVE-
KYLIE

"Right this way, Miss Roberts," the hostess tells me as soon as I arrive. "Your party is waiting for you."

We meander through the restaurant which has to be one of the most opulent I have ever been in. Michael and I are known to eat at nice places, but this is something I would have expected to see in Versailles. A table that could seat five is set up away from the other patrons, next to one of the most massive wine racks I have ever seen. Only one man is seated at it.

"This is a strange place for an interview, Senator," I tell the aging career politician.

"Because it isn't one. Please, have a seat, Miss Roberts," he politely offers as we shake hands. Tall, with graying hair and in his late fifties, he's more fit than most of the politicians in Washington. That's what money buys. From a notorious Maryland family known for its political prowess and extreme wealth, Senator Archibald Sinclair isn't afraid of dropping some coins to impress his guests. It's the main reason he's the Majority Leader in the United States Senate.

"I apologize for my staff being somewhat deceitful, but it was the only way I knew to get you here. Would you care for a drink? I took the liberty of having the sommelier pick out an excellent Merlot for you."

"It sounds like I may need one. Merlot sounds fine," I say, trying to hide how impressed I am that he knew that.

"Please bring the Merlot for the lady and bourbon for me," he commands with a likable charm.

"Of course, sir," the waiter says, before scurrying off. I heard the service here is very good, but money talks, and with what I am sure he's paying for this table, we are going to get a ridiculous amount of attention.

"So, if I am not here to interview you, what is this about?"

I should be more annoyed at the feeling of being used, but all he's managed to do is pique my curiosity. He's going out a smidge overboard with the courtship, so I know I'm being set up for something good. I hope he doesn't say anything that will force me to leave before dinner.

"Is Michael Bennit running for president?" Oh, boy. Where's that wine?

"I don't know."

"You've had to have discussed it with him," he presses.

"We're still nine months away from the midterm elections. There's a long road ahead before anyone should start talking about a presidential bid, including us."

"That's not stopping people from talking about it now. As you journalists say, the story has legs."

"People talk about a lot of things before they should. Do you want to know the number one reason why Americans hate politics? It's because politicians spend all our time thinking and talking about the next election when they should be thinking and talking about what affects the people they serve."

"We're hated for a lot of reasons, Miss Roberts, that's only one in a long list of them."

We pause as the restaurant staff bring our drinks, fill the water glasses, deliver a basket of bread, and take our orders. Since he's footing the bill, I don't even look at the price of my dinner before ordering. Senator Sinclair picks up with his line of questioning right where he left off.

"Did you hear your sister is in town?" That throws me for a loop for a second.

"Yeah, I ran into her at a Starbucks. The bigger question is how did you know?

The relationship, or lack thereof, I have with my sister is not a secret in political circles around Washington. As a journalist on the political beat, a feud with the former Press Secretary of a senior member of the House had been important information to know. Now that she is out of prison and I am dating one of the most influential members of Congress, I have no doubt everyone is paying attention to the moves she is making.

"She has reached out to several republican members of the Senate and offered her services," Senator Sinclair explains. "They all happen to be the ones considering a run for the White House in the future. Apparently she claims to have the means to defeat Congressman Bennit when he runs."

"If he runs, Senator," I say with a fake smile. "And I'm sure you didn't come here to discuss Madison Roberts."

"You're right, I didn't. Do you like the wine?"

"It's excellent, thank you."

"Try this bread, please," he says, gesturing to the basket at the center of the table. "I dream about this bread when I'm not in D.C."

"Yes, it's very good," I tell him after I oblige by tearing off a piece, applying a light coat of a peppered butter, and popping it into my mouth.

"Is Bennit going to support icandidates running against senators like he did in the House?"

I give him a little knowing shrug. I love his tactics. Get me to say yes a few times to warm me up and then start dropping the hard questions. He would have made a great car salesman.

"We believe he'll use the organization he builds by doing that to catapult him into the running for the White House."

"Or he's content where he is and is just starting the process of replacing senators who only know how to block legislation with ones who are willing to work with the House."

"They won't win. Running a senatorial campaign is far different than running one for a small House district."

"You think they can't win?"

"They can't compete in statewide races. Social media campaigns are cute, but serious runs for Senate seats take organization and money."

"I guess you have nothing to worry about then."

"You don't agree?"

"I've heard that before, Senator. Politicians and the media may think the social media movement is losing its mojo, but it's the people who get to make that determination."

"If they're still paying attention," he argues.

"Always a true statement whether the candidates are campaigning our way or by more traditional means. I think you know that and agree with me, which is why you're here."

"That's not accurate. I think you are overestimating the concerns the Senate may harbor about Michael Bennit replicating the successes he enjoyed in the House on our side of the building."

"Then you are asleep at the wheel, sir. The extreme sides of both parties and the independents are the new ying and yang of American politics. It's not a Republican verses Democrat battle anymore. Now it's both the left and right duking it out in a twelve-round prize fight against the middle. That's the new paradigm of American politics, and you're telling me you aren't concerned?"

"No, because there is a bigger threat to us than the independents in the House," Senator Sinclair admits.

It takes a minute for me to figure out what he's talking about. He leans back in his chair and stares at me while sipping his bourbon. He grins when I figure out what I'm here for.

"You're talking about the president."

"Are we off the record?"

"Were we ever on the record?" I fire back.

"He's flaunting his power, and members of both houses of Congress are doing nothing to stop him."

"Impeachment is nothing?"

"Not when there isn't even enough support in the House to pass it. Even if by some miracle they do, there's no will in the Senate to remove him. The Republicans are saber-rattling as they are prone to do, and desecrating a sacred part of the Constitution while doing it."

"And the Democrats are sitting idly by and watching as the leader of their own party is doing a jive on our founding document."

"Yes, and now you know why I'm here. This president is hardly the first to expand the power of the Oval Office. Former occupants from both parties are just as culpable in creating this current predicament. I know Michael Bennit considers me an elitist and an ideologue, and he's right. I'm both those, but this issue transcends partisan politics; it's about the survival of the republic and our Constitution."

"You're sounding a lot like Michael."

"I've been a senator for the better part of two decades," he sighs. "I don't agree with Congressman Bennit politically on much of anything, but the way he talks about America is downright ..."

"Inspiring?"

"I was thinking presidential. When it comes to determining what's best for the people of this great nation, as much as I hate to admit it, he isn't often wrong."

"I still don't know if he's running," I tell him, assuming he is trying the backdoor to get that information.

"I'm not sure we can wait three years anyway."

"If you're as concerned as you say you are, why don't you do something about it? You're the majority leader of the Senate. Are you telling me you can't muster the courage to take on a guy you helped put in the White House?"

"It's not that simple, Miss Roberts. The Democrats in the Senate are not going to challenge a sitting president from our own party. If we do, and a Republican gets into the White House in the next presidential election, things will go from bad to worse for us politically."

"Can you imagine what is going to happen if an independent gets in because you didn't act?"

"That was the reason for my first question," he says with a devilish grin. Damn, I fell into that one.

Our dinners are served and the conversation stalls. Senator Sinclair is a political heavyweight, but he's skirting the reason as to why I am here. I can't decide whether to force the issue or let him bring it back up.

"This is a great first date so far, Senator, but you need to know I'm taken." He smiles, so at least he appreciates the humor.

"What do you think will happen if Congress lets presidential power continue to grow unchecked?"

"You'll be genuflecting instead of applauding when the president enters the Capitol for the State of the Union address."

"That's … disturbing."

"Senator, it's your guy in the White House now, but what happens when it's the Republicans' turn? Every time the chief executive decides to expand his powers, half of Congress falls silent. Each time Congress fails to challenge that expansion, the worse it gets. You know that, so I'll ask one more time, why am I here?"

"Despite the misgivings I mentioned about taking on the president, we saw an advance copy of the State of the Union and didn't like what we read. I don't think Americans will like it either. Members of the Senate from my party are beginning to feel like the president is more of an anchor than an asset."

"An approval rating in the thirties will do that."

"Indeed. It also means I have room to negotiate certain things." Finally, there it is.

"I'm a journalist, Senator. I'm not in a position to negotiate anything with you on Michael's behalf, if that's what your intent of this dinner is."

"No, you're right, of course, but you're in the best position to quietly get me what I want."

"What's that?"

"A meeting with your boyfriend."

-FIFTY-SIX-
MICHAEL

"Nice place, Senator, but no matter how much you spend, I'm not putting out tonight."

"Kylie told me roughly the same thing last night," Senator Sinclair acknowledges as we shake hands.

"At least I know she's being faithful."

"Congressman Bennit, this is our idea of hiding in plain sight," Senator Stackhouse admits as we shake as well. "Nobody in this town thinks twice of the Senate Majority Leader and Majority Whip meeting a key member of the House for dinner."

"They would if they knew us," I offer.

"They would think about it more if we got caught meeting in some underground parking garage."

That actually makes sense. Senators Sinclair and Stackhouse are the two top Democrats in the United States Senate, and my public enemy numbers one and two. They are poster children for senior politicians—perfectly coiffed, gray-haired white guys in dark suits with toothy smiles and flashy personas. They are also very articulate and intelligent, even if their actions don't always show it.

"Only there's one problem. Everybody in D.C. knows the two of you are the bane of my existence. I fell out of my chair when Kylie told me about this meeting. Sitting here with you over a meal is big news around here."

"That is true, I suppose," Sinclair acknowledges.

"You had her convince me to come here tonight. What did you want to discuss, Mister Leader? And please tell me it is not about the recent escapades of Madison Roberts."

"You should probably be more concerned about her than you are, but no, this is not about her. Congressman, whether you realize it or not, we have a great deal of respect for what you've done. We—"

"You blocked all the bills we sent to you. That's your idea of respect?"

"We didn't block all of your bills," Senator Sinclair defends. He can't seriously want to argue this with me.

"No, you let the ones through that the president could justify vetoing. The rest you made sure never made it to the Floor for a vote and, if they did, you wouldn't budge in conference committee."

"Congressman, you may fancy yourself a man of the people, but you don't have the monopoly on believing you are doing what's right for them," Stackhouse snaps. I'm starting to get a good cop, bad cop vibe from them.

"And you believe your inaction is doing them a service?"

"It is, when we believe the laws you are trying to pass are not what this country needs." Stackhouse is definitely the bad cop.

"And executive orders are?" I question, a little too loudly.

"Gentlemen, please," Sinclair orders, trying to rein us in.

Senator Stackhouse is as liberal as they come. The only thing he hates more than conservative principles are conservatives themselves. In his mind, compromise is the closest thing to treachery you can get without selling nuclear secrets to the Iranians. Some Republicans in the Senate are the flip side of that same coin. It's very sad.

"That's why we wanted to talk to you. As much as we don't like the legislation coming out of the House, we are as worried as you are that the president is using this as an excuse to exceed his constitutional powers."

"He's a member of your party. Hell, you guys helped put him in office. Go talk to him. What do you need me for?"

They look at each other uncomfortably. When Kylie told me Sinclair was extending an olive branch, I wasn't willing to believe it. Now I'm beginning to wonder if the stress fractures forming in the Democratic Party are actually more like chasms.

"The president isn't making you guys a member of his royal court, is he?"

"We're not as included as we thought we would be," Stackhouse admits, averting his eyes in the process.

"Why the sudden concern, gentlemen? You've been abetting him in that goal for the past year. Are you having a change of heart, or is it because the president's poll numbers aren't that attractive in an election year?"

"Both." Wow, an honest answer.

"As Kylie may have told you, the president circulated an advance draft of his State of the Union Address. We have some … concerns … over some of the things in it."

"It must be something else to send you running to talk to me. Are you afraid you're losing your relevance?"

"Nobody wants to see their power decrease in this town," Senator Sinclair opines. "We work in the Senate, and there isn't a soul in that room who doesn't want to occupy the Oval Office someday. Perhaps you do, too, if what I'm hearing is accurate."

Nice try. Kylie didn't give away my intentions, and I won't take the bait either. I just sit and smile at them.

"Are you planning on running icandidates against our members this November?" Stackhouse asks, breaking the uncomfortable silence.

"Maybe. Why?"

"Because certain elements of our membership are scared that you will. Everyone has been watching what you've done in the House with a keen interest. You've gone from obscurity to the pinnacle of legislative power, and now there's some fear it could spread."

"That's a bold admission and contrary to everything you guys have ever said publically. I thought the party line was that independents couldn't win statewide races against entrenched incumbents?"

"Nobody wants to take the chance of being proven wrong and that provides you with *leverage* to negotiate." Now we're getting somewhere.

"What do you have that I need?"

"The one thing you don't have and will never get without us—our willingness to cooperate."

"You're suggesting some sort of trade? I decide not to actively help icandidates seek the seats of your members and in return you …"

"Take the shackles off our members on the legislation sent from the House and agree to bring veto override votes to the Floor without threat of filibuster."

Sixty is the most important number in the Senate. Like my chamber, laws are passed with a simple majority of the one hundred senators, but it takes sixty votes to block an unlimited debate called a filibuster. Unlike the House, which limits the time a member can speak, Senate rules allow any senator, or group of senators, to speak as long as necessary on an issue. The only way to end the debate is to win a vote of sixty members. A filibuster can go on forever if this cloture is not evoked.

My two dinner companions used the threat of filibuster to ensure the majority of the bills the icongressmen ushered through the House never even saw debate in the Senate. It was as much for political as ideological reasons. No wonder people think Congress isn't working for them.

"You guys just said you were acting in the best interests of the country? It sounds to me like you were more concerned about your own best interests."

"Sometimes those things are mutually inclusive," Stackhouse sneers.

"Yeah, right. Whatever you guys are selling, I'm not interested. I've been offered enough trades since I've been here. Maybe you've heard of a couple."

"I understand your reticence, Congressman," Sinclair appeals. "We aren't looking to influence you or control you. We are seeing if we can find a solution to our differences that is … mutually beneficial."

"You're going to have to do better than that, Senator. There are only seventeen Democrats in the Senate up for reelection this fall. Even with them on board, that is not enough to override a presidential veto, let alone send a message that he's exceeding his authority. To successfully take on executive power, we need a united front. You can't guarantee that because I don't think most of your members are going to be willing to do what needs to be done."

"There are a substantial amount of members that could be persuaded to see your line of thinking on a host of matters, including taking on the president … if there were additional incentives included," Senator Sinclair answers. His counterpart looks constipated at the thought, making this whole exercise far more interesting.

The real political deal-making is done just like this. There will be give and take on both sides, and neither will like what we end up with. Whether we end up with an agreement at the end of the night is anyone's guess, but for the first time, at least we're talking.

"First, we need you to understand and acknowledge that this meeting never happened. Any agreement reached cannot be discussed with anybody ... ever."

"Okay, now what kind of incentives are you talking about?" I ask. The men both lean back in their chairs, sharing a glance before looking back at me.

"What are you willing to trade?"

-FIFTY-SEVEN
CHELSEA

"Good morning, Chris," I tell Amigo One as he walks into his office.

"You just love dropping by unannounced, don't you?"

"It saves you the trouble of declining my meeting requests."

"Hm. Where's your other half?" he asks as he removes his overcoat and hangs it on a coat hook.

"He's out ambushing your partners in crime."

"A coordinated attack, I like that. I have a busy day ahead. What's on your mind, Chelsea?"

"It's about to get busier."

I explain the plan Congressman Bennit cooked up and briefed me on late last night. The look on his faces matches the one I'm sure I had when it was told to me. It may be borderline insane, but that's always worked for us in the past.

"That's the craziest thing I've ever heard. The Democrats will never go through with it."

"They will when I tell you what is being offered in return."

"Did she tell you what these lunatics have in mind?" Amigo Two bellows from the outer room before walking into his colleague's small office with Amigo Three and Blake in tow.

"We were just getting to that part," Amigo One laments. "Please, continue. I can't wait to hear this."

"What's the biggest concern of the House Democrats? Losing more seats to icandidates, right?"

"Yeah, probably."

"If they do this, Congressman Bennit will not actively work to set up independent campaigns against the other members this fall."

Amigo Three whistles. "That's a hell of a trade."

"I agree," Blake says. "Personally, I'd rather have him organize an army against the ideologues in the House, but he wanted to try this first."

"So, boys, will they do it now?" I ask, looking at the three of them and studying their body language.

"Are the Republicans on board?" Amigo One asks. I just give him a look.

"The president is trying to get James Reed to drag them through the mud. What do you think?" Blake answers.

"We don't have the sway we used to with the partisans. We lost our street cred when we joined Fight Club," Amigo Two explains. At least he didn't say no.

"Which puts you in the perfect position to bring this to them. You have something more valuable than party loyalty—you have the iCongressman himself in your corner."

"What you're asking ... it's a lot, Chels."

"Yes, it is, but you read the polls. You see the direction the country's leaning on this. The president doesn't have to get reelected in November. We all do. This is going to happen, either way. The GOP is on board. The independents are on board."

"Do you want to be standing with us or against us when it does?" Blake posits, taking up the argument. "Because the world will be watching."

"What do you think, guys?" Amigo One asks his cohorts. "Do we go with Bonnie and Clyde here?"

"My boss has gone all in with the Fight Club. He'll do it, but I don't know how many other Democrats we can convince."

"Agreed."

"It's an easy sell, guys. Cooperate now, or pay the price later. We're not trying to buy votes or influence decisions here. Congress is an out of tune symphony that we're trying to get on the same sheet of music."

"What you're asking us to do is embarrass the leader of the free world," Amigo Two argues. "Our principals are nuts enough to go along with it, but the others ..."

"There is no love affair between the president and the House Democrats. He hasn't lifted a finger to help them since he was elected and they have to be bitter that he's making them look bad. What we're asking is a small token of solidarity in return for job security come this fall."

"This is not a *small* token, Chelsea," Amigo Three corrects.

"Chris is right. This is an epic favor," Amigo Two adds.

"And there's no guarantee that icandidates won't run against the ideologues anyway. Or us, for that matter," Amigo One argues.

"No, there isn't. But we all know there is a big difference when Congressman Bennit gets involved in anything. If one tweet can send poll numbers soaring, imagine what a visit to campaign in the district would do."

Blake is right, and they are powerful words coming from a man who knows best what happens when Mister Bennit isn't taken seriously. This whole idea is a long shot, but the fact they are expressing interest is encouraging. Whether all this talk will translate into action when the time comes is another thing.

"He wouldn't do that."

"Your colleagues don't know that," I say with a wink. "And since when did Congressman Michael Bennit ever become predictable?"

"He could travel around the country like Taylor Swift on a summer concert tour." I need to talk to Blake about his simile choices.

"Okay. We'll jump off the cliff, but you're going with us. Grab your coats," Amigo One decrees, grabbing his own off the hook he hung it on only moments ago.

"Where are we going?"

"The House Minority Leader's office. If you want the Democrats on board, it starts with him."

-FIFTY-EIGHT-
KYLIE

"The Supreme Court has been announced, and it looks as if we are ready for the president to enter the House chamber," the anchor on one of the cable news network proclaims. "While we wait, we have Wilson Newman, the distinguished host of *Capitol Beat* here with us to provide analysis. Thank you for joining us tonight. The State of the Union Address is prescribed by the Constitution, is it not?"

"Yes, it is," the man with George Clooney looks and Barbara Walters's likability states, before turning to the camera. "Article Two, Section Three of the U.S. Constitution requires that, 'The President shall from time to time give to Congress information of the State of the Union and recommend to their Consideration such measures as he shall judge necessary and expedient.'

"For many of those years, the message was simply written down for the legislative branch and shared with the public through newspapers. In modern times, the message has become a platform for the president to outline his agenda for not only Congress to hear, but the nation as a whole. President Calvin Coolidge's annual message was broadcast on radio. Franklin D. Roosevelt first used the phrase 'State of the Union,' and his successor, Harry S. Truman, became the first president to deliver a televised address."

"Blah, blah, blah," Vince derides.

"No kidding, right? If Mister Bennit was even half this boring, I never would have made it through my junior year of high school," Vanessa confides.

"Give him a break, guys. Wilson is one of the most popular journalists in this country," I defend. I feel dirty for doing it.

"He's a bore," Vince concludes, as he sprawls out on the couch like he's going to take a nap. He has a knack for theatrics.

"The Constitution does not specify the time, date, place, or frequency for the State of the Union Address, although presidents have typically delivered it in late January after Congress has reconvened," Wilson drones on.

Tickets to the address are a hot commodity, and there was no chance we would be able to sit in the gallery where we had witnessed so many other of Michael's historic events. I may have managed to grab a seat, but I wanted to watch it with his staff. If he pulls this off, I want to be the first to congratulate the ones who made it happen.

"You're awfully quiet, Chels," Blake observes.

"I'm just a little nervous about what's going to happen next."

"Nervous as in afraid it's going to happen or not going to happen?" Vince asks.

"Neither. Both. I don't know. I just wonder if we've thought about all the consequences of this."

"Well, if they all go through with it, Congress will face the aftermath together," Vince states.

"And they'll be unified for something," Vanessa adds.

"I guess so."

"Here we go," I state, watching the action on television.

In modern times, the State of the Union Address serves as both a conversation between the president and Congress and, thanks to television, an opportunity for the president to promote his party's political agenda for the future. From time to time, the address has actually contained historically important information. Tonight may be historical for a completely different reason.

The talking heads on television stop yammering as the sergeant-at-arms enters the chamber and proceeds a quarter of the way up the center aisle. I notice that the entire center is filled with icongressmen. Oh, this is going to be interesting.

"Mister Speaker, the president of the United States!"

The chamber and gallery usually erupts in a standing ovation when the chief executive enters. Some presidents have taken fifteen minutes just to reach the front of the room. That's not the case tonight. Everyone stands out of respect, but their applause can be described, at best, as a polite golf clap. There is no fanfare whatsoever. The spectacle is just ... weird.

There are few offers to shake the president's hand as he makes his way up the center aisle. He looks annoyed at the lack of attention he's receiving. It is certainly a departure from the reception the leader of the free world gets at most State of the Union addresses. He steps onto the rostrum and shakes the hand of the vice-president and Speaker Parker seated behind him, and then launches into his speech.

"Mr. Speaker, Mr. Vice President, members of Congress, distinguished guests and fellow Americans. As we gather in this hallowed chamber tonight, our nation finds itself at a crossroads; be saddled with the indecision that has marred our government for far too long, or take bold steps to push our great county forward. Despite the challenges we face, the American public is with us and the state of our Union has never been stronger!"

The president utters the classic line incorporated into almost every address expecting the thunderous applause that usually accompanies it. This time, only a handful of the legislative branch even stand, let alone applause. The look on the president's face is priceless.

This is going to be recorded as one of the most awkward moments in the history of politics. The visitors above the chamber Floor seated in the gallery begin to doubt they should be applauding and the clapping fades quickly. They will take their cues from here on out by the reaction of Congress, unsure they are doing the right thing.

"Feel better now, Chels?" Vince asks, clearly excited this is actually working.

"A little. We're not home free yet."

The president continues with his first policy issue, which is ironically one of the bills that passed both the House and Senate only to meet the president's veto. He lambasts Congress for not doing their jobs and then throws in a couple of lines meant to placate the Democrats in the room. It doesn't work, and the president waits as the expected ovation never materializes.

"I just realized something. If you take out all the interruptions for applause, this whole thing goes a whole lot faster," Vince beams.

"People will be returned to their regularly scheduled programming in no time," I bemuse.

"Good. I have a *Celebrity Wife Swap* addiction to feed." I hope Vanessa isn't serious, but I can see her being a reality television kind of girl.

"We spend more on defense than the next ten nations combined," the president continues, now knowing something is very wrong. "While there can be no price on the safety of our countrymen, I believe we can, and we shall, do it smarter and with less cost."

The line was designed to get members from both parties on their feet. He waits for a show of life or support from the gathered legislators in the room. Even the staunch Democrats are joining their colleagues in this symbolic protest. Every single member of the House and Senate sit like statues in their seats.

"We … We will adequately fund the forces that guarantee our national security and our homeland security, but the money we spend on defense can better be spent elsewhere. We must look to the economic security for the American people."

The president is getting flustered. As we watch him prattle on about the budget to the stone-faced audience, the natives in this room are getting restless. For that matter, so am I.

As a journalist, it's hard to not want to break news first. Keeping the lid on this was incredibly hard to do. Fortunately, I love a good show. If what I think is about to happen comes to fruition, it will be one of the most memorable moments in American political history.

"Is it coming up, Chels?" I eagerly ask.

"If the advance copy I received hasn't changed, it's next."

-FIFTY-NINE-
JAMES

This is the most awkward speech I have ever heard. I almost feel bad for the president. Imagine talking to a clump of trees for forty-five minutes. There is an average of eighty applause lines in State of the Union addresses, and breaks for them are built into the official remarks by the speechwriters. Each and every time the president pauses when the teleprompter tells him, he's greeted with silence and the awkwardness returns again.

"I pledged to the American people that I would act alone if Congress failed in its responsibilities. We need the Legislative Branch of this government to tackle the issues that challenge our nation, not pass half-measures. I exercised my right to veto legislation because it is simply not enough. The American people deserve more. The bills you have sent me only scratch the surface of the major reforms needed to make this nation thrive once again.

"I challenge this Congress to do the right thing for the American people. To bring to the Floor of your respective chambers the bills I have proposed to help stoke the flames of this nation's prosperity. Together, we can make this vision, shared with the millions of citizens across our land, the reality they so justly deserve!"

A few icongressmen in the center of the chamber stand, and for a split second they look as if they may break into applause.

As the camera cuts back to the president, the smile that begins to creep across his face leads me to believe he thinks the same thing. There's only one problem—they aren't clapping.

A few Republicans join them and then some Democrats. Slowly, small groups of members from both houses of Congress begin to stand. None of them clap. None of them show any emotion at all.

Before ten seconds elapse, all except maybe a dozen or so of the five hundred thirty-five members of Congress are on their feet. Republicans, Democrats, and independents are all on their feet and standing united facing the chief executive. Then it happens. Almost on cue, they turn their backs to the president of the United States.

Seated toward the front, Michael Bennit is the last member to stand up. He exchanges glares with the president as the camera cuts back and forth between the two. America now knows who was behind this. Theatrically, Michael Bennit turns his back to the president as well.

In all my years involved in the political process, I have never seen something so despicable. This trumps the time when Representative Joe Wilson interrupted Obama during a speech to a joint session of Congress. As Obama was saying health care reform would not cover illegal immigrants, Wilson shouted, "You lie!" President Obama was angry at the outburst, but it was nothing compared to the humiliation this president is enduring and the rage he must be feeling.

Bennit was behind it all right. How he managed to get so many to cooperate is baffling to me. I can understand the moderates participating, and even the Republicans. But how the hell did he get some of the most liberal Democrats in the country to turn on their leader?

This will go right to the top of Politico's list of Top Ten State of the Union Moments, displacing such stalwarts as Clinton's "the era of big government is over" and George W. Bush's "axis of evil" comments. Bennit's staff won't need to push to make this go viral. The American people are going to react to this and I'm sure it will end up being tweeted, all over Facebook newsfeeds and on YouTube, among countless other social media sites. The mainstream media will be talking about this for weeks, if not months, as they measure the country's positive and negative reactions to the tactic.

That's going to add plenty of angst to an already stressed out White House. The president's approval rating is already at a historic low for the first year of a term, and this performance at the State of the Union will not do anything to bolster it. That's going to be a rude awakening, considering the president usually sees a bump in the polls following the face time he gets during prime television viewing hours.

The president waits for the congressmen and senators to return to their seats, but it's futile. They aren't sitting back down. No longer willing to let the excruciating pause drag on any longer, the president continues reading from the teleprompter.

He has given up on addressing Congress. He's now doing his best for the cameras he knows are showing the whole spectacle in high definition. He's just trying to get through this with as much dignity as he can.

"Steadfast in our purpose, the government of the people, by the people, and for the people, will press on. We know the price of inaction. We will rise to the challenge of securing America's future, and we will be victorious. God bless you, and the United States of America."

The sound of silence in the chamber is almost deafening. The thunderous applause normally seen at the end of every address is conspicuously absent with the exception of a smattering of applause from his most ardent supporters. Even the visitor's gallery, usually chock-full of supporters and dignitaries, still doesn't know how to respond and is doing nothing. They don't realize the history they are witnessing.

Without any further handshakes or greetings, the president walks up the aisle, past the ice-cold glares of legislators in what has to be the shortest address to Congress in over a century. The usual forty-five-minute oration only took just over twenty. Amazing.

As the president exits, the members of Congress begin to mill around and chat with each other. Democrats, Republicans, and independents are all conversing amongst themselves. They realize the magnitude of the moment. The battle lines have been drawn in the most public of ways.

"Well, that was the most … interesting … address I have ever seen," the anchor says to Wilson, as the image goes to window in the top corner of the screen. "The most applause interruptions on record is one hundred and twenty-eight times during Bill Clinton's nearly one-and-a-half-hour-long speech that was his last State of the Union. This set the record for fewest with … can we call this none?"

"I agree. It was something to behold. In all my years covering politics, I've never seen anything like it. That was a bold statement by the entire Congress."

"Do you think this could blow up in their faces? They have enjoyed an upswing in their approval rating over the past year, but how will people respond to humiliating the president of the United States?"

"I don't know what the reaction will be. I can guarantee that a lot of people will be talking about it tomorrow," Wilson forecasts. He's got that right. It's all anybody will be talking about.

"While we are waiting for the traditional Republican response, what do you think it will be?"

"I think they just made it in the chamber, and they united with the independents and Democrats to give it. We've always treated national politics as a fight between the two major political parties. What we witnessed tonight is a shift from that to something completely different."

"To what?" the anchor asks.

"It's now a battle to see who really leads the United States of America."

-SIXTY-

MICHAEL

"Receiving the majority of ballots cast, the vote to override the presidential veto of H.R. 255, the Small-Business Tax-Relief Act, passes," the clerk announces to the body on the Floor.

A cheer erupts from a majority of the members. The vote wasn't even close. This bill should have been an easy win to begin with, but party politics got in the way. Almost every person in this room would agree that small business is the engine of the American economy and they should be given every advantage they can to succeed in a competitive marketplace.

The bill we passed contained concessions to both parties, and passed both the House and Senate. Like so many others, it was vetoed by the president who didn't like aspects of the bill and wanted his own proposals adopted. With the veto override, it will be law the moment the Senate passes it. They are debating over it right now, with no threat of filibuster. Thus far, Senators Stackhouse and Sinclair are making good on their promise.

"That's two!" Cisco exclaims, draping his arm over my shoulder. "At this rate, we could fix everything in this country in a week."

"That was the low-hanging fruit, my friend," I tell him. "It gets harder from here."

"That may be true," Speaker Parker says, having come off the rostrum to shake my hand. "But it's a good start. Congratulations, Michael."

"Thanks, Mister Speaker, but I don't get the credit. The men and women in this room do. They actually may be starting to like working together."

"That may have something to do with the rising poll numbers they're enjoying," Cisco informs us.

"If it greases the wheels of progress, I'll take it. This is just the tip of the iceberg. We still have a ton of work to do. Federal spending, immigration, taxation, infrastructure and transportation improvements … the list goes on and it never seems to end. We can handle some of that by overriding vetoes or getting the Senate to vote on them, but the rest we need to find a consensus for."

"It's the price of decades of kicking the ball down the field for the next group to handle," Cisco concludes. "Hopefully we have enough cooperation to make a difference now."

"Speaking of which, I'm going to dinner with the leaders in the Senate tonight. I'm sure they wouldn't mind the two of you joining us," the Speaker offers. "In fact, I could use a couple of wingmen."

"I'm in," Cisco accepts without hesitation.

"What about you, Michael?"

"I'm afraid I have to pass. I already have plans tonight. I'm just going to swing by the office and then head home." I can't tell him why it's a bad idea to be in the same room with them if I can avoid it.

"Are you sure?"

"I am, thanks. You kids have fun. Don't do anything I wouldn't do."

"Not an overly restrictive suggestion, considering the antics you've pulled on this hill," the Speaker says with a belly laugh before the two of them head for the door.

* * *

"The House has voted to override two presidential vetoes and the Senate is expected to vote any moment now to do the same on one of them," I hear the program's host announce on the television, as I slip into the office. "This Congress was one of the most ineffective in history in the first session because of the Senate and no votes from the White House, and now they are suddenly working together. What is going on in Washington?"

Blake is watching one of the cable news shows which is trying to make sense of what they are currently seeing. Working with the Senate, the new majority we have formed in the House launched a plan to override the vetoes on bills we knew our members could support and began working together to iron out our differences on the rest. There are obviously still dissenting voices, as I would have expected, but not for the purely political reasons that have deadlocked Congress for so long.

"Congress is united in purpose for the first time in generations," I hear one of the analysts on television say. "The stunt Michael Bennit pulled two months ago during the State of the Union has been decried by many, but it has achieved the desired results. The log jam on Capitol Hill is finally breaking."

"What Bennit did was an embarrassment. He is a disgrace to the political system and should be reprimanded or expelled from Congress. I have no idea why people are talking about it like it's not a big deal," another analyst opines. He's the type of guy who loves conflict, and will provoke people whether he agrees with their viewpoint or not, just to make a show of it. He always has to be right, always has to have the last word, and always has to know everything. It's no wonder he's never liked me.

"The president was admonishing Congress on their own turf. And he vetoed most of the laws they did pass. A message needed to be sent and somehow Bennit organized its delivery. I don't blame him one bit for doing that."

An argument breaks out on the set of the show and Blake is riveted. I lean against the wall, just content to watch the firestorm unfold. Finally, the anchor wrestles back control.

"Do you think this is trumpeting Michael Bennit making a run for the White House?"

"If he can unify Congress, can you imagine what he's capable of as president?" I need to buy this pundit a set of pom-poms because he's my biggest cheerleader. Friendly, intelligent, and analytical, he's everything his bloviating colleague is not.

"His popularity took a hit after the president's speech, and rightfully so. Do you think Americans should trust a man who is a maverick with the reins of government? Would you trust him to make foreign policy decisions?"

"His popularity has surged since the initial dip following the speech. He took a calculated political risk, but it's paying off. He's exactly the kind of president I want to see." That's what I'm talking about.

"There isn't reward without risk in politics. Bennit gambled, and he's won. He will be the man to beat should he run for president," the third analyst opines, agreeing with the anchor. I've seen enough.

"Hey, Blake? Where's Chelsea? You two are usually joined at the hip."

"Sorry, I didn't see you standing there, Congressman. I think she's upstairs talking to a couple of staffers." It must be important. She only goes up there when it's serious or there is nothing pressing left on her calendar.

The fifth floor of the Cannon House Office Building is known as the "freshman dorm" since it's generally where all the new representatives to the House, who end up with worst office lottery picks, end up. The fifth floor was an add-on to the building and, as such, many of the elevators in the building don't even go up there. The offices are nicknamed "cages" because they are so small and cramped. It really isn't a desirable space, unlike the Rayburn Building, unless you are mavericks who don't really care, like the icongressmen. They wear their office address like a badge of honor, and the floor quickly became the political version of the Delta Tau Chi fraternity from *National Lampoon's Animal House,* sans the toga parties.

"Okay, thanks," I say, heading to my office to grab some reading material for tonight. There's plenty of pending legislation to sift through. Now I know how English teachers feel when the essays get turned in.

"Congratulations on the overrides. It has the media buzzing."

"So I heard. Thanks, but we still have a long way to go," I tell Blake, as I sift through a stack of pink phone messages on my desk. The important stuff to return is electronically forwarded to my calendar. The other calls are jotted down on these hideous pink sheets for me to get to when I get the chance.

"Yeah, but you have both parties in both houses talking to each other for the first time in a while. That has to feel good. Is the president still pissed at you?"

"I'm sure he hates my guts. He said as much the day after the State of the Union and there's no reason to believe his opinion's changed any."

The president went on the offensive following the speech. He must have stayed up all night, calling every political ally he could find willing to go on television to attack the members of Congress who had the audacity to embarrass him. Sympathizers in the media were willing accomplices, and the fight for the hearts and minds of the American people began.

"It's what he gets for rejecting your offer to work together."

"Yeah, it was too bad that information got released on social media," I say with a grin.

I privately extended the olive branch to the White House, because I thought we had made our point and wanted to show we were willing to work with him. I even met with several high-ranking advisors, including his chief of staff whom Chelsea trounced on that Sunday morning talk show a while back. They were clear about the president's refusal to work with us and reiterated their adamant demand that we toe the line.

That was fine. I tried the diplomatic and statesmanlike approach and they threw it back in my face. Statements about the president's refusal to work with Congress during that meeting leaked out on social media channels, and that was that. If you're not going to get on the train at the station, don't be dumb enough to stand in the way of it when it leaves. That was Vince's line to the media, as Congress began to act like the body the Founding Fathers imagined. Fortunately, the American people started getting on board and the whole game changed.

"Now he's going to have to start fighting for his job. Everyone is talking about you running for president."

"I know. We're still seven months from the midterm elections. This shouldn't even be a conversation yet."

"Congressman, can I be frank with you?"

"I didn't hire you to keep your mouth shut, Blake."

"No, but I have been punched twice by you before for speaking my mind."

That's a fair point. I had forgotten about the day in Arlington when I busted him in the head twice for telling me things I didn't want to hear. It wasn't long after that he introduced me to Viano and we began a quest to get me some help in the House, by trying to get a hundred independents elected. It turns out that Blake may be the single reason I'm still in Congress today.

"Blake, you'd be very unhappy to hear how thrilled the staff was about that, including Chelsea. The good news is she'd have a much different reaction now, so I think you're safe."

"Sir, this question about you running for the White House is one that's going to need to get answered. Like it or not, the focus isn't going to be on independents or social media candidates like it was in the last election cycle. It will be all about you."

"I know. The fact that Kylie's sister is running around town talking to every one of my political enemies that might have a design on the Oval Office isn't helping."

"No, sir, I'm sure it isn't," Blake agrees.

"Let me ask you something. You worked with Madison. What do you think she has on us that would make her run around selling her services to the highest bidder?"It's not a question I wanted to have to ask.

"Nothing."

"Nothing?"

"Yup. Absolutely nothing. Madison Roberts is a master manipulator and as ambitious as they come. She is on the outside looking in right now and knows that she's damaged goods. To be taken seriously, she'll say and do anything to weasel her way onto someone's staff."

"So you're saying she isn't a threat?"

"No, I wouldn't go that far. She doesn't have anything damaging on you, but I promise that she will dedicate her life to taking you down. The best thing you can do is get ahead of this thing and cut her off at the knees before she gets traction with one of your enemies."

"You're right. I just don't want have to deal with it right this moment." I nod at the stack of proposed bills and other files on the corner of my desk. I may like to read, but legislation is written so dry that I have to down espresso by the gallon to keep from dozing off.

"Understood. Thank you for asking my opinion on the matter, Congressman."

"We've come a long way, haven't we, Blake?" I call out to him as he turns to leave. "I'm glad you decided to work with us."

"Yes, we have. And despite getting shot and dealing with my aunt, my time with you and your staff has been the highlight of my life. I owe you all the thanks in the world."

He has had it tough, between the shooting on the stairs and having to balance his loyalty to Marilyn Viano with wanting to work with us. I have learned to trust him, and that isn't easy for me. Chelsea is living proof how teachers can learn from their students. Without her, I don't think I ever would have forgiven him.

"Do you think I should consider making an announcement of an exploratory committee this early?" I hate the idea, but Blake has a sixth sense about these things. If Winston Beaumont had listened to him, our first election would never have been that close.

"I do. Unless you want everything you say and do for the next year measured against that single question."

-SIXTY-ONE-

CHELSEA

"When you said 'Let's go for a walk,' I thought you meant to my spot on the stairs, not two and a half miles down the National Mall."

"It's a beautiful March day, Chels. We've been working so hard I thought you'd enjoy getting out for some exercise."

He's right, the weather is beautiful. After a long winter, the sunshine and mid-sixties temperatures with the arrival of spring is a welcome change. I only wish he had told me where we were going so I could have swapped footwear. As comfortable as these shoes are, I would have preferred to have changed into sneakers. Time to mess with him.

"Are you calling me fat?"

"That's it. No more hanging around Kylie anymore," the congressman says, sipping his latte.

"So, are you going to tell me why we're walking all the way down here or are you going to wait until we get back to the office to bring up whatever is on your mind?"

He says nothing as we walk down the sidewalk near the intersection of Twenty-Second Street and Constitution Avenue and come up on the Vietnam Veterans Memorial a moment later. Better known simply as "The Wall," the black granite memorial pays tribute to those who served in the jungles of Southeast Asia during the Vietnam War. It is inscribed with the names of over fifty-eight thousand Americans who were killed or went missing and is one of the most powerful memorials in Washington.

The reason this place evokes so many emotions is not solely because of the simple beauty of the wall itself. It's the medals, mementos, flowers, letters, and photos visitors often leave there in tribute to their fallen comrades, friends, and loved ones. The National Park Service collects these offerings, and some of them are so moving that they wind up being displayed up the road at the Museum of American History.

We take a moment to stroll down the length of the wall in silence, looking at all the names of men who paid the ultimate price for service to their country. Some volunteered. Others were drafted. All paid a steep price for their service. They were black, white, Hispanic, American Indian, and Latino. There were men and women, and they practiced every faith and religion.

As Mister Bennit once said, "People may discriminate, but bullets don't."

"Why did you want to come here?" I ask my mentor, sensing this outing may have had more of a purpose than I thought.

"I needed to be reminded of something."

I know what's coming next, but given the effect this memorial is having on me, and surely having on him, I don't use the traditional line we utter before he launches into a history lesson.

"Reminded of what?" is all I ask.

"Where this country was in the 1970s. After a decade of broken promises, conflicting messages, and outright lies about how the war was going, the American people were fed up with their leaders and decided to voice those opinions. Anti-war protests began erupting on college campuses and grew in strength until they spread throughout the country.

"Nixon finally succumbed to the pressure and achieved a settlement in Vietnam that allowed us to withdraw our combat soldiers. But then came the Watergate scandal, and politics interfered with fulfilling the obligations we made to the South Vietnamese as part of that agreement. Their government was broken and corrupt and didn't last long on their own against a battle-hardened foe. Two years later, the North Vietnamese stormed into Saigon and declared victory."

"It was a tragic war with a tragic result," I say, not able to fully understand it myself. "But I don't see how any of that applies to you."

"Destiny, Chels. Five American presidents grappled with what to do in Vietnam. Some wanted victory against the Communists, others to withdraw with honor. In the end, it was the Vietnamese who decided the fate of their country. It was always going to be that way. They were going to be the ones who determined their future, not some foreign power." Now I know what the point of this is. He's come to his decision.

"Congressman, are you sure you want to do this?"

"I've never been less certain about anything in my life, Chels. Why, are you scared?"

"Terrified, actually."

"Come on, you've never been one to shy away from wading into unknown waters," the congressman challenges as we walk past the bronze Three Soldiers statue.

"This is different."

"Is it? Did I ever tell you the story about Hannibal?"

"Lecter? The cannibal?"

"No, the other Hannibal."

"No, but I feel I'm about to double dip on the history lessons today."

"You absolutely are. Hannibal was a Punic Carthaginian military commander, generally considered one of the greatest military commanders in history," he explains, ignoring my comment.

"I thought you taught American history?" I interrupt.

"I did, but I was also a soldier before that, remember?"

"Touché."

"Anyway, during Hannibal's life, the Roman Republic established its supremacy over other great powers such as Carthage, Macedon, and Syracuse. At the outbreak of the Second Punic War, he marched an army from the Iberian Peninsula over the Pyrenees and the Alps into northern Italy."

"Wait! I remember this. He was the guy who used the elephants during the journey, right?"

"Yeah he did, although it wasn't as effective as you might imagine, even though it's what he's best remembered for. What earned him the respect in military circles were the three dramatic victories he won in the first years of the invasion. Hannibal had an uncanny ability to determine strengths and weaknesses of both sides, and to play the battle to his strengths while exploiting his enemy's weaknesses. Military historians have called Hannibal the 'father of strategy' because Rome adopted elements of his military tactics for use in their own armies, even though he was their sworn enemy."

"Are you going to make me ask?"

"The point? Somewhere along this journey we became the architects of modern American political strategy. You were the one who managed to implement it and be successful. People we consider our enemies will be adopting those strategies and using them as their own for years to come. If you can manage to alter the most change adverse system in the country, there's no doubt in my mind that you can do anything you put your mind to."

"I have a question," I tell my former teacher, fighting the desire to raise my hand.

"Shoot."

"What happened to him? Hannibal, I mean."

"He occupied much of what is now Italy for fifteen years, but a Roman counter-invasion of North Africa forced him to return to defend his home city of Carthage. He was later defeated by the great Roman general, Scipio."

"No, I mean, how did Hannibal die?" I ask. The congressman pauses and I know this story doesn't have a happy ending.

"He was betrayed to the Romans and poisoned himself."

"Yeah, that's what I figured. One of these days, you're going to use a historical anecdote that has a happy ending."

"I will when the day comes that I sit around the fireplace and tell my grandkids about you."

The comment makes me tear up. Mister Bennit is like a second father to me, and I'm sure he looks at me like a surrogate daughter. His pride in my accomplishments is only surpassed by my own dad's.

"What do you need me to do?" I ask, trying to change the subject before I get too emotional.

"Start by finding out if anyone has given Madison Roberts a job yet. And whatever you do, don't tell my better half."

"Are you that concerned about her?" I question.

"Madison? No, I just want to see where she ends up. If you were referring to Kylie, yes. I don't want to have the discussion with her about why I was inquiring about her estranged sister."

Kylie is the sweetest woman in the world, but when the subject of either her mother or sister comes up, her ugly side comes out. That's why Mister B doesn't want her to know. Should she find out, I imagine any discussion would be one-sided and rather unpleasant for the congressman.

"Understood. Anything else?" I ask.

"Yeah, start scouting a location back home to make the announcement. Everything will be easy after that."

"Or harder."

-SIXTY-TWO-

KYLIE

Most Americans couldn't name a single Pulitzer Prize winner. Unlike the Oscars, Emmys, and Grammys, the awards are passed out at a luncheon at Columbia University and the ceremony doesn't get prime-time television coverage packed full with star power or guest musical acts. Winners are notified a month prior, ostensibly so we have time to make travel arrangements, or in my case, find a dress I like.

In journalism circles, however, winning a Pulitzer makes you a rock star. Just ask Bill Gibbons who started acting like Mick Jagger when he won his. The staff at the *Millfield Gazette* insisted on throwing me a small party to celebrate and I felt obliged to attend. For a small-town newspaper, having a journalist who earned such a distinguished award writing for them is a big deal. And I owe the editor for agreeing to print the article in the first place.

Because they're so small a group from a sleepy town, the writers and staff for the paper are more like close friends and family than they are colleagues. They cheer each other's children on at sporting events and attend picnics together. It's a far cozier situation than I am used to, considering my job history, and I kind of like it. Okay, I like it a lot.

"So, is he announcing his run for president at this thing, or are you guys jerking our chain?" Damn. I almost made it through my cake before someone asked about that.

"Seriously, Randy, if he's planning a big announcement next month, why would I tell you now?"

"Because we asked nicely?"

"We know he applied for the permits to use Briar Point State Park. Isn't that where his first campaign began?" one the staff reporters asks.

"Yep."

"So, there's symbolism there. He's running, isn't he?" Randy prods. Even small-town media outlets can be relentless.

"Again, I'm not saying anything."

"Is he announcing the creation of an exploratory committee?" Randy presses.

The road to the White House historically began with a fancy public event, replete with red, white, and blue bunting and balloons, where the candidacy was declared in front of the media and an army of supporters. Today's aspiring presidential candidates ease themselves into the process by creating what's called an exploratory committee which allows them to gauge popular support. During this "exploratory" process, candidates are allowed to conduct polls, raise funds, and travel to events without the pressures of arduous disclosure requirements full-fledged candidates are required to endure.

"Okay, fine, off the record then. He's running, isn't he? He's going to announce his intention to form the committee."

"On the record, off the record, it doesn't matter. It's going to be the same answer," I tell my editor and the staff, getting a little annoyed by the inquisition. I'm getting it from everyone. Even Bill Gibbons called this morning and grilled me for fifteen minutes.

"You can't blame me for asking. A lot of people are salivating over the possibility of him running for president. He's ratings and circulation gold."

He's right. The coverage this is getting is ridiculous. Late night talk show hosts are basing their monologues on it. Social media is blowing up with Elect Bennit memes. The speculation is everywhere, although not everyone is jumping on the "Bennitmania Part Three" bandwagon.

Some not so friendly media outlets are being highly critical for a number of reasons, the primary being their ideological tilt. Politicians who have their eyes on a presidential campaign of their own are also weighing in on Michael's lack of experience. The White House is being downright hostile, especially as they watch all these vetoes being overturned and new bills on the verge of being sent to his desk with veto-proof majorities.

The most cynical people are claiming this is nothing more than a brilliant publicity stunt. They assert that the cooperation we are seeing in Congress is boosting incumbents' approval ratings and Michael is afraid more independents won't be elected. It's a laughable conclusion to reach since he was the one who unified them in the first place.

"So, since you won't come clean now, will you at least give us the scoop right before the announcement?" my editor pleads.

"Sorry, Randy. No scoops this time. You guys, and all of the other media, will have to wait to find out what the announcement is when the rest of the world does."

-SIXTY-THREE-
JAMES

"What do you want?" Diane snaps from thirty feet away. I swear pit bulls have less bark than this woman.

"Aren't you in a pleasant mood this beautiful evening?"

The temperatures are mild now that it is late April, and since most of the cherry blossoms are gone, the influx of tourists that descend on the city for the festival earlier in the month went with them. Washington, D.C. is one of America's most visited cities, but it has been nice to return to the normal numbers of camera-wielding visitors.

"I love this view of the White House. Most people like the south side of the building, but I have always liked the north," I continue, after she ignores my question and just stands there impatiently. "It looks more ... American."

"I'm not interested in small talk with you, James, nor am I interested in a stroll in the park. What do you want?" Part of me wishes she had been hit by a car when she crossed Pennsylvania Avenue. It's too bad that stretch of road is closed to vehicular traffic.

Lafayette Square is a seven-acre public space located directly north of the White House. It was originally called "President's Park" and was meant to be part of the grounds surrounding the Executive Mansion. It was separated from the White House estate when Pennsylvania Avenue was built through it and officially renamed in honor of General Lafayette of France in 1824. Over the years, Lafayette Square has been used as a racetrack, graveyard, zoo, slave market, temporary encampment for soldiers, and, most notably, a site of countless political protests. Right now, I'm using it to get what I need from Diane Herr.

"Does this have anything to do with Congress suddenly finding the courage to do its job?"

"Its job?" she asks incredulously. "Its job is to follow our lead. The people elected the president to set policy. He campaigned on taking charge of this country and was rewarded with a resounding win."

"Six percent is hardly a mandate, Diane."

"He won. That's all that matters. Then Bennit comes along and turns Congress into some hippie lovefest where everybody gets along. It's infuriating."

"I warned y'all not to underestimate him. He has a nasty habit of doing the impossible. It's why people are screaming for him to run for president." I'm in no position to sweet talk her. I know how this conversation will end, so why not rub a little salt in the wound?

"The thought of having to worry about the next presidential election when we aren't even at the midterms is causing him ulcers and making my life miserable. His announcement at the end of the month already has Glenn mobilizing the troops. We were even approached by Madison Roberts who offered her assistance in beating Michael Bennit and are actually considering her offer." That got my attention.

"Kylie Robert's sister approached you?"

"Us, and everyone else thinking of running three years from now. She seemed motivated to win when I met with her."

"I bet she is," I muse. "Although I am a little surprised y'all would be willing to work with a woman who just got released from prison."

"You are on your way to prison and we were willing to work with you," Diane elaborates smugly. "Nothing is settled yet, but she may be in a position to hedge Bennit's overtures about running."

"The media are driving that conversation, not Bennit. You know how it works. Once the honeymoon period following the election and inauguration are over, the press and talking heads are already looking forward to the next race. With a media darling like Bennit thinking about running, it happens even earlier."

"He's not a media darling!" Diane practically screams, getting us unwanted attention from some tourists taking pictures. "Who really cares that he has eight million Twitter followers or whatever. He's made himself vulnerable with the Albright affair and showed people his true colors with that stunt at the State of the Union. He's got everyone in this country fooled, and we are going to pull off that disguise and show the country that he's a wolf in sheep's clothing."

Diane is becoming unhinged over this. I remember how optimistic she was during the transition and following the president's inauguration. Things have not gone as either of them planned in the time since, and now the stress is taking its toll. If they are seriously considering bringing Madison Roberts into the mix, they are more desperate than I thought. The West Wing must not be a fun place to work right now.

"If you say so," I tell her. The impassive tone I use makes her even angrier.

Emotion is a fantastic weapon to use against an opponent. If you can upset your adversary, they begin to stop thinking about what they are saying and reacting instead. Diane Herr was already stressed, and now that she's angry, she is forgetting who she is talking to and that she should be minding her words. That is exactly what I need for what I have planned.

"We wouldn't have to even worry about him had you done what we asked you to," she says, stopping cold in the middle of the sidewalk so she can stare at me with those vengeful, even hateful eyes. "Glenn relied on you to handle him, James, and you never came through."

"What are you talking about?" Getting her to take the bait may be easier than I thought.

"All these plans you had to limit his power. None of them worked. Not a single one. We should have known you would fail. You couldn't manage to get him expelled when he was a nobody. Now, we are not only facing impeachment, but we have a unified Congress against us to deal with."

"And you're blaming me for that? We had a plan. You called me off. I was ready to leak what I knew about the Republicans in the House and fulfill my end of the deal." She doesn't need to know that Terry Nyguen was literally lurking in the shadows to ensure that didn't happen.

"The circumstances changed and so did the agreement. I told you that any promises were contingent on success. There wasn't any."

"So what does this mean? You're breaking our deal?"

She doesn't bother responding, and I already know what the answer is. I knew coming here what it would be. I want to hear her say it though. I *need* to hear her say it.

"I made the deal with you in good faith. The president made a promise to me in return," I prod. "If I agreed to use the information I know about the Republicans, the president would ensure I never see the inside of a jail cell. But I'm not going to get that pardon, am I?"

"I think you know the answer to that question."

"I thought the president was a man of honor."

"He's a man who wants results. You didn't deliver them." Neither has anybody on his staff nor the man himself, I don't say.

"Then there's nothing further for us to discuss," I conclude, turning to leave before stopping. "One more thing. I sincerely hope you burn in hell, Diane, because that's what you deserve."

"I'll be sure to save you a spot, James, because you'll be joining me there."

* * *

I walk northwest away from the park, passing H Street and up Vermont Avenue towards my old office on K Street. After making a right, I end up in Franklin Square. I look up at the topmost floor and the windows of my old office that overlook this very spot. The last time I set foot up there was a little over three months ago when David fired me and I'm still getting used to being on the outside looking in.

I look around, but I'm alone. I didn't expect to be followed, but after my run-ins with Terry Nyguen, I don't take anything for granted. I reach into my pocket and hit stop on the application that has been running for some time now.

The recording length is long, but the meaty part is only about five minutes of it. I use my finger to slide the finder to find the good part, and after some trial and error, find what I'm looking for. I press the play icon on the screen and sound begins belching from the speakers.

"The circumstances changed and so did the agreement. I told you that any promises were contingent on success. There wasn't any."

"I made the deal with you in good faith. The president made a promise to me in return. If I agreed to use the information I know about

the Republicans, the president would ensure I never see the inside of a jail cell. But I'm not going to get that pardon, am I?"

"I think you know the answer to that question."

I hit stop. The recording is a little tough to decipher, but it's audible. The contents are pure gold. Terry Nyguen may have temporarily stopped me from using old information I have on the politicians in this town, but he can't stop me from getting some new material.

I return the phone to my pocket and smile. With my inept lawyers unable to stall any longer, I have a court case looming sometime this summer. A little leverage might be just what I need. This recording won't be enough to keep me out of prison, but maybe I have enough now to make sure I don't stay there long. Blackmail is a beautiful thing, especially if the president is fighting for his political life against Michael Bennit. Timing is everything in life, and my time will come again, one way or another. With that thought, I look back up at my old office. It's vacant now. Nobody will be able to fill my shoes.

I am irreplaceable. Bennit may have won the biggest battles of the war, but the struggle isn't over. I am going to fight as long as it takes. I may win my case, and I may lose it, but there is one thing I know for certain. My time will come again.

-SIXTY-FOUR-

MICHAEL

The weather couldn't be more perfect. It's a gorgeous spring day, and thank God it is. I know for a fact that we didn't have a backup plan if it was pouring. April showers may bring May flowers, but that doesn't mean it doesn't rain in May and I don't feel like getting soaked doing this.

Briar Point State Park is big, but it's wooded and there are not many open areas to host a gathering. In absence of any better options, we have essentially taken over the parking area and surrounding picnic spots, and jammed about ten thousand people in them. Since there is zero room to park cars, the district office staff made arrangements for buses to shuttle people to the event from parking lots around Millfield.

Apparently, it's working without a hitch. The standing room only space filled up an hour ago, and now people are applying some good old-fashioned ingenuity in finding good viewing spots. The most daring and intrepid among them are climbing and hanging from trees like they are watching the Monaco Grand Prix from the Secteur Rocher.

Five minutes before the scheduled start of the speech, we all gather in the back of the temporary stage erected on the site. Most of my staff is here, along with Kylie, of course. As she promised, Chelsea brought her father, whom she convinced to be here on a Saturday. I'm thrilled he decided to come, because it gives me the chance to settle an unpaid debt.

"It's great seeing you again, Bruce."

"Same here, Congressman. It's been too long."

"Three minutes, Congressman," one of my staff members tells me. Chelsea delegated the setup of this event to my district staff, and they are buzzing around like bees high on Red Bull making sure everything is going according to plan.

"Come here a second, Bruce, I have something for you." Chelsea has a puzzled look on her face and appeals to Blake for guidance. I didn't tell him either. I trust them both with secrets, but not this one. Not when it comes to her father.

"For me?"

"Yup. Come on," I say, waving him to follow me.

We move farther behind stage where a small but bulky object is covered with a blue tarp. When everyone is gathered around, I pull it off. Bruce's face lights up like it is Christmas.

"It's only taken you four years."

"Do you have any idea how hard it was to find one of these? We need to have a serious talk about your affection towards early '80s furniture."

When news broke of my alleged affair with his daughter, I went to his house to face Bruce in person. After inviting me in and closing the door behind us, I was greeted by the four knuckles of his right fist. We ended up bruised and cut, but the end table, and lamp that sat on it, were the major casualties in the resulting donnybrook. He's since gotten a new lamp, but there's still an empty spot where the end table once sat.

"It's a perfect match. Thank you. I appreciate this. I will always have a soft spot in my heart for you, Michael, even though you were army."

"I know that it was tough for you to say that, Bruce, but I'm glad you were able to finally come to grips with it."

"Come to grips with what?" he asks.

"That God made the Special Forces because even Marines need heroes." The group laughs, except of course for Bruce, who has more of an anguished look on his face.

"I walked into that, didn't I?" he asks his only daughter.

"Yeah, Dad, you sort of did."

"Thank you, again," he tells me as we shake hands. "Now, you'd better get on that stage before the Marine decides to hit you again and break another perfectly good end table."

* * *

It took a full three minutes for the applause to die down after Chelsea introduced me to the crowd. I hate speaking to groups this large, and it made for an anxious time on stage. You would think after being a teacher up in front of students, nothing would faze me. Apparently, that's not the case. My stomach is churning.

"Thank you all so much for coming out here today. I know there is a lot of anticipation about what I'm going to say here today," I tell the assembled masses who greet my words with another enthusiastic applause. "It makes me a little nervous because I didn't actually write a speech."

Once again, Chelsea, Vince, and Vanessa told me not to prepare my remarks. Sticking to the "you're better off the cuff" reasoning, the note cards I prepared anyway were confiscated by Kylie five minutes after I got here. I knew she would, so I came prepared only to be thwarted again. Chelsea caught me with my backup set, so I guess I will have to do this from memory after all.

"There are many definitions of leadership, yet so few people can tell you what it really is. The dictionary defines leadership in generic terms as 'the leader of a party or group.' It's not the most helpful definition I have ever heard," I tell the gathering and get some much-needed laughter.

"Leadership is one of those nebulous terms we hear all the time, but means different things to different people. I think we can all agree that true leadership is much more than simply being in charge of a group of people. I like this definition: Leadership is the art of providing purpose, direction, and motivation to others, to deliberately create a result that wouldn't have happened otherwise.

"Just having the position does not make you a leader. Owning a title does not make you a leader. A CEO may manage his corporation, but the CEO who single-handedly turns a failing company into a Fortune 500 powerhouse is a leader. A principal may manage a school, but one who takes an underperforming school and turns it into a highly rated educational institution is a leader."

I get an enthusiastic applause. Now I know why they build these breaks into the president's speeches. When you have something to say, it helps to anticipate the interruptions so you don't lose your focus. Of course, his speech was written down and Kylie and Chelsea are holding mine.

"I know most of you are standing there wondering why I am talking to you about leadership. I began this journey by trying to show the American people the importance of their vote. How it needs to be used to pick leaders, not wasted on the trivial minutia so many candidates were relying on the public to base their decisions on.

"Since then, I have seen Congress begin to show the leadership qualities the people have long desired but only recently started to demand. It is making a difference, and it's because of your vigilance and your support. It has been a long road for me to travel, but I'm certain that Congress will continue on this path so long as you and your fellow citizens demand it."

The applause is a hearty one, and the crowd becomes more and more energetic by the moment. I glance behind me at the enormous American flag that is serving as the backdrop for this announcement. Then I look off to the side at Chelsea, Blake, Bruce, Kylie, Vince, and Vanessa. Most of them give me a nod. They sense the crowd is ready to hear what's coming. Maybe it's time to give them the news.

"For me, it's time to move on. I asked you to gather today because I wanted you to know that my time in Washington has been magical, and the opportunity to represent you has been the greatest honor of my life. But there are other things I need to accomplish, so I wanted you to know that I will not be a candidate for the Connecticut Sixth District this fall."

-SIXTY-FIVE-
CHELSEA

The crowd goes crazy with anticipation for what that means. Any serious candidate running for the White House won't run a second campaign at the same time. All these people are here to witness history be made—a serious independent running for the highest office in the land. They want to show their support for what we have done so far, and what we can do in the future.

"We have lost faith in our leaders in the United States. There have been too many empty pledges. There have been too many unfulfilled promises. There have been too many times where we picked the wrong person for the job, regardless of what we thought their qualifications were at the time. It has been mentioned, at least once or twice, that I may be thinking about becoming a candidate for president of the United States."

The crowd goes nuts again. The electricity being generated from the people standing here could light up Chicago for a day. It's crazy how excited they are.

"Somehow, people believe I'm the man that can restore sanity to the Executive Branch as I helped do with the Legislative; that I'm the one who can return our country to economic prosperity. That I am the one who can restore a sensible foreign policy that strengthens the bonds of friendship with our allies and strikes fear into the hearts of our enemies. That I am the one who can work with the Congress to pass sensible laws that address our nation's many issues and make it a better place to live than it is today. That I am the leader that can make that all happen."

Another cheer goes up from the crowd. Most Americans have seen at least one announcement speech in their lives, either in person or on the news. They know what's coming next. Blake reaches down and takes my hand in his. We know what's coming, too.

"I am here to tell you today, I am not that person."

The crowd deflates faster than an overfilled balloon. Stunned doesn't even do it justice, as people turn to the person next to them to confirm what they just heard. They're all about to get the explanation.

"You all came here today expecting me to announce I was running for president, and cannot fully appreciate how much that support and enthusiasm means to me. I have been called the ultimate social media politician, but I didn't want to make this announcement over Twitter. Some things require a personal touch, and this is one of them. I wanted to stand here in person and announce that I am not going to be a candidate for president."

The gasp of shock and subsequent murmur in the audience is slowly replaced by absolute silence. I get the feeling I know what the president went through at the State of the Union. Even the congressman looks a little nervous now.

"It takes a special person to be the president of the United States. It's a job where every decision is put under a microscope and every action subjected to unending scrutiny. Privacy is nonexistent, and there is no such thing as a day off. It's a taxing job, and one that any candidate looking to become president must be prepared to accept. At this point in my life, I am not.

"When presidents do their jobs right, they inspire a nation. When they do it wrong, they bring it to its knees. It's why we must ask the hard questions of our candidates and demand honest answers. It means we have to be confident in their abilities to handle complex economic issues and manage our foreign affairs with disparate cultures. Those abilities are best honed through experience, and I have very little of it.

"You deserve more than that. You deserve candidates who have the credentials to do the job. You deserve candidates willing to sacrifice their freedoms and privacy to preserve yours. You deserve candidates who will dedicate themselves to their job and pour every ounce of their soul into it.

"I started this speech talking about leadership. Leaders must know their strengths and weaknesses, and I shared mine. Now I will join you. I will join you and we will stand shoulder-to-shoulder to demand the leadership this country deserves. Together, we will ask the hard questions, force the candidates to give the tough responses, and we will go to the poll and vote for a true leader together. And while I am not going to have the honor of being one of those candidates working hard to earn your trust in leading this great nation, I will forever be honored to work with you to make it the greatest on earth. God bless all of you, and God bless the United States of America!"

The applause is thunderous. Once the shock wore off, it was a little like Yankee fans watching Derek Jeter's last game. They are sad he's not playing another year, but thankful for what he was able to do on the field. He may not ever be their president, but Mister Bennit will always be one of them.

"I think I'm going to wander through the crowd for a while," he tells me and Kylie after he steps off the temporary platform. The applause has only subsided a decibel or two, and the congressman is eager to show his appreciation, despite Kylie's look of trepidation.

"Of course you are," is all she says.

"Before you go, you got a text from the Senate Majority Leader," I tell him, reaching into my pocket to retrieve his phone which he handed to me before going on stage.

"Oh, yeah? What did it say?"

"Congrats on your retirement," I read from the screen. "I'm happy for you."

"I bet he is," the congressman replies, smiling before crossing the rope into the area where the crowd is gathered.

-SIXTY-SIX-

KYLIE

"I got your text. What are you doing back here?" I ask Michael as I step onto the iron bridge that crosses the river.

"Feeling nostalgic."

"I'm not surprised. You have a lot of history here. Do you think you ruined this place with your announcement today?"

Not that anything can ruin this place. The sun is setting behind the long ridge that runs to the west of town, and the leaves are now fully out on the trees. After a long winter, it finally feels like spring.

The crowds cleared out hours ago, but not until Michael did his best to shake the hand of every person who showed up. You would never know, by watching how he interacts with people, that he's the pure social media candidate, except that Instagram blew up with pictures of him and his supporters. Even Chelsea, Vince, and Vanessa got in on the act, being the pride and joy of this sleepy little Connecticut town.

"What do you mean?"

"Well, it was where you guys held your first staff meeting. We're standing on the bridge where Chelsea said she first threatened Blake with a knife and where you told her you knew she was going to leave us to attend Harvard."

"That happened a few steps over there to my right, I think. Things didn't quite go as she planned."

"No, it went better and she'd be the first to tell you that. I'm wondering, with all those memories, if you regret choosing this place to end your political career."

He takes a minute to ponder the question, leaning against the iron railing and looking up the river to the picturesque New England town he calls home. Sometimes I think I know him better than he knows himself. He may have only run for office because he lost a bet, but the job he ended up with grew on him.

"You're assuming I regret the decision at all?"

"Don't you?"

"No, regret isn't the right word. Are there things I will miss? Definitely, but everything has come full circle for me. There's symmetry to holding the final hurrah here. But that's not why I asked you to come."

"Oh yeah?"

"My life has been defined like chapters of a book. High school, then the military and college classes, followed by teaching and now this. If I am going to start another section in this novel, this is the place I want to do it."

"So long as I'm included in the book, it's fine with me."

"Are you kidding? I could never have done any of this without you, Kylie."

"Sure you could have."

Michael is one of the strongest men I have ever met. There is nothing on earth he couldn't do if he put his mind to it. He took on a challenge that so many before him had failed in, and took the necessary risks to make it work. He helped to fix what most considered to be a broken government.

"No, I mean it. You are my everything. I love you more than I can possibly tell you. All the support and the patience you've had with me. We've even survived getting shot at together. I couldn't imagine having done any of this without you and wouldn't want to dream of doing anything else without you in the future."

"Hopefully you never have to."

"That's my plan. Let's find out."

He moves so quickly, and I am so caught up in the romantic sunset, that I almost miss it. When I turn back to him, he's down on one knee. Before I can say a word, Michael pulls a ring box out of his pocket. He opens it, and the fading sunlight twinkles off the facets of the most beautiful diamond I have ever seen. All I can do is cover my mouth with my hands.

"Oh my God!"

"Kylie Marie Roberts, you are the love of my life and I want to spend the rest of my days with you by my side. Will you do me the honor of marrying me?"

"Oh my God, oh my God!"

My eyes dart back and forth between the man I love down on one knee and the perfect ring. He knows me too well. It's not too big or flamboyant and not gaudy. Like him, it's perfect.

"I ... I don't ... I don't know what to say."

"Well, not to influence your decision, I'm hoping you'll say yes. No pressure though," he says with a wink.

"Yes! Yes, of course I'll marry you!"

I hold my breath as he slides the ring onto my finger. Part of me expected him to drop it in the river or change his mind. That was how life was for me before we met. It was a long, uninterrupted series of disasters and train wrecks. No more.

We kiss and embrace in the warmest hug I've ever experienced. My spine is tingling, and the surge of sheer happiness makes me want to run through town and scream the news to anyone who will listen. The man of my dreams has asked me to marry him!

We have been through a lot. We've been tested the way most couples never have. We've even been shot at. But through it all, we've endured. I love this man so much it hurts, and today he made me the happiest woman on earth.

I never was the girl who dreamed of her wedding day. I always thought it was silly to define yourself by who you marry. I've seen friends marry and divorce and thought, why bother? Now I know why. When you meet that special person, it all comes together. For the first time in my life, I am excited about the prospect of marriage. No more politics, no more campaigns. Now, it is just about us and suddenly everything is right in the world.

-SIXTY-SEVEN-
MICHAEL

"This is insane. I feel like I should be doing something," Vince vents to anyone who is listening.

"How about starting your Christmas shopping?" Vanessa suggests.

"I've already done most of it. That's how bored I am. I usually don't start doing it until two days before Christmas."

"Earlier than I ever got mine done," I lament. Most of my shopping was done on Christmas Eve.

"Then you can call the network back to confirm the details of the interview tonight," Chelsea suggests. I am scheduled to do my very last interview as an elected representative tonight.

"I've already done that."

"Don't let him kid you, Chels. He's called so much that he's on a first name basis with the secretary over there," Vanessa informs my chief of staff.

"I can't help it. I'm bored."

Being bored is not a feeling any of us are used to. We had a very busy summer and it didn't slow down until Congress recessed to campaign before the election. If the 113th Congress is now regarded as one of the least productive in American history, then this one ended up being one of the most productive. The days were long, but the results were very rewarding.

"We all are, Vince, but the difference is, we aren't whining about it." Vanessa likes to torment him. Forget dating, I'm beginning to think they're married.

"You guys can complain all you want," I say, chiming in. "I am more than happy to sit here and do nothing for the first time in years."

"Shouldn't you be out looking for a job?" Chelsea asks me with a laugh.

"Nah, Chels, he's just going to leach off Kylie now that they're married."

"You know, Congressman, Vanessa has a point. She's a Pulitzer-prize winning journalist and can get a job anywhere she wants. You're an aging history teacher and washed up politician with no career possibilities." Ouch.

Kylie and I were married in a small ceremony in Millfield back during the summer recess in August. We postponed the honeymoon until late October while my colleagues were trying to get themselves reelected. Besides, the warm breezes of Aruba are a nice break from the chilly New England air.

"Thank you so much for your faith in my abilities, Vince. You guys are enjoying this, aren't you?"

"Just a bit."

They're right. Kylie has been the hottest commodity in journalism since winning the Pulitzer Prize for Investigative Reporting for her article on finding the mastermind behind my assassination attempt. Every major news organization on the planet has offered her a job, including her old employers, the *New York Times* and *Washington Post*. Right now, she's happy writing the occasional article for the only newspaper she has any desire to work with—the *Millfield Gazette*.

My prospects aren't any less impressive, despite what my former students are saying. I have been offered teaching positions at dozens of high schools across the country, administrator positions at colleges and prep schools, and lobbyist positions at almost every major firm in town. With all the offers flowing in, I'm just waiting for the Army to call and say they want me back.

I just haven't been able to bring myself to accept any of the offers. It's not about the money for me. I want whatever I decide to do to make me happy. I want a job where I can come home to my beautiful wife every night. I know I need to make a decision soon, if not for financial reasons, to get my staff to stop razzing me about it.

"You all know that's not true," I tell what's left of my staff defensively. "You've seen my offers."

"So why haven't you taken any yet?" Vanessa inquires.

"Yeah, you said you would start paying attention after you got back from your honeymoon. That was a month and a half ago or something," Vince adds to the usual one-two punch he and Vanessa have perfected.

"Yeah, but then we had Halloween, and All Saints Day, and Veteran's Day, and Thanksgiving, and football …"

"And all the excuses you never accepted for our homework being late," Chelsea quips, causing a nostalgic laugh among my three former students.

"Come in!" I announce as a knock at the door interrupts our gab fest.

"Yes, come in and save him from this line of questioning," Vanessa shouts. She read my mind.

"Congressman?" Sarah asks, after sticking her head in the open doorway. "There's a Charlene Freeman and Chalice Ramsey here to see you. They don't have an appointment."

"And they'll never need one. Please show them in, Sarah."

My staff started looking for new jobs when campaign season started in earnest. The floodgates opened once we started the lame duck session after the election. Sarah is one of five left in the office, and that includes Chelsea, Vince, and Vanessa.

My two former bosses come in and we exchange hugs and handshakes. I last saw Chalice at my wedding. As my former department chair and trusted confidant during my time here, she absolutely had to be at our small ceremony. I haven't had as much interaction with Charlene, the superintendent of the Millfield Public School system. Most of it was her threatening to fire me during my campaign or apologizing about it afterward. She and Chalice are longtime friends, so I'm not surprised they're here together.

"Can we talk to you alone?" my former mentor asks after noticing the room full of people.

"I have to go meet Blake for lunch anyway," Chelsea says before bidding her good-byes to my two guests.

"We are going to wander aimlessly around the Capitol and hope someone gives us something to do," Vince relays beforehe and Vanessa say their good-byes and run off to get into some sort of trouble.

"They sound bored," Charlene observes, as I show them to the seating area of my inner office.

"They are. Considering the pace we have kept up over the past few years, downshifting doesn't mean they've taken their foot off the gas. What brings you to Washington in the middle of a school week?"

"You do."

"I've been trying to get Chalice down here since the day I got sworn in and you both choose a lame duck session to finally come down?"

"Unfortunately, Michael, this is a business visit, not for a tour of the Capitol," Chalice clarifies.

"Congressman, certain developments back home have necessitated our reaching out to you," Charlene explains, getting right down to business.

"That sounds very ominous." They certainly have my attention. Public school officials rarely are authorized to travel for anything other than educational conferences, especially from a district as budget conscious as my old one was.

"It is. Robinson Howell has been terminated as principal of Millfield High School," Charlene deadpans.

"Did you guys finally find the German porn he has on his computer or something?"

They look at each other. I was kidding, but apparently I've hit close to the mark. It's the best news I have heard in a while. Howell handcuffed the teachers in that school, myself included. His adamant adherence to "teaching the test," to ensure good performance on the myriad of standardized tests the nation subjects its children to not only made student instruction dry, it stifled learning. That and he was a jerk. He won't be missed.

"I cannot discuss the nature of his ... departure. I can tell you that we are in the process of looking for a replacement."

"Chalice, are you finally getting the promotion you never wanted?" I muse.

"Actually, even if she did want it—"

"Which I don't," Chalice interjects.

"The Board of Education wants to go in a different direction," Charlene continues. "We have unique challenges we need someone to rise to the occasion to meet. Changes in curriculum, dealing with parents, bringing the best out of our teachers ..."

"I'm not sure how I can help, but I'll offer whatever assistance I can," I assure her as her voice trails off.

"The biggest thing you can do to help is accept the position I am about to offer you. We want you to be the next principal of Millfield High."

Whoa. I lean back. There are a host of reasons that will never work. First would be that I am not a good administrator. I don't like bureaucracy, and education these days is mired in it. Parents would hate me, because I maintain a set of standards that won't ever be reduced for anyone out of convenience. The list goes on.

Because of any of those reasons, it only takes me seconds to make my decision on this. I owe Chalice everything, and the superintendant was more than fair with me during the touchy parts of my first campaign. They have more than earned the courtesy of having me hear them out. Of course, they are going to get the objections that come along with it in return.

"There is no way the school board would ever approve that. They were the ones who upheld my suspension and then fired me before I came here."

"They already have approved it."

Wait, what? Why would they approve filling a position before even seeing if someone would take the offer? Charlene doesn't look interested in elaborating, so I look at Chalice for some clarification.

"A lot has changed since your first campaign, Michael. Some board members lost their reelections, others have come to the conclusion they were wrong to cast you out. Either way, when Charlene pitched the idea to them, the decision was unanimous to extend this offer to you. You haven't been formally approved for the position, but you would be if you accept."

"We can't offer much," Charlene continues, giving the best sales pitch she can with one arm tied behind her back. "Being a principal doesn't pay well, as you know, and Millfield pays even less. I'm sure you are getting very lucrative offers to work anywhere you want."

"Yes, I am. To the tune of several hundred thousand dollars, plus bonuses."

"We know we can't match … even a small percentage of that, but we're hoping we get a home team discount," Charlene manages to utter, once she picks her jaw up off the ground.

"I appreciate the offer, Charlene, I really do. I just don't know if it's a good idea."

"Think it over. We have someone in place running things on a temporary basis until a permanent solution can be reached. We're all hoping that solution is you

."

-SIXTY-EIGHT-
CHELSEA

"What the hell did I do with it?" I say to myself as I look behind another set of boxes.

"Do with what?" Blake's voice calls out from just inside the entryway to the outer office, scaring the crap out of me.

"Jeez, Blake, are you trying to give me a heart attack?"

"Sorry, love. You're going to make us late for the boss's last interview. What are you looking for?"

"My coat. It's freezing outside and I'm not going to shiver all the way over there," I explain as he strolls across the office to the corner with his hands in his pockets.

"You mean this coat?" he asks, smirking while he pulls my favorite white coat up off the back of the chair in the corner.

"Terrific! It was right where I left it."

The office looks more like a neglected storage unit than the workspace of a member of Congress. With only a week left of the lame duck session, Mister B asked us to start packing all the nonessential things. It was more of a project than we thought it would be.

"Shut up. Don't say it," I command playfully as I take it from him while trying to ignore the stupid grin on his face.

I follow him out of the office and down the corridor towards the lobby as I struggle to get my coat on while we walk. Blake didn't bother wearing his overcoat despite the chilly December temperatures. Looking over his well-tailored threads, he looks good. Really good. Complete with the little triangular pin of his father's old army unit on the lapel, the man knows how to wear a suit well.

"How many questions do you think he'll get about not running for the White House?" Blake asks me.

"It will be half the interview. The other half will be why he didn't run for reelection. Do you want to bet whether the president will be watching?"

"I know better than to make a bet with you, Chels. I know how those go and I don't want to end up in Congress," he says with a wink and a laugh. "But I don't think he'll tune in. He'll probably sign an executive order to have someone on his staff watch it."

President Obama may have caught a lot of flak about usurping congressional authority by signing executive orders, but this president brought it to a whole new level. Thanks to the efforts of Congressman Bennit, the other independent congressmen, and their allies, this has been one of the most productive Congresses ever. Unfortunately, it didn't stop the president from trying to expand his executive authority and set up a constitutional crisis the next Congress is going to have to deal with in the process. It's sure to become a hot button issue the candidates for president will be forced to address on the campaign trail a little over a year from now. Part of me is relieved the congressman decided not to run.

"I bet he's thrilled about not having to face the congressman in a debate," Blake says, interrupting my train of thought as we descend the stairs into the foyer.

"I'm sure everyone with their eye on the presidency is relieved. Madison Roberts is probably in therapy because of it." I regret saying that the moment it left my lips. Kylie's sister is as much a sore spot between the two of us as she is with Kylie herself.

"Probably," he mutters.

"Is she still looking for a job?" I can't resist asking.

"I heard she was," he mutters again. He might not want to talk about it, but I can't hold it back any longer.

"I honestly don't know what you ever saw in her! I mean, she's beautiful and all, but she's so ..."

"Not you?" he finishes for me.

"I was going to say dirty," I practically spit.

Since the moment Blake and I became a couple, I have made a point not to discuss his relationship he had with Madison when they were both on Beaumont's staff. It was a long time ago, and I wouldn't call what I'm feeling jealousy ... Who am I kidding? It's jealousy.

"Yes, she is beautiful. Yes, she is dirty, metaphorically speaking," he clarifies. "If it makes you feel better, I don't know what I really saw in her either."

"It doesn't."

"She was higher on the political food chain than I was. She was articulate, persuasive, ruthless, and conniving. It's everything I wanted to be, or at least thought I wanted to be," he tries to explain.

"And for the last nine months, she has been running around town offering a way to destroy the congressman to anyone who would sit down and listen."

"Madison was Beaumont's press liaison. She's very convincing. Back when we were on staff together, she knew better than most how to manipulate the facts to advance whatever agenda the boss wanted. She would have done the same thing against us for whoever employed her but, in fairness, she's not the only one wanting to take the congressman down. Do you know how the boss really got Congress working again?"

A shiver runs down my spine. There's no way he could know, could he?

"What do you mean?" I ask, trying to play it cool.

"It's hard enough getting people to agree on a direction when all understand the problem. It's impossible to do it when they can't agree on what the problem actually is. Congressman Bennit got them to agree on the facts. From there they could work on a consensus to fix them."

A wave of relief passes over me, and it actually warms me up as we exit the lobby and head down towards the Rayburn House Office Building where the congressman is doing his interview. A girl needs to keep her secrets, especially this one. I don't like withholding anything from Blake, but what Congressman Bennit told me can never be repeated. And I promised him it wouldn't be.

"Not everyone was happy he did that," Blake continues. "The Republicans and Democrats have been focused on keeping us divided for decades to appease their respective bases and increase the turnout at the polls. If a divided country is what you want, the easiest way to achieve that is to muddy the waters so the people don't know who to believe."

"And the easiest way to do that was confuse the facts. I get it, honey. I've been working here for longer than five minutes."

"Do you think he should have run for president?"

"Part of me wonders what would have happened," I tell him honestly.

"Do you know why he didn't?"

I give Blake a weak smile but don't say anything. Yep, a girl has to be allowed to have her secrets and he's just going to have to respect that. Hopefully for the rest of our lives.

"You do, and you aren't going to tell me, are you? Will I at least find out tonight?"

"Honey, I don't think anyone's ever going to hear the reasons for that decision."

"Okay, now you really piqued my interest."

"Sweetie, I better always have your interest," I tell him with a wink as we enter the Rayburn Building for the congressman's interview.

-SIXTY-NINE-
MICHAEL

Leroy was seventeen when he got his girlfriend pregnant. Instead of leaving her to fend for herself, he did the right thing and married her. Struggling and ultimately unable to make ends meet in the civilian world, he joined the army to provide for his young family.

Successful marriages in the Special Forces community are a rarity, and his was no exception. It fell apart after only a few years, but he never stopped providing for his daughter. She was a bright student and seemed to thrive in school, and Leroy spent every dime he could manage to ensure she got all the opportunities she could. He would have been so proud that she was the first member of his family to get into college. Between his G.I. Bill and scholarships she earned on her own, Arionna Charleston managed to attend and graduate from Fordham University in New York.

"I can't thank you enough for this opportunity, Congressman. This is the most sought after interview in the country and you didn't have to give it to me."

"You deserve a shot at the prime time, and I thought this was the best way to get you one."

After graduating, Arionna went to work at a respected cable news network she interned with her senior year. Media is a very competitive business, and even having the right recipe of looks and articulation to do the job does not guarantee success in the field. Sometimes success or failure comes down to who you know, and I hope this helps give her what she needs to get noticed. There are not enough prominent African-American journalists in the United States, and this can be the launch of a very successful career. Besides, I owe her father a lot, including my life.

"You are all grown up, Arionna," I tell her. Leroy would have gone crazy beating the boys off of her.

"That's because I haven't seen you in years, Congressman."

"I know. I'm sorry I missed your college graduation."

"It's okay. You came to so many birthdays and special events when I was a kid, I can let it slide. Speaking of special events, congratulations on your wedding."

"Thanks! We had a great time."

"I heard you kept it a very small affair."

"Those are usually the best ones. I really wish you could have come. Kylie would have loved to meet you."

"I'm sorry, I really wanted to, but I just started at this job and the hours are brutal."

"I understand, believe me. How are they treating you?"

"Okay, I guess. It's a lot of grunt work while I learn the ropes. The network is not very happy that you insisted I be the one who does this interview. A lot of people more senior than me wanted it."

One thing I learned from Kylie is that journalism is a cutthroat business. All the networks compete with each other for the biggest interviews and juiciest exclusives. Within each of those companies, the reporters and personalities in the trenches of delivering us the news are constantly jockeying for position and trying to land the big story all the others are pining for. The fact that she scored the interview of the year will not ingratiate her to any of them, but at least she's getting the exposure.

"The network will get over it once they see you in action, and all those senior people have had plenty of chances."

"You know I'm not going to take it easy on you," she whispers with a hint of embarrassment.

"I had over a hundred requests to do the last interview of my career. I rejected each one of them because I knew they'd only ask softball questions to appease their viewership. I wanted you because I knew you wouldn't."

"How do you know that?"

"Because your father was my best friend, and I know he wouldn't have. I figured his daughter wouldn't either."

"So you're prepared to answer any question I dish out?"

"I wouldn't have it any other way."

* * *

What the hell was I thinking? I should have gone with the cupcake interview instead of subjecting myself to feeling like a murder defendant under cross-examination from an eager prosecutor trying her first case. Just like Leroy, this young woman is relentless.

"Many politicians on both sides of the aisle think you are ideologically challenged. They claim that you are willing to compromise because you have no strong beliefs of your own. How do you respond to those critics?"

"I think there are politicians in this country who are ideologically rigid enough for all of us."

"You didn't answer the question," she says with a smile.

"Over the last couple of decades we've seen bitter partisan battles between Republicans and Democrats as each sought to advance an ideological agenda. They relied on huge majorities to get their way and, when they didn't have them, progress on solving issues ground to a halt. There was no dialogue and rarely any compromise. As a result, nothing got done, problems worsened, and the American people suffered."

"You still haven't answered it."

"I know," I say with my best charming smile. "I'm getting to it. I do have an ideology. I do have strong thoughts and feelings about issues. But it's not my opinions that matter. I'm here to serve the people, and what they demanded was progress on tackling the problems that plague us as a nation. I came here to do just that, and my ideology took a backseat to something I am far more passionate about."

"What's that, Congressman?"

"America."

"You held a press conference after Speaker Albright's suicide and explained to the American people how he was responsible for the assassination. You apologized for trusting him and asked everyone to forgive you, which most people did."

"Yes, and I'm grateful for that." I also know she's setting me up for something. I've already fallen for this trick twice.

"Don't you think you are violating that trust by leaving Congress now before the job is finished?"

"The job will never be finished, so I don't think that's what I'm doing."

"Many people do though. They placed their trust in you and are angry because you aren't seeing this through. Do you think they have a right to be angry?"

A journalist chasing a politician for an honest answer to a hard question is practically a national pastime. The problem is, if that politician is popular, the methods could alienate his supporters and cost the network dearly. Arionna is walking that fine line, and her producer looks like he needs a bottle of Rolaids because of it.

"I appreciate that so many have strong emotions about my service, but I think the anger is misplaced. So long as they pay closer attention to who they vote for, I think there are plenty of qualified candidates out there that can fill my shoes."

"Is that why you chose not to run for president and to leave politics instead?"

There it is. I smile at the question because, once again, she set me up beautifully for it. She doesn't accept the reason I gave for not running for the White House. Countless Americans would agree with her suspicion, and she is determined to get to the bottom of the real reason, right here, right now. It's something Kylie would have done, and that's how I know Arionna is going to have a great career.

I have no doubt that Sergeant First Class Leroy Charleston is looking down at his daughter from somewhere in the heavens above like a proud father. He's probably yelling like a rabid football fan, urging his team into the end zone. He wants her to win this battle of the wills. She wants answers, and I can't give them.

"To be a successful president, I think you have to want to do the job in your heart."

"And you don't?"

"It was never an aspiration of mine." I bet the current president of the United States will throw something at the television when he hears that line. I had him convinced otherwise.

"Neither was running for the House, Congressman. You did that because you lost a bet, and I think the American people are grateful for your American history class winning it, considering what you've done for this nation. Why would we expect anything different if you decided to run for the White House?"

Well, she did tell me she wasn't going to take it easy on me. I glance over her shoulder again to see the producer wishing he had a hole to climb into. Her questions aren't what the network had in mind, but they are what people want to hear the answers to, whether I like it or not.

"Because I am of the belief that the president should have some management experience and be well versed in foreign policy. They may not be Constitutional requirements, but I believe they are among the credentials we should value in candidates for that office." Despite how that might sound to the viewers, I really do believe that.

"Polls have your approval rating in the low eighties. You have sustained an approval rate over seventy percent since the weeks following the State of the Union. Many of those people want to see you run against the president and think you would win in a landslide. It doesn't seem like they're worried about your lack of experience and I think you can understand the disappointment many feel that you won't run."

"It's not a challenge I'm willing to take on," is all I say. The best thing you can do under a withering hail of gunfire is keep your head down.

"So you quit politics instead? I don't think many people would have expected a Green Beret to back down from a challenge." Of course, when you keep your head down, sometimes the enemy just throws a grenade.

She is definitely her father's daughter. Leroy used to call me out using a similar line all the time. And right this instant, I know Leroy is up there in the heavens somewhere laughing his ass off.

-SEVENTY-

JAMES

Today is going to be bittersweet. Almost two years after I was first arrested following Michael Bennit's press conference, and four months after the jury handed down a guilty verdict on all counts, the journey is coming to an end. On one hand, I am thrilled this is the last time I will have to look at the inside of the E. Barrett Prettyman Courthouse. On the other, I will likely be shipping off to somewhere far less pleasant. Such is the way of things at sentencing hearings.

The Courthouse is located at Third Street and Constitution Avenue, Northwest, not far from my former offices at Ibram & Reed and one block west of the United States Capitol. In the front of the courthouse on Constitution Avenue stands a statue of Major General George C. Meade, a pathetic attempt at Union leadership during the Civil War if there ever was one. His futility as a commander was only matched by the incompetence of my legal team. The effort they mounted in my defense of the charges I'm about to be sentenced for was futile.

I'm escorted into the courtroom by a bailiff that looks like he spends way too much time at fast food restaurants. I may not be a skinny man, but at least I carry it well. His gut rounds corners five minutes before he does. I think I saw him playing a mall Santa a couple of weeks ago during my Black Friday shopping spree.

I traded my custom-tailored Italian suit for a prison orange jumpsuit following my conviction. As my lawyers warned me earlier this year, I didn't have a prayer of being found not-guilty. It was a self-fulfilling prophecy. The defense they put up was less than spirited because they knew the outcome was all but predetermined. Forget about the jar, I got caught with the cookie in my hand, or so they concluded. That didn't stop them from taking my money though. For the results I got, I should have just gone with the public defender.

I glance to the back of the courtroom after greeting my horrible defense team for what should be the last time. There he is. Humans are creatures of habit, and my shadow is no different. He is sitting in the same spot he was when my verdict was handed down. Maybe he considers it his lucky seat.

I'm partly surprised Michael Bennit and Kylie Roberts aren't here to watch the show. I'm sure this is a moment they would enjoy. Then again, I was the one who made the battle a personal one. I don't think either of them could care less about me.

"All rise," the bailiff announces as the judge enters. After taking direction to sit, I plop into my chair and plan to zone out for the next three hours while my lawyers go through the motions of arguing all the mitigating circumstances surrounding my arrest and conviction, in a plea for leniency. From the look on the judge's face, it's not going to work.

When deciding a sentence, judges consider oral statements made in court by prosecutors, defense attorneys, and the defendant, in this case, me. Prosecutors use their time to highlight the aggravating factors in the crime and the criminal behavior. Defense counsel responds with arguments justifying a lighter penalty, namely that this is my first offense. Then I get the opportunity to throw myself on the mercy of the court.

No one can be more persuasive than I am. It's a gift I have applied to my trade for decades now. Convincing politicians to do my bidding became … well, as easy as breathing. Thus, I didn't bother to work with my lawyers to prepare what I would say to the judge. There was only one way I planned on responding.

"Mister Reed, as is your right, you are permitted to make a statement to the court before I impose the sentence. Would you care to take that opportunity?" the judge queries from the bench.

I rise as a free man one last time. One last chance to explain how this was all a mistake and how I should go free. How it's everyone in this town that corrupted me, not the other way around as the media portrayed. One last chance to set the record straight.

"No, Your Honor, I do not wish to make a statement."

There is a murmur in the courtroom that requires the judge to slam his gavel down to contain. They didn't see that coming. For the first time, I may actually understand the reasons Michael Bennit likes to do the unexpected. It is a very satisfying feeling.

"Mister Reed," the judge announces to me, "absent of any remarks in your defense, you force me to render my sentence based on the arguments already made. Do you understand that?"

"Yes, Your Honor."

"Okay, very well. You were an influential man in the operations of our government," the judge continues. "Unfortunately, the power that comes with such a position went to your head. You knowingly withheld critical evidence in the assassination attempt on a United States congressman, and then used that evidence to try to coerce him into entering an illegal quid pro quo relationship with you. I cannot imagine what unspeakable damage you could have done had he agreed."

Funny, I don't consider it "damage." I consider it progress for the greater good. Too bad there's nothing I can say to get him to see that.

"Thankfully, he did the right thing, and now you are here to answer for your crimes. The fact that you are a first-time offender does not move me. Although charges may never be brought, I am certain that this is not the first time you have engaged in illegal activities.

"Unfortunately, I cannot base my sentence on that. Based on the evidence presented and the conviction by a jury of your peers for your crimes of obstruction of the due administration of justice, I can tell you that I do consider you a menace to society. You do not deserve the consideration of this court for the leniency you requested today. While you may consider your crime victimless, I believe there are over three hundred fifty million of them. Your crime is against every man, woman, and child in this country, Mister Reed.

"Eighteen, fifteen-oh-three of the United States Code declares this to be a felony offense for which the sentence can be ten years imprisonment in a federal correction institution. Therefore, I hereby sentence you to the maximum ten years for each of the three counts of obstruction you were found guilty for, to be served consecutively for a total of thirty years. Bailiff, please remand the defendant into custody. This court is adjourned."

With a rap of the gavel, it's over. I can appeal the verdict, and I may consider taking that route if I can convince an appellate court that my defense was inadequate. For now, I'll just wait and see if the promises made to me by Terry Nyguen are fulfilled.

As I am placed in handcuffs, I look to the back of the courtroom once again. Terry is standing now, perhaps getting the best view he can manage of me doing the perp walk out of the courthouse. He gives me a nod. Terry may be a lot of things, but I hope more than anything he's a man of his word.

He came to me following my arrest with an offer that I had no choice but to accept. He knew people would be seeking me out to enlist my help in providing them with damaging information on political opponents. I was to let him know each and every time that happened and, in return, he would work behind the scenes to ensure my jail term was at the most hospitable location possible. If I failed to follow through on the arrangement, or I tried to double-cross him, he would ensure I was thrown in the deepest, darkest hole he could find.

Terry does not strike me as the kind of man who bluffs when playing poker. So much business in Washington is done in the gray, but he is a black and white kind of guy. If he says he can pull either of those off, I believe him. Not that there was a choice in the matter.

If he fails to follow through on his end of the bargain, I know exactly how to get even. The information I possess may be buried, but it's still safe. Even from prison, I am still a powerful man.

"Let's go," the bailiff orders.

"Yes, let's."

-SEVENTY-ONE-
MICHAEL

The last day of the lame duck session didn't have the drama of the last one. Marilyn Viano was not around to accost me on the way to the House chamber to plead for her continued involvement. There was no earthshaking rules bill that would fundamentally alter how our government does business to defeat. On another positive note, nobody shot at us either. I won't be enjoying Christmas, looming just days away, from a hospital bed like I was forced to do two years ago.

The downside is nothing really got accomplished, either. Representatives not returning for the next Congress, myself included, are not eager to vote on legislation. The reasons are twofold. The first is the moral argument that, after the election in November, they no longer really represent their districts. The second, more cynical reason, is the ones who were defeated may want to run for office again and don't want to have additions to their voting records to defend.

There is a great deal of uncertainty among the American people when it comes down to our battles with the president. The talk of impeachment died down after we began overriding his vetoes, although that is only treating the symptoms, not the disease. Unchecked expansion of presidential power is going to continue to be one of the dominant issues in our government.

For now, Congress has the political will to fight it. Who knows what will happen a decade from now?

The independent movement of social media candidates did not flame out like some pundits predicted, although it didn't experience another wave election like last year. A wave election is characterized by one major political party winning substantially more races than the other. There is no defined number of seats that constitutes a wave, but political analysts use the term to describe any year in which one party loses twenty or more seats in the House. They each lost many more than that two years ago. It wasn't as bad for them this go-round.

We didn't accomplish many of the things we set out to do. There are never any shortages of issues our citizens face that require a government solution. Of course, there is plenty of time wasted on things that don't require one. Regardless, I have supreme confidence that the icongressmen, led by Cisco, and the House, led by Thomas Parker, can handle anything thrown at them without the need for me to be around.

"I still can't believe you're leaving. We still have a lot to do here," my longtime friend tells me.

"I'm sure it's nothing you can't handle, Cisco. Right, Mister Speaker?"

"For once, Michael, I'm with him. I am going to miss our lively debates on the issues. I had forgotten how much fun it could be to have intellectual disagreements."

"You don't need me for that. So long as the Fight Club exists, I am sure you'll have plenty of them."

The caucus I created was more than a group, it was a concept. I designed it to be the place that caucuses were meant to be—a forum for representatives to gather and discuss issues amongst each other, without the prying eyes of the media or pressure from special interests and voters. That was how caucuses were originally designed, before congressmen started running to the press to tell them what happened during the meetings. I'm happy to have helped change that, and am sure the Fight Club will live on without me.

"You can pretend all you want, but you're going to miss it, Michael. You know you are."

"You may be right, but you know how the old adage goes. 'To all good things must come an end.'"

"Sure, but that doesn't mean I have to like it. You were our leader. El Jefe. The Big Kahuna. No offense, Mister Speaker," Cisco says to Parker.

"None taken."

"I may have started the social media movement and put it on its path, but it can't be perceived that it lives or dies with me. To prove to this country that independents are viable alternatives to the establishment, you guys need to stand on your own."

"Whatever," Cisco dismisses. He does that when he knows I'm right.

"And, Mister Speaker, I hope you'll continue to uphold your own promises to your office."

"With God as my witness." He's an ordained minister, so that's good enough for me.

I thought Thomas Parker was a partisan hack when I first came here. In some respects, he was. Since my expulsion, the respect we have for each other has grown. We don't agree on every issue, but we have set the standard for how lawmakers who disagree can still work together. My hope is that the trend we set lasts far into the future.

"You still really haven't told me why you're leaving."

"It was the plan, Cisco."

"No it wasn't. You promised the Democrats in the House that you wouldn't actively run icandidates against them like you did in the last election. There was nothing ever said about you not running again yourself."

"Yes there was," Speaker Parker says, measuring my reaction.

"What?"

I try to remain as impassive as I can. Nobody is supposed to know, and I'd rather keep it that way. The cat may be out of the proverbial bag as Cisco's head moves back and forth between us, like he's watching a classic volley between Nadal and Federer at Wimbledon.

"With the Senate Democrats, right, Michael? You made a deal with them. If they cooperated with you against the president, you would leave politics." I can't tell him. Well, I can, but I shouldn't. Hell with it. They've earned enough of my trust with everything we've been through. I owe them an explanation—the explanation.

"Mister Speaker, besides me, only four people on this planet knew about that."

"Wait! Four other people know what? And why wasn't I one of them?"

"I couldn't include you, Cisco. It was between myself and the Majority Leader and Whip in the Senate. To their credit, they never whispered a word about it. For obvious reasons I had to tell Kylie and Chelsea, but that was it. Nobody else could know."

"That's BS," Cisco groans.

"How did you figure it out?"

"I suspected it when everyone suddenly started cooperating right before the State of the Union. I was convinced of it afterwards when the Senate joined us in overriding the vetoes," Speaker Parker continues, clearly proud that he was correct in his assumption. "Following that, they were such strong advocates with their members for you. You are either a brilliant mindbender or you cut a deal with them. After you made your surprise announcement, I knew what you had traded."

"You really cut a deal with them that required you to quit politics? We had so much going for us. Why would you do that?"

"Because we needed their support and weren't going to accomplish anything without it. Those were the terms. Turns out the Democrats in the Senate were more scared of me than they were of the president."

"It was a lousy deal to make, Michael."

"This whole thing was never about me, not from the moment I lost the bet with my students. I wasn't in it for power or prestige. I wanted to restore American confidence in their government and prove that it could be of, by, and for the people once again. We needed a unified Congress to do that, so I—"

"Fell on your sword?"

"In a manner of speaking, yes. I asked a lot of people to make sacrifices. I asked them to become more involved citizens. I asked them to reject the establishment and elect mavericks to represent them. I asked them to forgive me for my own mistakes. And most of all, I asked them to trust us that we were trying to make a difference. They did all that, so when it was time to make a sacrifice of my own, do you really think I could refuse?"

"Yes, you could say no, go pound sand."

"I couldn't do that."

"Why not?"

"Do you know why George Washington leaving the presidency was such a big deal, Cisco?" I ask him, after thinking about it for a moment. "I mean, in modern times, we measure presidents by what they do in office. What's the big deal about leaving it?"

"And here comes today's lesson," Cisco says to the Speaker.

"I'm going to miss these," the big Alabaman beams.

"Washington lived in the time of kings—absolute rulers for which leadership was a birthright. He was a revolutionary, not just in fighting the war of independence, but what he did with the reins of power after it. By comparison, think of other military commanders and revolutionary leaders before and after him like Caesar, Napoleon, Lenin, Castro … When they seized power they held it with an iron grip until their death or defeat."

"Michael, you're not a president, despite my best efforts to push you in that direction."

"No, but as you said, I am the de facto leader of icongressmen. We came here to make Congress effective again, and that cause is bigger than any one man."

"I'm still not buying it," Cisco scoffs. I'm surprised. The cause is the one thing Cisco can relate to.

"It's the most unselfish act I have ever seen, Michael," the Speaker consoles.

"That's high praise coming from a minister."

"Well, I wasn't counting *Him*," Speaker Parker corrects with a laugh, pointing to the heavens.

"Minstrels," Cisco whispers.

"What?"

"Minstrels. They're going to write songs about him."

"I don't underst—"

"Please, Mister Speaker, don't ask. You'll only encourage him. And minstrels will never write about this. I trust the two of you can keep this a secret. The future cooperation in Congress depends on it."

"Fine. Mum's the word, under one condition. You run for office again someday."

"Was there anything in your deal that precludes you from running again at a later date?" the Speaker asks out of curiosity.

I think back to the deal I struck with the Democratic leadership in the Senate. Now that I think about it, there wasn't. I don't recall either Sinclair or Stackhouse making that stipulation during our dinner meeting.

"You know what makes you a politician, Michael?" Speaker Parker asks after a couple of hearty laughs. "You keep your options open. You know what makes you a great one? That you don't realize that's what you're doing. Here's a history lesson for you, although I'm sure you know it."

"I'm all ears."

"King George III once asked the American painting his portrait what Washington would do after winning independence from the British. Do you know what his reply was?"

"They say he will return to his farm," I immediately answer. Yeah, I know the story.

"That's right. The king was incredulous. He remarked, 'If he does that, he will be the greatest man in the world.'"

"For once, my liege, I get the point of one of these," Cisco proclaims. "And I agree with him. You may be the greatest man in the world, but you'd have been a greater ipresident."

-SEVENTY-TWO-

KYLIE

"Are you here to offer us a job too?" Chelsea asks Mister Dark and Mysterious as he slides in the door.

"No, but it could be arranged."

"No, thanks. I want to be able to tell people what I do for a living," Michael responds.

"Why do you always dress like you're a member of the Triads?" Chelsea asks, joking ... I think. She's rewarded with a dirty look, but nothing further.

"She's right. It's almost Christmas. You could at least put on a Santa hat to soften your image," I recommend.

"I like my image just fine."

"Leave him alone, guys. The look is great at keeping away muggers ... and small children," Michael jokes, poking fun at his ubiquitous seriousness.

"And Jehovah's Witnesses, street magicians ... curious puppies ..." Chelsea finishes.

"You guys are hilarious," he says as we erupt in laughter.

"We have to get going in a few minutes. What brings you here, Terry?"

"A warning."

"Oh, hell, I probably should sit down for this," I say, being literal as I take a seat on the sofa in Michael's inner office. It's one of the last pieces of furniture left in the otherwise barren office.

Everything else has been boxed up and moved out, making space for the next occupant in our little slice of the Cannon House Office Building.

"Why is it every time you stop by I feel the need to strap on body armor?" Michael asks.

"I have that effect on people. You're lucky you both didn't need it for the wedding."

"Oh, that would have gone well with my wedding dress."

"They can be custom ordered in white. By the way, I had a nice time."

"We were so glad you could come, and thank you so much for the gift."

"Yes, we needed a third gravy boat," Michael mumbles, prompting me to give him a slug to the arm. He actually gave us a nice check that went a long way towards paying for the honeymoon. Aruba wasn't the cheapest of travel destinations.

"So what are you here to warn us about now? Today was my last day, so there's no point in blackmailing me or taking potshots at us from a bell tower."

"No, but you have something equally valuable that will keep you on people's radar for years to come—a reputation."

"You can't be serious," Chelsea grumbles.

"I am, unfortunately. Michael, you're leaving behind an amazing legacy that will have enemies looking to tarnish for years to come. You may be getting out of the public eye, but always be aware that some people won't stop coming after you."

"Oh, great, something to look forward to," I lament.

"I'm sorry to be the bearer of bad news, but thought you should know," Terry relays to us.

"Anybody in particular I should be watching out for?" Michael asks, forever sensitive to Terry's warnings given his uncanny accuracy in foretelling fateful events.

"The usual suspects and some up and coming opportunists, looking to fill the void you're leaving behind. Did you hear that your sister landed herself a job finally?"

"No, I haven't," I reply harshly. "And frankly, I don't really care."

"The gig she was about to land working with the White House went up in flames after Michael announced he wasn't running," Terry continues, ignoring my implied warning to shut up. "The well dried up for her in the rest of the town too. Now she is working on behalf of a former congressman who may be looking to reenter politics eventually. I don't know if it will come to anything, but considering her history with you guys, I would be prepared for it."

"Terry, I am done with politics. What is there to gain by coming after me now?"

"Michael, you left a long train of enemies in your wake. Some you know about and some you don't. All I'm saying is you shouldn't be surprised if some of them don't stop coming at you, just because you decided to call it quits."

He's right. I will never be out of my sister's crosshairs for very long, and neither will Michael. Madison may not have a lot of things, like integrity, but nobody could ever question her tenacity. Regardless, I am eager to get off the subject.

"You came all the way to Capitol Hill to tell us that?" I ask, hoping there is nothing more serious coming out of his mouth.

"And to say congratulations and best of luck. I will miss having you guys around here."

"What will you do without us, Terry?" Michael asks.

"Whatever my employers ask me to."

"Including supporting the best interests of independent candidates around the country?"

That was what the former Seal Team Six commando had said his organization did when we first met him. To this day, we have never gotten any more insight than that. No surprise that the group he works for denies he's an employee at all. He will always be Mister Dark and Mysterious, and we will always be thankful for everything he's done for us—the stuff we know about and the things I'm sure we don't.

"It's what my think tank does," he says with a grin that I wouldn't begin to try to describe.

"Yeah, right," Michael says with a knowing head nod, one military man to another. "Take care of yourself, Terry. And thanks … for everything."

"It was my pleasure," he says with a slight bow.

* * *

"I forget, you've never been in this office, have you, Congressman?"

"No, I haven't, and please, call me Michael."

"I will, so long as you call me David," he answers in a pleasant and sincere voice. That is in stark contrast with my other interactions here, including the spacious room Michael, Chelsea, and I are now standing in.

"I've been here, and it wasn't a pleasant experience," I tell him. This room gives me the willies.

"Yes, so I've heard, Miss Roberts.. I'm very sorry for what James Reed put you all through. I wish I had been paying closer attention, but I never had much involvement with my father's business. Lobbying was never my thing."

"Reed started this firm with your father, didn't he?" Michael asks, inspecting a box on the big desk that looks like an intercom. That was an efficient way for the smug man to beckon his servants.

"Yes, he did. Unfortunately, after my father died, James used this firm as his own personal kingdom. He was a very smart man and could have built this into something special. Instead, he let the power and money he accumulated go to his head. You experienced the results."

"He had a very nice view," Chelsea observes from the window.

"Franklin Square is right below us with Lafayette Square and the White House in the distance. I think this view is one of the best in the city. The other offices on this floor are equally nice, although the view isn't quite as good. Did I mention that they're empty too?"

That gets all of our attention. We weren't really sure what the point of this meeting was. I assumed it was an official face-saving apology from the man left to pick up the pieces of this disaster. Michael had mentioned that he thought he might actually make overtures of job offers. Chelsea and I had laughed at him, but he may have been right. Great, I'll never hear the end of that.

"Is that what you're trying to fix by having us here?" Michael finally asks, earning a smile from David.

"James left me with a mess to clean up. We were the largest firm left on K Street, but his misdeeds have cost us a lot of prestige and a lot of clients. As I mentioned, lobbying is not my thing, but if I am going to resurrect my father's legacy, I have a lot of work ahead of me. I'm not sure I can make it work. What I do know is that it would be a lot easier with talented people who know what the definition of integrity is. I want the three of you to lead the rebirth of this firm."

"David, you realize I have a colorful history with Ibram & Reed and with lobbyists in general."

"That's why I changed the name to The Liberty Group. It's also precisely why I want you to fill the empty chair in this office. You have seen the ugly side of Washington politics firsthand and know what an explosive combination money and power can be in this town. I can't think of a better person to run this firm and build it the way my father would have wanted to see it built."

"I'm so not going to be his secretary, if that's what you have in mind," Chelsea states.

"No. Miss Stanton, I could not think of a bigger waste of your talents. Michael would be in charge of the direction of the firm, but you would be in charge of the entire lobbying staff. You know this town, and people respect you. Just mentioning your name would open doors."

"I'm not going to be his secretary, either," I tell David, figuring it was my turn.

"Kylie, we have a serious PR problem. You would be essential in rebuilding the firm and letting everybody know how we're changing and why.

"It is a very generous offer, David, but I have to wait a year by law before I can lobby my colleagues. Even if I didn't, I don't know if I'm ready to make the switch from legislating to lobbying." He actually sounds like he's thinking about the offer. That surprises me considering what he has told me he's looking for. Maybe the challenge this provides is appealing to him.

"I understand your reluctance. It would be a transition you could ease into. I expect it will take you a year just to get us on our feet, so that's not an issue. Before you make any final decisions, I'd like to show you the offer letters, if that's okay. I don't want the money to influence you, but I do want you to know what I think you're worth."

David reaches into his coat pocket and pulls three thin envelopes, each with our name typed on them. He hands them to us and we open them, reading the contents in silence. Wow.

I glance over at Chelsea because her eyes are popping out of her head. I walk over to her and crane my head so I can see the letter. Like mine, the number jumps off the page. The salary he's offering her, before bonus, is a half million dollars.

"That's a lot of zeros, David," Michael comments after reading his own page.

"You'd be worth every penny."

Most connected former government workers who become lobbyists make a few hundred thousand dollars a year. The fees companies pay for some of the top lobbyists can be upwards of a couple of million. When the two of us look at Michael's offer, I feel underappreciated. Like Chelsea, I am only being offered a half million dollars. Michael is being offered six times that.

"I'm sorry, David, I can't," Chelsea says, handing the letter back. "It's a very tempting offer, and a generous one, but I made a promise and I'm determined to keep it. Thank you anyway."

"I respect that. Thank you for at least considering my offer."

I look at Michael. I'm not surprised Chelsea didn't accept the offer, but I can't think of many people her age that wouldn't have. Her father would be very proud she kept her word to him, after the shock wears off. In fact, I can't think of many people of any age that would decline such a lucrative salary, us included.

It is a very tempting offer. I've never believed life is all about money, although having some financial security beats being a struggling journalist. We would be working together, which is both good and bad, but we could also stay in Washington. It's an important decision, and I'm not ready to make it right now.

"I don't want you to make a decision today," David says, reading my mind. "It means a lot to me that you even accepted this meeting. Please take your time. The offer is good until you tell me yes or no."

"Thank you very much, David.

"No, Michael, thank you."

-SEVENTY-THREE-
CHELSEA

This was once my spot, but now it's ours. I have loved this location on the steps of the west side of the Capitol since I came to work for Mister Bennit in Washington once I graduated. I came here on my first day when the reality of being a chief of staff for a congressman became overwhelming. I have visited it countless times, when I just needed a moment of peace.

Now it's fitting that it all ends here. It may be gray, dreary, and freezing out, but through all the hugs and tears, no one is complaining about the weather. Even the congressman is fighting his emotions. It's been a great run and now it's over.

"You look like you have the weight of the world on your shoulders, Chels. What's going on?"

"I don't know. I just wish … I wish we had been able to accomplish more while we were here."

"I think we did a lot," the congressman argues.

"Only in the past seven months. We spent the three years before that spinning our wheels. It seems like it was such a waste of time."

"Do you guys remember the e-mails and Facebook messages I got when I first was elected? Everyone was expecting me to come here and do great things. Others expected me to change the whole system on my own."

"I remember," Vince says.

"Americans are conditioned to believe one person can swoop in and save the day. I would have loved to propose some piece of groundbreaking legislation my first year that made the country a better place, but it wasn't realistic."

"So you're not Elle Woods in *Legally Blonde 2*?" Vince says with a laugh.

"It scares me a little that he's seen that movie," Vanessa quips. She's right. I'm a little concerned myself.

"Ignore him, please," Kylie says, rolling her eyes.

"I needed help. I needed you guys, Cisco, the icandidates, Speaker Parker, and even Marilyn Viano. Most of all, I needed the American people. Democracy is a contact sport, and it takes a team effort to move the ball down the field. We all have to be participants, or this whole thing will go down in flames."

"It still feels like it took too long."

"It always will, Vince. We are used to having everything now. E-mail on our phones, ATM machines, fast food … the list goes on and on. Government doesn't work that way, even in the digital age. It's built like that for a reason, and it works so long as our leaders are willing to have an honest debate and are open to a reasonable compromise."

"Haven't you guys had enough politics for one lifetime?" Kylie asks, shaking her head.

"It's a force of habit," Vince concludes.

"And we don't want to say good-bye," Vanessa adds, starting my crying all over again.

"Do we get a final history lesson?" I ask through my tears.

Vince and Vanessa laugh nervously. I'm sure they have the same acute awareness as I do that this will be the last one we ever receive. Even Kylie doesn't mind, and she gets to hear a lot of these.

"I suppose I owe you one," Mister Bennit concedes.

"Make it a good one," Vince demands.

"Yeah, one we've never heard before."

"That could be challenging," Kylie muses. She's right. We've heard so many.

"Democracy originated in Athens, but it wasn't easy going. Just like in our modern form of democracy, there was no shortage of corruption and abuse of power. Tired of the status quo, three citizens took it upon themselves to look after the well-being of people who couldn't or wouldn't speak for themselves.

"They were persecuted, called names, told they weren't capable or equal to the task. But each time someone tried to knock them down, they got up and came back even stronger. In part because of their efforts, Athens became the most powerful and respected nation-state of the Hellenic peninsula. Unfortunately, their names aren't well known, but their actions shaped one of the world's great civilizations."

"What were their names?"

"Tselsi, Binkentios, and Phanessa."

"I've never heard of them," I tell the congressman, racking my brain for any memory of that from back in my high school Western Civ class.

"I haven't either," Vanessa echoes. "What's the point of the story?"

Mister Bennit smiles and takes the time to look at each of us in the eyes. "You'll just have to figure that out for yourselves this time. Guys, it has been an honor working with you. And thank you so much for what you have done for me. There is no doubt in my mind that you all have even brighter futures ahead of you."

He hugs Vanessa and then shares a man hug with Vince. Tears pour down Vanessa's face. Even the tough, manly Vince is misty eyed. I'm not having any better success.

"Chels, I hate good-byes, so let's stick with 'until we see each other again' or we're both going to lose it."

"Deal," I say and give him a huge hug, like the kind I usually reserve for my father.

"Thank you," I whisper in his ear.

"No, Chels, thank you."

If the embrace had lasted ten minutes, it still would have ended too soon. With a quick wave, the congressman and Kylie head back up the steps, holding hands like they didn't have a care in the world. They had disappeared from view for a matter of seconds before I realized who he was talking about in his story.

"Okay, call me crazy, but I've never heard those names before in my life," Vince says.

"Yes, you have," I correct him. "You hear them every day."

"What are you talking about, Chels?" Vanessa asks.

"He made the story up. He was talking about us."

"How do you know that?"

"I bet if you do a search on Google for Tselsi, Binkentios, and Phanessa, they're Greek variants of our names. Tselsi is Chelsea, Phanessa is Vanessa, and I can assume Binkentios is like Vincent. In his own way, he was trying to say we made history."

"Son of a bi … I swear that man will never cease to amaze me."

"Agreed." No sooner do I say it than the sun peaks through the clouds with the promise of an even brighter future.

EPILOGUES

SHALL NOT PARISH FROM THE EARTH

-EPILOGUE-

JAMES

I guess Mister Nyguen came through after all. In July 2009, *Forbes* magazine listed the Federal Prison Camp-Pensacola as the second cushiest prison in the United States. I suppose for those not accustomed to five-hundred-dollar steak dinners, expensive Italian wines, and fine silk suits, this would be an okay place. I am not one of those people, but there are far worse places to serve out a prison term.

It took a month to get processed into the system after my sentencing and get my permanent prison assignment, so I only arrived in sunny Pensacola, Florida, a week and a half ago. The prison is actually part of an old naval base known as Saufley Field and is where naval aviators used to receive their basic flight training. I was assigned to a room housing eleven other inmates, in the dormitory-style prison that once had served as a barracks for the aspiring aviators. We are crammed in like sardines. My office overlooking Washington was easily three times the size of my current residence.

The prisoners here are almost all nonviolent offenders with no prior felony convictions or other criminal convictions of a serious nature. Thus, FPC-Pensacola is set up as a minimum-security work camp, with no perimeter fencing. It bears no resemblance to the supermax prison facilities most Americans associate with prison.

Inmates are eventually assigned to jobs ranging from menial tasks to more specialized ones based on their civilian skill sets. Support functions of the prison are all done by its residents, including the cooking, cleaning, and routine maintenance. The lucky ones get bused onto one of the surrounding military bases to ply their services there. I can only hope I end up being one of them.

New arrivals are assigned to the cleanup and raking of the compound while awaiting their assignment. My hands aren't used to the calluses I'm getting on them, so the sooner I get off this lousy detail, the better. At least I'm outside enjoying the beautiful Florida weather.

A group of us are picking up around the visitor area where inmates greet their visitors, when the guards put us on a break to prevent overheating. Anyone complaining about the Florida heat in January really needs to spend a winter or two up in Washington. Eager to sit down, I leave my rake and find a shady spot under a large tree. Unfortunately, my moment of solace doesn't last long.

"I was wondering when I would run into you, James. How many strings did you have to pull to land in this paradise?" Winston Beaumont asks, settling his large frame down next to me.

Prison food must agree with the disgraced former representative from Michael's district in Connecticut, since his waistline hasn't receded an inch. Beaumont was crafty enough to beat Bennit in the most watched congressional election in decades, but not enough so to keep him out of trouble when Blake Peoni switched sides. The result was a prison sentence for him, a resounding victory for Bennit in a special election, and an ongoing headache for me ever since. I suppose it's indirectly his fault that I landed me here under this same tree with him. I'm sure the Greeks acted out plays about that kind of tragedy in some Athenian amphitheater.

"It was the luck of the draw. I was more focused on getting a presidential pardon than worrying about where I would end up serving my sentence," I answer, omitting my understanding with Terry. "What brings you out here?"

"I had a visitor. You start getting them more and more once you finally settle in."

"I doubt anyone will be bothering to visit me," I lament, feeling a touch sorry for myself because it's true. I've not had any real friends in decades. I have always measured myself through the number of political relationships I've maintained, but none of those people will be caught dead associating themselves with me now.

"You'd be surprised. You were a very powerful figure in politics and some think you can be again. There is no shortage of opportunists who will seek out your advice and support."

"Is that really why we're sharing a tree, Winston? You're here to make some cockamamie horse trade with me?"

He snorts, and that tells me all I need to know. Winston Beaumont has always considered himself smarter than everyone else, and it led to his downfall. That arrogance and lofty opinion of himself is why he didn't listen to me once before and why he thinks he can play me now.

"Who saw you? Roger?" I ask out of curiosity, knowing he isn't ready to divulge the purpose of this ridiculous jail yard meeting.

"No, he's still locked up at FPC-Montgomery."

Roger Bean was Beaumont's chief of staff while he was in the House. Most of my dealings were with him, since Beaumont thought it was beneath him to have too much interaction with shady lobbyists. Roger was a capable guy and would probably have been a better politician than his blowhard of a boss. He had the looks, the connections, and the moral uncertainty to excel in pre-Bennit Washington, DC.

"Okay, then who?"

"My old press liaison." It takes me a couple of seconds to remember who that was. Beaumont lost his relevance in my life the day he was indicted.

"Madison Roberts?"

"Yeah, that's her."

"As in Kylie Roberts's sister? That Madison Roberts?" I'm rewarded with a devilish grin.

"It's Kylie Bennit now, remember? And yes, it's a small world, isn't it?" he responds, choosing not to elaborate further and forcing me to ask the next question as we continue this little dance of ours.

"What did she want? I'm sure it wasn't a conjugal visit." At least I hope it wasn't.

"To catch up on things. Did you hear they filled your old position at Ibram & Reed? Or should I say, The Liberty Group."

Now we're getting into it. My name and my legacy are both destroyed beyond repair, so it figures Ibram's snot-nosed son would change the name as quickly as he could. The thought of the firm I spent decades building into a political powerhouse and titan of America's lobby industry not having my name on it still smarts.

"No, I hadn't heard," is my weak reply.

"You'll recognize the name of your replacement. You know him well."

"Don't tell me it's Bennit," I demand. I don't want murder added to my list of crimes for choking the life out of this man.

"No, although from what I heard, David Karmitz offered the spot to him. Bennit didn't take it, so they went with another candidate who had all the right answers to every question he was asked," Beaumont relays, clearly enjoying having more information than I do for the first time in his pathetic life.

"Out with it, Winston."

"They hired Gary Condrey."

I wince, and he notices, causing him to snicker. Marilyn Viano's former chief of staff. I tossed Condrey out of my office after previously promising him employment for his assistance in dealing with her duplicity. I couldn't trust him, but remember wondering if I would be hearing back from him again. I guess that question is answered.

"Are you enjoying this?"

"Not at all," Beaumont answers without any conviction. "We have a common enemy, James. I don't take any pleasure in the misery he caused you. Michael Bennit was responsible for my undoing too."

"He shouldn't have, had you listened to my advice," I state, giving into my desire to seize the initiative back from him. I know things too.

Not everything that happens in political fund-raising is above board. If the American public thinks funding from political action committees is shady, then they would hate to know what happens when their elected representatives take outright bribes from corporate interests. It happens all the time.

Some of those interests had paid Beaumont a small fortune to help advance their agenda. With all the heat following the financial crisis in 2008, it was an easier and more cost-effective way to get guaranteed results. Unfortunately, the ploy hit a few snags along the way.

The first was the digging by an intrepid journalist who had somehow caught wind of what was going on. Winston hadn't realized just how close she had gotten, until her sister relayed a conversation they had to him. He had used his relationship with her paper to get her fired, and I had leveraged my own relationships to ensure nobody else hired her. It was the perfect solution until she had started reporting on the campaign of her now husband, Michael Bennit.

"I had no reason to believe at the time that Blake Peoni would have kept those documents," Winston disputes. "He was a loyal soldier until Bennit and his chief of staff, what's her name, gave him a crisis of conscience."

"Her name is Chelsea Stanton, and you're a trusting fool." Not to mention being in denial.

Campaign finance laws in the United States are Draconian. A politician has to account for every dime contributed and keep a meticulous list of where the money came from. To ensure he didn't make a mistake involving his illegal cash infusions, he had kept records of each and every transaction, transfer, and account the money was funneled to. When Kylie Roberts had turned up the heat with her investigation, he had ordered Peoni to destroy the records. The problem is, the ambitious piece of crap had kept them as an insurance policy, should he ever need it. Roberts and Bennit had convinced him to cash that in, and the rest is history.

"Maybe I am a trusting fool, but I'm also loyal. I could have told them everything I know and tried to save my own ass and you know it. You would have landed in here much sooner than you did, had I not kept my mouth shut."

Unfortunately, he's right. My firm has represented hundreds of companies and interested groups during my career as a lobbyist. Some of them are so desperate to achieve a desired result in Washington that they would do *anything* to make it happen, including outright bribery. In this case, it was a financial company that got their hooks into Beaumont. I know because I made the arrangements for it to happen. The Lexington Group was one of my best clients.

"And you think I should be thankful for that? How many of those nine elections you won would have gone your way without my support? I was the grease for The Machine and you know it."

Beaumont had an incredible base of media, politicians, and supporters in his pocket that he could call on in the event of a close race. He called it "The Machine" and didn't think he would need it in his race against Bennit. He was wrong and, like any machine, this one required grease. In this case, that grease was money.

"James, I'm not here to talk about what went wrong between us in the past."

"So what do you want? Do you need friends in here or something? Understand that I'm not going to be taking showers with you."

"No, no, no. I have plenty of friends in here. You have no choice but to make them and you'll learn about that necessity just as I did. No, I'm going to need something else from you."

"Like?"

"Like the names of everyone you worked with on the outside. Everyone you ever bribed, manipulated, or used." Now it's my turn to laugh.

"Why would you want that? More importantly, why on God's green earth should I give it to you? I could have used that information to cut my own deal with prosecutors." I actually gave it a pretty hard thought, but decided against it in the end.

"Because I will get out of here before you do. It may take a few more years, but I am going to be set free and will make my way back into the world. When I do, I have to rebuild myself and am going to need help to do it. Your help," he pleads.

"You don't seriously think you can ever hold public office again?"

"I'm not sure, but you never know. There have been stranger comeback stories. Remember the guy who was texting naked pictures of himself all the time?"

"That wasn't much of an example. He didn't win. If you think you'll ever be a public figure again, you're in desperate need of a shrink."

"No, I have no illusions about that. I don't need absolution through service to the people. I need payback. I have a score to settle with someone, and think you might find it in your interests to help me."

"Bennit."

"Look around you, James. We're both here because of him. Are you telling me you don't want to see him go down?" Now that's an interesting proposition and almost makes this intrusion on my private time worthwhile.

"He's not even in politics anymore, Winston." As much as I'd love another shot at Michael Bennit, I have no idea how or why I should bother to make that happen.

"No, but he does have a legacy that can still be attacked. He's the man who brought change to Washington," Beaumont sounds out sarcastically. "We are going to change it back, and there won't be any shortage of the old guard who have been cast out of politics willing to help. Madison is already working on it with me. It may take a long time, but I will find a way to destroy Michael Bennit, what he managed to build, or both."

I don't know what to think of Winston's overtures. Prison time gives a man time to think, and it's clear to me that he's done a lot of that. It can also drive a man to the edge of insanity, and he might be edging closer to that too. I have nothing to lose at the moment, but I have to think of the long term. I will get out of here someday and don't want to have burned all my bridges because of a rash decision.

"I can almost hear the gears spinning in your mind. Take your time and think about it, James. I don't need an answer right this minute. Weigh the pros and cons. Trust me when I say you'll have plenty of time to do exactly that."

Beaumont struggles to get up and brushes himself off when he finally succeeds. He looks around the yard as everyone begins to stir, signaling my brief respite has come to an end. In a moment, the guards will order us back to our raking.

"Visiting hours are over and I have to get back to my job in the prison library. Think about my proposition. We'll have plenty of time to talk more. Take care of yourself, James."

"You too, Winston," I respond, surveying the yard and the work to be done. Plenty of time indeed.

-EPILOGUE-
CHELSEA

"Hey, sweetie!" I say into my smartphone after answering it.

"Hi, darling. How's it going?" the voice on the other end responds.

"So far, so good, other than the fact it's freezing outside."

"You're from New England. You should be used to this," Blake admonishes, somehow thinking being raised in the Northeast makes you immune to frigid temperatures.

Boston weather in January is pretty typical to what we see back home in Millfield. The temps are in the mid-thirties and the skies overcast with clouds a medium shade of gray. The forecast for today is what they have been saying all week—chilly, with a wind that makes the temperature feel even colder, and a twenty percent chance of light snow.

"Yeah, right. Anyway, are you seriously going to call me after every class? You can't be that bored."

"After a year around Michael Bennit, you might be surprised. What do you think of college so far?"

Harvard University is a member of the Ivy League located about three miles northwest of Boston in Cambridge, Massachusetts. It was established in 1636 by the Massachusetts legislature, making it the oldest institution of higher learning in the United States. Harvard is also considered one of the most prestigious.

Technically, as an undergraduate, I go to Harvard College. In addition to that school, Harvard University includes ten other professional institutions offering graduate programs for students seeking advanced education in a masters or doctoral program. My father is almost giddy at the prospect of me continuing my education to the graduate and postgraduate levels once I finish the requirements for my bachelor's degree in a few years. His giddiness is unsettling, because the tough Bruce Stanton doesn't get giddy about anything. I made him a promise to complete college, but that doesn't extend to graduate studies. He will push me towards it, but I'll cross that bridge when I get to it.

"So far, it's pretty easy. After all the stories I have heard about stressing over papers and final exams, I can't help but wonder what I'm missing," I respond, causing the love of my life to laugh on the other end of the line.

"Well, in the defense of nearly every college student who started right after high school, they didn't have your life experiences. Not everyone can attend college after running three campaigns for a national office and being the chief of staff for one of the most important politicians in the twenty-first century."

"You know Mister Bennit is sensitive about all the new Founding Father talk the media is spewing these days. He would punch you in the head if he heard you say that."

"It wouldn't be the first time," Blake says with a laugh. That's true. He still says the two punches my mentor landed on him at Arlington National Cemetery were the hardest he'd ever been hit. And like a typical guy, he'd never admit it to Mister Bennit. "What class do you have next?"

"You know very well what one I have."

He's so cute. Blake insisted we go over my class schedule again last night for the hundredth time, because he wanted to make sure I was comfortable with where I had to be and when.

He's so excited about me starting college that I think he forgets I managed the schedule for a man who helped redefine politics on a national scale.

"I do. Make sure you call me when you're done. I'm dying to know how it goes."

"I will. Now, shouldn't you be getting back to work? I'd hate to see you get fired for talking to me all day instead of running the office like you should be."

"You know district offices aren't nearly as busy as things are down in Washington. I can spare a few minutes to check in on the woman of my dreams."

"I'm sure Congressman Phillips would love to hear you say that," I warn him.

Formerly disgraced and persona non grata in political circles, Blake has found his way back onto a congressional staff. After proving himself during his stint working for Congressman Bennit, countless members of both houses of Congress inquired about him going to work for them.

To be close to me while I am in Cambridge, he took a job running the district office for a liberal yet open-minded Democrat from the Boston area. It's a far cry from working with the still impressive numbers of icongressmen elected to the House, but his boss is willing to work with the Fight Club and even the Republicans to help get things done. We've come a long way. Before Mister Bennit got elected, Republicans and Democrats weren't even talking to each other, let alone finding the courage to work together.

"Aw, you're so sweet checking up on me, but I'm fine. In fact, I'm just walking into the building for my next class, so let me go."

"Fifteen minutes early. Your professor will love that."

"You're almost as bad as my father is," I say, part laughing and part shaking my head.

It's true. The moment he realized that I was really going off to Boston and not going to have another change of heart, he covered the house with every item he could find in the campus bookstore with Harvard on it. I know he is proud of my accomplishments with Congressman Bennit down in D.C., but every conversation he starts with someone now begins with, "My daughter goes to Harvard." Whether you love or hate your parents, they will always be universally embarrassing when you're young.

"I'll take that compliment," Blake replies, having nothing but respect for my father the ex-Marine. "I'll let you get to it. Have fun in class, honey. I love you."

"I will, and I love you too." I'm still getting a little used to saying that, after all Blake and I have been through. I like it though.

"And Chels?"

"Yeah?"

"Try to go easy on him."

* * *

This is the third college class I have ever attended, but I am starting to see a trend. All of my classes are going to be held in lecture halls. My schedule proclaims this room to be CGIS South S010, but the sign on the door advertises it as the Tsai Auditorium. It's a boring room, with whitewashed walls and faux walnut furniture. I am early, and the room is sparsely occupied. From the looks of it, there appears to be seats for about a hundred and fifty students, give or take a few. It is stadium-style seating, and the whole thing is reminiscent of my favorite movie theater back home. Judging by the size of the retractable screen at the front of the room, it may very well be.

I take my seat in the middle of the room and towards the front, which I am noticing is not a popular spot as the room begins to fill from back to front. I fiddle with my phone to kill time until the seats around me begin to get occupied. Looking at the time, I am now beginning to understand why nobody shows up early. The professor is already three minutes late.

When he walks in, it's like Caesar entering the Roman Senate. He drops his leather valise on the table and surveys the class. He has a confidence in front of small groups that reminds me of Mister Bennit, but that is where the similarities end. He carries himself with a certain arrogance my former boss and teacher never had.

"This is Government Ten, Foundations of Political Theory, so please ensure you're in the right place," he says as he paces in the front of the room. Middle aged, with a thick mop of gunmetal gray hair and a swollen waistline, he's dressed in a tweed jacket and brownish pants that barely match. As a fashion major, Peyton would be beside herself if she ever saw this. He does look the part of a professor though, for what that's worth.

"By now you've all read the description of this course," he continues. "Or at least I hope you have. It states that we're here to investigate 'the central problems of political theory that concern the justification of democracy.' We will read the works of canonical thinkers including Plato, Rousseau, and Mill to determine what the moral responsibilities of citizens are in selecting the representatives who exercise political power in their name.

"The last question we will seek to answer is whether or not democratic rule is a just form of collective decision-making, or whether we are diluting ourselves in believing the system is set up to work in our benefit. The last question I pose will be the first I answer," he booms from the front of the room. "The answer is no."

Now he has my attention, but apparently nobody else's. I can understand sleeping through art history or English literature when you have no interest in it, but this is discussing the very system each and every student here will live under. The apathy is appalling, but I shouldn't have expected anything different. Mister Bennit always told us that we never really understood how unique we were as a class.

"In the United States, and places like the United Kingdom that exercise a parliamentary system, society is set up to fail."

Is this guy for real? Is this the pessimistic crap they teach in college these days? No wonder everyone has lost faith in our system. This is ridiculous.

"Now, some of you may believe that this has all magically changed with Michael Bennit and his legion of social media candidates. If you don't know what I am talking about, you should crawl out from the hole you've been in for the past four years and turn on the news. Not that you should expect honest and fair reporting. All the media is interested in doing is propping this guy up to be some sort of modern day George Washington. It's a laughable exercise."

I'm not upset. Upset is way back in the rearview mirror. I've even cruised past angry and am heading straight for irate. I don't know if this professor knows I am sitting here or not, but he's about to get an education. I can't sit quietly and listen to a whole semester of this drivel.

No sooner do the words finish crossing his lips than my hand shoots up. I've heard enough and can no longer keep my redheaded tendencies reined in. I'd love to slug him, but since that's a surefire way to ensure my tenure at Harvard is a short one, I will have to settle for a verbal solution. I'm told education is all about a free exchange of ideas. Mister Bennit practiced that in his classroom, so let's see if Doctor Britteredge does in his. This is college, after all.

"Yes?"

"With all due respect, Doctor Britteredge, in the span of two minutes, you contradicted your entire premise that democracy is a failed system."

"And how did I do that, miss?" he asks with amusement.

"Human history has long witnessed the rule of tyrannical kings and military despots. The world has matured to understand that government is not about being subjugated to a single ruler, but having that ruler beholden to his subjects. That power, especially in the modern sense, should never be entrusted to one individual because it is so easy to abuse.

"There is no such thing as a benevolent dictator. Are you going to stand there and tell us that people living under the thumb of repressive regimes are better off than we are? I don't think so, sir."

"And you think allowing the masses to rule is any better?" he counters.

"Our system is not perfect, but no system devised by human beings ever will be because we are all inherently flawed, including those we choose to lead us. The United States will always have good presidents and bad ones. We will always elect good legislators and corrupt ones.

"But it is also *our* system. We have the power of the vote, and despite the attempts of outside influences to hijack control away from us, we have shown that we have the ability to exercise it effectively. To elect upstanding men and women dedicated to the people and not a party or special interest. Whether we can continue that trend is entirely up to us as a nation."

"That's a rather—"

"I'm not finished yet."

"Then, by all means, continue," he replies sarcastically, outstretching his hands theatrically to let me know the floor is mine. I choose to ignore his condescension.

"Groups of people looking to exert control and accumulate power have existed since the dawn of government. It makes no difference whether that system is a democracy, theocracy, oligarchy, or the Knights of the Round Table. That is the true nature of politics, and it will always exist. I, for one, want to live in a system where my voice is equal and can be heard without recrimination. I want to live in a system where I have a vote in the direction of my nation and the right to exercise it. Most of all, I want to live in a country where all of its citizens have a voice and can make the choice for themselves how to use it."

I have been hanging around Mister Bennit for way too long. The resulting silence from my rant is broken by a single sound of two hands striking each other. It is followed by a second, a third, and then many as the students in the room break into enthusiastic applause.

After studying my face during my little monologue, Doctor Britteredge finally figures out who I am. When the realization flashed across his face, it then turned to something else—respect. I think he realizes that he may have a worthy opponent sitting in his lecture hall.

"Miss Stanton, I hope you know that had I realized immediately that it was you with your hand up, there's no way in hell I would have called on you."

"Why not?" I snap, a little taken aback by his admission.

"Because you don't belong here," he says, again triggering my angry redhead gene. I fight the urge to stand up and start yelling at him. Come on, get it together, Chelsea. I take a deep breath before answering.

"I heard that a lot during my first year in Washington, sir. Each and every—" I stop when he raises his hand.

"You took that the wrong way. I'm not saying you don't deserve to be here. What I am trying and failing miserably to convey is the sentiment that there is no need for you to be here, given your considerable experience in politics already. You're probably in your mid-twenties and more qualified than I am to teach this class."

Damn straight I am. I survived two classes with Michael Bennit, and that was practically worth an award in that school. I took it a step further—I worked with him for four years. Not only could I teach this class, I deserve a medal. I use my better judgment and don't say any of that though.

"Miss Stanton, if it was in my power I would give you a doctorate from this institution right now and send you on your way. Your speech was the equivalent of a dissertation defense, and although I may or may not agree with what you espouse, I cannot argue with your passion or your knowledge.

"Unfortunately, Harvard does not let lowly associate professors make those kinds of decisions, so I will settle for making the one that is in my power. If I promise to give you the highest grade for this class right now, is there any chance I can get you not to show up for the rest of the semester?"

"Why? So you can continue to practice your disbelief in our system and preach it without challenge?"

"Am I not entitled to my opinion, and am I not tasked with the challenge of educating an ignorant populace as to how their government really works, or as it is in this case, doesn't work?"

"No, sir, you are perfectly entitled to share your beliefs, so long as you draw the line between fact and opinion. As a student, and someone who has been on the front lines of our political and legislative processes, I reserve the right to refute every word that comes out of your mouth."

"And we all thought this class would be boring," one of my classmates says from behind me to the apparent agreement of many in the room with us.

"Well, you clearly have the majority of this class on your side. Is there any chance I can convince you to sit there and say nothing for the rest of the semester?" he asks. I want to believe he's kidding, and his smile sort of indicates he is. But something tells me he would love it if I agreed.

"My participation is non-negotiable, sir. Besides, what fun would that be?" I respond, eliciting snickers from my classmates in the lecture hall. Politics may just be a class they need to take, but discussions and arguments in class makes the time go by much faster. I've learned that from experience.

"From my perspective, it would be much more fun," the professor mumbles. Again, I'm not sure if he's kidding.

"The whole idea of high learning espoused by this institution is the free exchange of ideas and opinions, so that its products can become integral contributors to the greater society. How would I be able to contribute if I'm not present here to do so?" I ask sweetly. After spending as much time in Washington as I did, I learned how to sugar coat answers very effectively.

"Oh, it's going to be a very long semester," Doctor Britteredge laments after a long, theatrical sigh. "Since I can't dissuade you from challenging my brilliant lectures, I have only one thing to say to you."

I wait to hear it.

"Welcome to Harvard, Miss Stanton."

-EPILOGUE-
MICHAEL

I had just reached the top of the stairs at the second floor when the bell rang. It only takes a few seconds for a high school hallway to go from being devoid of people to resembling Madison Square Garden after a Knicks game. Fortunately, the walk to my classroom was only a short walk down the hall.

I slipped into the door once the flow of students, fleeing class for their next one, slowed to a trickle. Looking around at the walls, I realize I'm home again. With few exceptions, every poster and piece of décor is right where it was when I left here over four years ago. I was surprised to find that on my first day of work a couple of weeks ago. I don't know why I'm still surprised.

The room is set up in a horseshoe instead of the rows of desks emblematic of most classrooms. I always found the arrangement more engaging and personal. Students tend to be more attentive when they have to follow your movements around a room, instead of staring straight ahead. I had heard from Chalice during my first term that my replacement had adopted the style. I guess he liked it.

"If you think it's weird for you teaching here, you can imagine how I feel," a voice from the corner sounds out.

"Hi, Emilee," I say in surprise. I can only imagine the adjustment of going from being a high school student to a student teacher in the same room. "Sorry, I didn't see you there. How are classes?"

"They're good. Eric is already letting me teach lessons and, honestly, I'm still trying to get the hang of it. You always made it look so easy. I didn't realize how much work goes into teaching."

"Good teachers never let their students know how much work they put into it," I say out of experience.

Emilee is in her senior year at New York University, majoring in education. When it was time to do her student teaching, this is where she wanted to be. Chalice pulled a few strings for me to make sure it happened.

"Have you talked to any of the gang lately?" she asks. She's had a lot on her plate since she started her student teaching stint, so we really haven't had a chance to catch up.

"Unfortunately, no. I tried calling Vince and Vanessa the other day, but neither picked up."

"I'm sure Congressman Reyes is keeping them plenty busy," Emilee concludes, having heard how thrilled he was when they agreed to join his staff after I left my seat.

Vince and Vanessa were cherished members of my staff and, through the course of my nearly two terms, built a stellar reputation for themselves as capable staffers. More than six dozen members of the House, and even a handful of senators, tried to woo them to join their teams. In the end, I wasn't surprised when they decided to run Cisco's office in Washington together. They are engaged to be married, after all.

"Have you heard from anyone?" I inquire.

"I talked to Chelsea over the weekend. She's really excited about starting classes at Harvard."

"I bet. The professors at that school have no idea what they are in for."

"No kidding," she laughs. "Amanda is interning at some big firm up near Hartford. I'd be shocked if they don't offer her a job when she graduates."

"If they don't, there are about a thousand of companies who will. Have you heard from Xavier? It's a shame about his knee."

Xavier was killing it on the court at Syracuse. Rumors were swirling that the star senior would go high in the NBA draft. That was until the game against St. John's where he collapsed to the floor clutching his knee. A torn ACL is not a career ender for a professional, but nobody is going to risk a contract for a kid coming out of college.

"Not for a couple of weeks. Last I heard he is looking into law schools. He wants to become a prosecutor."

"God bless him."

"Other than that, Peyton is just trying to finish up her degree. She has a job lined up down in New York and Brian has already formed a startup with some friends."

"I heard. He's going into social media marketing."

Brian was always the tech savvy one of the group. We could never have run either campaign without him, nor would I have survived my ethics hearing without his help. I have always thought the socially awkward teen would end up being wildly successful in life. Looks like I was right.

"Yup, but did you hear who else joined his company?"

"No, who?"

"Peyton and Amanda. They're going to be silent partners."

"Wow. Talk about putting the band back together. Can you imagine the contacts those three can cultivate?" The thought is mind-boggling.

The bell rings and I realize that all my students are already seated and waiting for me to begin.

"Time to get to work," I tell Emilee. "You work here, so don't be such a stranger."

"I won't, Mister Bennit," she promises.

"Em, I'm not your teacher anymore. You can call me Michael."

"Whatever you say, Mister Bennit," she says with a smile, as she heads for the door.

"Okay, where did we leave off yesterday?" I announce to the class as everyone finishes settling in. I catch the knowing glance from Emilee as she heads into the hallway and closes the door behind her.

"We were discussing the three ways the Confederacy could have won the Civil War," Olivia says from the seat to my right. Chelsea's old seat, if I remember correctly. Go figure.

"And what did you learn?"

"Despite the military successes Lee had with the Army of Northern Virginia, the best ways for the South to win was getting a European power to intervene or creating enough of a stalemate that Lincoln loses the election in 1984," Tyler surmises. He's my new Vince.

"The Union almost cracked at Gettysburg. That would have won it for them," Logan argues. Whatever Tyler says, you can count on Logan disputing it.

"But they didn't."

"They almost did. What would have stopped Lee from parading his army right into Washington if the lines broke on Cemetery Ridge?"

The class joins the personal argument between Tyler and Logan as the room erupts in chaos. It reminds me a little of Fight Club. We could be just as rowdy sometimes. The one thing every teacher on the planet understands is a room full of adults can act just like a room full of kids under most circumstances.

"Mister Bennit, can I ask a question?" Sophia interrupts from the rear of the room, with her hand extended. The group immediately pipes down.

"Sure. Shoot."

"How much of this is testable?" Her question causes me to smile.

"All of it. Why, are you scared?"

"No way!" Kaitlyn exclaims with the same tenacity Vanessa had in this room. "We'll take whatever you throw at us."

"Strong words considering you haven't seen one of my tests yet," I retort.

"It doesn't matter," Caden offers. "We'll ace it."

"I doubt that very much, Caden."

"Are you willing to put something on that, Mister Bennit?" Tyler chides.

"You mean am I willing to bet on it?" I ask, instantly regretting it.

"Yeah, a bet." The excitement in the room instantly rises as everyone perks up at the prospect.

"Not a chance."

I know where this road leads. It was an epic journey, but one that I'm in no rush to ever take again. Part of me wonders where I would be in my life had I given that answer to Chelsea, Vince, and company four and a half years ago.

"What's the matter, Mister Bennit, chicken?" Logan goads. I'm not falling for that line again as Olivia, Tyler, Caden, and Kaitlyn join their classmates in their taunts of various clucking sounds.

"Yes, yes I am." And I mean it.

* * *

When the bell rings after D period, reality sets back in. I make my way back down to the first floor and into the main office. Behind the long counter where many of the administrative dealings with students happen is my secretary's office. Adjoining her office is mine.

"How was class, Principal Bennit?" Elaine asks as I stroll in. I inherited her services from my predecessor, and I can say with no hesitation that he would have been a much bigger train wreck without her. She was the one running the school during his tenure.

"Elaine, please, for the hundredth time, call me Michael. And class was just like old times," I say, unable to suppress my smile.

"Well, the stack of paperwork on your desk will wipe that smile off your face, *Principal Bennit*," she says with a wry smile of her own as the phone rings.

Leaving her to her own duties, I begin to tend to mine. I chose this job willingly after Charlene's offer, but there were some stipulations I made the school board accept before taking the position. The first is that I am the one responsible for establishing the high standards and commitment to success of all students at Millfield High.

The second was I could have full authority to improve scholastic achievement by focusing on the quality of instruction by the teachers. That made the teachers' union nervous, but since I was once one of them, they have given me the benefit of the doubt so far. As a result, we have joined forces to define the standards and help students reach those lofty expectations.

The third concession was that I got to pick my vice-principals and department chairs. I have replaced the slackers with those who can get the job done and, as a result, the workload has balanced to a manageable level for everyone. Students get more attention and, by design, are already showing improvement in both academics and behavior. I've only just started, and there is still so much more to be done.

The final, and most important stipulation, was that I be able to teach at least one class. Of my demands, it was the one the school board balked at the hardest. Apparently they don't believe administrators should be involved in the educational process. I happen to believe the opposite is true. It was a deal-breaker and they finally acquiesced, resulting in my taking over the class I just left. It's the most fun I have all day.

"Are you used to your new digs yet?" Chalice asks after a gentle rap on the door, interrupting my train of thought. It's a change of pace. I was the one who usually visited her back in the day.

"Come on in, Chalice," I offer as she enters, admiring the décor. I dusted off a few old army displays and hung them around the room. "And I am, for the most part. It's been hard expunging the stench of Old Spice and failure Howell left here."

Robinson Howell became principal of Millfield High right before I got hired. From the moment I started my first class on my first day, we were at odds. He liked to exert control and force learning through intimidation, whereas I liked to inspire students to learn. Beaumont's smear campaign against me presented him with the perfect reason to force me out, but removing his enemies only masked his personal failures for so long.

"The décor is fitting. You are the conquering hero."

"What do you mean?"

"You don't know? Since when do I have to give one of my brightest history teachers a lesson?" Chalice mocks.

"Since the day I got hired," I reply. "Regardless of what position I hold, you'll always be my mentor. I should call you Master Splinter."

"If you name me after a rat from a movie sporting young, hormonal, sword-wielding reptiles, we're going to have a problem." I hold my hands up in surrender. I get the feeling she's serious.

"I was about to say, you're a conquering hero and you don't even realize it because you've never studied your own history." I lean back in my chair, reflecting as she continues.

"You ran your first campaign against Winston Beaumont, who tried to drag you through the mud by creating phony scandals. He went to prison and you took over his district office.

"Then there was Johnston Albright. He tried to kick you out of Congress and even have you killed. When he committed suicide, you were the speaker pro tempore and would have been elected by your peers in a walk if you wanted it.

"Once James Reed was indicted, the son of the other founder offered you his position and, presumably, his office. You could have changed the face of modern lobbying if you had wanted to."

I give Chalice a little head shrug. I am used to giving the history lessons, not receiving them. I have to bite my tongue before I ask her to get to the point like so many have asked me over the years.

"Finally, it was the man who occupied this very office. Robinson Howell did everything he could to get you fired from this building. Now, you sit in the very chair he did."

"I switched the chair out," I say playfully, causing Chalice to roll her eyes.

"Michael, you beat everyone who crosses your path and thinks they can take you on. Each of your enemies underestimated you, dismissed you, and ended up losing to you." I can't fight the urge anymore. I have to ask.

"Chalice, does this story have a point?"

She rises out of the chair, straightens her suit jacket, and looks at me with knowing eyes. There is no way to measure the amount of respect I have for this woman. She may technically work for me now, but she will always be my superior.

"As teachers of history, we focus on the past because they serve as indicators and warnings of the future. As you've always said, 'History does not repeat itself, but the themes in history do.' The stories of most of those people still hung on the walls of your old classroom upstairs have run their course, but your story still isn't finished. The question is, how will that story end, and will it be here?"

She looks around the room with an approving nod. "I have to run. I'll see you tomorrow."

I lean back in my chair again and look around the room, same as she was. It's funny how we never look at our own lives in a historical context. Once again, Chalice has given me a lot to think about.

-EPILOGUE-
KYLIE

The drive from my newspaper office in the center of town to Millfield High School is not a long one, but traffic can be problematic when there is an accident. It's only half past two in the afternoon, but to catch Michael before he leaves for the day, I need to make sure I'm there before three.

I keep my distance from the car weaving through traffic in front of me. The roads are still slippery from yesterday's snow squall, making this lunatic's driving even more dangerous. It dawns on me that we'll have to upgrade to a bigger vehicle soon. I'm going to miss this car. The first time I ever met Michael in person was when he slipped into my passenger seat in the parking lot of the Perkfect Buzz. I'll miss not having to make a car payment too. Not that we have to worry about money.

Offers from publishing companies to purchase the rights to his memoirs started flooding in less than an hour after Michael announced he was not running for another term. It's not hard to figure out why. Not only does his life since his days in the army resemble something right off the fiction rack, but his built-in social media platform and captive audience on a national scale had publishing companies of every size drooling.

Michael decided not to make it autobiographical, instead opting to tell his story to a writer he selected with the help of the publisher. We all got interviewed to get our perspectives—me,

Chelsea, Vince, Vanessa, and even Blake. When the book was finished, I read the advance copy even before Michael did. It was good, but there was just one piece missing—what to call the book.

Michael has had a lot of titles since I've known him. He was the iCandidate when we met and became the iCongressman once he got to Washington. Although never selected for the position, his temporary filling in for Johnston Albright earned him the name iSpeaker. When the book was finally complete, the search for a suitable title that would help define his tenure in Congress still hadn't been settled. It was a raging debate that lasted for weeks.

Everyone involved in the project to bring Michael's story to print had an opinion on what to call it. I heard everything from naming it *The Great Uniter*, after the old nickname he earned when the new Congress formed, to the more ridiculous *The Man Who Flipped Washington*, which poked fun on his ethics hearing antics. The options got sillier from there.

In the end, the publisher settled on a title that was sure to capture the nation's attention while making it clear who it is about. For Michael, it was the only moniker he really ever wanted. They entitled the book *The iAmerican*.

Despite all the fanfare surrounding his retirement and the book release, the former Congressional representative from Connecticut's Sixth District is not without his critics. Some people, ranging from political elitists to jaded cynics in the media, have decried his withdrawal from public life as failing to finish what he started. Others, some of them former ardent supporters, have mistaken his not wanting to run as cowardice despite his countless explanations to the contrary.

Fortunately, the naysayers aren't going to stop him from embarking on the small book tour the publisher set up. The majority of people in the country liken him to George

Washington—a depiction Michael flat out rejects whenever it comes up. Regardless, copies of his aptly titled memoir have been flying off the shelves faster than the publisher can print them. Within a few days of its debut, *The iAmerican* shot up to number one on the *New York Times* Best-Seller list.

He loves meeting people, and will no doubt enjoy his respite from my recent moodiness. I've been warned against travelling, so he will be going solo. He shouldn't miss the big day, unless I end up being early. He'll be devastated if that happens.

I squeeze out from behind the wheel of my car, after pulling it into a visitor parking spot right across from the main entrance of Millfield High. It's freezing out, and I try to wrap my heavy wool coat closer to me as I brave the biting wind on my way to the entrance.

I make it through the inner door and immediately start shedding the layers of clothing I'm wearing. Why the Millfield Public School system maintenance department feels compelled to heat the building to blast furnace temperature I'll never know. I barely have my coat off in time to look up and see the stunning blonde dressed in heels and wrapped in a stunning yet still professional blouse and pencil skirt. C'mon, really?

"Hi, Kylie!" Jessica Slater announces with unabashed enthusiasm as she walks over to me, the click of her heels against the tile floor echoing off the rounded brick walls of the main entrance foyer.

"Hi, Jessica. How's school treating you?"

"Better. It's nice to have a principal who listens to his staff and doesn't cave to the whims of every parent with a complaint," she explains.

"I can only imagine," I respond with a smile.

I will never really like Jessica Slater. She was my husband's former fiancée, is more put-together than I will ever be, and I will always harbor the same fear about him leaving me for her. It doesn't matter how irrational those thoughts are, I will never get over them. And they are irrational, especially now.

Despite my misgivings, Jessica and I have made peace with each other. She has moved on, although I get the feeling she will always be looking for a man that can measure up to Michael. She accepts that, and I don't think she would ever try to interfere with our marriage. Despite the truce between us, I will always keep my eye on her. Like Ronald Reagan once said, "Trust, but verify."

"Normally, the sight of this would scare the hell out of me," I hear Michael announce as he walks out of the door leading into the main office, his own long wool coat is draped over his arm.

"Which part?" Jessica asks. "Your wife talking to your ex-fiancée or the fact we could be trading notes about you?"

"Both, actually," he says with a smile, giving me a kiss before rubbing my swollen tummy. "And how's my little guy doing today?" he asks his unborn child.

"Kicking up a storm, thank you very much," I relay.

"Do you know for sure it's a boy?" Jessica asks in a tone of genuine curiosity.

"It's a guess, although I suppose it could be a she who's destined to become the future starting midfielder for the Women's World Cup team in a couple of decades."

"Well, I need to get going. I have some parents to call. It seems my D period Western lit class doesn't like doing their homework."

"That's because *The Odyssey* is an epic ... bore," Michael fires off sarcastically. Jessica gives him the same look I've given him a thousand times.

"Don't worry, Jessica. I'll take care of him." I mean that in more ways than one.

"It was good seeing you again, Kylie."

"You, too," I respond politely, before she wheels on her heels and saunters off. I will tolerate her. I will stomach having her work with my husband. I refuse to have to like it.

"Well, that wasn't awkward or anything," he says as I wrap my arms around him.

"Oh, is the most recognizable high school principal in the history of American public education a little dismayed that his former fiancée and his wife might actually be getting along?"

"No, but I know you both, so I'm the one in the best position to say it creeps me out. What brings you here, my love?"

"Well, I was hoping I could steal you away for a nice stroll over at Briar Point," I say, lying. The look on his face lets me know he sees right through it.

"Hon, it's ten degrees outside, and that's without the wind chill. You don't want to walk. You want me to take you somewhere to get some crazy ice cream, pickle combination, don't you?"

"That's very perceptive of you, Mister Bennit."

"I know you too well, Missus Bennit."

We share a kiss. After everything we've been through, right here, right now, I'm the happiest I have ever been. We've been through multiple campaigns, smear attacks, efforts to expel Michael, and assassination attempts all while navigating the deceit and treachery that is as much a foundation of our political system as our founding documents are.

But in this moment, the journey was all worth it. I am married to the man of my dreams. I live in a quaint town in one of the most picturesque parts of the country. I have a low stress job that I love doing. There is no more politics, no more deal making, and no more media to appease. We are for ourselves and, soon, we'll have a child to share it all with.

"Principal Bennit?" I hear Michael's secretary announce from the door of the office, causing us to let go of our kiss.

"She still refuses to call me Michael," he whispers. "What's up, Elaine?"

"You have a call."

"Can you take a message for me, please?"

"I normally would, but I thought you might want to take this one."

"Why? Who is it?"

"He said he was the Speaker of the United States House of Representatives."

I look at Michael with fearful eyes. This is how it starts. One small request leads to bigger ones, and before you know it, he will be dragged back onto the national scene either willingly or out of a sense of duty.

"He said it was urgent," Elaine pleads.

Michael smiles at me, eschewing my foreboding look as he slips into his coat and buttons it. I follow suit, as he helps me climb into my own comfy coat. He gives me a quick kiss before offering his arm. Michael is one of the most unpredictable men I have ever met, and this reaction is no different.

"What would you like me to tell him?" Elaine prompts once more.

"Tell him I left for the day."

Acknowledgements

To all good things must come an end, and words cannot express the gratitude I have for each and every one of my readers for choosing to be a part of Michael Bennit's journey (or at least this part of it). I can only hope you found the four books of this series both entertaining and enlightening. I have some exciting new books coming and I sincerely hope you will choose to read those as well.

To my greatest love, Michele, I want to thank you so much for your eternal support and for actively sharing this experience with me. You have been there for me from the beginning of this adventure and have kept me energized and motivated to bring these works to the world.

Everyone has heroes and I dedicated this book on behalf of my father, Ronald, because he is one of mine. Family is important to me, and my father, my mother, Nancy, and my sister, Kristina, have been with me every step of the way on my own journey writing these novels. Thank you so much for your support!

As my military career winds down, I want to thank everyone I have served with over the past twenty years for your sacrifices in the defense of our nation.

A special thanks to my editor Caroline, Gary, and the rest of the staff at BubbleCow who were so dedicated to making this whole series come together the way it did. My deepest gratitude also goes to Diana for the copyediting job on this book and to Veselin Milacic for creating the fantastic covers for the last three books of series. I appreciate their talents and professionalism more than I could ever express.

A Note from the Author

To be honest with you, I didn't really want to end Michael's journey. I also didn't want to stop writing Kylie's character or watch as Chelsea grew as a person each page I typed. Each and every character was fun to write in very different ways. It was almost disturbing how enjoyable it was to write about James' constant scheming and his interactions with political types like Diane Herr and Harvey Stepanik.

So why did the series end when so many would have wanted to see him go all the way to the White House? The simple answer is because he wanted it to end. Michael Bennit never aspired to be a politician. He never sought to be the Speaker of the House. He certainly never had his sights set on the Oval Office. To keep pushing the envelope was to destroy the person he really is and I didn't want to do that.

The more complicated answer involves believability. I have asked the reader to suspend a little of their cynicism from the very beginning of this series. I intended to reward that by making as much of the journey as realistic as possible. While I tried to present plausible events and circumstances leading to Michael's rise to power, I thought the road to the White House would have been a difficult one to justify. As he mentioned in his speech at Briar Point, someone running for that office really has to be willing to make great sacrifices to to be elected to it. I could not imagine a scenario where Michael and Kylie were ready for that... yet.

I spent considerable time at the end of The iAmerican to try to tie up as many loose ends left from the prior three books as possible. Now we know what happened to Winston Beaumont and that Madison Roberts is trying to make her way back into the game. I gave as many updates as I was comfortable giving. I wanted to give as much information as I could about how people were moving on without boring my readers to tears.

Before I forget, I wanted to clear one thing up before I get emails on it. Yes, Michael did attend Johnston Albright's memorial service when it was held. I had actually written much of the chapter before discovering it wasn't adding anything to the narrative. The whole thing had the feel of Marilyn Viano's memorial when I finished writing it without any of the purpose like we saw when Kylie ambushed James. In the end, I dropped it even before my editor saw it.

So, is this really the end? He is settling into a new job and is starting a family. Chelsea is finally starting school while her peers are finishing their degrees and are about to enter the workforce. Could they ever come back together again?

The answer is that I don't know. The one thing I learned during writing this series is not to ever count Michael Bennit out. You probably shouldn't either.

About the Author

Mikael Carlson is the award-winning author of the novel *The iCandidate* and the rest of the Michael Bennit Series. This is his fourth novel.

A nineteen-year veteran and current noncommissioned officer in the Rhode Island Army National Guard, he deployed twice in support of military operations during the Global War on Terror. Mikael has served in the field artillery, infantry, and in support of special operations units during his career on active duty at Fort Bragg and in the Army National Guard.

A proud U.S. Army Paratrooper, he conducted over 50 airborne operations following the completion of jump school at Fort Benning in 1998. Since then, he has trained with the militaries of countless foreign nations.

Academically, Mikael has earned a Master of Arts in American History, and graduated with a B.S. in International Business from Marist College in 1996.

He was raised in New Milford, Connecticut and currently lives in nearby Danbury.

Dreams are the window to your subconscious. What happens when they are the window to someone else's, and that someone is a traitor?

The Eyes of Others

–A Paranormal Military Thriller–

Coming Spring 2015

WARRINGTON
PUBLISHING

Sign up for the Mikael Carlson newsletter to discover other works and learn about future projects at:

www.mikaelcarlson.com/connect

Follow Mikael on:

Facebook: authormikaelcarlson

Twitter: @mikaelcarlson

Google +: mikaelcarlson

For signed copies and other cool stuff, check out the bookstore at MikaelCarlson.com/store.

Made in the USA
Middletown, DE
13 April 2021

37455408R00245